Alabastron

Judith Goulding

Bridge-Logos

Alachua, Florida 32615

Bridge-Logos

Alachua, FL 32615USA

Alabastron
by Judith Goulding

Copyright ©2009 by Judith Goulding

Printed in the United States of America.

Library of Congress Catalog Card Number: 2009924004
International Standard Book Number 978-0-88270-9833

Dedication

To my best Friend and Supporter

Jesus Christ

Who makes all things possible.

Author's Note

And so she "stood behind at His Feet." She had brought with her an "alabastron" (phial, or flask, commonly of alabaster) *of perfume.... We have evidence that perfumed oils—notably oil of roses, and of the iris plant—were largely manufactured and used in Palestine. A flask with this perfume was worn by women round the neck, and hung down below the breast.... Hence it seems at least not unlikely, that the 'alabastron' which she brought, who loved so much, was common among Jewish women* (The Life and Times of Jesus the Messiah, *p. 390).*

In studying for this novel I found the above reference to the term alabastron deeply buried within a massive, learned body of research by Alfred Edersheim, a well-respected New Testament Oxford scholar. Other sources suggested that a container of perfume sometimes had to be broken to unseal and release the fragrance. It seemed to me that my principal character, Mary Magdalene, might have worn an alabastron. Even more interesting is the concept that the alabastron represents brokenness, bleeding, and ultimately blessing. In that sense Jesus, the Messiah, was an alabastron as He hung on the cross.

PROLOGUE

A.D. 68

Greetings from Jonas bar Simon to my dear son, Benjamin; may God our Father and our Lord Jesus Christ give you grace and peace. Your mother sends her love. She wants you to know that you and your family are constantly in her prayers. I bear witness that her prayer beads are dwindling in size daily due to fervent handling. As you can imagine, she has worn down the agates designated for your sisters considerably also. She tells me to instruct you to give both Jerusala and Bethany embraces and kisses from us when next you see them and their families.

I had forgotten how glorious summertime in the hill country of Palestine can be. The heat is a soothing balm to my tired bones, and the cold ache in my back and legs has melted away. I must commend you, my son, for insisting that we take this trip; it is proving to be beneficial to my health and in other respects as well.

We arrived in the town of Magdala eighteen days ago welcomed by the elders of the church that meets secretly in the home of Gaius Valerius, a Roman magistrate and follower of the Way. Gaius has been instrumental in sorting out the legalities pertaining to my inheritance. In response to the letter I sent him last winter, he found a buyer for the majority of the property bequeathed to me by my parents.

The only part of the estate that I have kept is the villa and its surrounding gardens. Minor proceeds from the remainder have gone to pay taxes and management fees. Some profits I have kept to give to you and your sisters, and others I will seed into the churches we have established in Britannia.

I am greatly heartened by the love and fellowship I have found among the believers in Magdala. Accordingly, I have earmarked a generous gift to the Magdalan brotherhood as well as to the church in Jerusalem, which is undergoing great hardship and famine at this time.

We are quite comfortable here and glad to be back in the homeland of our childhood. At certain poignant moments I become a boy again, an abandoned waif playing among these marble columns, lonely and in need of someone to care. Then the nostalgia turns to joy because I remember how I was adopted and became heir to all the love and privileges of a true son.

This morning I am sitting on the veranda with your mother at my shoulder. Dew glitters among the grasses like jasper from heaven, and stately cypresses shade the lakeside road in the same cool way they have for generations. Buxom hedges abound in wild profusion, lifting cheeky flowers to catch the first rays of morning warmth. Some things never change.

I close my eyes and breathe my mother's fragrance, the special blend of white roses she distilled into costly perfume and encased in alabastrons to be worn about the neck on a braid of silk. Many stories have been told about her, my son, not all of them true, as you well know. That is one reason I have decided to write certain things down, both as I recollect them from my boyhood and as my parents explained them to me later.

An examination of the villa reveals that, while it is sound, there is much to do: broken pediments, peeling plaster, seeping tiles, tangled weeds and vines to uproot and burn. But tasks of this kind are always present, my son, to draw us away from more important duties. I must use these long, uneventful summer days to better advantage. The chores will wait.

I have purchased a roll of papyrus. The perfume *atelier* at the rear of the villa with its benches and table will be my workspace. It looks out upon the fountain and the back gardens through large open windows. I don't care if the honeybee visits. Its ceaseless droning will keep me steady. And the cheerful bustle of the garden sparrows will keep my spirits from flagging. Your mother promises to help; it will be good for us to remember together. I know, however, that these halcyon days will not last forever, or the inspiration to put them to rare use. They are gifts and, as such, must not be squandered.

I tell you truly, my son, even at this apparently peaceful time in Palestine, trouble is brewing. In the larger cities there is a seething unrest. Several revolutionary bands have been attacking caravans along the Via Maris and other trade routes. My father's old party, the Zealots, as well as other like-minded groups, are continually stirring the cauldron of insurrection. It has been thirty-eight years since our Lord ascended into heaven before the astonished eyes of his followers. During that time we of the Faith have gone to many distant lands spreading the message of God's love and salvation. Others, however, fight against peace and the transformation of the heart. They foment rebellion, hatred, and violence. Many of the brothers and sisters here say that a war of epic proportions will occur in Palestine within the next year or two.

Before that happens, however, your mother and I should be back in Britannia. We plan to sail in early spring. Meanwhile, I look forward to a balmy winter, improved health, and the opportunity to do my necessary scribbling.

You should receive this letter from the hand of Merwyn, the tin merchant. He sails from Tyre next week with a shipment of linen and olive oil. We have laid hands on him and prayed for traveling mercies.

The believers here send greetings. Please give my blessings to our churches in Brigantia and Atrebatia. I thank God without ceasing for their love for us. Remember to pray everyday for the church in Rome, which is under fierce persecution.

Finally, dear Benjamin, may God bless you above all you can ask or imagine and give you peace and wisdom. May your wife and children prosper and be in good health during our absence, and may the husbands and children of our daughters be guarded by angels. Your mother and I give thanks always for the family God has given us. I sign as always—Jonas bar Simon, your loving father and a follower of the Way.

Chapter 1

A.D. 28

"Not by might nor by power,
but by my Spirit," says the Lord Almighty.
Zechariah 4:6 NIV

Simon bar Cleopas sat alone in the dim interior of the wine shop, a half-eaten cake of barley bread at his elbow, an empty cup held loosely between his hands. The other patrons, mostly traders and vendors of the town, took their noon meal outside, enjoying the open air and friendly conversation. Simon, however, was a visitor in the region and not particularly a social man. He considered his solitude better company than frivolous bantering with strangers, especially lately when there was so much to occupy his thoughts.

The shop had provided him a modest, economical place to eat since arriving in Magdala ten days ago, and sitting at the same corner table in the shadows of the windowless shop had become routine. Shallum bar Jekemiah, the proprietor, had served him efficiently. He had also answered Simon's questions concerning the Nazarene without demanding explanations or further discourse.

According to rumor, the Nazarene rabbi was in Capernaum, a few miles north of Magdala. Simon would have already gone there except for the fact that he had met Batasha, the perfumer. Simon had first encountered her on the lakeside promenade as she walked home after closing up her perfume shop at the end of the day. She had freely engaged him in conversation, a breech of Jewish social etiquette that he had found both scandalous and intriguing.

She was a striking woman of fair hair and blue eyes. Her demeanor, unlike that of a modest Jewess, was proud and worldly. She told him that her Jewish father had been an importer, her mother a tribal princess he'd met on one of his trips to the outer provinces. Although educated in a synagogue school, Batasha embodied none of the traditional Hebrew values. Instead she was an independent businesswoman—sophisticated, outspoken, and pagan.

In short, she epitomized much of what he despised in the present culture of Palestine. Still, he would not give up walking with her every evening to the colonnaded veranda of her villa as the last vestiges of day painted a rosy glow on the naked marble gods and goddesses in her garden. Her father had built the impressive Greco-Roman villa, but she had added the lush gardens and outbuildings later in order to manufacture perfume.

He made a sound of impatience—a sibilant, half-spoken oath between his teeth. Shallum, interpreting it as a summons, hurried over to refill his cup with wine before going outside to serve other patrons. Absently Simon took a sip. *Blessed Jehovah, what was he doing tempting himself with this woman?* He had often mocked various patriarchs of old for their weakness for women. David had become obsessed with Bathsheba and had plotted murder to have her. Solomon had let the dark beauty from the South fill his palace with heathen idols. Samson had lain placidly on Delilah's couch as she had sheared him of his strength and destiny. Was he going to allow himself to become like them?

He focused on the reason he'd come to Galilee in the first place. His party of revolutionaries in Judea had entrusted him with the important mission of discovering if this new prophet was really the Messiah. What would they say if they knew Simon was wasting their funds staying in this little town to be near a woman? The Zealots were not men to toy with—they took their mission seriously.

He lifted his head as four Roman soldiers came into the shop and swaggered to the counter. Shallum stumbled over his robe to serve them. Simon resented Jews like Shallum who sold their birthright for a mess of pottage—greedy, materialistic Jews who didn't honor tradition, the purity of the race, or the supremacy of Jehovah God. Instead of fighting the Roman invaders, they became their slaves. He leaned farther back into the shadows, his black eyes glittering obsidian.

How he hated them, these Romans who had stolen the land given to the Jews by God Almighty, these usurpers who burdened the people with taxes and filled their cities with idols and heathen temples where once altars to Jehovah had stood. They strutted the length and breadth of Palestine in the name of justice, liberty, and tolerance, all the time robbing the Hebrew people of their identity. He wished them all in hell—the godless foreigners as well as the adulterous Jews who pandered to them.

The soldiers stood with their backs to him, talking loudly while lifting their cups to drink. The leader of the group wore an ornate sword bearing the insignia of a high- ranking officer. He and his companions were dressed in the short tunic Simon found so revolting on a male. Their burnished helmets, plumed with scarlet, rested on the countertop as they drank and postured and made boisterous jokes. Shallum hovered over them like a vulture—watchful, obsequious—his hands like claws grabbing their money.

Simon's body tensed into a posture of rigid anger. Their arrogance, their self-proclaimed power, even their short-cropped hair and beardless faces incensed him. Half-listening to the loud repartee, he waited quietly; he would not get up and leave at this time and risk having to speak to them, or Shallum, in a civil manner.

The officer in charge did most of the talking. His name was Marcellus. Simon's mouth twisted in derision. *A pretty-sounding name*, he thought. His mother must have mistaken him for a girl. Simon listened as Marcellus extolled the virtues of the tetrarch Herod. Shallum's quick nods of agreement further infuriated Simon.

Any Jew worth his salt despised Herod Antipas. As ruler of Galilee, this son of Herod the Great was openly immoral. He had stolen his brother's wife and was living with her in unabashed, incestuous adultery. Yet he proclaimed himself to be a priest-king and observed Jewish holidays even though he barely knew the significance of them. John the Baptist had denounced him in a loud voice in the wilderness desert of the Jordan. But the ruler had soon silenced the prophet by throwing him into a dungeon at Machaerus.

Simon listened again to the banter of the soldiers. The lesser officers appeared to be teasing Marcellus about one of his girlfriends. Apparently the lady, if she could be called that, had recently broken off their relationship. Marcellus assured his companions that the situation was merely temporary.

"She will return to me," he proclaimed lifting his cup in salute. "To my golden Venus, as sweet as the perfume she sells."

Not a muscle moved in Simon's body. Only his eyes changed, widening slowly as perception dawned.

"To Batasha, my heathen goddess. You will invite me once again into your warm sweet arms to share pleasure."

Simon snapped. All his pent up rage against Roman domination now mingled with jealousy. He sprang forward, his robe flying, his hands fisted and ready to do murder.

"I'll kill you!" He hit the cup in front of Marcellus's face shattering it into his mouth. Then his bloody hands went for Marcellus's throat. "I'll kill you," he repeated between clenched teeth.

The three remaining soldiers, frozen for a moment in astonishment, quickly grabbed Simon's shoulders and tried to pull him off. But Simon was a large man, a stonecutter by trade, and extremely strong. As they began to rain blows on Simon's head, he released Marcellus and turned and charged them with a vengeance, attacking them alternately with quick timing and deadly precision. Having learned to fight in the back alleys of Jerusalem, Simon followed no rule but the rule of might. The swings of the seasoned soldiers occasionally connected with a part of his body but had little effect in slowing him down.

Marcellus, now somewhat recovered, grabbed Simon from behind, pinning his arm across Simon's neck. Simon twisted and brought his elbow back swiftly into Marcellus's stomach, lifting him upward. Marcellus's breath came out in an audible grunt. Well-accustomed to combat, Marcellus refused to relinquish his hold on Simon, however, and continued to grapple with him until the others could assist.

In a concerted effort, the four men wrestled Simon to the dirt floor where they all rolled and thrashed in bloody savagery. The room filled with dust and grunting curses in both Aramaic and Latin. Shallum added to the melee by emitting alarmed shrieks and hopping about like a hysterical pond bird.

"Hold him!" Marcellus exclaimed throwing himself over Simon's torso. His barked order sprayed blood on Simon's cheek and neck. The soldiers immobilized Simon's arms and legs and shifted to press into his chest as Marcellus slowly rose to his feet gasping for breath.

"Stop that caterwauling, you old fool!" he yelled at Shallum. "Get me a towel!"

Quieter now, yet still muttering incoherently, Shallum hastened to obey. Flat on his back, Simon gathered strength and made one last attempt to unshackle himself. He succeeded in rising to a half-sitting position before the soldiers again drove him down. His muscles knotted beneath their hands and gouging knees.

"Hold him fast!" yelled Marcellus. "Are you going to let one crazy Jew get the best of us?" He swabbed the towel over his face then ran his tongue inside his mouth to check the status of his teeth. "Vile Hebrew dog," he muttered.

Undaunted, Simon cursed and made a spitting sound with his mouth. This was a gestured understood in any language. Wordlessly, his eyes never leaving Simon's face, Marcellus pulled his sword from its sheath. Simon stared. The tempered metal flashed as it slowly descended toward his heart.

Shallum began shrieking again. "Oh no! Merciful Jehovah, don't kill him!"

"Run him through, Marcellus! Quickly! Then we'll throw him in the gutter where he belongs," urged one of the soldiers.

"Oh no, no! Not in my shop, not in my gutter." Shallum pulled the thin, grey hair at his temples. "Please, take him outside the city if you must kill him!"

Simon focused on Shallum in disgust. It was all right with the shopkeeper if these Romans killed a Hebrew brother as long as it wasn't an inconvenience. Then he looked into the tawny, foreign eyes of Marcellus and knew he was about to die. With this realization, his body stopped fighting and became still. He felt sorrow now. Sorrow for the way he would die. Not on a battlefield for the freedom of Palestine and the glory of Israel, but in a squalid wine shop for a woman of dubious reputation. He closed his eyes and asked Jehovah for forgiveness.

"That's right. Pray! Ask your invisible God to deliver you from your fate." Marcellus teased the point of the sword through the rough fabric of Simon's robe and broke the skin of his chest. Then he levered himself behind the sword like a farmer behind a plow. It would take his full force to run the blade through Simon's considerable bulk.

"No!" Shallum screamed. "I beg you! You can't kill his man in my shop! News of it will be all over town. Already some of my customers have witnessed the fight. They left when you drew your sword. If you go ahead with this, they will inform the elders of the synagogue that you murdered a Hebrew, and there will be no end to the trouble!"

Marcellus paused. The pressure of the sword lessened. "He's right. I've been ordered to keep the peace in Magdala, not to instigate riots. Herod doesn't like trouble with the masses."

"Then let's take him to the fort and imprison him. He can't get away with attacking a Roman officer."

Marcellus stepped back and sheathed his weapon. "No." He had begun to think more rationally. "My command here has been without incident. I'm in Herod's good graces. There will be no report of this, nor will I take this mongrel prisoner."

"But you can't just let him go!"

"Of course not." He smiled grimly down at Simon. "By the time I get through with you," he said spitting in the dirt beside Simon's ear, "you'll wish I'd killed you with one merciful thrust. Haul him to his feet," he ordered his men. His fists clenched into tight, vengeful weapons. "Keep a good grip on him. This may take some time."

The beating was brutal. When Simon finally slumped to his knees half-conscious, the soldiers released him and joined Marcellus in striking and kicking him till blackness closed in.

The next morning he opened his eyes to the first amber light of dawn. Floating on a sea of pain, he remained in a motionless stupor for a while, assessing and adjusting to the seriousness of his circumstances. He lay on a low wooden cot in a small supply room. He assumed it was the backroom of the wine shop, and that Shallum had dumped him here either to revive on his own or expire.

Grimacing, he slowly rose to a sitting position, bent forward, and cradled his battered head in his hands. Remembering fully what had happened, he gave a labored sigh and repented heartily of his stupidity. Testing every movement before undertaking it, he stood to his feet and inched his way painfully to a nearby basin of water. He washed his swollen eyes and the dried blood from his beard. His face was mushy and tender to the touch, and his jaw felt loose on its hinges. The garments he wore were bloody rags.

His traveling bag lay on the floor containing two scrolls of sacred Scripture, his toiletries, and the expensive suit of clothing he wore only on the Sabbath. Shallum had apparently fetched it from the inn where he was staying. At the foot of the bed Simon noticed a new tunic and a robe of poor, rough linen. This unexpected provision of common traveling attire surprised him and his low opinion of Shallum elevated somewhat. At first he ignored the new clothes, preferring to leave Magdala as soon as possible. Then pausing, he changed his mind and cast aside his bloodstained garments.

Giving his body a thorough washing, he tried not to mourn over the violet bruises on his torso and the gash from the sword next to his heart. He drew the new undershirt over his head, feeling its rough, abrasive texture against his wounds. Next he put on the robe, then his belt, tying it securely. He checked the hidden pocket within the folds to make sure his few remaining coins were intact. One was missing. He scowled, once again heartily despising the wily little shopkeeper. The coin was worth much more than Shallum's trouble and meager purchases, but Simon was in no condition to haggle.

Fighting pain and nausea, he left the shop and approached the north gate of the city. His troubled gaze swept far out to the right where the Sea of Galilee had begun to awaken in shades of amethyst and pink. The tall, buff-colored *Magdala*, which gave the city its name, rose among giant cypresses nearby and made a stately sentinel. Originally it was intended to guard against approaching enemies, but the watchtower had become a monument of irony: the enemy now lived within its walls as well as inside the surrounding fort Herod had built at its feet.

Keeping his head down, Simon avoided eye contact with two soldiers guarding the gate. He had no desire to engage the Roman army again. Indeed, merely walking from the marketplace to the gate without limping pathetically took an effort that made his head ache and his legs tremble.

Once in the countryside with a cool breeze in his face, however, he experienced a modest resurgence of strength. Soon he reached a fork in the road. The one to the right led to the elaborate lakeside estates where Batasha lived. He paused briefly, glaring angrily in that direction. Women! he thought. *A faithless, whoring breed. Jehovah God should have let Adam keep his rib and thereby saved the whole male race a lot of grief!*

Dismissing her from his mind, he struck off toward the hill country in a determined, hobbling gait. He would find a place to camp. Then after a few days of rest, he'd go to Capernaum in search of the Nazarene.

As he pressed farther and deeper into the isolated terrain, the sun became a blazing punishment over his head. He must find a place of shelter soon, safe from the elements and the wild jackals that often roamed the hills. Stumbling, he fell hard to a sitting position, almost losing consciousness. When his vision cleared, he saw a young boy a little distance away watching him. Lifting his arm, he gestured faintly. "Who are you?" he asked in an exhausted voice.

"I am Jonas." The boy walked closer touching Simon tentatively on the shoulder. "You are hurt. There's a cool place nearby." He tugged. "Come with me. I will show you."

The aroma of baking bread wafted into the cave. Simon rose from his pallet and walked to the entrance. Leaning against a rock, he looked out over the valley. The day had been quiet and restful. A turtledove mourned nearby, and crickets played a melancholy symphony in the underbrush. The hills wore gold crowns as they pulled the purple robes of evening about their feet. In a clearing beyond the cave Jonas hunkered over several cakes baking on a flat rock. He took a stick and made a well in each one. Then he cracked eggs into them, built a protective wall of stones to hold in the heat, and sat back, smiling up proudly.

Simon chuckled at the youngster's ingenuity.

"I hope you're hungry."

"I certainly am," Simon answered.

"Tomorrow I'll try to get us some meat."

"Eggs are fine."

Simon did not question Jonas too closely about where he got his provisions. He figured that the eggs came from someone's nearby henhouse; the grain was probably stolen from a not too distant field; and the milk—well, there was no telling what unsuspecting goat had gotten her teats attacked by this resourceful boy. The thievery made him uneasy. Jewish law, however, allowed for a certain fringe area of any crop to be gleaned for use by the unfortunate. The fact that he and Jonas fit into this lowly category at the present time was indisputable.

"It's ready, sir!" Jonas lifted the cakes onto a clay plate and poured the milk into bowls.

Simon sat on a rock near the fire and began to eat with appetite. This was a good as the other food Jonas had cooked during the past five days.

"Your wounds are healing very well," Jonas said while chewing his food. "The cut over your eye is still very angry though. I'll bet it'll leave a scar. But your eye is no longer black." He grinned and ducked to take a quick drink of milk. "Now it's only a funny shade of yellow."

"The cut should have been sewn," Simon admitted, a trifle regretful that a white scar would bisect one of his eyebrows, probably for the rest of his life.

"I could have done it if I'd had a needle and some thread."

"I don't doubt it for an instant." Simon laughed. Then suddenly he fell silent. Looking up from his plate, he asked, "Where are your parents, son?"

"I don't have any."

This was the answer Simon had gotten every time he'd asked. He chewed slowly. "You mean you don't have a father?"

"No."

"Your mother, where is she?" Simon pressed further. He was determined not to be put off again. He wanted to know more about this engaging youngster who had obviously been living in the hills for some time, probably as a runaway or an orphan.

"She's dead."

Simon dropped the bite of bread on the way to his mouth and set his plate aside. "How did she die?"

Jonas, having already finished eating some minutes before, sat before the fire hugging his knees. "They stoned her."

"Who stoned her?" Simon asked quietly.

Jonas pressed his lips together and stared into the fire, his dark, luminous eyes gathering tears. "The elders of the synagogue in Capernaum. They called her a harlot and dragged her into the streets and stoned her." He jumped suddenly to his feet and ran down the hill, a small gravel landslide at his heels.

Stunned, Simon remained seated for several moments. His heart broke for the boy. Night was closing in. He knew he had to go to the child and offer some kind of comfort. But he didn't know how. Tenderness was foreign to him.

He found Jonas seated in a thicket of myrtle, his head on his knees, crying. Simon reached down and pulled him up. Reflexively, Jonas clamped his arms around Simon's waist, burying his face in his robe. Holding his thin shoulders and trembling back, Simon let him weep. What could one say to a child who had been through such horror?

"They called her bad but she wasn't. She was my mother, and she loved me. She took money from the men because we needed food. After they killed her, they drove me away." He looked up at Simon, his face contorted with grief. "I miss her," he whispered.

Simon turned toward the camp with the boy close to his side. It was dark. A glowing pillar of smoke from the embers of the campfire led the way back. Simon knew instinctively that words at this time would be woefully inadequate. He continued to keep a fatherly arm around Jonas as they silently walked.

Simon didn't have ready answers for life's pain; all he could offer was the caring of human contact. When they reached the cave, he helped Jonas get ready for bed. He spent time tucking the blanket around Jonas as his own mother and father had done to comfort him when he was a child. Then he said a prayer of blessing and patted him on the shoulder before preparing to withdraw.

"Don't leave," Jonas mumbled in a sleepy voice.

"Very well." Simon had not planned to go to sleep so early, but when he settled on his own pallet, his eyelids soon grew heavy. *The Pharisees in Capernaum had been grossly negligent*, he thought, drifting off. In Jewish law, synagogue charities must always make provision for taking care of orphans.

Chapter 2

The wickedness of man was great in the earth.
Genesis 5:6 KJV

Herod Antipas had built Tiberias in only eight years, yet it was a city of ageless beauty. Grecian in style, its marble domes and colonnaded verandas glistened white against the Sea of Galilee, like a goblet of diamonds against a sea of blue silk.

Many pious Jews shunned Tiberias because it had been constructed on ancient burial grounds and therefore was considered "unclean." Mary Batasha bas Hillel was glad she was forward enough in her thinking not to be bound by this kind of religious superstition. She had been looking forward to her visit to the capital, and not even her aunt's frequent hand-wringing and entreaties had deterred her from coming to enjoy her stay as a guest in Herod's palace.

Grete had been afraid that Batasha would have one of her "spells" while attending the festivities. Batasha had never experienced an attack away from home, and Grete worried that there would be no one to care for her. Stubbornly, Batasha insisted upon going on the trip anyway and took leave of her aunt in stony silence without offering a farewell embrace.

Arriving at the palace, she stepped out of the chariot onto snowy white paving stones. A slave led her horse and chariot toward a hedged side street, at the end of which stood a bustling stable, Palladian in design. Another slave wearing Herod's insignia across his chest led her driver, Alexes, in another direction to the servants' quarters. Batasha walked up wide, blue-veined steps toward two massive bronze doors folded open to receive guests. Immediately, she was embraced by her friend Joanna, the wife of Herod's steward.

Joanna gracefully excused herself from the receiving line and led Batasha through the atrium gardens. Hand in hand, they skirted a magnificent fountain decorated with cavorting marble fauns and turned down a lavishly appointed hallway where Joanna opened a door and ushered her into a private apartment.

"Chuza and I reserved one of the best accommodations for you," Joanna said smiling.

Batasha, although not unacquainted with luxury, looked around in silent awe. Translucent Persian silks swathed a huge couch in the middle of the room, and a number of panther skins splashed black on a white-tiled floor. Oriental tapestries festooned the walls, and oval mirrors stood in every corner.

A slave delivered the cedar box containing her clothes; another came with a decanter of wine, goblets depicting Bacchus ensconced amid jeweled grapes, and a silver platter of various cheeses. "I am speechless," Batasha said, half-laughing in wide-eyed wonder.

"Enjoy," said Joanna. "I have to get back to the other guests now," she added quickly, "but I'll return for a chat before the banquet begins. The baths are located at the end of the peristylium. They are fed by hot springs beneath the floor and offer a relaxing way to get rid of the dust and weariness of travel." She gave Batasha a quick hug before hurrying away.

A short while later Batasha entered the side of the bathing hall designated for females. She saw about eight or so unadorned women lounging by the pool. Slaves rubbed perfumed ointment on their backs and shoulders. Batasha, unaccustomed to nudity, quickly looked away. A few other women swam languidly in the water, holding their necks swanlike in order to protect elaborate coiffures from the splashing of lion-headed spigots. These women, too, by all indications, were naked.

Overwhelmed by the unfamiliar situation, Batasha desired nothing more than an abrupt withdrawal. Then she caught the scent of the perfume the ladies were using and decided she must stay and brazen it out. She had come to promote business, after all, and her perfumes were far superior to any being used here. Quickly she disrobed and went into the water as fast as she could to conceal herself.

The gossiping women nearby had barely noticed her, so she relaxed and began to move about tentatively in the warm water. Soon she became riveted by their conversation, unable to avoid eavesdropping since their strident voices carried clearly.

"Did you notice Claudia? Last month at Phineas's party she looked at least four months pregnant. Now she's as flat as a skipping stone," said the apparent leader of the group.

"Abortion," said one of her companions. "Everyone is doing it. There is a new instrument that is very efficient."

"I suppose you heard about Julia," said another. I knew she wouldn't be faithful to Flavio for long. She's the restless type, you know."

"Flavio is notorious as well. Why do you suppose he leaves Rome so often to visit his country estate? It's certainly not to check the vineyard. He has set up a mistress there."

Batasha decided to move away. She considered herself a worldly woman, but their talk was disturbing. As luck would have it, the bevy of matrons also chose that time to migrate, coming again into her immediate vicinity. Now they were again talking about Claudia's alleged abortion.

"But you know how much Antony wants sons. I can't imagine her having the nerve."

"My dear, then you don't know Claudia very well. She definitely isn't the maternal type. Too vain. She would do anything to keep that lovely figure intact. Let's face it, one's stomach is never the same. Why, if abortions were as much in style years ago, I would have gotten one myself. Two actually. Everybody knows that motherhood is not the exalted state the poets would have us believe. One ruins her body breeding babies, goes through the most excruciating agony delivering them, and then suffers the pains of Tartarus putting up with them. Thank the gods that we've got slaves to take the brats off our hands."

Batasha glanced over at the group, then quickly away. Two of them were embracing openly, and it was not anything like the hug of friendship she'd recently shared with Joanna. "Excuse me," she said maneuvering around them. There was a sudden lulling of conversation, then silence, as she ascended the steps.

"Where are you from, dear?" the most vocal of the group asked her. "We're from Rome, invited through our friend and Herod's ambassador, Phineas Lysanus."

"Magdala is my home. I am Batasha." She reached for a towel from a stack on a nearby table and began to dry off.

"Is that one of our outer provinces?" another of the group asked in a tone of disdain.

Batasha smiled. "No. It's a little town nearby. Herod invited me to his annual spring banquet because I'm good friends with the wife of his favorite steward." She wrapped the towel around her tucking it securely. "Personally, I have never met the king."

"Listen to her." They laughed. "The king! Did you hear that? You have the right idea, my dear." The leader hoisted herself up the steps, the others following in her wake. "Just address him as Lord and King and you'll get into his good graces right away." A slave hurried to her side and began toweling her off. "Of course he's merely a tetrarch, but the wiser ones of us are aware of his tremendous appetite for adulation. We call him Your Majesty and act subservient. As a result, he invites us to this diverting little party every spring.

"Yes, Herod is king of this god-forsaken little province, and Herodias is his queen," added another in voice stinging with sarcasm. Everyone laughed.

Batasha guessed that they were jealous of Herodias. The tetrarch's present wife—that term being debatable—was reputed to be a great beauty.

Batasha sat down and began to oil her legs.

"Oh, what is that delicious smell?"

"It's roses," said one.

"No, ginger," argued another.

"It's a special scent I blended myself," said Batasha. "I'm a perfumer. My shop is in Magdala."

"How far away is that?"

"Only three miles northwest. Here, she offered. I'll give you each a sample." They held out their hands eagerly as she poured some of the attar into their palms. "It's made from a white flower cultivated only on my estate. According to family tradition, one of my ancestors brought the first cutting all the way from ancient Babylon's hanging gardens. I call it the Magdalan rose. We constantly distill the nectar this time of the year and on into the summer until the blooms are spent. We have plenty of this perfume available if you have time to visit my shop. My manager, Suzanna, is in charge while I am gone and will be happy to serve you. Then you can go back to Rome with the essence of a flower found in no other part of the world. This perfume is very rare, very expensive."

"It's luscious," one pronounced, stroking her palm down her neck. "I must have some." The others agreed with murmurs of delight.

As she gathered her things and departed, she knew they would be making a trip to Magdala at the soonest opportunity. As a result, she and Suzanna would make a pretty profit from the influx of new customers.

On the way down the hall she met Joanna coming for her promised visit. Her friend seemed somewhat preoccupied although she made a valiant attempt at cheerfulness as Batasha asked her to sit down and have some refreshment.

"What's the matter, aren't you feeling well?"

Joanna sighed before taking a sip of wine. "Oh, I don't know. I just don't seem to be as excited about this sort of thing as I usually am. Last year and the year before, it was different. I was happily involved." She waved her hand. "But this year I'm not a part of it. It's as if I'm standing aside looking on. I can't explain it, but I sense that Chuza feels the same way."

"Has anybody said anything to upset you?" Batasha remember the women she'd encountered in the baths and wondered if one of them had said something to upset her friend. "I've met some of Herod's illustrious female guests from Rome," she remarked. "They're not exactly paragons of virtue."

"They make me sick," Joanna said with hearty disapproval.

"Then one of them did say something." Batasha bristled. Joanna was sweet and naïve. She sometimes had trouble coping with the real world.

"No." Joanna played thoughtfully with the rim of her goblet. "No one has said anything to me directly. It's just that I don't fit in with them."

"And no wonder!" Batasha exclaimed. "You haven't taken a lover, or had an abortion. I'm extremely glad you aren't like them. Why," she added indignantly, "I think I just witnessed two females openly engaged in a type of love play."

Joanna gave a mirthless laugh and shook her head. "That must have been Octavia and Phaedra. Such relationships are looked upon with tolerance in these circles, between women as well as men. Last year my attitude was one of indifference. But now the whole lot of them make my skin crawl." She placed her cup on a low table and sat forward earnestly. "But they are not the ones who have changed. It is I. And also Chuza. It began when we met the Galilean rabbi."

Oh no, not the Galilean again! thought Batasha. Joanna introduced him into every conversation. Giving all this importance to some itinerant prophet was ridiculous. Yet because she loved her friend, she was determined to be sympathetic. "I know you believe he healed little Paulus..." she began in a patronizing voice.

"But he really did!"

"Of course." Batasha bit into a piece of cheese to avoid meeting Joanna's direct and somewhat fanatical stare.

"I know you don't believe it," Joanna challenged. "But if you had been there and seen our little boy burning up with a fever one minute and awake and asking for honeyed milk the next, you would believe too." Her eyes flamed passionately. "It was a miracle performed by the prophet from afar. The hour he pronounced Paulus healed, our son was transformed from a dying child to a normal, healthy one. And at the same time a mysterious renewal took place in Chuza and me.

Joanna obviously thought she'd experienced something mystical where this upstart prophet was concerned. In Batasha's opinion, Paulus would have come out of the fever in any case. Joanna and her husband were making a happy coincidence into a miracle. "Try to realize," Batasha said gently, "that this Galilean is just a man, and not some kind of god."

"No," Joanna countered with conviction, "he's much more than a mere man. You'll see."

If the Galilean rabbi put one in this irrational state, Batasha didn't want to see. Religion was something she had no use for: it was so binding, so restrictive, so—obsessive.

After Joanna left to help Chuza with last minute preparations for the banquet, Batasha began to dress. Her garment was a simple toga made of diaphanous silk the color of pearl. It draped over her figure in folds, gathering narrowly at her waist and criss-crossing her breasts to meet behind her neck in a coral and jasper brooch. A female slave arrived to assist, and Batasha allowed her to arrange her hair into large curls cascading from the crown of her head like spun gold.

Next the slave applied cosmetics to her face and quietly and wordlessly hennaed her nails. Afterwards she bowed and departed as another servant delivered a plate of fruitcake and a fresh decanter. Batasha walked the perimeter of her apartment dressed in her new finery and gazed at herself. The brass mirrors, polished to a high gleam, reflected her as a burnished goddess gilded upon a frieze. She felt as if she were in another world, far away from the dusty streets of Magdala and the shouting, haggling traders that comprised her daily society.

She hoped she would get an audience with Herod so that she could present him with a gift of appreciation for his hospitality. Kneeling on the floor, she bent to search within her traveling chest. A moment later she rose to her feet and looped a slender, delicately carved alabastron about her neck by its long, gold cord.

A tentative knock on her door presented another slave, bowing deeply and waiting politely for permission to enter. He was good-looking, about her age, with classical features and short, black hair falling forward in ringlets on his forehead. Smiling she ushered him in.

"Lady," he said, bowing again respectfully, "I am Troilus, the court artist. I have come to ask if you want your body painted."

Batasha suppressed a puzzled smile. "You paint bodies?" she asked faintly. "I have never heard of it before."

Keeping his head down, he explained, "It has become the newest fashion among the ladies of Rome. The bare skin is adorned with paints of various colors depicting a scene or design. It is a temporary adornment for a special occasion and washes off without difficulty. Herodias has ordered me to paint the body of any guest who wishes it." He stopped abruptly as if suddenly remembering it was not permitted for a slave to talk freely.

"I see." Batasha knew that familiarity with slaves was not generally accepted, but curiosity prompted her to engage him further concerning this curious phenomenon. "And how did you become involved in this most amazing occupation?"

He lifted his face keeping his gaze on the floor. His expression, while impassive, revealed vestiges of pride and passion. "I have a natural artistic ability. Many of the murals in this palace are my work. The depictions of the gods on Mount Olympus on the walls of the peristylium are by my hand, and the vines and fruits twining about the columns were all done by me." He raised his eyes to stare morosely out the window. "Then Herodias arrived. She was much enthralled by the new art in Rome of painting the body. Herod sent me to Egypt to learn the skill, and now it necessitates most of my time."

Batasha sat down on a small sofa. She didn't offer him a chair because she knew that, as a slave, he would refuse it. Passing through the peristylium, she had noticed the lovely delicacy of the murals and columns to which he referred. Now he was using that talent, she supposed, to paint women like those she had met in the baths.

"How many of them have you painted today, Troilus?" she asked quietly.

An expression of aesthetic distaste passed across his face. "I didn't count, my lady. Eight or nine, I suppose. I have become rather famous for my unicorns. Would you like a unicorn, my lady?" Now he allowed his eyes to meet hers and she noted a glint of self-effacing humor.

"Do you think I'd look good in one?" Her mouth lifted at the corners.

"No. The simplicity of your dress is all the adornment you need," he said bowing low.

"You are dismissed, Troilus," she said gently. "I hope the fashion will not last long and you will be back to working beautiful art onto plaster very soon."

Moments later another slave arrived with a request. It seemed that one Phineas Lysanus, a member of the Praetorian Guard, requested an audience with her. She immediately admitted him.

"Are you Batasha, the perfumer, from Magdala?"

"I am." She nodded her heavy crown of curls graciously.

"As a personal friend of Herod and an acquaintance of his favorite steward Chuza," he began, gesturing one linen-draped arm, "I have been assigned the privilege of escorting you to the banquet."

The Praetorian Guard was an elite group of noblemen making up Caesar's personal bodyguard. This was a man of consequence and Batasha was flattered. "It is I who would be honored. You are very kind. I hope it isn't too much of an imposition."

"On the contrary." His appreciative gaze slithered over her in frank admiration. "It will be my pleasure. I saw you when you arrived, and knew then that I wanted to meet you."

She led him farther into the room. "Won't you have some refreshment before we go?" she said motioning for him to sit down. "It's still quite early."

He made himself comfortable on the divan and accepted her proffered cup of wine. She wondered if this was the same Phineas she'd heard the women mention earlier at the baths who had given an elaborate party in Rome. He looked like a man who enjoyed Bacchanalian events. There were lines of dissipation about his eyes and mouth, and an air of ennui in the way he arranged himself among the couch pillows. He was not as young as Batasha imagined a member of the Praetorian Guard would be, not a day under fifty, she judged. She wondered if he rinsed his hair in the juice of pomegranate bark: it was too falsely black to be natural.

"Isn't the wine delicious? I understand Herod imports it from Massilia."

"Very delicate," she agreed politely, taking a seat on a cushioned chair some distance away. Something about this man made her uncomfortable.

"He can well afford it," Phineas remarked. "This province is not as poor as he would have Emperor Tiberias believe. Why, the taxes from the purple dye alone must be enormous."

Batasha murmured noncommittally. Knowing nothing of political matters, she changed the subject. "Do you come every year to Herod's banquet? I gathered from some of the ladies that this trip is considered a pleasurable excursion for many Romans each spring."

He left the couch and came to stand directly at her side, so close that the flesh on her bare arm cringed away. "Herod always invites me," he said, "because I use my influence in Rome to gain him favors from the Emperor."

His oily voice and predatory stealth made her instinctively wary. Quickly she stood up. "I was hoping to see the gardens. I glimpsed them today while the slaves were installing the colored-glass sconces. I wonder if they are lit by now."

"Shall we investigate?" He offered her his arm, which she accepted as a matter of custom. As they strolled the lighted pathways in the garden, she began to relax. The air was heavy with perfume, the shrubbery a riot of flowers and trailing, star-studded vines. People of rank and importance paused often to have a word with Phineas, and he always introduced her to them with deference.

"You are well-known," she remarked.

"Yes. I frequently entertain, and that has made me popular. Ambitious people seek me out in order to be remembered on my guest lists. My extravaganzas are famous." He encased her hand with his, smiling down. "It tries my imagination to come up with new ideas."

It would be impolite to withdraw, although Batasha desperately wanted to jerk away. Remaining silent, she began to experience a vague apprehension, an inexplicable dread.

"I believe they're beginning the feast now," he remarked lifting his head and attuning his senses. "I hear the music. I'm afraid we'll have to suffer through one of Herod's long, self-exalting speeches before we get to the first course. But after that, everything should be quite enjoyable. I have heard that he has imported some extraordinary dancers from Crete."

Batasha also heard the strong cadence of cymbal and drum. It was a raucous noise, very unlike the timbrel and lyre she was used to hearing at Jewish festivities.

"Aren't our Roman ladies handsome tonight? I much admire the fashion of body painting that has come into vogue. There is Livia portraying a magnificent unicorn." Phineas smiled in admiration and waved.

Batasha also recognized the woman: she was the most talkative of the group she had met at the bathing hall, the moral leader. Upon her bare stomach Troilus's delicate handiwork had become something comically grotesque in its undulant movement. Embarrassed, Batasha quickly averted her gaze—she did not know whether to laugh or weep.

Chapter 3

They hatch the eggs of vipers and spin a spider's web.
Isaiah 59:5 NIV

The *triclinium* was ablaze with torches. Phineas led Batasha to a place near Herod's table. She saw Chuza and Joanna across the room and gave them a little wave of acknowledgement. Joanna looked wan and pensive. Chuza laughed and talked to people around him with forced gaiety. She was beginning to understand how they felt—misgivings of her own about coming to Herod's spring banquet had definitely taken root and were growing at a rapid rate.

The Roman fashion of dining required guests to recline on couches perpendicular to the table. Propped on the left elbow with their heads near the table, they used the right hand to partake of the food. Familiar with the custom since it had become widespread in Palestine, Batasha readily took the couch Phineas indicated as he assumed the one beside her nearer Herod.

Positioned to her left, or, more precisely, to her back, was a thin, austere looking gentleman with white hair. Since they were to be dinner companions, she twisted around and gave him a friendly smile. He grimaced in return then glanced about in silent disinterest at the flutter of chattering people taking positions and exchanging greetings.

"Good evening, Tacitus," Phineas said over her head to the man. He reached for a handful of nuts from a nearby silver bowl and tossed one in his mouth. "I'm surprised to see you here."

Before Tacitus could reply, Herod rose to begin his welcoming speech. The room fell silent, almost worshipful. He spoke of politics, trade and revenue, and anecdotes of people and events unfamiliar to Batasha. As she didn't understand much of what he was saying, she concentrated her full attention on his physical appearance.

His face was unusually narrow, his eyes close together over a prominent nose. His neck, arms, and legs were thin while his body appeared quite incongruously corpulent in comparison. He gestured artfully as he spoke with heavily jeweled hands. In watching him Batasha thought of an iridescent snake she had once seen in her garden that had just swallowed a rat.

She remembered hearing stories about his father, the one called Herod the Great, who had ruled all of Palestine. Customarily, when the Romans conquered a territory, they preferred to have indigenous rulers whenever possible. Herod the Great, half-Jew and half Idumean, had ingratiated himself with those in power. Both politically astute and rabidly ambitious, he had made peace with Rome and secured the title of King of Palestine. Then he had gone on to build aqueducts, roads, grand government buildings, and whole cities after the Hellenistic style. He had even constructed the magnificent Temple in Jerusalem, unparalleled in beauty and richness.

But the heart of Jewry had never loved and revered such a man, for he was a murderer. In plots of jealous intrigue, he had killed his brother-in-law, his mother-in-law, his uncle, his favorite wife, Mariamne, the entire family of the Maccabees, and several of his own sons. His last years were marked by an insane paranoia. Upon hearing a rumor that a king had been born in Bethlehem, he had ordered his soldiers to murder all the male infants of that village under the age of two, an atrocity of horrifying wickedness that was still talked about today.

After the death of Herod the Great, Palestine was divided into sections. His son Herod Antipas inherited Galilee and Perea; and another son, Herod Philip, ruled the northern district of Iturea. Both of them, however, were subservient to Imperial Rome in matters of law, taxation, and fealty. Rome controlled the wealthy and troublesome area of Judea, which included the holy city of Jerusalem, through an appointed procurator named Pontius Pilate.

Batasha focused her attention next upon the queen. Herodias had left Herod Philip, her rightful husband, and was now living with his brother, Herod Antipas. Practicing Jews were offended by the incestuous nature of the relationship and further outraged that Herod had not divorced his legal wife before claiming Herodias his new queen. Adultery was a serious breech of the law.

Batasha noted that Herodias was indeed beautiful, as the rumors had indicated, but it was a beauty empowered by an air of raw authority rather than loveliness and serenity. Her features were bold. Her mouth was wide and expressive, her brown eyes alert and cunning. Thick auburn hair, combed back from her face, framed flawless skin and a clear, patrician forehead. Her painted body was voluptuous. Truly, there was little else covering her besides the slave's colorful designs: only a veil of transparent material and a few strands of precious jewels.

Herod ended his speech amid shouts of acclaim, which she joined with polite enthusiasm. Slaves dressed in silk crimson tunics arrived bearing platters of food: seasoned vegetables, roasted fowl, the rare meat of oxen, larks' tongues swimming in a savory sauce, breads stuffed with herbed pork, and other exotic fare.

The slave Troilus was present, acting as Herod's personal cupbearer and assigned to dispense wine to the guests immediately surrounding the royal couple. He showed no recognition as he filled Batasha's goblet, but she sensed his awareness of her and a certain guarded friendliness.

Phineas habitually leaned over her too closely when he reached for food, and Batasha was relieved when he left his couch to pay homage to Herodias. Having eaten very little herself up to this time, she relaxed somewhat in Phineas's absence and selected a slice of red meat, finding it tender and succulent in her mouth.

"The food is delicious," she remarked to Tacitus on her left.

"Yes indeed," he returned. "But I have an aversion to rare meat. It's barbaric and lies too heavily on the stomach—like something dead. And I find the lark's tongues absolutely distressing. Imagine how many of the lovely creatures were slaughtered to feed this gluttonous throng. Imagine how many sweet songs were extinguished." Sadly, he sliced a small piece of white cheese and nibbled at it sparingly.

"You'll have to forgive Tacitus." Returning to his couch, Phineas placed himself closer to Batasha than ever. "He's of the stoical school of philosophy and takes all his enjoyment from depriving himself of pleasure. It gives you a sense of superiority, doesn't it, Tacitus, to exalt yourself above the decadence you find here and in Rome?"

"It doesn't take much to rise above it," the poised, fragile man answered with a sniff. "Pity there aren't more around who honor the Rome of old, when her nobility was her crowning glory, when her men were moral and just."

Phineas laughed. "Tacitus, you are quaint and naïve. One must adjust to the times. And right now the times offer us pleasure." He stroked Batasha's arm with the back of his hand. "Forgive me, my dear, I am frightfully hedonistic. It is my only virtue." Batasha shivered with disgust. To disguise her aversion, she turned to listen to Tacitus who continued to denounce Rome.

"I tell you it will eventually destroy her—this canker of immorality eating from within, this lazy dissolution. If we do not go back to the old values of bravery and honor and family, everything that gave Rome her predominance...."

"Shush!" interrupted Phineas with a motion of his hand. "Quiet now. No more sermons. The dancers are going to perform."

The Cretan dancers were sensuous and provocative beyond anything Batasha had ever seen. The males wore nothing but loincloths; the females were bare from the waist up. Their oiled bodies gyrated to the beat of the drums and the reverberations of the cymbals.

The crowd, sated with food and drink, became a lascivious drunken mob. Couples openly kissed and embraced. Some of them left the room altogether, seeking darker, more private places to further indulge their appetites. The music and revelry continued to crescendo. Batasha, not one given to praying, began to do so now with silent, fervent supplication. "Oh blessed Jehovah, in the name of all that is sane and decent, deliver me from this tumult, and I promise I'll never again have anything to do with these people."

Phineas and Tacitus continued to argue their philosophies. In the course of their conversation, she learned that Tacitus had come to beg audience with Herod on behalf of his son. As a soldier who had fallen under the censure of Emperor Tiberias, he had been banished to the outpost in Capernaum. After talking with Herod, Tacitus made a hasty exit, his thin nostrils flaring with distaste as he skirted around several lounging bodies.

During a lull in the music the sweating dancers broke away for refreshment, and Phineas took Batasha before Herod. Her head was throbbing. While walking to Herod's ornate couch, she became aware of that particular haze of unreality that signaled the onset of one of her spells. In that moment of realization, she experienced a moment of panic. Quickly her blue eyes searched for Joanna. Her friend was nowhere to be found; she and Chuza had slipped away unnoticed.

Knowing well the progression of her attacks, she calculated that she still had some time before being totally debilitated.

This peculiar, one-dimensional way of seeing things, and its accompanying headache, would proceed in intensity for one or two hours before a seizure finally overtook her.

She knelt before Herod as Phineas introduced her to the royal couple. Unclasping the alabastron from around her neck, she presented it to Herodias explaining that it was a rare perfume she wished to offer the queen as a gift.

Pleased, Herodias unstopped the alabastron and, after applying some of the essence to herself, rubbed Herod's hand with a small amount of the oil. Batasha barely heard their murmurs of acceptance as the fragrance of her very own perfume, which she had spent hours lovingly preparing, filled her nostrils and made her nauseated. Never had her beloved scent affected her in such an adverse way.

They withdrew from the royal dais and returned to their couches. Phineas had replenished her cup with wine, and she reached to take a drink.

Someone whispered in her left ear, "Refuse the wine. He has put the powder of the mandrake in it."

Startled, she looked up. Troilus was bending over the table to take away the utensils left by Tacitus.

"Don't drink it," he warned again softly before withdrawing. "He is trying to drug you."

The crowd had begun to cheer as the dancers came back with a magnificent tiger in tow. Batasha swallowed sickly and cast about for a way to excuse herself without drawing undue attention. She vowed that if she got out of this situation with her life, she would never again venture from her safe, well-insulated estate with its pink, marble walls and innocent flowers.

When Phineas became obviously distracted by the fierce roars of the tiger, Batasha surreptitiously emptied her wine onto the floor. Then she requested that Phineas take her to her room as she wasn't feeling well.

Seeing her cup empty, he smiled, took her by the hand, and helped her to her feet. She swayed before bringing herself under control. Oh, why hadn't she listened to her aunt? Why had she come to this unwholesome place and put herself in this kind of jeopardy?

Phineas led her back to her apartment and in a sudden, practiced move pinned her against the door. She writhed, trying to fend off his wine-sour kiss. He opened the door and pushed her through.

"Now we're alone. You won't fight me, will you?" he said advancing toward her.

She shook her head in disbelief.

"No, of course not. You want me. You must." He grabbed her shoulders and kissed her neck.

Batasha pushed him away, slapping at his face. Now anger fueled his lust. He threw her down on the couch and crushed her with his body.

"Oh, no, please," she said sobbing. Scared, sick, senseless with shock, she tried to push him away with weak, trembling arms.

A moment later she heard and felt the impact of something hitting him. She froze in disbelief as he slowly released her and slid to the floor unconscious.

Looking up, she saw Troilus standing before her, armed with a bloodstained, marble figurine. "Oh, dear God!" she cried, struggling to a sitting position. "What have you done? They'll kill you for this." She lifted her hands helplessly toward heaven. "Oh, blessed Jehovah, why did I ever come to this awful place!"

"I couldn't let him hurt you," the slave explained calmly.

"Oh, but don't you see? You will surely die, and I will never be able to forgive myself."

"I'll survive," he said grimly. "I've lived through many things."

She looked down at Phineas. Blood oozing from a wound on the back of his head stained his fine toga. He wasn't moving. "Is he dead?" she asked in a small, thready voice.

Troilus knelt and lifted Phineas's wrist, then placed his hand near his nose. "No," Troilus answered dispassionately. "He will live and once again prey on other hapless victims."

"What makes a man so vile?" she asked.

"Lust," he answered. "Lust and boredom. And a heart as black as hell."

Her eyes filled with tears. "He tried to rape me." She choked on a sob. "How can I ever repay you?"

"By going away from here," he answered. "By not becoming one of them. There are too many of their kind already—those who make slaves of others. Feed on them. Molest them."

He hauled Phineas to his feet and threw him over his shoulder. "I'll take this rodent outside and deposit him under a palm bush. Make sure you remove any evidence of his being here. He drank quite a lot at the banquet. When he wakes up in the morning, he'll assume that he passed out and hit his head. Fear of being humiliated and derided as a common drunkard by his peers will keep him silent."

"But won't he remember coming here?" she asked.

"I doubt it. Strong wine creates confusion and forgetfulness." Troilus went to the window and parted the arras. "Besides, he'll be more concerned about keeping the matter a secret from his friends than trying to remember. But go away, lady. Go away very early in the morning in case he wants to question you," he said from the windowsill before dropping silently into the night with his burden.

Blackness swallowed him up before she had a chance to say more. For a few moments she just stared. Then her vision blurred, reminding her that a seizure was imminent. She moaned. Hadn't she suffered enough this night? Pacing the floor, she tried to fight it. The second stage was already upon her. Color and proportion became distorted. The walls moved, the mirrors glowed, colorful tapestries became feverish, and torches threw grotesque shapes and shadows.

In a panic, she ran blindly to the door. She'd call for Alexes and have her chariot prepared immediately. But that would draw attention from the revelers still in the banquet hall. They would ask questions and the wounded Phineas might be found. No. She'd have to suffer alone. In the morning she'd go quietly while everyone slept, as Troilus had suggested, leaving a message that she had been called home unexpectedly.

Joanna! She'd find Joanna, and she would come and help. But no. She'd die of mortification if her friend saw what was to come. Oh, God, she cried silently, where are you. I'm all alone. Don't you care?

A frog-shaped creature leaped into her peripheral vision, his lips stretched with a grin. "Oh, go away," she moaned. It spanned over her head in an arc and disappeared on her left in a flash of unnatural light. Terror dried her mouth. She forced herself to douse the lamps then stumble to bed.

They would be coming soon—coming to torment her in unholy glee. The green thing returned. He was their herald. She clearly saw his morbid, scaly body and horned head before he again leapt away. She fell back on the couch, her head rolled and she turned rigid.

Then they were all there. A shiny, blue creature moving like a serpent, venomous, odious. Leather-like, skeletal birds flapping above, their clammy wings breathing decay into her nostrils. A personification of death enlarged in front of her, its skin brown, a thousand years old, its face a boiling hole of quicksand. They were not human, not animal, but gross distortions of living beings. One had only eyes, huge and protruding, in sockets of thick skin, eyes that filled her head with liquid madness.

They were Satan's henchmen. She knew them by name: Chemosh, Dagon, Anammelech, Nergal, Siccuth, Meni, Malcham. They did horrifying things in her mind, things that had happened long ago in some evil land in the darkest night. They tortured her with visions of obscenities: bloody mutilations, unnatural sexual rites. They offered naked infants upon an altar of fire. She saw their helpless bodies floundering, their little eyes glowing like coals.

The evil spirits continued to attack until their energy began to wane. Their torment became sluggish shapes and movements, then muddy swirls that slowly ebbed out of her mind.

Finally she was left to a deathlike sleep. She awakened a few hours later. A grey, pre-dawn mist mingled with the sweat of her body, sticking her hair to her forehead and neck. Slowly she rose from the couch. Her torn banquet gown was sodden and soiled. It clung to her like a shroud.

Exhausted, she walked to one of the mirrors. In recent years her attacks had become more intense. This was the worst one yet. Pale, lifeless eyes stared back at her. At that moment, hovering between madness and sanity, between darkness and light, between a world of evil and a yearning for peace, she admitted something to herself that she'd never before been able to accept—her mother had committed suicide. Suffering from the same affliction, her mother had walked into the lake twenty years ago and the demons had taken her under. Now Batasha knew that all the whisperings and rumors concerning the event had been true.

Now she understood. These satyrs were in the blood. They hosted themselves upon a victim until they drove her to destruction. As a grown woman, she could identify with her mother as she had never done before. They were alike—they had the same tainted blood.

It didn't matter that the affliction was unfair and unjust, that they'd never done anything to deserve it. The only reality was its evil existence. She had tried to fight. She had prayed and wept and pleaded. But at this moment, facing her defeated reflection in the mirror, she admitted there was no help, no hope. All was desolation and despair.

She went to the baths and washed the stench from her hair and skin, anointed herself with scented oil, and dressed in a clean linen smock trimmed in purple. Back in her room she braided her hair and wound it about her head in the old-fashioned style her mother had worn. Fresh grief, unabated since she was a child of ten, momentarily overwhelmed her. Her mother had been lovely, her arms white and scented and protective, her eyes laughing and blue as the Sea of Galilee on a summer day.

Breaking away from the pain of remembering, she packed her traveling chest and made a final inspection of the room for traces of what had happened to Phineas. Satisfied that there were no telltale signs, she went in search of Alexes. The palace was quiet. She saw a servant girl asleep outside the banquet hall. She woke her and told her to go and fetch the driver of Mary Batasha bas Hillel.

The sleepy-eyed youngster hastened to obey, and soon her slave appeared. He was in a stupor and not altogether sober. The celebrations of the previous evening had apparently extended to the servants' quarters.

As they departed, dawn broke over the lake, touching the domes of the city with mauve sadness. Alexes drove the chariot through the north gate with its famous intaglio of bending reeds. Batasha gave a backward glance. It was a whitewashed tomb, beautiful on the outside, but rotting within.

Chapter 4

That which I see not, teach thou me.
Job 34: 32 KJV

Simon had become restless during the time of inactivity while his body healed. He was not a man given to abstract ponderings or deep meditations. He preferred to work in stone—tangible evidence of his thoughts and plans. Yet he revered the Scriptures and had brought two scrolls along on his journey, one inscribed with the prophecies of Isaiah and the other a collection of the Psalms of David. This morning he was reading one of the Psalms and committing it to memory. When he had gone to school as a boy in the little town of Emmaus, most of his lessons were by rote. He had memorized the Laws of Moses and had learned to recite them verbatim. The rabbi, however, didn't encourage further contemplation. Interpretation was the duty of the scribes, who reduced the sacred commandments to rules and regulations for daily life.

Having completed his chores, Jonas came to peer over Simon's shoulder. "I wish I could read," he said wistfully.

"Come here, boy." Simon circled his huge arm around Jonas's waist and made him sit down. "You have fixed me some very fine meals and tended my cuts and bruises. Now I'll repay you by teaching you the Hebrew alphabet." He cleared a large square of sand between them as Jonas hunkered down to watch.

Simon drew several rounded letters in the sand and proceeded to put them together into three-letter root words. "This is the ancient language of our fathers. It is no longer spoken except in the synagogues during Sabbath services. All of our Scriptures are written in this language. Boys and girls are encouraged to learn it at a very early age." As time passed, they remained deeply preoccupied. Simon took on the pedantic tones of a rabbi while Jonas quickly absorbed each exercise as a new revelation. The morning shadows shortened beneath the trees then slipped to the other side.

At last Simon stood up, put his fist into the small of his back, and stretched. Jonas, insatiable in his desire to learn, still crouched over the sand slate practicing his newly acquired skills.

"An intelligent boy like you should be in school," Simon remarked. "Tomorrow I'll go into Capernaum and speak to the leaders of the synagogue. It is their responsibility to see that you are properly educated." He looked around at the squalor of Jonas's living conditions. "And this cave!" he exclaimed. "This is no way for a young boy to grow up! The elders should find you a suitable foster home"

Jonas jumped up. "No sir! I won't go back to live in Capernaum. The Pharisee that rules the synagogue is a bad man. He is the one who led the mob that killed my mother."

"Then all the more reason for him to do his duty by you. The synagogue must provide for orphans. That is the law."

"No!" Jonas repeated stubbornly. "I'll never put myself in the hands of that devil!" He stalked angrily from the mouth of the cave and down the hill toward town.

Jonas returned some time later carrying a string of fresh fish and a small bag of wheat kernels and dried figs. Silently, he built a fire and began to roast the fish.

Simon concluded that he had stolen them. Fish didn't bite this time of day, nor did Jonas have the wherewithal to catch them if they did. Simon had winked at the other provisions because they were allowed by the latitude of the law. He strongly objected, however, to Jonas becoming a common thief

"Where did you get those fish, boy?" Simon asked in a voice heavy with accusation.

"Somebody gave them to me." Jonas carefully turned one over, and its fresh aroma wafted up from the hot rock.

"Did you go down to the lake and take them from some honest fisherman while he wasn't looking?"

"No!" Jonas protested defensively. "I swear they were given to me."

"Hasn't anyone ever taught you that stealing is against the sacred law?" Simon relentlessly interrogated. "That one commits a terrible sin when he takes what is not his?"

"My mother taught me this. And all the other commandments. I'm not a thief. I got the fish from a very old lady who lives on the outskirts of town. A generous fisherman gives her a fresh string twice a week. He's a kind man, and she has no way to provide for herself."

Simon wavered. "Who is this woman? What is her name?"

"Sephar. She's the mother of the Pharisee I was telling you about. She lives in a poor hut on the edge of town. Her health is bad, and she walks all bent over with a crippling disease. Sometimes I work in her garden and she pays me with fish since the kind fisherman brings her more than she needs."

"If her son is an elder, why doesn't he provide for her?" Simon asked. "The law requires us to take care of our parents in their old age."

"I've told you," Jonas answered patiently, "the Pharisee is bad. Even though he lives in a fine house and is very rich, he won't help Sephar. He claims to give the money he would use for her to the synagogue. She could starve to death for all he cares."

"I see." Simon knew of this loophole in the law. If a man took an oath that a portion of his income was corban, or dedicated to God, he could avoid family responsibilities. Subdued by Jonas's logic and highly uncomfortable that he'd wrongly accused the boy, Simon abruptly changed the subject. "Are those fish ready yet?"

Quick to forgive, Jonas grinned and began to serve up the food. Simon sat down, and after he had said the customary blessing, they both began to eat. Jonas chattered amiably on a variety of subjects. He mentioned that the fisherman supplying Sephar was a man named Peter. He lived on the north side of town with his wife and mother-in-law in a new house. His fishing business was very successful.

"Have you met him?" asked Simon.

"Oh yes. Sometimes I get odd jobs working at the inn. I've seen Peter there on many occasions. He's a large man. As large as you. But his beard and mane are fiery red, and he makes me think of a lion."

"Does he roar like a lion?" Simon asked his eyes twinkling.

"Oh no," Jonas said munching on roasted wheat nuts. "He laughs a lot, but he doesn't roar. The inn is a stopping place for travelers going to and from the East. Peter sups with them and engages them in conversation. Abdul's inn is well known for its friendly debates. Everyone likes Peter. One evening as I washed the cups, he threw me a shekel and told me that now I was the richest boy in Capernaum. And I guess I was because a whole shekel is a great deal of money. It bought the clothes I'm wearing and the woolen blankets that keep us warm as well as the cooking utensils. Peter has given me money several times since then. And he says funny things to make me laugh. Once I saw him give a Phoenician sailor a bag of denarii. The sailor had lost his foot in a cargo accident." Jonas offered Simon the last of the fish then took it himself when Simon shook his head. "I like Peter. He's nice."

Simon thought that Peter must be exceedingly nice, or else a man habitually in his cups. Giving a purse full of denarii to a total stranger was beyond generosity. Just one denarius was an average day's wage.

"I haven't seen Peter in several weeks though," Jonas said yawning. "He doesn't come to Abdul's anymore. A great rabbi is staying at his house and a lot of people are always gathered around. The rabbi is a healer and a teacher. His name is Jesus. He's from Nazareth." Jonas stifled another yawn. Night had closed around their friendly fire.

"You'd better get some sleep, son." Simon motioned for Jonas to leave the fire and seek his bed inside the cave. "Where did you say Peter lived?"

"On the north side of town, near the lake," answered Jonas settling into his blankets.

Simon tidied the camp and dressed the fire so that, as it died, the gentle radiance of its coals would provide some warmth drifting into the cave. A healer, a miracle-worker, he thought. Could this Nazarene really be their long-awaited King? As he lay upon his own pallet, he silently recited several lines from the Psalm he'd committed to memory that morning: Why do the nations conspire and the peoples plot in vain? The kings of the earth take their stand and the rulers gather together against the Lord and against his Anointed One. The One enthroned in heaven laughs; the Lord scoffs at them. I have installed my King on Zion, my holy hill. Ask of me, and I will make the nations your inheritance, the ends of the earth your possession. You will rule them with an iron scepter; you will dash them to pieces like pottery.

He fell asleep dreaming the dreams of a warrior. The Messiah would restore Palestine to God's chosen people. He would be more powerful than Judas Maccabee who had defeated the Syrian army occupying Palestine over a century ago, braver than Gideon who had routed the Midianites with just two hundred torch-bearing shepherds, mightier even than David who had purged Israel of heathen enemies then made of her a great theocracy.

Accompanied by an army of young, zealous Hebrew men, the Messiah would rise like a giant with clouds on his shoulders and sunlight in his hair. He would lead the attack against the Roman invaders who had fouled the land with idolatry, burdensome taxes, and immoral practices. He would stand astride the Jordan with Jerusalem before his face and Mount Hermon at his back. And the enemy would tremble at his glory. Their horses would falter; their chariots would crash in the dust. Their blood would soak the earth. Simon smiled in his sleep.

Simon rose at dawn. He quietly gathered his things, planning to be well on his way before Jonas awakened. He went down the hillside to a stream to bathe. Keeping the body clean was a religious duty. After meticulously washing and dressing, he took a smooth orangewood comb out of his rucksack and raked it through his thick, black hair. Then he pulled the comb through his beard so that it wouldn't lay in tangled curls unbecoming to the well-groomed Hebrew. Finally he dressed his hair with an ointment of sandalwood to give it luster and fragrance.

Satisfied that now he looked respectable, he grabbed his traveling bag and headed north. After a few steps on the brushy path he suddenly stopped. There sat Jonas, perched on a large rock, grinning down at him.

"Good morning, sir."

"Good morning, son," Simon returned sorrowfully.

"Were you going away without saying goodbye?"

"You were sleeping so well that I hated to wake you." Guilt stabbed at his heart. He reached into his belt and pulled out a half-shekel coin. "Here take this as payment for your kindness."

Jonas pushed his hand away. "I don't need your money."

Embarrassed and uncomfortable, Simon deposited the coin back inside his belt and proceeded to go forward. "I have to go now, son. God's blessing be on you."

Arriving at the top of the hill, Simon became aware of certain sounds behind him: crackling twigs, dislodged stones, the whipping of leaves being pushed aside. He turned and saw Jonas following a short distance away. He was carrying a ragged little bag of possessions tied to a stick.

"And what do you think you're doing?"

"I'm going with you. I've decided to become your servant and follow you wherever you go."

"I can't have a small boy underfoot," Simon explained impatiently. "I'm on an important mission."

"I'm not small. I'm nearly a man! And I won't be underfoot. You've seen how useful I can be."

"I can't afford a servant. I can't afford to feed you, much less pay you wages," he said with finality. Abruptly he continued walking.

"But you don't have to pay me." Jonas ran after him on light, anxious feet. "You can teach me things." He danced around in front of Simon, hopping backwards as Simon's long strides ate up the ground. "You can teach me to read. You can teach me to be a stonemason. I need a trade. You said so yourself."

"It takes strong arms to cut the stone," Simon answered curtly. The last thing he wanted was the responsibility of this boy.

"Then I'll grow strong arms. Look," he said, reaching beneath his woven sash, "I can pay my own way. I can help you with expenses." Panting and holding out his hand, he continued to run ahead of Simon. "And I can make more if we need it."

Simon halted and stared at the boy incredulously. Jonas had several half-shekels in his grubby, outstretched palm. Defeated, Simon looked down, wagging his head from side to side. This clever little baggage was determined at any cost to break away from his present circumstances. Simon had to admire the persistence and nobility he exhibited in spite of the helplessness of his situation. His heart suddenly melted.

"All right, then!" he said in mock exasperation. "You can travel with me for a while. But just until I can find you a home, you understand?" He took Jonas by the arm and led him back down the hill toward the stream. "Meantime I won't be seen with you the way you are. I doubt if you've had a proper bath in months."

He made Jonas strip and get into the frigid water. Then not satisfied with the boy's efforts, he took off his clothes and got in too. He scrubbed Jonas's head roughly ignoring his yowls of protest. Afterwards, he sat Jonas on a rock, took the razor out of his rucksack, and cut the boy's long, glossy hair, ordering him to be still if he valued his ears. He said that long hair on a child was an abomination. When Jonas became a man he could grow it to the shoulders, which was the accepted style for a respectable Jewish male.

As Jonas looked up at him happily, Simon silently berated himself. *Taking on the boy was madness. Traveling was arduous enough and sometimes dangerous. And what would his partner, James, say when he showed up in Jerusalem with Jonas? They had talked about taking on an apprentice, but certainly not a skinny, underfed child with arms no bigger than sticks. Perhaps once back in Jerusalem, he could find Jonas a home. Surely someone would want to adopt the boy and love him.* Simon's heart swelled with pity.

"Now, you must mind your manners at all times," he said gruffly, "or I'll thrash you."

Jonas grinned.

"Today we are going to the house of Peter, the fisherman, because I want to see the prophet Jesus. He may become King someday, and you are to behave toward him accordingly."

"Oh, I will," Jonas promised.

"And keep a silent tongue in your head. It's unbecoming for a boy to make a nuisance of himself asking a lot of annoying questions."

Jonas nodded, smiling up in wordless obedience. His damp hair glistened in the sun. Simon reached down and ruffled it.

At mid-afternoon a blazing heat rose up from the pavement of Capernaum in shimmering terraces. A large population had packed the street in front of Peter's house. Women with sick infants clutched to their breasts pleaded for admittance over their crying babies. The lame struggled to keep from falling as people jostled and pushed them off balance. Blind men strained forward with sightless eyes. Simon was horrified to see a leper skirting the perimeter of the crowd amid indignant shouts of "Unclean, unclean!" A confused clamor of voices assaulted Simon's ears, and the stench of humanity rose in his nostrils.

He drew Jonas to his side and ordered him not to let go. Jonas wrapped his arms around Simon's waist and stuck there like plaster. Simon inched his way through the throng making some headway due to his sheer size and bulk. At length he reached the entrance to the courtyard where he saw a perspiring, ruddy-looking man trying to organize the crowd.

"That's Peter," Jonas said. "I recognize his voice."

"Friends!" Peter's light-brown eyes showed concern and frustration. "Please form a line. The master will see you all!" Cries and growls rose from the crowd. Peter ran his hand through his fiery hair. "James! John!" he called throwing up his hands. "I can't do anything with them."

Immediately Simon heard two of the most thunderous voices that ever issued out of the mouths of men. "Stand back! Give way so that the sickest may enter first!" Simon spied two tall, sinewy Hebrew males, one younger than the other. The reluctant crowd began to respond to their vehement orders and repetitious shouts. Amid the confusion, Simon slipped through the gate unnoticed, dragging Jonas with him.

The press inside the courtyard was just as great, but here the people were quieter. By virtue of his great height, Simon observed a small inner circle gathered under a terracotta roof. In the midst of them stood the prophet, his arms reaching out to people in distress, listening to them individually as they presented their petitions.

Simon inched closer. There was a palpable excitement in the courtyard. It pulsed in the air. Every breath Simon took infused him with trembling anticipation. His legs, always so faithful and strong in every situation, weakened beneath him.

At that moment, Jesus paused and lifted his head. He turned his gaze toward Simon as if deliberately seeking him out. The prophet's eyes shocked him with their intensity. They were as pure as heaven, as deep as eternity. It was as if something hit Simon in the stomach with a force like the most powerful tool used to break up stone. He had to lock his knees to keep them from falling. A sob rose in his throat.

Suddenly, a woman, running from the house into the courtyard, shattered the moment. She was shouting vehemently in an angry voice: "Get off my roof! I said come down from there!" She shook her fist toward the sky.

Simon followed her direction and saw four men making their way across the roof dragging a stretcher. Stopping at the spot above Jesus, they began pulling up the terracotta and laying it aside with care.

"Hooligans!" she shrieked. "I tell you, I won't have this rabble destroying my house," she said turning to address the crowd at large. "Where's my son-in-law?" Her eyes cast about searching. "Peter, make them stop at once."

Peter ran up the back stairway and began to tread cautiously across the roof in the direction of the men. When he got to the stretcher, he knelt down. Lying upon it was a paralytic, his limbs thin and wasted, his face a mask of suffering. After a moment's hesitation, Peter rose to help the men with the ropes that would lower the stretcher through the hole.

"You're going to drop him!" the woman screamed. "Peter, come down from there. You're going to fall and break your neck."

The two loud fellows that Simon had seen earlier attempted to guide the woman back into the house. A tousle ensued. "Peter," one of them shouted, "come and do something with Leah. She's upsetting the crowd."

After making sure the paralytic had been delivered safely before Jesus, Peter ran down the outside stairway. Soon he and a young woman encircled Leah who, still muttering imprecations and warnings, allowed them to lead her away.

Simon focused his attention on the scene unfolding beneath the damaged roof. Jesus was looking up. He seemed amused. From the open hole, sunlight poured over his face, clearly revealing his open smile and expression of warmth and compassion.

"What faith!" he called up to the four men still on the roof. His eyes crinkled, and the white smile in his beard broadened. "I am amazed at your determination and belief." Then he looked down at the man on the cot. "Friend, your sins are forgiven. You've been made right with God this very moment."

A shocked gasp came from a group of Pharisees sitting in a shady recess under the pergola near Jesus. "Who does this man think he is?" said one in a voice of reproach. "Only God can forgive sins. This man has no authority. He can't speak for Jehovah God!"

"That's the Pharisee I was telling you about," Jonas whispered. "He is probably with his friends from Jerusalem."

Jesus turned his head and confronted the six men dressed in finery and sitting on comfortable pillows. He stared at them for several moments. They began to shift about uncomfortably, agitating the blue fringes on their white garments.

"Why are you sitting there complaining against me?" he finally asked in a calm, soft voice. "Why do you have unbelief and resentment in your hearts? I've said this man's sins are forgiven. Which is easier: making a paralytic well, or forgiving his sins?"

Simon and Jonas moved quietly to a better vantage point next to the wall. Simon wondered about the question. *Which was easier?* he asked himself. Then he realized something. It really didn't make any difference—God can accomplish either one with very little strain.

Jesus continued to stare at the knot of Pharisees as if waiting for an answer. They wore pinched expressions and refused to respond. Dismissing them with a wave, he turned to the silent, breathless crowd.

"I want you to know that the Son of Man has the right to forgive sin—that I can do what I claim." His outstretched arm lowered over the paralytic like a scepter. "Get up!" he commanded. "Get up and pick up your mat and go your way."

Somehow the man got his skeletal legs beneath him and pushed to his feet. He shouted. He laughed. His arms stretched toward the light streaming through the roof that surrounded Jesus. "I'm well!" he cried. Immediately he fell to his knees before Jesus in gratitude. Then still sobbing, he turned to his four friends who had joined him, all of them crying and talking at once. They helped him roll up his cot, but he insisted upon carrying it himself. The awestruck crowd parted as they left.

Simon felt faint. He leaned his back against the wall needing the solid, familiar support of the stone.

"Did you see that?" Jonas asked in a whisper.

"I saw it." Simon's voice was thick with emotion. "Dear God, our Messiah has come at last."

Chapter 5

"How beautiful on the mountains are the feet of him that bringeth good tidings."
Isaiah 52: 7 KJV

It had been six weeks since the banquet at Tiberias. Batasha remembered it as a bad dream. She hoped that Troilus had escaped detection in the heroic part he had played in her rescue. She hadn't had a seizure since then but was overwhelmed with a sense of hopelessness and depression. Every morning before opening her eyes to the glad sunshine and the routine business of another day, she sensed that something large and evil crouched beyond the edge of her mind, something dark and menacing and ready to engulf her in a horrible unknown. As she moved through her daily tasks, the threat retreated. But the next day it returned and sat again at her bedside as, curled up in fear, she traveled from the darkness of sleep to the dawn of consciousness.

When she had arrived home from Tiberias, pale and lifeless as a marble statue, her aunt had known that she had suffered a "spell." Batasha had readily admitted it but would not discuss the details or divulge anything else that had happened. Ignoring her aunt's worried looked and solicitous comments, she threw herself into her work. The harvest was more profuse than it had ever been. The flowers must be gathered while beginning to open because to wait until they came into full bloom would be to waste their essence upon the summer air.

Her slave Alexes was in charge of overseeing the workers, keeping a record of the baskets, and making sure that her three distilleries operated continuously. She spent as much time as possible in her laboratory blending the perfume. The attar of the white rose of Magdala comprised the heart of her signature perfume. She added it, however, to a base of almond oil, tinctured with ambrette seed to give it staying power. A few drops of cardamom and clove topped off the secret formula, after which Batasha immediately bottled it in opaque alabastrons imported from Egypt.

The alabastrons were made from a polished, marble-like substance, pastel in color with darker veins running through. The perfume was preserved within a carved out, hollow interior, capped with a jewel or marble stopper, and sealed with beeswax. There it remained inert until the seal was broken and the essence rebirthed and permeated the air with infinitesimal tears of fragrance.

Working among the scents was therapeutic for Batasha. Laurel, chamomile, and rosemary had a calming effect; the oil of sandalwood strengthened her. Ylang-ylang made her smile. These and other attars, balms, and oils arrayed the shelves her laboratory, along with beakers, droppers, measuring scoops, weights, and decorative boxes, tins, and pendants like the alabastrons.

She had established an atelier in her villa, and this is where her friend Joanna found her one morning in mid-summer. "Joanna!" She exclaimed looking up with a smile.

"Grete told me I'd find you here," Joanna said. "I hope you don't mind the interruption."

"Of course not." She motioned for Joanna to sit beside her on the bench while she continued her work.

"I'm surprised you're home. I thought you might be at the shop." Joanna focused on Batasha's hands as she measured the components of her perfume.

"Suzanna, the Cyrene, has taken over the management of the shop," Batasha explained, "so that I can spend all my time with production. We have agreed to be partners. She has also expanded our inventory to include exotic imports such as spikenard and frankincense that her husband and sons bring back from their journeys to northern India. Suzanna had grown tired of traveling with them year after year along the trade route from the coast of Africa to the Indus. Since I have been procuring the alabastrons from them for some time and we have a close relationship, I suggested that she work with me while the men make the arduous trips. How are you?" she asked, looking up briefly. "What has brought you to Magdala?"

"Herod has left Tiberias for his palace in Machaerus, and Chuza and I are residing in Capernaum till he returns at the end of the summer. Since I haven't seen you since the banquet in Tiberias, I persuaded Chuza to stop here for a brief visit before we ride out into the country," explained Joanna.

Puzzled, Batasha continued to measure ingredients. "Chuza and Paulus are here too?" she asked.

"They are waiting for me outside. Paulus wanted to see your horses. We were hoping that you would come with us to Karn Hattin since the weather is so beautiful," Joanna said excitedly.

"Karn Hattin?" Batasha inquired in puzzlement. It was a mountain with two peaks located in the countryside. There was nothing near it to provide entertainment.

"Please come with us," Joanna urged. "Jesus has a camp there and he's preaching to great multitudes. People are coming from Tyre, Sidon, the Decapolis, and even Jerusalem and Idumea to hear him."

The fact that Batasha was unaware of the growing popularity of the Prophet didn't surprise her. She had exiled herself inside her villa day after day and had not gone anywhere for some time. "I have work to do," she said shaking her head.

"Batasha, please," Joanna said softly, setting aside beakers and other paraphernalia to indicate she wanted her friend's full and undivided attention. "I know the banquet was a disappointment to you, and that is probably why you left early."

"The nobleman Phineas was a horrible old man," Batasha responded indignantly. "I can't imagine why Chuza arranged for him to escort me."

"But Chuza didn't know!" Joanna protested. "Phineas asked about you, and since he was a member of the Praetorian Guard and a favorite of Herod, it seemed like a good idea."

Batasha heaved a sigh. "Oh, I don't blame Chuza," she said. "But Phineas was truly evil."

"Then you'll be glad to hear that he fell after the banquet and cut his head badly. It put him out of sorts for the rest of the holiday."

Bereft of activity to keep her hands occupied, Batasha silently wrung them in her lap. "Come on," Joanna coaxed, "take a day off and go with us. It will be lovely."

Restless, Batasha got up and began to pace. She didn't want to leave the comfort of her villa, the absorption of her work. Yet it was a fine day, and she longed for the enjoyment of society.

"If you're concerned about the rumors going around about you and Marcellus, the centurion, please don't be."

Batasha stopped in mid-stride and turned to face her friend. "What are you talking about?"

"Didn't you hear about the fight that took place in Shallum's wine shop?" When Batasha shook her head, Joanna continued. "Marcellus was in there bragging about being your…er…lover, when a traveler named Simon bar Cleopas got into a fight with him."

"My lover?" Batasha said in a choked voice.

"It was a terrible scene. Marcellus and his friends nearly killed the man. News of it has reached all the way to Capernaum."

Batasha had wondered why the stonecutter had left Magdala without a word of farewell. "Was Simon hurt badly?" she asked.

"No one knows," Joanna said. "But apparently he was able to walk, for the guards saw him leaving early the next morning. Since the incident, people have spread the tale, adding their own embellishments. I'm afraid it has damaged your reputation. You know how people always believe the worst."

"I'm not surprised," Batasha admitted ruefully. "I've always been different. They never really accepted me because of my mother."

Seeing her friend's distress, Joanna hooked her arm through Batasha's and they walked into the peristylium. "All the more reason to show them you are unaffected by their gossip. Go with us today," she urged in wheedling tones. "We will have a good time."

"Are you sure you want to be seen with me?" Batasha said half-joking.

"Don't be a goose," she chided softly. "Chuza said that the reputation of more than one woman has been ruined by idle talk in wine shops. There are some men who like to brag about women when in the company of others. It makes them feel impressive and important."

"Mama! Batasha!" Paulus ran toward them, his chubby legs churning across the pavement. "Papa says hurry or we'll miss everything!"

"Whoa there, my fine little friend." Batasha reached out, caught him around the waist, and hauled him into her lap. "Let me see you. Goodness sakes, how you've grown!"

Paulus wiggled off her lap and stood up proudly. "Jesus made me well. See how well I am?"

"Yes indeed!"

"Are you going with us? Oh, please do! Mama says we can sit on a blanket and eat sweet figs. And you can sing with me, and we can play the clapping game." He danced with excitement. "It'll be fun. Jesus will talk though, and then we have to be quiet because he's an important man. The most important man in the world. Papa says so."

"Very well." Batasha gave him a quick hug before turning him around and slapping him on the bottom. "Go tell your papa that I'll have my chariot harnessed before you can say, 'Run donkey, hide donkey.'"

As they approached Karn Hattin, Batasha was astonished by the sheer magnitude of the crowd milling about. Most of them were noticeably of the am ha'arez—the common folk—but many well-dressed foreigners, in addition to clusters of the religious elite wearing their customary blue-tasseled robes, were also present. She was surprised. *How could a poor prophet attract this large assemblage of people?*

The drive up the mountain was pleasant. The terrain was lush with greenery and vivid color. Myrtle bloomed in shades ranging from mauve to scarlet, and canna, poppy, and anemone splashed regally over the hills and meadows, creating a wide palette of colors washed in sunshine.

Halfway up the mountain they found a shady spot under the low boughs of a sycamine tree, tethered the horses, and began to spread out blankets and food. Paulus ran about in excited exploration, exclaiming happily at every songbird and butterfly. Other parties had settled in small groups, snatches of their conversations entwined on the breezes. Chuza walked further up the crowded slope and stopped to talk with a middle-aged man Batasha had never seen before.

"That's Chuza's old friend, Nathaniel," said Joanna. "He's been following Jesus off and on for over a year now. Chuza says he's the only man who has managed to live his life without ever saying a harsh or judgmental word against anyone."

Batasha's blue eyes smiled as she observed Nathaniel. He had the physical appearance of a purebred Jew—smooth olive complexion, dark eyes snapping with energy, and a prominent nose. His bald head, with its silver halo that offered little protection from the sun, had already begun to turn pink. His demeanor was unpretentious and friendly.

She focused on arranging a platter of sliced cheeses and olives. Having left his friend, Chuza soon joined them as she and Joanna continued to set out the food.

"Guess what?" he said. "Jesus has chosen Nathaniel to be one of the inner circle of twelve men to accompany him on his journeys."

"Well, he couldn't have picked a better man," Joanna remarked, placing folded napkins on the blanket. "Just look at those ants," she said irritably. "They have sent out signals all over Palestine that we have arrived with food. Paulus," she called to her son who was playing nearby, "come and sit down before everything gets spoiled. Who else did Jesus choose?" she asked.

Chuza dropped to the blanket, sprawled into a lounging position, and reached over to steal an olive.

"Stop that! Wait till we say the blessing."

"Peter, the fisherman," he said savoring the meat of the olive while working the pit forward in his mouth to be extracted between his thumb and forefinger.

"Well, of course. If ever there was a man devoted to the Rabbi, it is Peter. He has given up everything. He not only ignores his business now, but Leah has been complaining lately about how often his travels take him away from Deborah and their new house."

"Leah complains about everything," Chuza remarked. "Deborah and Peter are in perfect accord on this issue."

"Still, as a new bride, she can't be too happy about his frequent absences," Joanna pointed out.

"Deborah understands him," Chuza argued, helping himself to more olives.

Joanna swatted his hand with the napkin she had been using to ward off flying insects. "He's irresponsible," she said prickly from the heat and the task of laying the picnic, not to mention waging war against the ants.

"Not irresponsible," Chuza objected. "More like impulsive. And generous," he added, snagging a piece of cheese.

"Generous to a fault," Joanna retorted. "His brother Andrew is the practical one of the two."

"Jesus chose Andrew as well."

"But with both of them gone, who will manage the business?" asked Joanna. "Paulus!" she called in a high-pitched voice. "Come here this instant. We're ready to eat."

"Their partner, Zebedee of Bethsaida, will keep the business afloat." He grinned at his play on words since it was a fishing business and then continued to pilfer more food. "Both of Zebedee's sons, James and John, will also be going with Jesus. I just found out that they are cousins of the Rabbi on his mother's side."

"Which probably explains why he chose them," Joanna said acidly. "Oh, young John is nice enough, I suppose," she conceded. "But James! Who'd want that loudmouth around?"

"Why are you so cross?" Chuza asked knitting his brows.

"I'm not cross!" She swatted a fly, which impolitely oozed its entrails onto her clean white tablecloth.

Chuza looked at Batasha, who'd kept discreetly silent during their exchange. His expression pleaded wordlessly for help.

"Why, here's Paulus now!" Batasha exclaimed catching his arm as he ran by. "It's time to eat, darling." Unceremoniously, she lifted him off his feet and made him sit on the blanket. "There!"

"Look at your hands!" Joanna said to Paulus in a horrified voice. "Go wash them. Where's the water, Chuza?"

Chuza scratched his chin thoughtfully.

"Oh, for pity sakes! Don't tell me you forgot the water!"

"Well, how was I to remember?" he asked defensively. "You had me dragging everything out of the house except the jewelry and the cooking pots. Let's go ahead and eat. A little dirt never hurt anybody. Why, when I was a boy, I must have eaten a ton of it."

"It's an abomination!" Joanna retorted angrily. "I wasn't brought up to eat with unclean hands as you were. Don't forget I'm a strict Jew. "

"How could I when you're always reminding me!" Chuza's ears reddened. He had interpreted her remark as a direct insult to his mixed ancestry. Little Paulus, looking tearfully at his hands, murmured something about only wanting to build a fort out of leaves and twigs.

Batasha, distressed at seeing their lovely outing being destroyed by petty bickering, hastened to designate herself a peacemaker. "I'll go borrow some water. Sit down, Joanna," she ordered. "Chuza give her some wine, and say the blessing right away. Everybody is hot and hungry."

A party nearby had brought a firkin of water and were pleased to give some to Batasha. She carried it back in a pitcher, and then soused a cloth and cleaned Paulus' hands and face. Meanwhile Chuza also wiped his hands, and, with a sigh, Joanna followed suit.

"My good linens! They'll never be the same."

"What ninny would bring expensive napkins on a picnic anyway?"

Joanna's chin quivered.

"So!" Batasha interrupted loudly. "Who else did the prophet choose, Chuza? You only named five." She handed Chuza the bread bowl and motioned for Joanna to select some cheese. "Didn't you say he picked twelve?"

Chuza nodded. "There's Matthew. He was one of the Mokhes in Capernaum who collect taxes on caravans leaving north of town with their goods. He started to follow Jesus several weeks ago." Chuza's eyes darted toward his wife anticipating some scurrilous comment about Matthew. Preoccupied with her food, Joanna offered no comment. "Many were displeased when Jesus befriended him," Chuza went on, "since tax collectors are considered to be the worst of cheaters, as you well know."

"Surely this prophet can find better men than that to follow him." Batasha shook her head in disapproval.

"I don't know," Chuza mused thoughtfully. "Jesus is a man of keen insight and discernment. Apparently he saw something redeemable in Matthew. Of course, Matthew was overjoyed, and immediately resigned his position with the government in order to travel with Jesus. Then he held an elaborate dinner and invited all his friends from the customhouse to meet the Rabbi. The Scribes and Pharisees were outraged that Jesus had defiled himself by sitting down to eat with sinners. News of it reached religious leaders in Jerusalem who sent a delegation to investigate Jesus.

"It doesn't sound as if this prophet is winning the support of the establishment," Batasha observed. "If he's to assume important political status, he will have to follow the rules of the Scribes and Pharisees."

"Jesus doesn't need to please the religious leaders by following their rules," Joanna interrupted. "He doesn't have to answer to anybody. He can write his own rulebook."

Batasha ignored this fanatical statement from her friend and asked Chuza to go on with his list of disciples. "Aren't there any upstanding citizens in the group?" she asked wryly.

"There's Philip of Bethsaida," Chuza answered. "He's from a wealthy and highly respected family of silversmiths. Then Thomas and Judas of Kerioth. I don't know much about them, except that Thomas is a twin. And James bar Alphaeus, a stonemason. He is called James the Less because he is much shorter than the other James whom Joanna referred to as a loudmouth. James the Less has a son named Thaddeus, whom Jesus also chose. And there's another stonemason called Simon the Zealot." Batasha realized that this was the same stonemason named Simon that she knew, the one who had nearly gotten killed in a fight with Marcellus. During their walks he had mentioned that he was looking for the prophet Jesus. "Do you know anything more about him?" she asked, curious.

Chuza's brows knitted. "I think Nathaniel said that he and James the Less are business partners. They are from Jerusalem. Simon is a fiery fellow, a revolutionary who is particularly interested in Jesus becoming a Messianic King."

"Hush, Chuza!" Joanne said. "There's Jesus. He's going to talk to us."

The prophet was standing on a huge flat rock between the twin summits of the mountain. Although perhaps a little taller than the average Hebrew male, he was an unremarkable-looking man dressed in a poor brown robe. Distance prohibited her from seeing his face clearly. She joined the vast throng as they rose to their feet and fell into a hushed expectancy.

His speech was precise Aramaic, lacking the usual provincial accent prevalent among Galileans. After he finished a saying, he immediately translated it into equally faultless Greek for the benefit of those from the Decapolis and the well-educated. Even the ancient Hebrew phrases that seasoned his sermon were as correct as those spoken by the Priests and Scribes. His distinct, baritone voice carried over the hillside with great clarity:

"You are fortunate if you realize your spiritual need because then you will experience God's salvation. And when you sorrow for your sinfulness, be happy because God will surely comfort you. God will bless you in your humbleness, and someday you will help rule the earth. Be joyful when you desire righteousness more than anything else because God will give it to you. And then you will show mercy to others and God will continually show it to you. He will bless you when your intents and emotions are pure, and He will reveal Himself to you. And you will be fulfilled because you work for peace, and God will consider you his very own offspring. When difficulties arise because you belong to God, be assured that his Kingdom is your inheritance."

"He speaks in riddles," Batasha whispered to Joanna.

"Just listen." Joanna's eyes never left the mountain.

Paulus had grown restless. Batasha motioned that she would take him back into the shade under the tree. Joanna nodded, still concentrating on every word the prophet spoke. Quietly she and Paulus began to play, drawing pictures in the dirt with sticks and exchanging smiles at the funny faces. She no longer listened carefully to the Rabbi. His enigmatic statements had no practical value in the real world. He was a dreamer—an idealist.

After a while Paulus lay on the blanket and fell asleep. Quietly, Batasha began to gather the remains of their picnic. No longer hearing the sound of the Rabbi's voice, she looked up. He stood with his arms outstretched in benediction. Batasha rose to her feet respectfully. Then his men surrounded him and he disappeared from sight. People slowly began to move around and mingle. Some exclaimed that he was a great teacher, much more learned than the Priests and the Scribes. With others, the afterglow wore off quickly as they became occupied with life's petty annoyances and frustrations. Still others cried out for healing.

She scanned the teeming multitude trying to spot Alexes. Upon locating him, she indicated that she was ready to leave. As she headed toward her chariot, however, Joanna grabbed her arm, pulling her back toward the colorful fringes of the crowd.

"Jesus may come this way soon," Joanna explained. "Don't you want to meet him?"

Reluctant to offend her friend, Batasha silently complied. She glanced back to find Alexes following behind. "We'll be leaving shortly," she said with a smile. "Please remain close by."

The faithful servant nodded. "I think you should stay, mistress. I just saw the prophet restore a withered hand. Perhaps he can heal your headaches. Let's wait on him."

Batasha was astonished. This was the longest speech she'd ever heard the servant utter, and she had known him practically all her life. Her father had rescued him from a battlefield in Gaul.

Out of gratitude, Alexes had sworn to serve her father and his family the rest of his life. His quiet, unwavering loyalty had been one of the few constants during her difficult childhood.

"Does anyone here need the Master's touch?" A gentle-spoken, bandy-legged man came into their midst. He was quite short and wore an incredibly vivid, multicolored robe. "I am James bar Alphaeus, one of the Master's disciples. If anyone is sick or afflicted, please step forward. Jesus will be coming soon."

Joanna piped up without hesitation. "My friend here," she said gesturing toward Batasha, "suffers from severe headaches. Please ask the Rabbi to heal her."

People began to gather around. Batasha felt the flush of embarrassment sweep up her back and across her shoulders into her face.

"What's wrong with her?" a curious bystander asked. "She doesn't look sick or afflicted."

"She has headaches," Joanna repeated stubbornly. "They are serious."

Batasha jerked Joanna's arm trying to get her to be quiet.

"Oh ho! Headaches, is it?" a man in the crowd jeered. "Is the Rabbi now expected to heal a woman of her female complaints?" The crowd laughed and began to lose interest.

Joanna grabbed the little disciple's colorful sleeve. "Please tell Jesus that she suffers dreadfully," she begged.

"Is this true, daughter?" the disciple asked Batasha.

Batasha looked down, too mortified to speak. Joanna hurried to explain. "Yes, it's true! She has seizures. And it is said that she is possessed. Her mother had the same sickness and killed herself."

Batasha's head jerked up. "Joanna, what are you saying?" She tried to turn away. Joanna held her arm firmly as if preparing to wrestle if necessary.

"James! Are there any sick over that way."

Batasha saw Simon shouldering through the crowd, his black hair glinting blue in the sunlight. Recognizing her immediately, his dark eyes narrowed, giving him a diabolical look made even more intimidating by a white scar driving through one of his eyebrows.

"Her friend says she's demon possessed," James explained gesturing toward Batasha. Hearing the mention of demons, the crowd perked up and edged closer. Possession and exorcism always afforded a spectacle.

"This is Batasha, the perfumer from Magdala," Simon told James. "She has a reputation in this area as a woman of sin. The only demon she might possess is one of lust." He motioned to his friend abruptly. "Let's move on and find someone who really deserves the touch of the Master."

James frowned uncertainly. "Do you believe in the Master's powers," he asked her softly.

"Don't waste time, James," Simon interrupted.

Draping her stole over her breast as if to hide wounds, she lifted her head and spoke with a dignified calm she was far from feeling. "You ask if I believe in your Jesus," she said to James. "No, I do not." The crowd rumbled angrily, but she stood her ground. "Your master just delivered a sermon about God, and his love and mercy. And you, Simon," she said addressing him, "as one of his closest followers, have just shown me the kindness of Satan. How can I believe a man whose very followers make a mockery of what he teaches?"

Holding her robes with trembling hands, she turned. The murmuring people parted as she proudly walked away, not stopping until she boarded the chariot and Alexes took the reins. For a brief moment she looked back. She saw the face of Jesus. He was standing on a hill motionless, looking at her with an expression of love and compassion. It was as if he knew and understood everything. She felt like a child again held in her father's arms. The moment was a tiny fraction of time, but it encapsulated an eternity of pain. "Master," she whispered holding his gaze as the chariot turned and began to descend the mountain.

Chapter 6

Behold, the Lord's hand is not shortened
that it cannot save.
Isaiah 59: 1 KJV

The hills of Galilee lay to the west in shadows of purple as Jesus led his twelve over the Plain of Gennesaret. The disciples had sent the clamoring, demanding crowd away to their camps or to inns in neighboring towns. It had been a long, hot day and they were tired. Their feet plodded heavily through the thick, dewy grass as they headed into a cool southerly breeze. The sun lowered onto the hilltops and began to expire in swathes of gold and scarlet. There were no sounds except the peaceful chirring of the cicadas and the disciples talking intermittently among themselves.

Remaining silent, Simon walked a little apart from the rest of the men. He was preoccupied with unwelcome thoughts of Batasha. Encountering her again had been disturbing. As much as he tried, he could not dismiss her from his mind. He breathed her perfume on the evening air. Her face and hair were in the sunset, her figure in the Galilean hills.

When they made camp, he and James the Less built a fire as Jonas and Thad brought firewood. Peter and Andrew unstrapped sacks of provisions and the hungry men gathered around to eat a meal of bread and dried fish. They talked companionably during the evening meal as full stomachs and a cheerful fire restored their strength. Jesus continued to teach. The stars came out and made a twinkling chuppah, or canopy, over their heads as they listened.

"You are the light of the world," he said, "like a city on a mountain, glowing in the night for all to see. Men don't take a light and cover it with a basket. They put it on a lamp stand and share it with everybody in the house. So let your spiritual enlightenment shine forth among men. Let them see the good things you do and be thankful to God for your deeds."

He broke a piece of fish that had been dried in the sun and preserved with salt. He offered some to John, the disciple closest to him, then ate a morsel himself. "You are salt," he said to them with a smile, "to season and preserve mankind. But if salt becomes bland and tasteless, what good is it? It has no purpose. It may as well be considered useless dust."

The Master's energy seemed undiminished by the demands of the day. They had all been up since dawn, yet he alone showed no signs of fatigue. His eyes were alert, his voice and bearing still forceful. Simon was amazed at his vigor and stamina.

The fire burned low. Peter dozed fitfully into his beard then startled himself awake with a snort. Nathaniel smothered a yawn, and Jonas had already fallen asleep with Simon's thigh as a pillow. Jesus stopped talking and glanced about tenderly at his weary followers. He motioned for James the Less to make his son Thaddeus more comfortable since the young man had fallen asleep in an awkward position. Next he bent over Jonas, who, although too young to be named a disciple, was nevertheless included in the group. As Simon rearranged Jonas's head and shoulders, Jesus tucked the child more securely in his robe. Then he took off his mantle and covered his cousin John against the damp night air before walking off into the night.

The rest of the men, one by one, rolled themselves in their robes and fell asleep. Simon continued to sit moodily before the diminishing fire. "How does he do it?" he whispered to his partner. "He's up before we are, works all day like an army of men, then goes out and prays half the night."

Spreading his cloak beneath him, James the Less responded, "He doesn't seem to require as much sleep as we do."

"Did you see how he captivated the crowd today?" Simon asked in a low voice. "He's as charismatic as our ancestor David." Simon's eyes glowed in the firelight. "I'll wager you that within a year he'll be ruling Palestine from a throne in Jerusalem."

"And what will Herod do when Jesus takes over?" James the Less asked satirically. "Bow down?"

"That swine will be dead," Simon said in a harsh whisper. "And so will Pilate, the Tetrarch of Judea."

"I can not imagine our serene Rabbi taking the throne over the bodies of dead men," James the Less pointed out. "He isn't that type of leader."

"He was born to rule," Simon argued. "He is a direct descendant of David according to James and John who are of the same lineage. And anyone can see that he has great leadership qualities."

"True. But I'll wager that war and bloodshed aren't in his plans."

"But fighting the Romans will be necessary," Simon insisted. "What's wrong with ridding the world of heathen vermin anyway? God will thank us for it."

"Maybe. Maybe not." James the Less refused to commit to Simon's views. Yawning, he lay down making snuffling sounds. "I hope my brother Joses is taking good care of our business. You know how lazy he is. Every time he cuts the stone for even an hour, he complains of backache."

"That's your mother's fault. She has spoiled him."

"True," James the Less conceded. "She has always doted on Joses. I suppose because he's the youngest."

"Women!" Simon exploded quietly. "They're useless and frivolous, the whole lot of them. They're worse than the ten plagues of Egypt."

James the Less levered himself up to one elbow. "I guess I may as well forget about trying to sleep since you're determined to talk half the night." He glanced longingly at James and Peter who were snoring in gruff harmony. "Why don't you at least lie down?"

"I'm not sleepy. How did you feel when Jesus called you this morning out of so many followers?" Simon asked.

"I don't know," James said thoughtfully. "I felt a tremendous gratitude certainly." He seemed to search for words. "Something wonderful is going to happen. I have a great sense of anticipation. When you came back to Jerusalem and told me about him, I felt an unexplainable compulsion to come with you. Then my mother informed me that he was my cousin, and I knew I had to come and see him for myself."

"Being related through your father," Simon remarked, "it's strange that you and he never met. Surely his family visited Jerusalem whenever they came up for the feasts."

"His father and my father were brothers," James the Less explained. "Years ago they had a bitter argument. I remember it vaguely as I was only ten-years-old at the time. "It had something to do with my uncle Joseph's choice for a wife."

"Didn't your father want his brother to get married?" Simon asked.

"I don't remember clearly. There was some sort of scandal. My father became inflamed over it. He said some terrible things to my uncle Joseph about his engagement to a young maiden named Mary. His behavior frightened me because my father was a gentle man, and I had never seen him act that way. I had previously met Mary, Joseph's espoused, and could not understand how anybody could object to her. I remember her as a quiet, unassuming Jewish girl." James the Less smiled as his memory took him back. "There was something special about her, an inner serenity, a purity."

Simon gave him a wry look. His partner had a tendency to idealize women. Simon had heard him on many occasions eulogize his dead wife Tabitha.

"I can see Jesus' resemblance to the maid." James went on. "He has the same dark, silky hair that sparks with threads of gold and auburn in the sunlight, the same high forehead and tranquil eyes. But she was small. And since all the men in our family are also small, including my father and Joseph, I wonder where the Master got his considerable height?" He laughed quietly. "From Jehovah God, I suppose."

"He'll make a fine king," Simon pronounced. "More splendid than David or Solomon."

"He's like neither," James said smothering a yawn. "Need I remind you of David's abominable behavior with Bathsheba, not to mention his murder of her poor, unsuspecting husband. And Solomon! He brought grandeur and wealth to Israel then wallowed in it until it consumed his desire for God. Jesus is like no other that has ever lived," James went on. "All the prophets and kings put together can't compare." He settled down grumpily and closed his eyes.

"Are you going to sleep now?" Simon asked.

"Yes, and you'd better too. We have to go to Capernaum tomorrow, and that's more than a little stroll."

Simon raked his hand through his hair wearily, but didn't lie down. He continued to sit and stare at the smoldering coals.

Suddenly his partner threw off his cloak in irritation and sat up. "What's wrong with you?" he asked in a loud whisper. "I've never seen you like this. Usually you're asleep before any of us, like a felled cedar of Lebanon. What is it? Is it that woman?"

"What woman?" Simon asked, immediately on the defensive.

"You know very well who I'm talking about. Jesus doesn't send us into the multitude to insult people, you know. If she hadn't left when she did, there's no telling what that crowd would have done to her. Do you want a stoning on your conscience? Think of how happy the religious leaders in Jerusalem would be to hear that the Master and his followers go about inciting riots and murder. You know they're constantly looking for any charge to lay before Herod against Jesus." Turning his back on Simon, he wound himself in his robe head and all. "Go to sleep," he commanded in muffled tones of finality.

Without thought or plan, Simon left the dying fire and started walking. His strong, muscular legs took him over the moonlit fields until he found himself on the lakeside of Magdala. The great tower and the fort beneath it were asleep. He followed the edge of the lake, its quiet surface gleaming like black onyx in the moonlight. Finally he halted in a little cove surrounded with reeds situated in back of Batasha's estate and sat down on a crumbling bench.

Perhaps James was right. The Master had not called them to judge the people, but to minister to them and lead them forward for healing and deliverance. Whatever Simon thought of Batasha, he had been wrong to reject her in the Master's name. He should not have gotten emotionally involved.

The moon hung high, like an oval platter of silver light. It was late, perhaps as late as the second watch. He'd be tired tomorrow. He leaned forward, rubbing his face in his rough, callused hands. Suddenly he heard something—a low moaning from off to his immediate left in the direction of Batasha's villa. He lifted his head and peered through the gloomy vegetation. An apparition in white floated down the slope toward the cove. His heart gave a lurch and he stiffened in fear.

At first he thought it was a ghost, and his legs tensed for flight. Then he saw a long curtain of hair silvered by the moonlight. It was Batasha. But something was terribly wrong. The back of his neck prickled as she moaned again and called for her mother. Then she said "abba," which meant papa in Hebrew.

Motionless Simon continued to watch as she reached the edge of the lake and glided into the water. He slid off the bench crouching forward like a runner. Now she was waist deep. Her gown billowed out before the water engulfed and swallowed it. Suddenly she flung her white arms toward the moon and seemed to pitch backwards out of control. He held his breath, waiting in vain for her head to break the surface and take a life-sustaining gulp of air. The water churned and she moved out farther as if being dragged.

Every impulse in his body sprang into action. He dived into the water headlong, his eyes wide open, seeing nothing beneath the surface but the blackness of hell. His hands searched; his head was ready to explode from lack of oxygen. Suddenly he surfaced with a mighty gasp and, cold with panic, dove again, deeper this time, his strong arms groping.

At last he touched her hair, then the tissue fabric of her gown. He clutched and tried to pull her into his grasp. She fought with the strength of seven demons and he almost let go because his need for air was overpowering. He gave a sob and inhaled water. Then he imprisoned her next to his body and kicked with all his strength to propel them upward.

Coughing and nearly losing consciousness, he held her limp body as he swam toward the shore with one arm. When his feet suddenly touched the lake bottom, he felt surprise and relief. He struggled out of the water, his sodden robes and Batasha's dead weight making him stagger as he fell into the grass with her at his side.

Drawing deep breaths, he turned her face toward his. She was pale and lifeless. "Oh, you foolish woman!" Quickly he rolled her over and pressed her back. "Breathe!" he ordered in a desperate voice "Please!"

Water gushed out of her mouth. She gave a weak cough, and he felt her waist expand with an indrawn breath. "Blessed Jehovah," he said as she gasped and began to cough.

After a few moments he turned her over to face him. Her eyes flew open, wide and terrified. "Dear God, has Satan sent you also to torment me?" She pushed at him weakly. "Go away."

"What is wrong with you? Stop fighting me. Are you mad?"

"Oh Simon," she begged grabbing his robe. "Please go, please go. You mustn't see me like this."

"Come on. I'll carry you to your aunt. You're cold and hysterical." As he gathered her in his arms, her head jerked back, her body contorted, her eyes rolled in their sockets. He let go fast. Sitting back he watched her go into a seizure, her lovely face contorting into a grotesque mask.

After the initial reaction of shock, his heart melted with pity. Her friend had been right: Batasha suffered from possession. He never would have known. Gently, he bent over to pick her up. She stopped thrashing, but remained stiff and unyielding like twisted iron in his arms.

Her aunt met him on the veranda, her face gaunt and stricken in the lamplight. She prattled on hysterically, first in Aramaic and then in some unknown tribal language. "Brighitta, Brighitta! My little, golden-haired sister. Batasha, Batasha!" She moaned and sobbed. "Such suffering, such death. Brighitta and her child, but not me. Not me." She stroked Batasha's sodden hair and pale face. "You mustn't kill yourself, you mustn't, you mustn't. I knew you would do this terrible thing."

"Silence!" Simon brushed past her. "She's not dead. Where is her room?"

Holding the lamp higher, Grete rushed beside him through the atrium and the peristyle to Batasha's apartment. "Jehovah sent you to save her!" she said. "Thanks be to God! Thanks be to blessed Jehovah!" Then she lapsed again into her tribal tongue as if not wanting to exclude any possible deity from her expressions of gratitude.

Simon laid Batasha down on the bed. Her body went limp, as the evil spirits seem to relax their hold. He watched as her breathing softened and her face became as white and waxen as the flowers that adorned her bedside table.

"How long has she had this sickness?" Simon asked.

"Since she was twelve." Grete knelt and held her niece's hand, calmer now but still distraught. "She started having the spells when she became a maiden."

"Is this one over?"

"No. She will have seizures one after the other throughout the night. They attack her at night when the moon is full. Then they leave at dawn."

"I'll be back," Simon said abruptly, turning on his heel and striding from the room with purpose and determination.

He hurried to the camp looking for Jesus. The Master hadn't returned from his prayers. Simon quickly changed into dry clothes and went to search for him. Calling continuously in a soft, urgent voice, he began to despair of ever finding Jesus in this random, haphazard way. Suddenly, as if by some miracle, he spied the Master kneeling by the gate of a sheepfold. Moonlight shimmered over his shoulders and bowed head.

"Master?" Simon called in a hesitant voice.

Slowly Jesus rose to his feet. Encouraged, Simon came closer. "Master, there is a woman in Magdala who needs your help." Simon could see his face clearly now: the prominent cheekbones, noble aquiline nose, and his ever-changing eyes, deep and knowing.

Simon rushed on to explain, "She is possessed by evil spirits. She nearly drowned herself tonight. I have never seen anyone so tormented." He fell to his knees, bowing his head. "Will you help her? Please?"

Jesus reached forward. His hand warmed Simon's cold, trembling shoulder. "Of course I will."

Upon again arriving at Batasha's, Simon unlatched the gate and led Jesus into the torch-lit courtyard of the villa. "This is Jesus of Nazareth," he said to Grete who met them at the entrance. "He's come to heal Batasha."

"He's a physician?" Grete asked. "We've tried physicians already."

"Not like this one. Stand aside."

She gave Jesus a startled look. He nodded, and something in his calm demeanor must have given her reassurance. Batasha's room was dimly lit by an oil-burning lamp. The moment Jesus came near her, she went into another violent seizure. The slave Alexes standing on one side of the bed and a tall, statuesque

African woman on the other held her down as she twisted and writhed beneath their hands.

"What is your name?" Jesus commanded pointing at Batasha.

She cried out, and then several unearthly voices clamored to speak. "Chemosh, Dagon, Anammelech, Nergal, Siccuth, Meni, Malcham! Why are you bothering us, Jesus of Nazareth? Have you come to destroy us? I know who you are—you're God's Holy One!"

"Be silent!" Jesus said sharply. "Come out of her this instant and never enter her again."

Batasha leaned over the bed gagging and choking from deep within her stomach. Simon experienced a moment of panic. Surely this violence would kill her. Then uttering a deep, exhausted groan, she fell back against the pillows unconscious.

"Is she dead?" Simon asked.

"Where is your faith?" Jesus said. "Have faith in God. Listen to me! You can pray for anything, and if you believe, you will have it. But when you are praying, first forgive anyone you are holding a grudge against, so that your Father in heaven will forgive your sins, too."

Simon nodded. This was a familiar teaching of the Rabbi, and one that Simon accepted but did not fully understand. There are some things that could not be forgiven because of being cruel and unjust like the Roman occupation and their subjugation of Israel. So Simon knew that Jesus was speaking in general terms about forgiveness and that there were naturally exceptions to this precept.

Jesus walked over and sat on the edge of Batasha's bed. He took her white, boneless hand and held it between his own. Her eyes opened, confused and unfocused. As she stared at Jesus, her expression cleared and changed to wonderment.

"Mary," he said to her softly.

Her eyes welled up and spilled over. "No one has called me that since I was a child." When he responded with a smile of tenderness, she went on. "I've been so helpless and tormented. But you came. And you sent them away. Things will be different now." Overwhelmed, she turned her head into the pillow and sobbed. "How can I ever repay you?"

Jesus rose and told Grete to give her something to eat. He then acknowledged Alexes and the stunned African woman with a friendly nod. They both bowed and fell to their knees. Simon felt the power in the room too. It was clear and palpable as the aftermath of a crystalline bell."

Jesus turned and motioned for Simon to follow him. Simon stumbled like a sleepwalker before finally managing to keep up.

Chapter 7

Arise, shine, for your light has come,
And the glory of the Lord rises upon you.
Isaiah 60: 1 NIV

During the next ten days Batasha rearranged her life: consulting with her lawyer, conferring with her father's old friend Ashima, and speaking at length to her slaves. She and her aunt, for once, were in complete agreement. Grete's only lament was that she herself was too elderly to travel with Batasha and that they would be separated for long periods of time.

The first day of July dawned clear and warm. Batasha looked down the road winding north from her villa with a feeling of having been there before. The dusty surface lay quiet and cool with newborn shadows from the cypresses marching along either side. She thought of her childhood, the patches of sun and shade, the nostalgia of green smells and moist earth. Then she thought of her future, the bright adventure of it now that she was well.

Smiling, she turned and hugged her aunt, kissing her dry, parchment cheek. Ignoring Grete's gathering tears, she walked purposefully to her newly acquired four-wheeled wagon. She sat beside her business partner, Suzanna, who was to do the driving.

Then waving to the assembled members of her household, she turned and set her face toward a life of promise and destiny.

They reached Joanna's home in Capernaum around noon. The sun was straight up and blazing. It was a relief to be received into her friend's cool arms and sit in her shaded peristyle. Joanna refreshed them with a cup of apricot juice, iced with snows imported daily from Mount Hermon in straw-packed, leather skins.

Avoiding Batasha's eyes, Joanna focused her attention on befriending Suzanna. The African woman, although amicable, had some difficulty with Aramaic and kept her heavily accented responses brief. Finally running out of things to say, Joanna looked down to hide her discomfort.

"I thought you'd never want to see me again," she suddenly blurted out, "and I wouldn't blame you for it."

"You're my friend," Batasha protested softly.

"You hated me when I told the disciple about your condition."

"Only for a moment."

"I'm sorry." Joanna looked up. "It's just that I wanted so desperately to help."

"I know." Batasha gave her a reassuring smile.

Joanna took a sip from her cup quickly blinking away tears of distress.

"Did you see my new wagon?" Batasha asked brightly, changing the subject.

"How could I not? It looks as if you and Suzanna are preparing to join a caravan to the Far East!" Joanna exclaimed. "What's under the goatskin? Alabastrons on their way to Damascus?"

"The goatskin is a tent. Underneath are supplies we will need to live comfortably for quite some time. Cooking equipment, foodstuffs, clothing, blankets, wash basins." Batasha's voice escalated with excitement. "And hidden in a lemonwood chest at the bottom of it all is a treasury of gold and silver." Batasha and Suzanna exchanged grins.

"Where are you going with all that?" Joanna asked.

"I can't tell you," Batasha said, "because I don't know yet myself."

"Are we playing a game of riddles? How many guesses do I get?" Joanna lounged back into the cushions, adopting an attitude of humorous patience. She knew that her friend's news would burst forth soon of its own volition, like a chick hatching from the confines of an egg.

"Jesus came to my house." Batasha leaned toward Joanna intently. "And within moments he healed me." Her voice was breathless with wonder. "You can ask Suzanna. She saw it."

Quickly uncrossing her legs, Joanna sat up. "Batasha! I knew this would happen to you!" She looked quickly at Batasha's African partner, catching her rich chuckle and white smile. Suddenly they all three, clasped hands, and huddled together laughing. "But why did Jesus come to your house?" Joanna asked.

"It's a long story," Batasha said. "Simon the Zealot brought Jesus to the villa as I was having a seizure. The Master immediately ordered seven demons out of my body and restored me to life and health. The demons had taken me into the lake to destroy me. But I am well now and happy for the first time since I was a child."

"Oh, this is wonderful!" cried Joanna. "I've prayed so many times for you to be healed."

Batasha regarded her with fondness. "Perhaps that's the mark of true friendship—how much we pray for one another." She searched beneath her sash for a handkerchief. "Just look at me. Crying again. You know I've never been one to indulge in weeping," she said sniffing and blotting her face. "It's awfully untidy, but since I met the Master I've been crying a great deal. All the tears in my life that I should have shed, but didn't, are now gushing out like the headwaters of the Jordan." She smiled, continuing to dab moisture from her eyes and cheeks.

"I said that he would change you, didn't I?" Joanna said.

"Yes, you did. He called me Mary. How could he have known that except by extraordinary knowledge? I haven't been called by my Hebrew name for years. And when he did, it was with such love and acceptance that I knew I couldn't go on rejecting the God of my childhood. Somehow I knew that Jehovah had been waiting all these years for me to come back to Him—to come home, so to speak."

"What are you going to do now?" Joanna asked. "And why the wagon and supplies?"

"I'm going to find him and properly thank him. Then I'm going to ask him to take me along on his travels," Batasha said.

"But you're a woman," Joanna protested, not taking her seriously. "All his disciples are men."

"That doesn't matter," Batasha responded with a determined lift of her chin.

"I've already arranged everything. I handed the shop in Magdala over to Ashima, my father's old friend. He is trustworthy, and I have never forgotten his kindness to me after my father left. Since he is elderly, I hired his grandson to help. I also gave all my slaves their manumission and told them they were free to go. They refused to leave, so I have agreed to keep them on for wages." Her eyes filled again recalling their loyalty. "Alexes will be the foreman now, completely in charge of the production of the perfume. Goodness knows he's helped me blend it often enough. Inventory may run low until Suzanna's husband and sons return from the Indus Valley, but there will be enough income to keep the household running smoothly. Suzanna will be coming with me as she also has pledged herself to serve the Master any way she can."

"Heavens!" Joanna exclaimed. "You don't even know if the Master will let you go with him. I hope you and Suzanna are not headed for a terrible disappointment."

"What do you mean?"

"He may not want you, Batasha." Joanna warned.

"Why shouldn't he? I have a lot to offer." She lifted her head in the old, proud way.

"Your money won't impress him, Batasha. He's not that type."

"It's not just the money. I have talents and skills. I'm educated." She trailed off in a tone of hesitation. "I could look after the domestic side of things. And Suzanna is a wonderful cook." She paused, her brow creasing with uncertainty. "Oh, Joanna," she burst out, "he just has to accept me!"

Joanna remained quietly thoughtful for a moment. "Well then, if he considers your proposal, will you ask if I can come too?" she asked. "Just for the summer," she added quickly. "I mean, if he'll let you and Suzanna, I don't see why I can't come too."

"Are you serious?" Batasha asked. "What about Paulus?"

"Paulus is going to Jerusalem to visit Chuza's mother and his sister. He usually spends at least two months with them this time of year. And Chuza will soon be off to Tiberias to serve Herod. I've already told him that I don't want to go this time. I don't think he wants to either after that horrible debacle last spring. But of course I'll have to talk all this over with him before fully committing." She turned to Suzanna whose limited mastery of Aramaic kept her silent much of the time. "Does your husband mind that you want to follow the Master?" she asked.

Suzanna, older and more mature than Batasha and Joanna, simply smiled. "He doesn't about it know yet," she answered in thick accents. "But because I am fixed here" —she touched her heart—"he will agree."

Joanna nodded. "Chuza will not object either," she said, "for he loves the Master as much as I do."

Muttering to himself, Simon measured the lintel over the entrance of the house. Leah had pointed out the crack the moment they had walked into the house that day, homing in on Simon like a bird of prey. Could he fix it? Of course he could. He'd done such a lovely job refitting the roof tiles after those ruffians had torn them up. Simon mimicked her under his breath.

His strong, stonecutter's arms trembled with fatigue as he held up the knotted measuring rope. Couldn't she see that he was blind with weariness? Didn't she know they had set out from Nain that morning and had tramped twenty-five miles at a fast pace to make it back to Capernaum by evening? The Master had not even stopped for a bite of lunch but had kept on going with long, bone-breaking strides until, at last, on the outskirts of the town, he had turned to survey in some surprise his straggling, unevenly spaced disciples, the last being Judas of Kerioth panting a long distance behind.

None of them, not even Peter, who was known for his impetuous remarks, had dared to ask Jesus to slow down. All of them were still awed by what had happened that morning on the way out of Nain. Jesus had called a dead man back to life, a miracle of such astounding magnitude that none had spoken to him or to each other the whole day since it had happened.

"It'll have to be replaced, you know." The mild voice of James the Less startled him from behind.

He jumped, letting his arms fall in aggravation. "What do you mean, sneaking up on a person like that? They should have called you James the Quiet and the other James the Loud instead of distinguishing you by your size." He turned and again held the rope to the stone. "I know it must be replaced. That's why I'm measuring it. One doesn't try patching a lintel. Too risky." He grunted, made a mark, and then moved the rope. "That old shrew will have me spending the whole day tomorrow bracing up the house and inserting a new one. I don't see why she didn't ask you," he grumbled, his empty stomach giving a corresponding growl. "After all, you come from a family of stonemasons, too."

"Not really," James the Less said. "My forefathers were carpenters. My uncle Joseph was a carpenter, and my cousin, the Master, is a carpenter by trade. My father branched off into the business of fitting stone after the family split up and he moved to Emmaus."

"Same thing. You've always been in the building business." Simon's tired, clumsy fingers dropped the piece of papyrus holding his figures. He uttered an oath of impatience then quickly repented as he'd promised God that he would moderate his sometimes intemperate language.

"Here, let me help." His partner bent to retrieve it. "You're as jumpy as a cat. All of us are after what we witnessed this morning."

"I tell you, my eyes have seen many things since I met Jesus, things impossible to believe, but this one outshines them all," said Simon. "The man was dead. Thoroughly and completely dead. No man, even one in a deep sleep, could have breathed through all those grave clothes."

"Oh, he was dead, all right," James the Less returned. "I was close enough to see his chest heave with the first indrawn breath as his spirit came back into his body. He struggled to get out of his winding clothes quickly enough then."

Simon concentrated his attention on coiling the measuring rope over and over his hand. "It's all so mysterious," he said thoughtfully. "Where does the Master get his phenomenal power? How did he command the man's spirit back into his body? And why? Many people die every day. Why restore this particular man?"

"I don't understand how he does so many miraculous things except that it's from God," James the Less said. "But I think I know, at least in part, why the restoration of the young man took place. It was because of the mother. Jesus was overcome with pity for her. The boy was all she had left in the world. With him gone she would be alone and at the mercy of the Pharisees and their charity. Her grief, instead of being loud and ostentatious like that of the hired mourners, was quiet and infinitely profound. Did you notice during the procession how she kept one hand on the wicker bier as if trying to hold him back from the grave? Jesus is a man who deeply sympathizes with the shocks and tribulations we go through in this life," James stated. "He was moved for her. Perhaps she reminded him of his own mother and how she would feel at losing a son."

Nodding in agreement, Simon set the rope aside with his other tools. Hunger and nervous strain had made him feel queasy. Deborah, Peter's wife, a young Jewess of perhaps eighteen, padded up to them on slippered feet, her head modestly covered with a maroon mantle. She was biddable and unassuming, two traits Simon appreciated in a woman.

"My husband says to come to the upper room." She kept her shy, doelike eyes downcast. "The evening meal is being served."

Simon needed no further prompting. He followed after her as James the Less fell in behind. They washed hastily then sat down Oriental fashion around a low table laden with food. Jesus wasn't present, and his empty place at the head of the table was conspicuous.

"Where's the Master?" Leah asked Peter, placing a platter of mealed fish on the table.

"He has been invited to dinner at the home of Simon the Pharisee," Peter said apologetically. "I forgot to tell you."

"Humph!" Leah said making her opinion of her son-in-law's thoughtlessness clear. "Then bless the bread now. Any further delay and the food will get cold."

Simon bristled silently as Peter said the conventional prayer. He couldn't understand his fellow disciple's patience with his bossy mother-in-law. Peter didn't seem to be a particularly longsuffering man by nature. He guessed that the burly, fiery-bearded fisherman tolerated Leah out of respect and love for his wife and a desire to keep peace in the household.

"My ward Jonas tells me that the Pharisee is a man to avoid," Simon remarked as he helped himself to a piece of fish and a fragrant roll of leavened bread.

"True," said Matthew who had pushed up his sleeve to spoon buttered leeks onto his plate. "And he has officials visiting from Jerusalem. Members of the Sanhedrin. My friends informed me of this when I went by the customhouse after we got back today. No doubt the Pharisee and his delegation want to sift Jesus and find some fault in him."

They began discussing the prudence of Jesus mingling with rich and powerful men who wished him ill. Leah upbraided Peter stoutly for letting him go. Nathaniel, who refused to believe evil of anyone, remarked that no harm would come of it. On the other hand, Philip, the urbane and wealthy disciple from Bethsaida, expressed grave concerns. Judas didn't comment. He was totally immersed in the meal.

There was a certain taint of avarice about Judas which Simon could not admire, a greed for the comforts of the flesh that eclipsed every other consideration. His fingers dripped as he ate honeyed figs one after another. Thomas, the twin, expressed doubt concerning the wisdom of the Master's decision to eat with the Pharisees. He always pointed out the worst that could happen, not by design, but because of his natural inclination to dwell on negative possibilities.

The meal was coming to a close. They had eaten well and thoroughly chewed over the problem. Peter impulsively slammed his fist on the table. The cups rattled and the oil lamps blinked.

"I don't like it," he declared in a gruff voice. "Why did James and John have to go on to Bethsaida? We could use their advice in this."

"But surely the Pharisees will not attempt to harm Jesus," James the Less said. His was always the calm voice of reason.

"Who knows what people will do?" Peter argued. "His own friends and neighbors in Nazareth tried to push him off a cliff. People he'd grown up with! They were led by the family of his own brother-in-law." Peter's already strident voice escalated. "Now tell me, would you expect something like that to happen? Sometimes people turn into self-righteous, vicious animals!"

A worried silence fell over the table. Deborah moved to her husband's side and put her hand on his shoulder. He reached up to cover it with his own. "Perhaps," she ventured tentatively, "you and a few of the others could go to the Pharisee's house and stand outside. If all goes well, no harm will come from being there. If not, you'll be on hand to help our Master. Peter looked up into his wife's gentle, wide eyes. Sitting directly across the table, Simon clearly saw the transformation Deborah's touch and soft words had wrought in him. Behold, the lion had become a lamb.

"Peter, you're a lucky man to have such a wife," Nathaniel pronounced into his beard. "She has come up with a good solution."

"I'll go." Simon offered wiping his hands hastily before rising.

"Yes, you and James the Less come with me," Peter said. Assuming the reins of leadership was Peter's natural inclination in the Master's absence. "Three of us will be enough. Any more might excite comment. Causing trouble is not our intention. And bring your ward Jonas," he suggested to Simon. "If there's a problem, he can run back to get the others."

Peaceful onlookers packed the courtyard in front of the Pharisee's house. As was the custom in Palestine, the Pharisee entertained visiting dignitaries under a small, protected roof attached to the house proper, completely visible to the public. By showing off his important guests and the richness of his table, a host attempted to elevate his social status and arouse admiration and envy among his friends and neighbors. In this instance the Pharisee was obviously flaunting his connections with the delegation from Jerusalem instead of the poor itinerant rabbi.

After shouldering their way through the three-deep crowd of people, the disciples came to a halt when they could clearly see the dinner scene being played out under the torch-lit pergola. The host had seated Jesus to the left of the Jerusalem group in what would be considered the lowest position of honor.

Peter snorted, noticeably offended by this humiliating placement. "Don't they know that they have a great prophet in their midst, one anointed with more power even than Elijah?" he said to Simon.

The officials sometimes made an effort to address Jesus or ask him a question in intellectually condescending tones. Further elevating their attitudes of importance was their attire. They wore the customary blue robes with deep white fringe denoting religious superiority. By contrast, Jesus was dressed in the simple, rough clothing of the common folk

Simon leaned toward Peter and spoke in a low growl. "Look! The Pharisee has ordered his servants to give Jesus inferior wine. See how they are serving the guests from Jerusalem from different decanters?"

Peter immediately bristled. "They're giving best portions of meat to the Pharisees too. The servants often ignore the Master altogether." Peter ground his teeth in anger. "A little more of this and I'll charge right into the middle of them and upset the table all over their expensive finery."

Peter's anger fed Simon's, which was never far beneath the surface. "Why doesn't he strike them dead? If he has the power to raise a man to life, surely he can slay these hateful, irreverent peacocks with a wave of his hand!"

James the Less pulled at Simon's sleeve. "Come away, both of you, and cool down. You're angry and don't know what you're saying. While the Pharisee has certainly insulted our Rabbi, he obviously has no intentions of hurting or attacking him. And the crowd is peaceful. Come away," he urged both of them, "before you make a spectacle."

Simon resisted for a moment, his gaze lingering on the Master who seemed a bit weary and forlorn from his long day's journey. He wanted Jesus away from these inconsiderate people. He wanted him at Peter's house where Deborah and Leah would care for him. Leah, whom Jesus had healed of a raging fever on a past occasion, was always scrupulous in her service to the Master. No wine was too good for him, and she always served him first with the choicest morsels of meat. Simon had to give the domineering old nag credit for that much. She treated the Master like a king.

He felt Jonas tugging at his robe. "Are you coming, sir?"

Simon looked down at the boy who had become so dear to him. "Yes," he said smiling. "Go ahead. I'll follow behind you." Turning, he immediately ran into a woman trying to bully her way forward. He placed his hands on her shoulders to keep her from stumbling. A familiar perfume filled his nostrils. "Batasha!" His hands dropped as if on fire.

"Simon, I didn't know it was you." She looked up startled.

"What are you doing here?" This was the first time he had seen her since the night of her healing.

"I came to bring a present to the Master." She clasped an elaborately fashioned alabastron to her breast with protective hands. "I wanted to thank him for saving me." Her eyes welled with tears. "And I want to thank you also, Simon, for bringing him to me."

"It was my duty," Simon replied gruffly. "Are you sure you want to go before all these people with your gift? There are Jerusalem Pharisees attending. The host might not like the interruption."

"I'm sure," she said. "I can not wait. It doesn't matter to me if my presentation is public. Nor do I care what the Pharisees think." She tilted her chin forward mulishly. "The Pharisee sponsoring this dinner will not welcome me here, I know. But I shall honor the Rabbi in spite of it, because it feels right in my heart to do so."

Simon stood aside to let her pass. Then he located Jonas and immediately caught up with him. "Who was that woman you were talking to?" Jonas asked.

"Just someone," Simon answered curtly. "You don't need to know anything about her." He had no intentions of trying to explain Batasha's complex and somewhat tarnished persona to a boy.

Batasha walked into the courtyard toward the tableau of dinner guests lounging on their couches around a low table upon a dais. Held forward in both of her hands lay the alabastron. As she stopped at the feet of Jesus, every person in the assemblage, as well as those looking on from the courtyard, fell silent. The Pharisee was her enemy. He had hated her father, and now was doing his best to destroy her with half-truths and rumors. At being thus within the hostile walls of his house her courage faltered. Then Jesus drew her into his deep, calm eyes and she forgot everything except him. She barely heard the discreet cough of one of the dignitaries or the embarrassed laugh of the Pharisee.

The carefully rehearsed speech similar to the one she'd recited before Herod when presenting Herodias with the gift of perfume lay in a million fractured syllables in her mind, torn asunder by a tempest of emotions. Feelings of inadequacy engulfed her. She was unworthy. Her life had been selfish and unwholesome. Her walk from childhood to adulthood had been through a tunnel of unbelief and pride. When had she lost the simplistic faith of a child? When had she forgotten the faithful, simple prayers a wide-eyed child uttered into heaven?

She had no right to approach this pure man. She was a sinner. Her neglect, scorn, and self-absorption had made her a sinner, as surely as if she'd killed or stolen or committed heinous crimes. She had given no thought to the God who made the universe, to her childhood friendship with him. Nor had she really been concerned about his other creations or about making the world a better, more loving place for mankind to inhabit. Mary Batasha had been the center of the universe, her ambitions, needs, and schemes. And now she realized how spiritually poor she was. With that realization she finally understood the first thing the Master had said that day on the mount. "Blessed are the poor in spirit." Looking into the Master's dark, mysterious eyes, she knelt at his feet, bowed her head and began to cry.

How I wish I could proclaim my great love and regard for you, O gentle man from Nazareth! she cried inwardly. *But I'm weighed down. And sorry, so sorry. I've exalted myself. I've been proud. But now I know how insignificant I am.* Weeping openly, she remembered the next statement he'd made on the mount that day: "Blessed are they that mourn."

How can I adequately express my grief? she said silently. My throat is full of tears. I can't speak. You found me and healed me of my affliction, when I cared nothing for you or the life you represent. How does one repay such a selfless act of compassion? How does one return such love?

A shining curtain of hair fell forward hiding her shame. She used it to wipe the tears that made muddy rivulets on his dusty feet. In great sorrow and gratitude, she concentrated every effort on the menial task of cleaning his feet. The thick, calloused soles were heavy with particles of sand collected from his travels. No one had ministered even a drop of water to refresh him. She broke the seal on the alabastron and rubbed his feet with the aromatic perfume. Gently she worked away the grime with her tears, now mixed with the oil, and then wiped his feet with her hair.

Fragrance permeated the room, releasing deeper waters within her soul. She forgot where she was and that her acts of humility were being observed by a silent throng of witnesses. Continuing to empty the alabastron, she ministered to him until his feet were free from soil. Then she embraced his ankles and kissed the white arch of his foot, placing her tear-stained cheek against his instep.

The Pharisee's face twisted with distaste. He was embarrassed that Batasha had entered his house and so debased herself before this beggarly prophet. Several of his exalted guests asked in whispers who she was. He replied that she was a woman of dubious reputation, little more than a harlot. He said that if Jesus were truly a man of God he would shrink from the touch of such a sinful woman.

Jesus broke into their whispered conversation. "I have something to say to you." He looked up from Batasha's bent head at the Pharisee.

The host feigned politeness. "Then say it, by all means, Teacher."

In a courteous, well-modulated voice he posed a problem: "There was a certain businessman who lent out money at interest. One of his debtors owed him five hundred denarii, and another owed him fifty. They neither one had the means to pay him. Out of the goodness of the lender's heart he cancelled both debts. Now, which one will love him more?"

"Why, the one, certainly, for whom he forgave and cancelled more." The Pharisee smiled patronizingly at this absurdly simple question.

"You have decided correctly," Jesus said. He turned to Batasha who was still kneeling at his feet. "Do you see this woman? When I came into your house and removed my sandals, as is the custom, you didn't afford me the common courtesy of giving me water for my feet; yet she has wet my feet with her tears and has wiped them with her hair.

"You gave me no welcoming kiss. She has kissed my feet tenderly and caressed them over and over.

"You didn't anoint my head with even the cheapest oil, but she broke an alabastron of the sweetest perfume over my feet.

"You're like the debtor who owed little. You see yourself as already righteous, as one who doesn't need pardon. Therefore, pardon means nothing to you. If it were given, you wouldn't feel any relief or gratitude for the favor. On the other hand," he said regarding Batasha with tenderness, "this woman looked into her heart and found it heavy with sin. She realized there was much to be forgiven. The love she gives in return for her pardon is proportional to the need she had." He fixed his host with a steely look. "Those who think they require a small amount of forgiveness, give but a paltry amount of love in return."

Jesus leaned toward Batasha. With his hand under her chin, he tipped up her ravaged face and made her look at him. "Your faith has saved you. You're clean now. Forgiven. Go your way in freedom and peace."

Batasha rose, covered her head with her mantle, and left the courtyard. She walked quickly until she reached the deserted street in front of Joanna's house where she was lodging. Before going inside, however, she sat on a stone bench and removed her mantle. Looking up, she bared her face to the vastness of the universe, the swathes of glittering dust, the ancient rhythms and cycles of the heavens, the velvet, indigo mystery of the deep. A profound benevolence enveloped her, a security she had never before experienced. The moist night air baptized her face and cooled her scalded eyes. She felt poured out and, at the same time, whole—like a hollow alabastron filled with a new essence, an elixir of peace and love.

Simon and the other disciples who had stayed the night at Peter's house lounged among cushions on the floor after breakfast listening to the Master and planning the itinerary of their upcoming journey. Paramount in Simon's mind was getting to the quarry to purchase the lintel for Peter's doorway before the sun rose high and the stones became hot to the touch and their surfaces too blindingly white to the discerning eye.

Just as he was about to rise and excuse himself, Deborah entered announcing in her usual demure fashion that there was a woman outside who wanted to speak to the Master.

"Tell her the Lord will see her this evening when he speaks to the people and heals them," said Peter.

"I already suggested that, my husband," Deborah said, "and even though she is very kind and polite, she most insistently desires an audience with the Master this morning. Her name is Batasha, and she is from Magdala."

Simon, in the act of getting up to leave, slumped back down. "Rabbi, this is the woman whom you delivered of seven demons at her home in Magdala. I can't imagine what she wants now." He turned to Peter. "Send her away. She isn't the sort of woman you'd want in your house and in the presence of your virtuous wife."

"Forbid her not," Jesus said.

Simon bit his lip in silence. All thoughts of stone and lintels fled his mind. Why was Batasha always showing up at odd times to disrupt and discomfit him?

Entering the room, Batasha knelt briefly in obeisance to Jesus. She wore a translucent veil over her long hair and a simple robe of white linen. When she stood again, she quickly scanned the room full of men and caught Simon's hostile glare. Her chin inched up a notch in its usual stubborn fashion, and she planted her feet solidly in a determined stance. Her blue eyes were composed and clear.

"Why have you begged admittance into my home at this early hour?" asked Peter, not unkindly. "What can be so important?"

"I am sorry to inconvenience you," Batasha answered, nodding deferentially toward Peter. Swallowing nervously, she wondered if the Master would also consider her rude and aggressive. She so wanted him to think well of her. "I apologize, Rabbi," she addressed Jesus softly, "but I have a boon to request of you, something extremely important to me."

Jesus looked down, his finger absently tracing a pattern in the carpet. "What do you want me to do for you?" he asked.

Batasha hesitated. For a moment her courage faltered. Maybe it would be better to run away than to be rejected by the Master and scorned by these men. Her resolve to work for him, however, superseded every other consideration. "I want to travel with you," she announced bluntly. "I want to be a follower like these men." She gestured toward the disciples. "I want to serve you, to walk your path."

Simon exploded. "This is preposterous! You can't go where we go. You're a woman!"

"So?" she challenged. "Yes, I am a woman. But I have a right to learn from the Master, too! I have a right to sit at his feet and absorb his teaching."

"You have no rights!" Simon thundered. "This is a mission for men, strong men. You'd faint by the wayside. Go back to your cool villa and sip new wine and play among your unguents and potions."

An embarrassed silence pervaded the room. Peter spread his arms placatingly. "Surely you understand," he said to Batasha. "We simply can't take women with us. Right now we're planning a journey into all the towns and cities of Galilee. It'll be hot and arduous. I've forbidden my own wife to accompany us, and she is intensely devoted to the Master. Female company would be a hindrance."

"There, you see?" Simon said in more temperate tones. "Peter's wife knows her place, as a true daughter of Israel should."

"I also know my place," Batasha said undaunted. "It is with the Lord. If Peter's wife feels the same way, then Peter should reconsider and let her go. I have a friend named Joanna who also loves the Lord and keeps up with his every move. She wants to travel with him too for a while. Because of her great devotion and desire to serve, I think it should be allowed."

Simon lifted his hands toward heaven in horror. "By all that is holy!" he exclaimed. "She would have us become a caravan of vacationers like the Romans who visit Herod every year. I can see it now: a merry band of sightseers wandering into the byways of Galilee to preach to the poor and afflicted. And with all the flighty trivia women bring with them on a trip, it'll take a day to pitch camp and a day to break it. They'll have to stop in every town to shop and have their hair braided. And Jesus will get the reputation of having his own harem accompanying him." Simon paused out of breath.

"Simon!" admonished Nathaniel. "No one would dare accuse the Lord of being so immoral. The Pharisees would criticize him for many things, but never that!"

"I wouldn't be too sure," said Thomas doubtfully. "Ever since he ate dinner with Matthew and his friends they have called him a glutton and a winebibber. What's one more sin added to the list?"

"They're just trying to discredit him," Nathaniel reasoned. "They know in their hearts that the Master is pure."

Batasha saw that she was losing ground fast. She appealed to James the Less with pleading eyes. He looked away. Were they all against her?

"Object all you like," she said, refusing to be defeated. "I know I'm right. Think of all the things women can do that men can't, all the creature comforts they can attend to. My partner Suzanna also wants to come, and she is a very good cook."

"Merciful Jehovah!" Simon interrupted. "How many women does she want to bring? We have Andrew to do the cooking."

Some of them frowned thoughtfully as they considered Andrew's culinary talents. Batasha saw her advantage. "Suzanna's skills would put Herod's chief baker to shame," she said. "And we have amassed funds to provide for the poor."

Judas's eyebrows rose. As acting treasurer of the group, he was always interested in money. The impassioned tone of her voice also drew grudging looks of admiration from Nathaniel and James the Less. Simon's hands clenched helplessly at his sides as he tried to think of an argument to crush her.

"Women can mend and wash clothes," she pointed out. "We can keep the campsite clean and the tents tidy when you are too tired to deal with such chores. We can provide cheer and comfort when you are weary."

Rubbing his chin, Peter seemed to be considering the logic of Batasha's scheme. "It is difficult being apart from Deborah so often," he admitted. "And she is such an angel. How could she be in the way?"

"The women are to be commended for their devotion and willingness to serve the Master," James the Less agreed generously. Simon groaned.

Jesus had remained motionless and quiet during their exchanges. His head was still bent. Dark hair flowed clean and shiny like curtains down either side of his face, concealing his expression. Batasha could see only the tops of his cheeks which seemed full and wide as if he might be silently amused. She dropped to her knees in front of him, leaning forward ardently.

"Please let me go," she begged softly. "You know how much I love you. If I can't learn from you, I don't want to live."

He looked up slowly. His deep-set eyes glinted with humor and something else: complete acceptance. "Mary," he said with the familiar voice of loving approval she was beginning to recognize.

Laughing through her tears Batasha folded her hands together in front of her face. "Oh, thank you! Rabboni! My own dear Master!"

Chapter 8

*Praise him with the timbrel
and dance.*
Psalm 149:3 KJV

Jesus and his band of followers camped in a grove of acacia trees bordering a wide, sugar-sand beach midway between the commercial cities of Tyre and Sidon. To their right lay ancient Sidon ten miles to the north, a city renowned for its wicked idolatrous devotion to Baal. To the south within dim visibility was the metropolis of Tyre, an island city that had become attached to the mainland by a causeway built by Alexander the Great more than three hundred years before. Both cities prospered with bustling sea trade brought in on the mild waves of the Mediterranean. Tyre was famous for exporting its purple dye manufactured from the millions of murex shells existing in great white and lavender heaps on the nearby beaches. Sidon trafficked in all kinds of goods both exotic and nefarious such as ivory, gemstones, ebony, and slaves.

Every day Jesus went into one of the two cities to speak in its synagogue. Due to the many dispersions of the Hebrew people throughout the history of Israel, there was not a major city in the known civilized world which didn't have a unified group of practicing Jews. These little communities kept a firm

grip on the traditions of their forefathers: adhering to their
rituals, eschewing all heathen interference, and taking care to
keep family bloodlines pure. As God's chosen people, Jews
invariably prospered and did well in business. A community
of Jewish bankers controlled the riches in Tyre and Sidon,
looking down their crooked noses at Gentiles, whose money
they manipulated and multiplied. The Gentiles, in turn, were
contemptuous and fearful of this strange but necessary group
of people whom they needed for financing and loans.

There was a copious well in the center of the camp filled
with deep, quiet water, abundant and sweet. Andrew had chosen
this particular spot to pitch the tents because of this rare find.
No one could imagine why the well had been dug and then
abandoned. Andrew reasoned that at one time it might have
been the site of a thriving dye works because fresh water was
essential in the manufacturing of the purple dye. Whatever the
reason for its existence, everyone was grateful and it became a
focal point, or lodestone, of their daily living.

Not only had Batasha and Suzanna come along in Batasha's
lurching four-wheel wagon, but also Joanna. Deborah had
accompanied Peter, and James and John had invited their mother
Salome, a hardworking, practical little woman who had thought
to bring her chickens.

The Zealot showed signs of strain. He stomped irritably
about the camp scattering the chickens, which by accident or
sheer perversity frequently got in his way. But he was the only
one who seemed unhappy with the cozy little tent city; everyone
else was pleased with the good food and dry, comfortable
goatskin shelters.

It was evening and suppertime. The disciples had returned
from Sidon without the Master. When Salome asked her oldest
son where Jesus was, James replied that the Master had stayed
behind to dine at the home of one of the wealthy bankers of
the city.

During the general before dinner hubbub of exchanged
greetings and washing up, Batasha walked down to the beach

looking for Jonas who liked to play in the shallow waves and scour the tidal areas for washed-up treasure. Spying him at the shoreline intent on building some sort of architecture in the sand, she called out:

"Jonas! It's suppertime!"

Caked with sand, he stood up. After diving into the swell of a rolling wave, he ran in her direction, his loincloth clinging to his slender flanks like a second skin. He grinned up at her shaking the water from his hair and eyes.

"Be still!" she ordered brusquely attacking his head with a linen towel before turning him around to dry his back. "Heavens! You're getting as dark as Suzanna. Soon everybody will think you are a little Nubian boy."

"It's fun." His tanned face intensified the white of his teeth. "I wish you would go in with me sometime. Thad swam with me yesterday after they returned from Tyre, but he says he must always go with his father James the Less to accompany Jesus and I shouldn't count on him as a playmate. And I've begged John to swim with me, but he's too grown up and serious." His dark eyes looked up at her tragically. "Nobody wants to have any fun."

She slung the towel over one shoulder and held his chin in her hand. "I'll go in with you soon," she promised before bending to kiss his brown nose.

"Tomorrow?" he asked excitedly.

"Perhaps." She laughed. "Now scat! Change into dry clothing before supper. And don't forget to hang your wet loincloth over a tree branch," she called as he scampered up the hill. Her smile vanished quickly as she saw Simon standing nearby, his arms folded over his chest in disapproval.

When she started to pass him, he caught her arm. "Don't treat him like a baby."

She flung off his hand. "Why not? He is a lovable child. He needs affection."

"In a few years he will be at the maar stage in a Hebrew boy's development. It will be time for him to be a man," Simon explained inflexibly. "I am trying to prepare him for that responsibility since I am the only father he has."

"In the meantime he is still a boy," she argued. "A boy who has missed a great deal of affection in his young life. And if I want to dote on him and mother him a bit, I shall."

They stared at one another, blue clashing with black, neither one willing to back down. Simon broke the impasse with a command: "Don't make him weak and womanish."

"Love will make him stronger," she asserted trying to bring her temper under control. She knew it would grieve the Master if there was bickering among his followers. She looked down searching for words of appeasement. "I'll try not to interfere," she finally conceded before turning to climb the hill. "Come and eat now. Suzanna has prepared her best recipe of chicken and saffroned rice. And I've made a sweet pastry with honey and nuts. You must be tired and hungry."

They entered the camp walking some distance apart in silent wariness. Batasha glanced at him and caught a strange, fleeting expression on his face, a certain confusion mingled with self-reproach. She avoided him during the meal as, seated around the fire, she listened to the men discuss what had happened that day.

Peter said that Jesus amazed the common people, and his simple stories confounded the wise men in the synagogues. Today he had told the people about a farmer sowing seed in various types of soil. Even after he had ordered them several times to listen, many had not understood that he was acting out the parable before their eyes. His words were seeds that would grow into truth and freedom if their hearts were spiritually receptive

Batasha hazarded a glance at Simon and observed his smile. No anger or disquiet marred his expression. At that moment she conceded that he was possibly the handsomest man she had ever seen. She turned her head away quickly.

"I'm not sure I fully understand the symbolism of everything the Master says," old Nathaniel said honestly. He rubbed the humped bridge of his nose thoughtfully and shook his grey beard. "Sometimes I'm not clear at all about what the Master really intends for us to know, what he expects us to believe. So much of what he teaches is simple and we accept it. Yet upon close examination, it becomes abstract, and too complex for analysis."

"I know what you mean," Thomas agreed. "Sometimes I wonder who he really is and how I am supposed to respond to him."

"You stay confused," Simon criticized. "Jesus is the long-awaited Messiah. Right now he's gaining the popularity and trust of the people both of the wealthy class and the *am ha rez*. When the time is right, he'll allow them to proclaim him King over Judea, Galilee, and all outlying districts. He'll reign with a pageantry we haven't seen since the days of Solomon. Then as the Persian Cyrus of ancient times or Alexander of Greece or the Caesars of Rome, he'll take over the whole world and everyone will pay homage to him as their true king."

"And as his disciples, you twelve will be his generals," said Salome excitedly. The hard-working, wiry little woman made no secret of her good-natured ambitions for her two sons, James and John.

Thomas, chaffing from Simon's abrasive criticism, spoke up. "The ancient prophets foretold of a Messiah who would rule the earth in glory," he allowed. "But Isaiah also told of a suffering Messiah, poor and lowly, who'd bear the burdens of the people and bleed for their sins,"

"I can see Jesus in this role before I can picture him as the avenging conqueror Simon presents," James the Less said as he nodded respectfully toward his partner in silent apology. "Simon and I have debated these two differing concepts many times."

"Nonsense!" Simon asserted. "The Messiah will deliver us from our Roman bondage and establish his own theocracy. That much should be apparent to us all." His eyes swept the circle in search of support.

Peter sighed. "Let's not argue among ourselves. None of us knows the Lord's mind. It is beyond our comprehension to completely understand him. All we can do with certainty is serve him with our whole heart and make sure we are good fertile soil for his teaching," he said in conciliatory tones. "Whether he is a conquering Messiah or something else, he'll let us know in due time."

"Peter is right," Philip agreed. "I've studied at the university in Alexandra and have sat at the feet of the learned scribes in Antioch. No one agrees on exactly what the Messiah will be like. Almost everyone, especially young zealots, feel as Simon. They want him to be a political King, one who rules with benevolence and wisdom instead of the forced servitude of the Romans."

A thoughtful silence fell on the group. "How do the people in Tyre and Sidon receive him?" asked Deborah quietly. "Does he heal those among them who are sick? Do the crowds follow him about as they did in Galilee?"

"He's different here," said Peter musingly. "It's almost as if he's holding back his power."

"It's because this area is predominately Gentile," said Simon presumptively. "He won't give himself fully to the heathen world because he came to minister primarily to the seed of Abraham."

Philip disagreed. "I don't believe he would deny anyone simply on the basis of their blood or tribe. After all, my mother was Greek and he chose me. The Magdalene is of mixed parentage and he healed her of seven demons." He paused regarding Batasha with open friendliness. "I believe he's holding back because they aren't prepared to accept him as a true Prophet of God. They weren't taught stories of Jehovah from the cradle as our Jewish children were. As a result, they have no sense of spiritual matters. They live by their senses and by their senses they are made happy or uncomfortable. Their religious beliefs, if any exist, are based on superstitions. Upon seeing the Master's miracles, they might immediately assume he is a magician, or worse, a sorcerer. I think he's sowing seed here among the Gentiles, if I may refer again to the parable. He will patiently and painstakingly prepare the soil and plant the seed. Then he'll go away and let it germinate for a season. When he comes back, if all goes well, he'll reap a harvest for the Kingdom of God."

Batasha gave him an admiring smile. She especially liked Philip. He was a scholarly man with a gentle, wry humor, who had spent his entire life searching for knowledge and answers to the meaning of life.

As an accomplished musician, Deborah could play a number of instruments, all of which she had brought along on the trip. It had become customary for her to entertain them each night after dinner as they sat before the fire. Tonight she selected the *kinnor*, a type of lyre made of a sounding board with an empty space in the middle strung with sheep gut. When strummed, it produced a melodious sound soothing to the soul. Batasha wondered if it was this type of lyre that David played before Saul to ease his mental stress.

Deborah often sang an accompaniment to her music in a clear, soft soprano voice. The effect was beautiful, inspiring a fleeting, benevolent envy within Batasha's untalented being. Batasha could give a fair imitation of a dying frog, and that was only when she really concentrated on doing well. Aware of her shortcomings in this area, she was careful not to join in the singing when many of the others of the party did so with amazing success. Simon had a wonderful baritone voice, possibly due to the depth of his chest, and John's tenor was sweet and rich. The Master himself loved to sing hymns before the fire and could provide a miraculous range of harmony. Due to his absence this night, the music, although certainly pleasant, seemed to have lost a dimension.

If Batasha had any ability at all to express herself musically, it was through dance, which she enjoyed immensely and performed quite well. As a child she had loved to go to weddings and parties because of the dancing. During Deborah's playing, she often held her back rigid to keep from swaying and hid tapping feet under her robe.

The music picked up as Deborah changed to a traditional Hebrew tune with a strong beat. Nathaniel and young Thad began to clap. Batasha could hardly keep her feet still. Suddenly, Jesus came up from behind and took her by the arm urging her to rise. He held her to his side smiling down, his face radiant in the firelight, and they began the sideways and backward steps performed so often at Jewish feasts and celebrations. With her arm twined around his waist, she followed his excellent lead and sure steps. Laughing with the pure delight of a child, she pulled up Jonas in passing. He stumbled, but soon caught on. He, in turn, grabbed Peter who, with his customary keen enjoyment of life, participated with enthusiasm. Soon several others joined in and it became a line dance.

The Master led, his white smile flashing brilliantly in the firelight. It was one of the few times in her life that Batasha had felt pure joy. Sequential thought ceased. The past was a lost memory, the future a distant anxiety. There was only the moment, the dance, and holding on to the Lord. If he had decided to strike off into the vast, besprinkled night, she would have followed him confidently with sure trusting steps.

The music finally stopped amid laughter and clapping. "Lord, did your dinner go well?" she asked breathlessly. "Did you get enough? I could fix you something if you're hungry."

"Master," Jonas interrupted hugging his waist. "Will you go swimming with me tomorrow?"

Before he could answer, Deborah suggested that he at least have a cup of wine. They all gathered around as if drawn to a magnet. Salome offered to rub his back with oil, for he would sometimes allow his aunt to do this after a long day. Shaking his head and laughing, he ruffled Jonas's hair and bent to kiss Salome's cheek saying that his only need was to go to his Father in prayer. Tacitly they understood, for he would often draw apart at night to meditate before making his bed alone.

The next morning Batasha and Joanna harnessed the donkeys and set off toward Sidon for a few supplies and a poking exploration among the booths in the marketplace. When they arrived in the teeming city, Batasha bought some rice, nuts, and a frivolous wind chime hung with silver bells that captured her fancy. She also picked out some choice pomegranates to take back to Jonas. Joanna found a brass-studded girdle she thought would look good on Chuza and a tiny jade box of malachite for her eyes.

The bazaar swarmed with color, and the loud staccato of several different languages clashed in the air. Batasha lost herself in the ebb and flow, delighting at the variegated garb and spectacle of humanity. At times, though, she silently wept, because the crowd was liberally sprinkled by the lame and deformed, who huddled on the pavement groveling for a copper coin or a crust of bread.

At one point her eyes caught an old beggar peering at her. She couldn't see him clearly as he was half-hidden behind a stall. A tremor of recognition forced her to advance a step in his direction. He quickly fled, and the hustle and bustle of the throng blotted out his existence.

"What's the matter?" asked Joanna. "You look as if you've seen a ghost."

Batasha stammered. "N…Nothing. For a moment I thought I saw someone I knew. He was standing over there at the stall where you bought Chuza's girdle," she said pointing. "But now he's gone."

"Well, who was it?"

"Oh, I don't know," said Batasha dismissively waving her hand. "Nobody, I guess. Just a strange, nameless old man."

Joanna shrugged. "Have you gotten everything you wanted?"

Batasha peered absently into her woven shopping bag. "Yes, I think so."

"Then I think we had better be heading back," said Joanna. "Suzanna will be needing our help with the evening meal."

They mounted the animals and made their way down the congested, noisy streets out of the city. The early September sun had turned merciless. Joanna continually mopped her brow with a perfumed silk handkerchief, clearly unused to the rigors of traveling in the open heat at midday.

"Whew! I feel as if I'm going to melt right down to a spot of grease," she complained.

"I may go in swimming today," Batasha mused. "It's a good day for it, and I've been promising Jonas. If I start the bread, will you finish it?"

"Certainly," said Joanna. "But what will you wear in the water?"

"I have a short tunic. Do you want to go in to? If so, we'll hurry up with the bread and both take a swim. Jonas would love it. Poor little rascal. He keeps telling everyone how wonderful the water is but no one will pay him any mind."

"No, thank you! I only swim in the little blue pool Chuza built me just after our wedding. I can see the bottom clearly, and it's not over my head. No vast oceans with great thrashing waves for me. And all those transparent wriggling things, and those leggy creatures with the large pincers. Ugh!" She shuddered and looked at her friend askance. "I guess you've heard about the huge sea monsters people have sighted in the Great Sea—tremendous leviathans with long serpentine necks, and tiny evil heads with beady eyes and razor-sharp teeth?"

Batasha gave a bubble of laughter. "Yes, I've heard those old stories invented by bored sailors too long at sea. But I think the beady eyes and razor-sharp teeth are your own exaggeration."

Joanna grinned. "Well, it stands to reason that they'd have them. How else could they see an innocent white leg under the water and bite into it for a nice juicy meal?"

Batasha laughed and called her a coward. They reached the stretch of beach before the pine grove where they were camped and could now clearly see the tall trees enclosing the site. The donkeys, their senses keen for shade and water, stepped up the pace.

Batasha had been plagued with a sense of unease off and on the whole way back. She had an inexplicable feeling that she was being watched. Her azure eyes darted to the rocks of a massive tumbled-down wall to her left, instinctively looking for a reason for her discomfort. Suddenly she screamed, clapping her hand to her mouth. The grey, scraggly, seemingly bodiless head of an old man was peering down at her from atop a rock. It was the same face she'd seen in the marketplace.

"Batasha! What's wrong?" Joanna exclaimed turning and looking back in alarm. Upon seeing that her friend was still mounted and had not been jostled off into the sand, she sighed with relief. "I thought you'd fallen and hurt yourself."

"No, I'm all right." She waved distractedly, scouring the rocks again, not seeing any sign of the weather-beaten face whose familiar dark eyes had struck painfully at her childhood memories. It was nothing, she reasoned, merely a mirage rising in the heat off the white boulders.

"These foolish beasts," Joanna grumbled, jogging along unsteadily while dabbing her forehead. "They're enough to break all your bones and clabber your insides."

Within two hours after arriving back at camp Batasha was dressed in her tunic and down at the water's edge. Ignoring Jonas's excited taunts, she sat down on a linen towel and smeared her arms and legs with oil, being careful to put a heavy application on her nose, which was already freckling at an alarming pace from being too much in the sun.

Jonas continued to pester her unmercifully, throwing water in her vicinity where it broke into diamond drops caught by the sun, only to splatter and disappear into the thirsty sand. She warned that he would be a very sorry little boy if he didn't mind his manners because she knew very well how to make short work of wicked children.

He laughed impertinently, tossing another handful of water, dousing her thoroughly and making her gasp. When she got up

and advanced toward him with purposeful determination, he
giggled and lunged into an oncoming wave, trying to get away.
Catching up with him within minutes, she cut his legs out from
under him and gave him a proper dunking.

Then they rode the waves and crouched in the backwash for
a time digging fingers and toes into the shifting sand, finding
all sorts of interesting treasures. Soon the beach was littered
with a cache of shells, smooth stones, and bits of driftwood
they'd discovered.

At last Batasha came out of the water and flopped down on
her towel. She told Jonas to go on and play while she rested.
She closed her eyes and let the Mediterranean sun absorb the
droplets from her cooled skin. Soon she became languorous and
sleepy and entered into a state of semi-consciousness. Vaguely
she heard voices in the distance, but took no notice since it was
too early for the men to return.

"What in the name of all that's holy are you doing?" Simon's
harsh voice shattered her peace.

Her eyes flew open to meet his, black and scowling. She
bolted for her robe, donning it hastily.

"Well, well, what have we here?" said Philip walking up.
His manner was amused and friendly. "A mermaid? A siren?
A piece of golden flotsam?"

"How's the water? Asked Andrew arriving with some of
the others.

"Nice." Batasha shook her damp hair. "Very nice." She
glanced nervously at Simon who was still seething, his nostrils
dilating like some great behemoth ready to charge.

"Now there's an intelligent girl," Nathaniel wheezed joining
the circle. "Whew! I've never been one for beach bathing, but
on a day like this it's not a bad idea."

"Ho!" Peter called from a distance away. "Is this what the
women do all day while we're gone? Gad about on the beach
like a bunch of wealthy Romans on the Isle of Capri?"

Batasha responded to his teasing. "You should try it. It's
very refreshing."

"Master, Master!" called Jonas from the waves. "Come on in! It's fun!"

Jesus went to the shoreline and disrobed down to his loincloth. He waded into the surf and dove into an oncoming wave, his strong, sinewy carpenter's arms slicing the sea with muscular ease.

Impulsively Peter cried out like a wild Bedouin, flung off his robe, and hit the water with great showmanship. Then they were all going in, even old Nathaniel, whooping like a schoolboy on holiday. Thomas held back dubiously, but Andrew and Peter grabbed him by his arms and hurled him in clothes and all.

Batasha surveyed the scene with great enjoyment. Even Simon, eager to join his friends, had joined the happy melee. But when Batasha caught herself watching him more than the others and with greater interest, she hurriedly turned away and went to help the other women with the food.

After a while Deborah went down to tell them supper was ready. She came back dripping. Peter in his exuberance had pulled her in.

"They've all gone crazy," Salome muttered scrubbing a cooking pot. "You'd think they'd never been in the water a day in their lives. And my boys are fishermen! Constantly working the boats and nets. Always getting wet." The pot gleamed and she tackled another with fierce determination.

"They've been working hard," said Batasha. "And it's so hot. Everyone needs to play occasionally."

Salome said "Humph!" as if the concept of play hadn't occurred to her since infancy. "I wish they'd come on," she said. "The hens are getting cold."

"I don't think the Zealot is going to be very happy about having poultry again," remarked Joanna. "He barely touched that delicious dish Suzanna fixed last night."

"The Zealot doesn't like chicken whether it's cooked or walking around," said Salome. "The next time he kicks out at one of my white-leggers, he's going to get this!" The spunky

little woman doubled her fist into a tight knot and shook it in
the air as if it were a lethal weapon.

Batasha stifled a giggle. Salome's fist against Simon would
be about as effective as an acorn dropping on the backside of
a Lebanese bear.

"Why is he always so angry?" Joanna wondered aloud.

"He's very intense," Deborah commented. "Perhaps all
Zealots are." She had rinsed the salt from her hair at the well
and wrapped it in a towel.

"Why did the Jesus choose a surly one like that?" Salome,
in her ever-constant need to be busy, began to meddle with the
platters of food Suzanna had arranged and covered with linen
napkins. The heavy-set African looked on, the whites of her
eyes flashing dangerously.

"Did you ever stop to wonder why he chose any of them?"
Deborah asked. She had come back from her tent in a crisp dry
tunic gathered at the waist with braided leather. "My husband
has never been a saint. Far from it! He visited the taverns too
frequently and has a reputation for impulsive and boisterous
behavior. I thought I was the only one aware of his good
qualities. But Jesus saw them immediately and called Peter
right out of the Sea of Galilee one day while he was fishing,
telling him he would make him a fisher of men. You can look
at every one of the disciples and see faults." She paused to
reconsider. "I suppose Nathaniel might be an exception," she
amended. "I don't know by what standard the Master chose his
followers," she continued thoughtfully, "but it was not based
on perfection."

"He can see into the inward man, into the heart. He can
tell whether a person is hungry for God and desperate to know
Him," said Joanna walking toward the path that led to the beach.
"I'd better go down and call them out," she volunteered bravely.
"They must be starving."

Cannily, Joanna survived intact. Soon the men had rinsed
with fresh well water and were settled around the fire in clean
robes, eating hungrily. Peter announced that they had decided

to break camp tomorrow and go back into Galilee. Batasha was sad. She'd been happier these two weeks than she'd been since childhood.

That night she stood at the shoreline looking out at the vast expanse of sky and sea. The two were distinguishable only by a ribbon of reflected moonlight ending at the horizon like a path to infinity. The moist breeze lifted her long curtain of hair and cooled her dry, melancholy eyes. She turned and saw a man coming down the slope and knew immediately who it was. Philip's manner of walking was unmistakable. He was the only one she knew who walked with his head tilted at a quizzical angle as if always asking wry questions about the world around him.

"Going for another swim?" he asked.

"No, I just needed to get away for a while."

"Will you walk with me?" He came along side her and they began to amble down the beach together. "Tomorrow we go back."

"Yes." She sighed.

"You don't want to?"

"Oh, I know it's time to go," she said. "It's just that I've enjoyed myself."

"You've enjoyed the flies and the gnats and the sand sticking to your skin?" he asked cynically with upraised brows.

She laughed. "Of course not. But the people. Our group. I've gotten to know them, to think of them as family. We've been close here. It may never be the same again."

"So you've formed opinions of us?" he asked.

"Not really opinions," she answered.

"Observations, perhaps?" he pressed. When she nodded, he continued. "I just wonder, then, what your observations are concerning me?"

Realizing that he was flirting, she smiled. "Well, I think you're enormously nice and exceptionally well educated."

"And you like me?" His eyes sparkled merrily in the moonlight.

She felt a pleasant little butterfly in her chest. "Do you want me to?"

He threw back his head and laughed. They had reached a turning point and began to walk back toward camp. "Yes, as a matter of fact I do."

For a moment she was struck with shyness. Never had she imagined that this charming and sophisticated man might be interested in her. "Why did you call me a siren today?" she asked changing the subject.

He chuckled. "I was making a joke. When I was a child, my Greek mother told me amazing stories of her ancient ancestors and their many gods, whom, I must say, were a pretty undesirable lot. They were particularly capricious and vengeful where one of our legendary national heroes was concerned. His name was Odysseus. While traveling back from the Trojan War, he suffered many trials and misadventures. A Greek named Homer wrote it all down in a magnificent epic poem about eight hundred years ago, and I studied it as a literary work at the universities in Alexandria and Athens. But of course then it didn't have all the scariness and thrill that my mother put into it at bedtime when I was a boy."

"Didn't your Jewish father have something to say about your mother filling your head full of heathen gods and such like?" Batasha asked.

"Oh yes, he disapproved heartily and ordered her to stop many times. But she was a born storyteller and I was an avid audience."

"Then a siren is one of the ancient Greek goddesses?" she asked.

"Not a goddess. A nymph. A lovely sea nymph. There were three of them. They lived on an island and sang beautiful songs which lured sailors to their deaths on the rocks. Odysseus stopped his men's ears with wax so that they would not hear and be driven to destruction."

"Ha! Then you did well to call me a siren," she said. "Because my singing could certainly drive a person to ruin."

They had reached the path leading to the camp and turned to face each other."

"Are you coming up?" he asked.

"In a moment," she said. "You go ahead."

He took her hand. "I hope we will be seeing a great deal more of each other, Batasha." Releasing her hand, he departed.

Bemused, she turned and strolled toward the water's edge. "Merciful heavens," she whispered as a sudden, fearful thought occurred. With all the work she had been doing lately had her hand felt like one of those spiny creatures she and Jonas had found in the sea today? Oh, why hadn't she rubbed on some lotion before leaving camp? What must Philip think?

"Well, it didn't take you long to slip back into your old habits, did it?"

Startled out of her frivolous angst, she whirled to face Simon, his black eyes sparkling with angry chips of obsidian. "What are you talking about?" she asked bewildered.

"I'm talking about Marcellus," he said harshly. "And now Philip. You are a temptress and will always be."

She sighed inwardly. There seemed to be no escaping Simon's low opinion of her. She had tried silence and she had tried conciliation in an attempt to raise herself in his esteem and promote peace. Neither had been effectual. She decided, therefore, that confrontation could cause no more harm than was already done.

"And you are a disagreeable brute," she said tartly, "as unfortunately it appears you will always be." He stepped forward, but she held her ground. "And concerning Marcellus, there was no reason for you to start a fight with him," she challenged. "That was your decision. Please don't blame your rash conduct on me. And although it is none of your business, I might mention that Philip has treated me with both respect and consideration, which is a great deal more than I can say for you."

"You lured him down here," he accused. "He saw you in that skimpy swimming dress today and couldn't help himself."

Simon's strong emotions had rendered him almost speechless. He paused a moment then exploded, "You're no better than Bathsheba, parading before a man and tempting him!"

Her mouth dropped open in outrage. "I am heartily sick of everybody down through the centuries blaming Bathsheba for one of the darkest scandals in Jewish history," she began, launching into a tirade. "There is nothing in the record that indicates she planned to seduce King David. It was David who was out scouring the rooftops for naked women. It was David who had her brought to his palace and got her with child."

"Be quiet," Simon ordered in a soft, threatening voice.

"It was David," she continued in his face, "who arranged for her husband to be killed."

"I said be quiet."

"It was David who sinned. It was David's lust!"

Suddenly he crushed her to his body and kissed her, intensely and thoroughly. There was no anger or brutality in it—just sheer, raw passion. When he released her, she ran.

The camp was asleep. Once inside the tent, she fell on the blankets catching her breath. When her heart ceased pounding and her blood cooled down, she turned over on her stomach, buried her face in her arms, and began to laugh soundlessly. *Dear heaven! What would he have done had she spoken up in defense of Eve?*

Chapter 9

Remember the Sabbath day,
to keep it holy.
Exodus 20:8 KJV

Back in Capernaum the party split up, each having his or her own business to attend to before uniting again at Peter's house in a couple of weeks. Batasha stayed with Joanna, planning to go on to Magdala to spend a few days with her aunt and see to the perfumery. James and John went with their mother to Bethsaida at the northern tip of the Lake of Galilee. Philip accompanied them, for this was where his father had his prosperous importing business. Matthew stayed at his own house in Capernaum. Others of the disciples dispersed to the homes of friends and relatives. Simon and James the Less planned a trip into Judea to visit their families.

As Batasha packed her belongings in preparation for her departure for Magdala, she held up the little wind chime she had bought in Sidon. Its tinkling music cascaded in a pleasant shiver from top to bottom.

"That's lovely," said Joanna entering the room. "I remember you buying it when we visited Sidon."

"Yes," said Batasha regarding it fondly. "I'm going to give it to my aunt. With all our traveling around I hardly have a place to hang it. Aunt Grete will put it on the veranda where she can enjoy its pretty music every day."

"I came in to tell you that Simon is here," said Joanna.

Batasha deposited the chime into the chest where it collapsed discordantly. "Who?"

"The Zealot. He wants to see you. He's waiting in the peristyle."

Batasha went immediately and with some trepidation, not sure what to expect. She and Simon had not spoken since their encounter on the beach and had assiduously avoided eye contact. She found him standing with his back to her, huge and formidable in his loose-fitting robe. He was accompanied by Jonas, an unexpected development that relieved her apprehension a great deal.

"Good morning, Simon," she said graciously. Jonas ran and wrapped his arms around her waist. "Hello, scamp." She welcomed the boy with a hug.

Simon had turned. "Batasha," he acknowledged her with a curt nod.

"Won't you sit?" she gestured to a bench by Joanna's blue-tiled pool.

Simon shook his head. "I don't have time. James the Less and I are to leave immediately for Emmaus. Thad will be staying behind in Capernaum to help Peter. The crowds have heard that Jesus is back and have already begun to gather. James and I need to visit our families and check on the business, but our trip will be hurried as we want to return as soon as possible." He hesitated. "Jonas told me that you invited him to spend a few days in Magdala. Did you mean it?"

"Why certainly," she answered. "I'd be very happy to have Jonas at the villa."

"It's just that our pace would be hard on the boy," Simon explained. "I wish to spare him the stress of constant and arduous walking day after day."

"I understand," she assured him. "Jonas is more than welcome to stay with me while you're gone."

His gaze met hers then skittered away to focus on Jonas who had gone over to inspect Joanna's pool with great admiration. Simon's expression softened as he watched the boy peer into the water at the colorful tiles continually fracturing into hundreds of shades of blue.

Perhaps this was a good time to attempt a civil conversation, Batasha thought. "Simon," she said beginning tentatively, "I never properly thanked you for rescuing me that night at the lake and for bringing Jesus to deliver me from my affliction. I owe you my life. Please accept my heartfelt appreciation." She hoped that this simple expression of gratitude would, at least, open a positive dialogue between them, if not an amicable relationship.

"It was Jesus who wrought the miracle," he said, gruffly dismissing the topic with a wave. Precluding further discourse on the topic, he walked over and abruptly placed a rucksack at her feet. "Here are Jonas's things. I will fetch him in two or three weeks."

Before she could adjust to his preemptory manner, he had crossed the peristyle and gone out the front entrance without a backward glance. She shook her head, dragging in a deep sigh. Then she turned to Jonas who lay on his stomach at the edge of the pool swirling his hand through the water.

"You can't go in," she said implacably.

He grinned.

"I mean it. Joanna's little pool is primarily for looking, not for a boisterous boy thrashing about like a leviathan. When we get to my house, you may swim in the lake. And there are plenty of secret hideouts on my property where you can play. There is even an old tree house my father built for me when I was a child."

"A tree house?" Jonas jumped to his feet. "What is that?"

"It is a place of safety between heaven and earth, where one can dream dreams," she said. "I'll show you when we get there."

☙

Simon and James the Less traveled south along the western shore of the Sea of Galilee. They crossed the Jordan at the ancient city of Beth Yerah to follow the eastern bank of the river, thereby observing the law that prohibited a strict Jew from touching the soil of Samaria. Once within sight of the white cliffs of the lower Jordan Valley, which produced much of the limestone used in Palestine, they turned west to cross the river again into Judea, the precincts governed by Pilate.

James the Less began talking about the Essene community at nearby Quamran, rising from the desert in a wide, white plateau. Only members of a special brotherhood were permitted inside the monastery. John the Baptist had been one of them before coming out to travel up and down the banks of the Jordan proclaiming his message of repentance and the coming Messiah. John was still alive in a dungeon at Machaerus, one of Herod Antipas's palaces. It was said that the Tetrarch had taken a personal interest in him, but Simon and James the Less shook their heads in concern when they contemplated the great prophet's chances of survival.

The two disciples bypassed Jerusalem, dovetailing into the road leading to Emmaus. It was late evening when they finally came within sight of their humble little stoneyard and the small, well-kept house at its farthest end where James lived with his family.

"Ah," James breathed painfully. "You see how my brother Joses has let the grass grow up around the stones. What would a customer looking for a suitable monument think when seeing yonder Lebanese marble so ingloriously wrapped in vines and thistles?"

"He's let the whole place go to hell!" Simon ground out fiercely. "We paid a pretty price for that particular stone, a price we might never have recovered anyway once the Roman customhouse wrung their taxes out of it. I'll break your brother's addlepated skull for this!"

"Calm down, my friend." James grasped Simon's arm, which was granite-hard with anger. "Remember my poor, elderly mother. Didn't we expect something like this anyway when we left the business to Joses?"

Simon remained broodingly silent, promising nothing. They both walked forward and entered James's modest but sturdy little house. James'ss mother cried out, greeting her eldest son with eager arms, clasping his head in her hands, her sunken mouth kissing both his cheeks soundly.

Simon glanced around the interior of the house, noting with surprise that it had been newly furnished in their absence. The familiar rush matting no longer adorned the floor but an expensive Persian rug instead. Elaborate tapestries hung on the humble, mud-plastered walls, and every dark corner was filled with gold and brass bric-a-brac cluttered upon finely wrought, polished tables.

When his mother left to fetch them wine, James joined Simon's perusal of the room in silent wonder. She soon returned with the refreshments: a little silver tray with matching cups inlaid with red enamel, and a gold filigree basket containing delicate pastries. They took their seats silently on brocade pillows gathered around a low marble table. Simon took a drink from his cup, discovering the wine rich as warm silk.

"Mother, where did all this come from?" James waved his hand about incredulously.

"Joses bought these things for me," she replied with obvious pride. "He lives in an apartment in Jerusalem now and makes very good money at his new job."

"Joses has left you?" James said astonished. "But he mustn't leave you alone, Mother, I forbid it. And what is this new job? Our family has always been in private business. Our father impressed us with the importance of working our trade."

She placed a sweetmeat into her toothless mouth working it happily. "Don't take on so. I'm living luxuriously now, and my health is good, as it always has been. Besides, Joses visits me two or three times a week. Now, tell me about the Prophet. There are rumors of him all over Judea. Is he really the firstborn of your father's brother Joseph? Is he really the Messiah? Just think of it. A kinsman of ours being the Messiah."

James ignored her queries about Jesus. "Tell me about my brother's new job," he insisted.

"Joses has made many important friends in Jerusalem," she said, touching the heavy neck chain at her throat and preening. It was studded with pale agates that Simon thought resembled dead eyes. "He's been given a job overseeing new construction on the Temple. Isn't it grand?"

Simon inhaled sharply. He suspected as much. Nobody got rich quickly in Jerusalem unless he joined ranks with the Romans and began kissing their backsides. James's greedy, rat-faced little brother had sold out to the enemy.

"I'm leaving!" He rose abruptly.

James followed him to the door. "Don't worry," he said in low tones. "I'll handle this."

Simon turned away in disgust and began walking with vigor toward his own home. He knew well enough how his partner would handle Joses—the way he always did—with indulgence. Never mind that the young pup had left their business to ruin, a business they had put the sweat of their backs into. They hewed lintels, foundation stones, commemorative monuments, and occasionally a round gravestone to cover the entrance of a tomb. Hard work, it had not made them rich, no—but it was honest and respectable. Most importantly, it was free from Roman domination.

When he entered the cool interior of his parents' house, his anger subsided. His mother's embrace surrounded him with the calm fragrance of cedar wood.

"Simon!" his father called from a back room. "Is that Simon I hear? Come here, you rascal."

Simon entered his father's room to find him lying in bed. He masked his concern behind a warm greeting. His father stayed to his cushions like this only when he was in deep pain. "Who are you calling a rascal?" he quipped, gently sitting on the side of the bed.

"We were just talking about you, weren't we, Hannah?" his father said happily. "How rough and wicked you were as a boy." His father shifted among the pillows excitedly, trying to rise up on one elbow.

"Don't move about so, Cleopas. You'll aggravate the pain."

"Bah!" he responded waving away her warning. "Look at him, Hannah," he went on proudly. "Our son has the beauty of David and the strength of Samson."

Simon grinned. His father's statements were invariably extravagant and wildly exaggerated. "Thank you, Father."

"Tell me, son," Cleopas said leaning closer to Simon, "have we found our Messiah?"

Simon nodded his head with a smile. "Yes, Father, we have."

"Ha!" Cleopas collapsed triumphantly on his pillows. "I knew it. I knew he would come. And soon I will walk to see him. I'll walk down the road to Jerusalem and pay homage to my Messiah!"

Simon looked up, communicating with his mother in secret sadness.

The evening before the Sabbath Hannah adorned every room with pots of flowers and greenery, for according to the Law, each home must meet the dawn of a Sabbath dressed as a bride. The Sabbath lamp was lit, and Simon went to his room to wash while his mother took a pan of water into her room to do likewise and to help her husband whose body was too bent and paralyzed with arthritis to perform even the simplest tasks.

Dressed in their finest garments, they sat at the best table Hannah could afford: mutton in sauce, fresh greens and leeks drenched in olive oil and vinegar, and unleavened bread. After the prayer, they began to eat. Simon asked his mother about the state of their finances. His father interrupted with assurances that they were managing nicely with what he made on days he was feeling better. No longer able to work in stone, Cleopas had taken to doing odd jobs for old friends. The work was degrading but honest, and he was too proud to complain.

After the meal, Simon lingered at the table while his mother helped his father get ready for bed. He got up and lifted the lid of the ceramic pot in which Hannah kept her household money. Discovering a pitiful amount, he deposited most of what he had left over from the trip and quickly closed the lid.

He thought of Judas, the keeper of the Master's treasury, who wouldn't be pleased to know that Simon had donated ministry funds to his parents. Judas had even grumbled about giving James and Simon the traveling expenses necessary to make the trip home. But Jesus had intervened saying that the monies donated by his wealthy followers must be used among his disciples as needs demanded, and that the rest must be distributed among the poor.

At the Master's reprimand, Judas had left the scene in a pout, and Simon had experienced his first flickerings of ambivalence toward Judas. After all, the donations had been given to Jesus, not Judas. The disciple's resentment had shown both a disrespect for the Master and an inordinate preoccupation with acquiring and hording money. Simon was beginning to distrust Judas.

Sabbath morning broke and Simon and his mother left Cleopas in his sickbed and hastened to the synagogue. It was the rabbinic rule to go with quick steps and come back after the service slowly and somberly. Hannah took a place in the women's gallery while Simon entered the pillared room designated for the gathering of adult males of the seed of Abraham.

The officials were assembled, their faces toward the congregation, their backs to the *Aron Haggodesh*, or Holy Chest, which contained the sacred scrolls. Simon's eyes found the *Archisynagogos*, or Chief Ruler, one Haddad ben Joachim, who had held his office for as long as Simon could remember. The lines around his alert, old eyes crinkled with silent recognition as they met Simon's. At the far left stood the *Chazzan*, or Minister of the Scrolls, Shammiah, who also acted a schoolmaster. This venerable man had patiently taught Simon how to read and write and how to recite the Law verbatim with the proper Hebrew intonations.

Simon was filled with a sense of peace. His large bones relaxed against the hard stone benches as Haddad ben Joachim began the familiar liturgy. This was home—this traditional observance of what was right and Godly.

After the service several old friends, as well as synagogue leaders, asked him about Jesus. News of the famous Rabbi had reached them, and, as a close follower, Simon discovered that he had become something of a celebrity in his hometown. Simon recounted some of the great miracles such as the healing of the centurion's servant and the cleansing of the leper. He was careful to avoid mentioning anything, which might provoke discord. He left the raising of the widow's son out of his account, afraid that the Master's restoration of life to the dead might stretch their faith to the breaking point.

He accompanied his mother home in a state of mild euphoria. The observance of worship on the Sabbath always elevated him to a higher plane of existence, one in which he communed with God with his whole being. As they walked, he blessed the sun which stood in the heavens in perfect majesty, not a degree too far to the right or left. He blessed the calm fingers of the breeze in his hair. He looked up and blessed the benign blue sky, then the grass in the fields and the grain almost ready for harvest. Everything on the earth was just as it should be. God was in control and he was at peace. Simon gave up struggling on the Sabbath.

They ate cold leftovers for dinner as cooking wasn't allowed this one day of the week. Afterwards, Cleopas took to his bed again for a nap, Hannah walked down the street to visit a friend, and Simon rested an hour in the tiny courtyard among his mother's carefully kept flowers and potted shrubs. Closing his eyes he saw Jesus standing in a green Galilean field among the lilies. He looked at Simon as from a great distance. He gave Simon an open, frank smile of approval and waved. Simon's heart swelled with love. Jerking awake, Simon realized he'd dozed off. He lifted his arm to swiped beads of perspiration from his forehead before going back into the house to check on his father.

Cleopas slept shallowly. Simon watched his chest in its slow up and down movement then softly sat beside him on the low bed. His father had grown much worse in his absence. His hand lay outside the cover, gnarled and twisted, the knuckles big as walnuts. His mother said the crippling had spread into his back. Would his entire body eventually look like his hand? Simon covered it tenderly with his own. It was stiff and cold, like winter sticks.

Why did a man have to endure pain and sickness in his old age? Why couldn't he live vigorously and in good health to his dying day? Why couldn't dying happen in an instant, instead of by inches? The angel would come in a moment and say it was time, and a man would go with dignity to meet his God.

"Oh, Father. *Abba*. Daddy." Simon bent over his father's hand and quietly wept.

"At least wait until I'm in my grave before you mourn me, my son."

Simon looked up into his father's irrepressibly humorous eyes. "I was grieving for your hand," Simon said blinking the moisture from his eyes. "It's not the hand I remember. The one that taught me how to work the stone."

"The one that taught you how to behave, is more like it," Cleopas responded with a chuckle. "You were such a fearless and rebellious boy. There were times I wondered how you would turn out. Even now I worry about you. But you are a man now and I am a cripple. If your ears need boxing, God will have to do it."

"Father, I can take care of myself."

"No man can take care of himself," said his father. "You see before you an example of that. If I could order my circumstances, would I be lying here like this? Would my hands be useless, misshapen claws; would my spine be solidifying into a piece of twisted iron? I have fought this, my son, I've fought it with all my might. So much for a man taking care of himself!"

Simon bent toward his father earnestly. "Jesus is planning a trip to Jerusalem in a few months to attend the winter feast. He'll come and make you well."

"Bring him then," Cleopas said wearily. "I need him. Keep holding my hand, my son, I can feel your warmth dissolving the pain."

Simon held on gently until his father fell into a deep sleep. Then he said a prayer of faith and laid the hand down, now loose and relaxed as Cleopas slept.

His mother came in and whispered in his ear. "Eleazer ben Samuel is here to speak with you."

Simon stifled a groan. He knew he had to talk to his fellow Zealot sometime, but not today, not on the Sabbath. Reluctantly, he got to his feet and went into the courtyard.

"Simon!" Eleazer boomed upon seeing him, "my old friend."

"Sh!" Simon motioned. "My father is asleep. He's not well."

Eleazer lowered his voice. "What can you report on Jesus?" he asked showing no interest for the health of his friend's old father. "We have all been anxiously awaiting your report. Is he the Messiah?"

"Yes." Simon sat down on a low stone bench motioning for Eleazer to join him.

"I knew it!" His friend's eyes kindled with fanaticism. "I saw him raise a cripple at the pool of Bethesda last Passover. Some said it was a hysterical healing, that after a time the old man's bones would again collapse under him causing more damage than before. But he is still walking."

Eleazer leaned forward aggressively. Simon backed away. He didn't want to be drawn into Eleazer's fierce energy, not today. Today was the Sabbath.

"Have you told Jesus we will support him? That we have a well-armed and well-organized force, willing and eager to fight?" Eleazer asked.

Simon lifted his hand briefly to pinch between his eyes. "Jesus doesn't speak of politics. He spends much of his time helping the sick and the poor and those who cry out to him for spiritual comfort. Some of his followers see him as the suffering Messiah."

Eleazer remained silent for a moment. "And how do you see him?" he asked suspiciously.

Simon sighed. He'd been afraid to face this question. With the other disciples he'd argued that Jesus was to be the avenging deliverer of Israel. Now he wasn't so patently sure. He'd eaten with Jesus, swam with him. He'd watched his tender expressions and had brought the sick under his healing hand. He had become his brother as well as his disciple.

"Well?" demanded Eleazer.

"I only know that he has tremendous inner power," answered Simon searching for words. "He speaks of a kingdom, but I have no idea of his plans and strategies for bringing it into existence. He is not a violent man."

Clearly offended, Eleazer got to his feet. "If I didn't know you better, Simon, I'd say that your association with this prophet had turned you into a coward."

Simon also rose up. He wouldn't deal with Eleazer today. Perhaps tomorrow he would decide to fight his fellow Zealot for accusing him of cowardice.

"We tried to make the Baptist our leader," Eleazer pointed out, "and he denied us. Look where his righteous refusal got him. Cast into a pit to be victimized by Herod. If the Galilean is too meek to take the reins of power too, we'll find us another leader. There is a man named Jesus bar Abbas. He has already killed three Roman soldiers on the Jericho Road, and even though he is not as popular with the masses as your Jesus, he's more like us."

Simon was enough of a logician to see the flaw in Eleazer's reasoning. Man did not confer the Messianic title—God did. If Jesus didn't fit the Zealots' preconceived notion of what the Messiah should be, it didn't make him any less the Messiah. Simon folded his arms across his chest and remained silent.

"What's the matter with you, Simon? Where is your loyalty?"

"My allegiance belongs to no man but Jesus of Nazareth," said Simon implacably.

"Then you have betrayed us!" Eleazer clenched his fist in Simon's face. "Damn you!" He spat at Simon's feet and stalked out of the courtyard.

Simon drew in a deep, trembling breath and slowly unfolded his arms. He looked down calmly, stepped around the offensive matter that had missed his big toe by a fractional distance, and went into the house. Suddenly he felt tired. *What a great deal of energy one has to expend to keep from fighting*, he thought wryly.

Evening was coming on and his mother had lit the lamps. She smiled and motioned for him to sit by her on the couch. He did so leaning back wearily.

"Did you notice how lovely Lila looked this morning?" she asked.

"Who?"

"Lila. The daughter of our old friends, Jesse and Sofa."

He remembered now. There was a tacit agreement between Jesse and his father that their families would someday unite by the marriage of their offspring. His mother broached the subject infrequently but too often in Simon's view.

"Yes, the child is very attractive." He dimly recollected a young girl with a smooth complexion and modest brown eyes. He gave his mother a wary look as if to warn her away from a subject he wasn't in the mood to discuss.

"She has already turned sixteen, well into marriageable age according to custom. Another year and she'll be considered an old maid. Jesse has been discouraging other possible suitors in hopes that you'll speak for her. You know your father's wish."

Simon bit the inside of his cheek, twisting his mouth in irritation. Did all the forces of hell conspire to ruin a man's Sabbath? Now Satan had set his own mother against him. There was nothing more disconcerting than her gentle nagging. The warmth and peace he'd felt this morning had all but dissipated. Life's problems and a thousand aggravations had no respect.

"Won't you consider arranging an espousal before going back to Galilee?" she urged gently.

"Mother, I don't want a wife. Please convey to Jesse as tactfully as possible that I have no intention of asking for Lila in marriage and I never have had. Taking a wife now, or in the immediate future, is out of the question. My work is with Jesus. All our traveling about would make me a poor husband. Perhaps someday, when Jesus brings peace to Israel, I'll consider it. But that could take months, years perhaps."

Hannah smiled at him maternally, blissfully deaf. "But surely the Master doesn't discourage marriage," she said gently cajoling. "It is the most important stronghold of our society. Jehovah ordained that a man and a woman cleave to one another and produce children."

He sighed. "Of course Jesus sanctions marriage. Peter bar Jonah, who is perhaps his closest disciple, is married; and his brother Andrew is espoused to a maiden named Tassa, whose father is a weaver in Bethsaida. But right now I don't want the complications and responsibilities of acquiring a wife."

"But Cleopas and I would so love to have grandchildren about us in our old age," she said appealing to his sense of duty. "Won't you at least think about it?"

This had always been his mother's method of bending him to her will. Where his father had simply cuffed him and sent him spinning, his mother would *chirp, chirp, chirp* like a cricket in the ear. He groaned and nodded grudgingly.

They were suddenly interrupted as Cleopas stumbled into the room crying and waving his arms erratically. Simon sprang from the couch grabbing him, thinking that his father's constant pain had finally driven him mad.

Cleopas jumped up and down fighting him. Simon managed to wrestle him to the floor. "Get off me, you big Goliath!" his father yelled.

Simon tried to get him around the waist and carry him back to bed. He was frightened. He had heard that people sometimes exhibited incredible strength while in the last throes of dying. "Father! Let me help you!"

"Look! Look!" Cleopas cried holding his hands in front of Simon's face. The room fell silent and motionless. Simon stared. Cleopas wiggled his fingers and laughed. The knots were gone. Hannah took one of his hands, turned it over and back again, then burst into tears.

Simon got to his feet, lifting his father with him. "Jesus did it," said Simon in a hushed voice of awe. "I prayed, and he did it. Distance is not a factor. His power is absolute."

"Ha, ha!" Cleopas burst into exuberant laughter, whirled around and leapt into the air. "My legs! My back!" He arched and bent his torso. "When Jesus comes to Jerusalem, I'll walk to meet him and kiss his feet," Cleopas vowed, dancing with excitement, "just as I said I would. And I will recognize him instantly, for I saw him as I slept, standing in a field of lilies."

Chapter 10

*Mightier than the thunder
of the great waters.*
Psalm 93:4 NIV

Summer had departed from Palestine, dragging the humid heat of September behind like a reluctant child. Batasha and Suzanna sat in the atelier blending perfume. Business had been good during their absence, and inventory in the shop in Magdala demanded replenishing. The villa was quiet. Suddenly she heard the distinctive baritone of a familiar voice coming from the peristyle. In the process of counting drops into a fresh alabastron, her hand poised motionless for a moment before she laid down the syringe.

"Please excuse me, Suzanna," she said to her partner. "I think I have a visitor."

She hurried across the stones into the colonnaded courtyard finding her aunt chattering futilely in an attempt at small talk.

"Good afternoon, Simon," she interrupted with a polite smile. "Aunt Grete, would you prepare us something refreshing. Some juice, perhaps, and some of Suzanna's honey cakes."

As Grete hastily departed, Simon waved her offer aside. "I've come for the boy," he said tersely.

She motioned to a wrought iron chair. "Jonas went outside to play after lunch, but he should be back soon. Won't you sit down?"

Simon gave an impatient huff and, after eyeing the delicately scrolled chair with some disgust, seated himself on a cushioned bench.

"Didn't James the Less return with you?" she asked.

"He left Emmaus three days before I did," Simon replied. "He missed his son and wished to be reunited with him as soon as possible. I didn't want to cut short my visit with my parents."

"Then you haven't seen Jesus yet?" Grete reentered bearing a tray, set it on a table between them, and departed.

"No," answered Simon ignoring the tray. "Is he well?"

"Yes, he's fine. Jonas and I went to Capernaum last week for a visit. People are pouring in from the Decapolis every day to hear him teach. And the Sanhedrin has sent another delegation up from Jerusalem to try to ensnare him."

"Their persistent harassment bothers me," Simon admitted, his intelligent black eyes deepening with concern. He leaned forward, expecting further information.

Batasha complied by saying, "When Jesus speaks, many of the am ha rez chant that he is the Son of David, and the Messiah. The officials shout them down, claiming that he is a son of Satan."

"That makes no sense!" Simon exploded softly. "Why would a son of Satan be casting out evil spirits? He would be working against himself."

"That's exactly what Jesus said. He added that it was a grievous sin to call something Holy evil." She took a sip of juice then a nibble of pastry. If Simon wasn't going to partake, she would.

To her surprise he bent over the table following her lead. Not a man to do anything by halves, he swallowed a deep draft of juice and ate two honey cakes in record time. Then he leaned against the cushions, visibly relaxing.

"His mother came up from Nazareth to see him too while you were away," she said conversationally. "I met her outside Peter's house. She was alone and seemed so forlorn that I asked her if I could be of some help. She told me then who she was and that she was waiting for Jesus to come out and talk to her. She said that two of Jesus' brothers were pushing through the crowd in an effort to get to the Master and tell him she was there."

Simon slowly shook his head. "Jesus rarely speaks of his family," he said. "I believe there is some dissension among his brothers concerning his mission. I think he finds it hurtful."

Batasha nodded. "You are right. When I told John to tell him that they wanted to get through for an interview, Jesus made the remark that his followers were his true family because they believed in him. He sadly, but steadfastly refused to see them."

Simon had retrieved his cup and sat holding it in his hands loosely. "How that must have cost him," he murmured.

"It clearly distressed his mother also," Batasha continued in serious tones. "She was crushed when the other sons returned to her with the news. They were angry and said that Jesus was crazy, that he should be put away. It had started to rain, as it had off and on all day, a grey, miserable drizzle. I don't think I shall ever forget the anguish on her face when they pulled her away. She kept looking back through the soaking dreariness, hoping to catch a glimpse of him as the brothers kept up their abusive diatribe. She seemed torn apart." Batasha looked up. Simon was attending to her closely, taking in every word and nuance. "Later he wouldn't eat supper," she added, her voice lowering with sadness. "And he went apart without speaking to spend the night alone."

"He is such an excellent man," Simon remarked softly, "so perfect in all his ways that sometimes we forget he is human too, that he feels pain, heartbreak, and rejection just as keenly as we do.

They shared a rueful smile in perfect accord, feeling comfortable in talking to one another for once. A basis of rapport had finally been established between them because of one grand fundamental thing they had in common—Jesus, and their mutual love for him.

"Sir! Sir, you've come back!" Jonas barreled through the atrium into the peristyle.

Simon stood and caught him in a wide, fierce hug, swinging him around, both of them laughing. "Of course I've come back," boomed Simon. "Did you think I would abandon you?" He set Jonas on his feet and held him away. "You've grown stouter."

Jonas's straight, pre-adolescent body had filled out noticeably during his short stay with Batasha. She had insisted that he eat good food and rest well. As a result, he was bursting with vitality. His thick, black hair lay against his head in glossy curls, and his dark eyes were full of life, the whites clear and healthy.

Simon grabbed his head and kissed him on both cheeks. "You look good!"

Batasha watched them in silent bemusement.

"Go get your things," Simon ordered brusquely. "I want us to reach Capernaum by nightfall." He turned to Batasha as Jonas ran out of the room. "Has the boy behaved? I've taught him to be obedient."

Batasha nodded. "I enjoyed having him." She did not add that Jonas had gotten into more than one heart-stopping predicament. He had fallen out of the tree house catching himself on a limb to dangle precariously above the ground until Alexes ran to his rescue. And there was the morning he'd mounted Mercury without permission. The stallion, accustomed to only Batasha and Alexes, had thrown him off into a heap on the stable floor. Batasha had given him a sound scolding for that, which he had accepted with good humor promising never to go near the horse again without supervision. Considering all, however, she knew that she was going to miss his lively exploits, if not the ones that had stood her hair on end.

Jonas returned with his bag of belongings. Simon hefted it, giving her a quizzical look.

"I bought him some new clothes," she admitted. When Simon smiled, she grinned back. "I hope you don't mind."

He shook his head. "I thank you."

Jonas surprised her with a hug. "When will you come to Capernaum?"

"Soon," she promised kissing his forehead. "I never let much time go by without visiting the Master."

The lakeside teemed with people. Jesus, Peter, Andrew, James, and John had gotten into Peter's boat and had pushed out a little distance so that Jesus could continue to teach without the constant press of the crowd.

Simon and Jonas sat on a rock by the shore listening, accompanied by Matthew who was writing down the Master's words on parchment. Other disciples moved about ready to quell any disorderliness, an unnecessary precaution, since the throng was as peaceful this day as the calm lake. Jesus spoke to them in parables until evening and the much of the crowd had dispersed to go into the city to buy supper before the vendors closed their booths. Peter brought the sturdy boat to shore, and Jesus disembarked. Simon stepped in front of him, making a clear path for the Master through the remaining people.

They went to Peter's house for supper. Peter's mother-in-law was in a snit. Several of the crowd had trampled her new flowerbed. Batasha had brought her cuttings from Magdala, and at being shown the poor, mutilated bits of sticks and leaves, Leah had flown into a temper. Nevertheless, she had dedicated herself to preparing the Master a meal of delicious food with a minimum of grumbling.

As they ate, Thomas and Philip asked Jesus to explain some of his teachings. Simon felt annoyed. Couldn't they see that the Master was hungry? He preached all day to the multitudes, and then couldn't even finish a meal without having to elaborate further in private.

"Let him eat," Simon growled.

Jesus lifted his hand, indicating that he didn't mind deferring his hunger. "I want you all to listen, and listen well," he said in a tone that demanded their full attention. He penetrated Philip with his keen gaze and then Thomas. "I want you to understand the simplicity, yet the profound importance of my words. I don't go into lengthy explanations for just anybody. You are my chosen ones and I have great plans for you." He fixed his eyes on them one by one, pausing when he reached Judas.

They all turned to stare at Judas at the end of the table. He was thoroughly engrossed in his food, dipping bits of bread in honeyed curds and dropping them into his mouth with great ecstasy. Upon finally realizing that they were watching him and that he had not been paying attention, he drew back guiltily then shrugged.

Simon snorted. The man would sell his soul for a plate of bread and gravy.

The Master resumed speaking. "The Kingdom of Heaven is like a treasure chest buried in a field. A man uncovers it and realizes what he has found. He goes and sells everything to buy that field. In the same way, a dealer of fine pearls will search for a large one of great value. When he finds it, he'll sell every gem and lesser pearl he has to obtain it. The Kingdom of God is like that priceless pearl.

"There is also this to consider about the Kingdom of Heaven," he went on. "It is something I've said before, but it bears repeating. At the end of the age a great dragnet will be thrown out to gather in the people. Some of you are fishermen, and all of you should be able to imagine what it will be like. Those who are righteous will be kept. But those who are wicked will be thrown away. Just as you fishermen keep the good fish and throw away the bad."

"Where will they be thrown, Jesus?" his cousin, John, asked.

"Into *Ge Hinnom*, the lake of fire. And their sorrow and anguish will know no bounds. I don't want anyone to suffer that," he said emphatically.

"But Lord, most of the time I'm afraid I am not a righteous man," Peter spoke up impulsively. "How are we to become righteous and good so that we may escape hell?"

"I am the Way," Jesus said.

They all sat in various postures of stupid silence. Sighing imperceptibly, Jesus bent again to his food, his dark, sun-burnished hair cast in a golden glow by the lamplight. The rest of the meal was completed in silence.

After supper they left the house. Although dusk had descended, pockets of people still lingered and began to bear down on Jesus with rude determination. Simon wondered if the Master ever felt like a hunted man. Lines of fatigue scored his face, and Simon's heart swelled with concern. At least Simon had been able to get away to Judea. But Jesus had taken no such respite from the demands of his mission.

"Lord, let's get into the boats and sail to the east side of the lake," Peter suggested suddenly. He pointed to his three fishing vessels bobbing nearby.

When Jesus assented with a nod, Peter naturally fell into a role of leadership. "We'll take the two smaller vessels," he said. "They'll be faster." He told Simon, James the Less and his son Thad, and Andrew to come with him and Jesus. The remaining disciples joined James bar Zebedee and John in the other boat.

As they were about to shove off, Jonas stepped into the stern. Simon ordered him out. It was too late, he said, and Jonas needed his sleep. The boy obeyed and stood on the shore wearing a tragic expression. As the sails popped and filled with wind and the boats skidded away from shore, the forlorn boy pleaded with his eyes.

Jesus called out. "Jonas! I need you to do something for me."

"Yes, Master?" His face brightened.

"Go back and tell the women we've gone to the other side of the lake. If you don't they'll be concerned. Do that now. I'm depending on you."

Jonas turned immediately, cut through the grumbling crowd, and scrambled over the rocks—an insignificant speck in the twilight, made important only by the Master's need for him. Jesus chuckled as Simon, too, broke into laughter.

"That boy is going to be a mighty man of God someday," Simon predicted with the pride of a father.

The sails held taut with a stout but gentle breeze. Night descended in earnest as the boat's prow pushed silently through the water, only a hush of foam gliding along its sides. Being from an area of Judea devoid of large bodies of water, Simon was unaccustomed to sailing, yet soon he relaxed and began to enjoy himself, feeling very much in charity with Peter for suggesting the adventure. He glanced across at James the Less, who was also an inexperienced seaman. They exchanged expressions of surprised delight. Peter sat in the rear of the tiny ship manning the helm with great confidence. Jesus, curled comfortably on a net in the stern, his head resting on a leather pillow, immediately went to sleep, snoring softly as one profoundly exhausted.

The white ghostly sails of James's ship floated airily a little distance away on the starboard side. Snatches of their conversation carried across the breezes intermittently, only a phrase here and there discernible.

"Peter! Look ahead!" James suddenly called.

Sooty clouds had belched out of the inky horizon. They were full of internal lightning, flashing in eerie shades of green and silver and touching off distant thunder.

Simon had heard that the Sea of Galilee was infamous for its savage and sudden storms. The basin in which the sea nestled, most of the time peacefully, was fringed by the hot arid cliffs of Gadara on one side and the cool hills of Galilee on the other. Sometimes currents swept down from both elevations clashing violently over the water.

Angry, white-capped waves began to whip up, tossing them to and fro. Peter called to James. "Ho! Brace yourselves for bad weather."

Simon witnessed the subsequent, rapidly transpiring events with growing alarm. He cast a nervous glance at Jesus who still slept soundly, spray dousing his tranquil face. Then he looked at Peter who had enlisted Andrew to help control the rudder. Their arms bulged with the effort to keep the craft steady.

James the Less shouted as a wave leapt over the port side of the boat and swamped him. He clasped the edge of the boat in a frantic embrace. "Thad!" he yelled to his son. "Hold on!" Thad screamed as lightning stabbed close beside him followed immediately by deafening clap of thunder. He fell at his father's feet chattering prayers for deliverance.

"Keep your positions," Peter ordered them, "one on either side to provide ballast!" Two walls of water hit him successively filling his mouth and nearly knocking him overboard. Another streak of lightning rent the sky from top to bottom followed by thunder so fierce it impacted them physically. Amazingly, Jesus continued to sleep in a shallow pool of water, his seemingly boneless body rolling with the pitch of the boat.

James bar Zebedee's voice came through faintly. "Master! Master! We're nearly capsized!"

Simon's side of the vessel rose suddenly to a frightening height. He arched his heavy torso out into the water-soaked darkness in an instinctive effort to weight the ship down. James the Less and Thad lay at his feet looking up in stark terror

The ship crashed down whipping in around full circle like a toy. Peter panicked and let go of the rudder. He fell on Jesus shaking him roughly. "Master, wake up!" he shouted. "Don't you care that we are drowning?"

Jesus jerked up on his elbow, his eyes suddenly open and alert. He rose and braced his legs in a wide stance. The wind buffeted him, clawing at his sodden robes, and the boat heaved beneath his feet. The storm gathered around him, rolling up with malevolence.

Simon sensed a primal energy moving in from all sides. It was silent, cold, evil. This was more than merely a bad storm; it was an instrument of destruction. Wiping the lake water and the moisture of fear from his eyes, Simon did something he'd never done in his life—he cowered.

Jesus raised his right arm, seeming to expand with majestic authority. "Stop!" he said more loudly than any previous thunder. This one word reverberated through the sky echo upon echo. The malicious clouds reversed and began moving back upon one another. Infinity opened up into an ever-widening, peaceful circle above their heads.

He turned to the boisterous waves and pointed his finger. "You! Be still!" A great layer of quiet folded over the water in a blanket of peace.

Now the boat rocked gently like a cradle; the stars came out twinkling humorously. "Oh, you faithless babes," he said turning to confront them. "Why were so afraid?" He lay down on his side again in the stern, bending his arm for a pillow.

"All's well!" shouted James from a great distance, his boat having been blown off course.

"All's well!" Peter answered, cupping his hand around his mouth.

"Peter!" James called back across the water. "What happened?"

"Jesus told the storm to cease!" shouted Peter.

There was a moment charged with silence before James responded. "Thank you, Lord!"

Simon saw a flash of white split the Master's dark beard and heard his soft, exasperated laugh.

By evening the next day Batasha was frantic. She had arrived at Joanna's house in Capernaum earlier to discover that Jesus and the disciples had set out across the Sea of Galilee late last night.

A violent storm had blown in from the east into Capernaum from the area in which they were sailing.

She paced Joanna's mosaic floor wringing her hands and frowning. Leah had promised to send Jonas with word as soon as they found anything out. If the boy didn't come soon, she would go over to Peter's house and wait there with Leah and Deborah. Suddenly she halted, listening intently. Joanna entered the formal living room off the atrium where they received visitors when the weather was too cool to sit in the peristyle. Philip followed on her heels; they were both smiling.

"Everything is fine," Joanna said with relief.

"Thank God!" Batasha exclaimed.

"Yes, we are all blessedly intact," Philip assured her in his usual unruffled manner. "Although it was a bit harrowing for a time," he added. "We got wet and cold and were nearly frightened out of our wits, but not a hair on our heads was harmed. Jonas was coming to tell you but I volunteered instead."

Joanna asked if he would like some refreshment. Glancing her way, he politely declined, explaining that he'd just eaten at Peter's. Then he focused once again on Batasha.

After a pregnant pause, Joanna broke the silence. "Praise Jehovah that you all made it back safely. Now if you'll excuse me, I have to go give Paulus his bath."

Batasha lifted her brows. Joanna never bathed Paulus this early in the day. Joanna returned her quizzical look with a knowing smile and left the room as if hurriedly pressed with the onerous duties of motherhood.

"Please sit down," Batasha said motioning to the couch, "and tell me what happened."

Philip, an image of sartorial perfection in a rich robe of finely woven purple and scarlet sat beside her crossing his legs. A ruby prism pierced his right ear and an intricately wrought belt embroidered with gold floss encircled his slender waist, riding his hips as was the style among fashionably wealthy males. He wore his hair shorter than the other disciples and his pleasant patrician face was beardless.

"I was sorry to hear that we caused you women so much anxiety," he apologized.

"Peter suggested that we get into the boats and go across the lake. He wanted to give Jesus a chance to rest, and we all thought it was a good idea."

"I just arrived in Capernaum today," Batasha said. "It didn't rain at all in Magdala last night. But Joanna said the storm was very bad here."

"It was worse out on the lake," he responded with a mirthless laugh. "I was in James bar Zebedee's boat, who attempted for a time to subdue the storm with invective. Trying to out-thunder the thunder, I suppose."

"Where was Jesus?" asked Batasha.

"He had set out in Peter's boat. Simon later told me that he was sound asleep. Peter had to rouse him with considerable force to get him to wake up and help us."

"But Jesus is no sailor?" Batasha commented in a questioning tone.

Philip's tapered fingers tugged absently at the ruby earring. His hands were slender and smooth, free from calluses—the hands of a scholar. "Apparently he is more in tune with the natural elements than anybody knew. The Zealot said that he stood up and ordered the storm to be quiet and in a moment it was over." Philip continued to toy thoughtfully with his bejeweled earlobe. "I thought it was odd that the storm stopped so suddenly. There wasn't the gradual cessation of wind or the final sheets of rain you see when most storms die down." He shook his head. "So strange," he murmured. "We were all quite amazed."

That Jesus had power over the laws of nature didn't strain Batasha's credulity in the least. If he could cast seven well-ensconced evil spirits out of her body, he could certainly command any vagrant turbulence in the sky.

"We beached our ships on the shore of Gadara this morning," Philip continued. "Peter caught some fish and Jesus built a fire and cooked it. We protested that he was making himself our servant, but he assured us that he didn't mind. The fish was the best I've ever eaten, melting sweetly in the mouth. We filled up while warming ourselves by the fire. Jesus continued to serve us, mothering us a bit. No doubt, considering our cold, miserable condition, he thought we needed it."

"Philip," Batasha scolded gently, "as a man of learning, you should be writing all this down. Someone must preserve these astonishing events. Time has a way of making us forget important things."

Philip laughed quietly. "I'm afraid I'm no historian. Matthew has appointed himself to that task. He has been taking notes for over a year." At Batasha's doubtful expression, he added. "As an ex-publican, he's more assiduous about keeping accurate records than I could ever be."

He leaned back, draping his arm across the cushion behind her comfortably. "The Master told us we had little faith," he remarked. "Do you know where it is?" he smiled at her satirically. "I would like to find this thing called faith and please him. Is it some bit of tissue way down in the human heart, small as a tiny thread, grown atrophied and shriveled from neglect and disuse? Or perhaps God created man with two brains," he suggested, "one called intellect and one called faith. Over the centuries the faith one shrank to the size of an almond while the other grew to completely fill the skull cavity as our species preferred to rely on our own resources instead of our Creator. I'd like to think that we all have a little sleeping seed of faith in us somewhere—just waiting to burst into glory."

He rose reaching for his outer cloak. "I must be going. I've overstayed my welcome and must have tried your patience sorely."

She followed him through the atrium into the vestibule. "Nonsense, Philip. It was considerate of you to come across town to assure us that you are all safe."

Smiling, he took her hand and held it briefly before departing. She walked back to the receiving room to discover Joanna waiting eagerly. "He's interested in you," Joanna pronounced wearing a pleased expression. "What did he say?"

Batasha took up some needlework she had brought along to keep busy. Painting pictures with thread had always been her most restful pastime. "He spoke about faith," she answered looking up briefly.

Scarcely able to hide a pang of disappointment, Joanna pressed. "How do you feel about him," she asked curiously.

Batasha stabbed her embroidery. "I don't know."

Chapter 11

He remembers that we are dust.
Psalm 103: 14 NIV

Another great throng had gathered at the lakeshore to listen to Jesus teach. Out in the countryside colorful tent camps dotted the golden hills of Galilee as they lay harvesting under the cool autumn sun. Batasha kept a watchful eye on Jonas, as Simon and the other disciples stayed close to Jesus, knowing that crowds of this size were unpredictable and inherently inconsiderate.

Batasha saw one of the rulers of the synagogue push by. It was Jairus, a pious man, who had never heckled Jesus as the other Pharisees had. His thick, prematurely graying hair blew wildly in the wind, and lines of stress scored his forehead and radiated from the outer corners of his eyes.

"Lord!" He waved frantically above the crowd. There was an edge of hysteria in his voice as he pushed himself through the crowd. Jesus ordered the people to give way, and Jairus arrived before him breathless, falling at his feet.

"Please, Lord! My little girl—she is sick." He He drew in a ragged breath.. "The doctors say she is dying. Please come!" He began crying, continuing to plead incoherently. "Lay your hand on her, Master. She is my treasure—sweet and fair and fragile.

An angel since birth.... the apple of my wife's eye.... our heart of hearts." His voice broke and he sobbed openly.

Jesus lifted him to his feet. "Where is she?" Jairus pointed and Jesus began walking with him, holding his shoulders and comforting him with soft reassurances.

The crowd buzzed, sensing they were about to witness another miracle. Batasha felt a surge of anger. All they seemed to care about was what thrilling thing they would see next and how they would enjoy gossiping about it. Didn't they really care about this poor father's pain? Did any of them comprehend what Jesus was about? Had any of them ever done a selfless thing, pulled something precious out of their souls and handed it over to someone in need, expecting nothing in return?

They jostled and pushed her forward. The disciples made a human wall around the Master. She grabbed Jonas and motioned for him to squeeze between James the Less and Thad. After Jonas had wriggled his way to relative safety, she protected herself from abuse the best she could.

Someone from behind gave her a violent shove, hurling her into James the Less. She grabbed him around the neck and didn't let go. He looked into her blue frightened eyes, recognition immediate.

"I'm sorry!" she cried above the stir of the throng. "They're pushing me."

James the Less maneuvered her in front of him and called to Simon. "Can you take care of the Magdalene? The crowd is too rough."

Wordlessly, Simon reached out granite-like arm. He pulled her, none too gently, to his side, and there she remained like a wounded bird as they continued to inch forward.

Looking down and to her right, Batasha was astonished to discover a woman crawling on her hands and knees, working her way at cross-purposes to the crowd and being kicked and trampled from all sides. Every time they knocked her over, she struggled up to make her way again inexorably toward the Master.

Batasha dove out of the safe haven next to Simon's heart. He grabbed for her wrathfully, uttering imprecations against her and all womankind. Batasha threw herself down to protect the woman with her own body and tried to lift her to her feet.

"Get up! Do you want them to kill you?"

"No, no!" The woman fended her off, lashing out with her frail arms. "I have to touch him. Just one touch—that's all it will take."

Batasha realized that the woman was determined to get to Jesus and would never rise to her feet until she had done so or died in the attempt. It was dangerous and futile to fight her, so Batasha crawled on her hands and knees too, helping her push forward. When they reached the wall of disciples, she lashed out at Simon's feet causing him to stumble.

"Batasha! Are you crazy?"

She feinted as he lunged for her, and pulled the woman into the tight circle where Jesus walked. The woman reached out in a desperate effort, her frantic fingers working. "Please," she sobbed piteously. "Please, please!" The Master continued to walk, apparently unaware.

Batasha wrenched the woman's arm and thrust it toward Jesus' retreating robe. The woman's dire need had somehow transferred to her. Her only thought was making sure that the seeking hand made contact with Jesus, if only for an instant. She saw the fingers close around one tiny, dangling tassel and heard the woman's cry of joy.

Suddenly Jesus turned around. "Who touched my clothing?" he said loudly.

As the jostling, noisy movement ground to a halt, Batasha scrambled to her feet pulling the woman up with her. Simon surveyed the sea of people, perplexed.

"Master, in this press, it could have been anyone, even though we have tried to prevent mishap."

"You see all these people, Master," Peter said gesturing with his arm. "Yet you ask who touched you? We have all pushed against you time after time."

Jesus did not move. "Someone touched the edge of my garment. I felt the healing virtue go out of my body. Who was it?"

A profound hush settled over the crowd. Batasha glanced at the woman crouching behind her. When she took her hand, the woman burst into tears, stumbled forward and fell at Jesus' feet.

"I did it! I'm the one!" she cried. "I knew that if I touched you I'd be healed. And I am! I felt the well-spring of my disease dry up." She covered her face with her hands. "Oh, please don't be angry. I didn't mean to steal your power."

Jesus lifted the woman and made her look at him. He smiled compassionately. "You had faith, daughter of Israel. You believed in my restoring power. Now go in peace and be free from suffering."

Two servants from Jairus's house broke through the crowd. Batasha didn't wait to hear what they said. She covered the woman's bowed head with her mantle and led her away.

She discovered that the woman's name was Veronica. She had been afflicted with chronic menstrual bleeding for twelve years. She and her husband had given all their financial resources to doctors seeking a cure. Their home had been in Antioch, but when they had heard that there was a healing prophet in Galilee, they had sold out and moved to Capernaum.

Following the woman's directions, Batasha found the house with little trouble. She pushed through the curtain serving as door, followed by Veronica who was still highly wrought emotionally.

"Wife!" A slightly built man dressed in a beggarly robe ran forward and helped Veronica to a rush mat in front of a low burning brazier. "Where did you find her," he asked Batasha. "I've been half out of my mind with worry. I was afraid she'd gone into the multitude to seek Jesus. She's not strong enough to hazard the crowds, and we have been trying to think of a way to gain a private interview with him. Then I woke up this morning and she was gone." He knelt by his wife putting his arm around her and looked up at Batasha. "Thank you for bringing her home."

Batasha smiled. "Today she met the Master and he healed her. "As one of his devotees, I was able to be instrumental. My name is Mary Batasha bas Hillel of the tribe of Benjamin."

"It's true!" Veronica said. "From now on I will be normal in my courses. And we shall have the child we always wanted." Her husband's forehead touched hers and he began to weep silently. "No more physicians, my husband, who take a hundred denarii and tell me to swallow the drip of a rabbit. No more prescriptions of frogs' livers or the salt of a viper's sweat. Do you remember the Egyptian who spread the ashes of a charred wolf's skull over my stomach? We knew he was a fraud, and we didn't look at each other for fear the knowledge would show in our eyes. Always hoping for a miracle. But now I can take my place in the synagogue with the other women, for now I am clean. And I will become strong and firm of flesh as I was when you married me. And we will have a son." Softly she began to sing an ancient Hebrew hymn, a psalm of praise.

Quietly unnoticed, Batasha moved toward the door. Before leaving she reached beneath her sash and found a leather pouch studded with olivine. It was full to nearly bursting. She placed it on a crude little table then threw the ragged hanging aside and went out.

That evening she walked over to Peter's house. Rumors that the Master had brought Jairus's daughter back from the dead were all over town. She expected to see the usual great crowd clamoring at Peter's gate, but it was strangely desolate, as if even the miracle-seekers were too stunned, too awestruck, too satiated to take in any more.

She entered the house unhampered. Leah had not yet lit the lamps, and she found Simon and James the Less sitting listlessly on the couch. Philip and Thomas were at a table huddled motionless over an open scroll as if trying to see in the gathering gloom. Thad lounged nearby twiddling his thumbs while Judas Iscariot made a great art of cleaning his nails with a knife.

"Where's Jesus?" Her voice sounded hollow to her ears.

"Gone to the hills to pray," said Thad looking up briefly.

"James and John have gone home for the night," Simon added. "Matthew also went to his house. Jonas is outside playing."

"They're saying that Jesus raised Jairus's little girl from the dead."

She was met by silence. Finally Philip spoke up. "They didn't hear it from us. The Lord charged us to keep quiet. Jairus's servants must have spread it abroad."

"Then it's true? He really did?" she asked.

"Yes," said James the Less drawing in a heavy sigh. "He did the same thing in Nain last spring. That time it was the only son of widow. We were all witnesses."

"Then you saw Jesus raise this child?" she pressed.

"No," Thomas answered. "We waited outside and kept back the crowd. He took only Peter, James, and John into the house with him."

She went over to Philip who bent silently over his book. She touched his arm. "What's wrong with you all? Have you lost faith in the Master?"

"No." Philip groaned. "We know what he did. The maiden was dead and now she is alive. It's just that we've seen so much— so many things that confound the laws of nature. He turns our human thought processes upside down," he said rubbing his temples. "A man's brain can take just so much. And still he leads us on and on. To what end none of us knows."

"Where's Peter," she asked.

Simon gestured lethargically. "In his room."

"Get some rest, Simon," she snapped. Her concern for them had made her voice shrewish. "You're all exhausted. The body is like a stubborn mule." With reference to Simon, she thought this analogy particularly apt. "When it gets overtired, it balks and won't go anymore." She turned on all of them sweeping her arm. "Go to your beds and sleep. Just like a bunch of men—you're too foolish to realize your own need."

"But we haven't had supper," Judas pointed out.

"Food will not help. Only sleep will refresh you."

Philip got up slowly rolling the parchment. "She's right. I'm so tired I can't think straight."

Leaving the room Batasha went upstairs to Peter and Deborah's chamber. At her knock, Deborah silently motioned her in. Peter lay on the bed fully clothed, one arm thrown over his face. She tiptoed to the bed.

"Don't mince about as if I'm on a sickbed," he teased gruffly.

"A fierce old lion like you doesn't get sick," she said. "Just lazy. I can't imagine why your saintly wife puts up with you."

Deborah smiled as he chuckled tiredly. "The woman you helped today," he asked, "how is she?"

"She's whole," Batasha answered. "She had suffered for years with an issue of blood. I left her in the arms of her husband making plans for the future. They were poor, so I left some money." She knew that Peter would not think this gesture odd, or that she had mentioned it to seek praise. He, himself, was thoughtlessly extravagant.

"Good, good," he said, heaving a deep sigh.

"What happened today after I left?" she asked softly.

He lifted his arm and she saw his eyes. They were filled with an inner radiance. She had often seen this glow upon Jesus and had mentioned it one time to Joanna who had not noticed. Having been tormented by beings from another realm before meeting Jesus and adhering to him, Batasha had come to believe that she retained a residual sensitivity to the world beyond. She instinctively knew that Peter was now reflecting the power of Jesus, which the prophets of old had referred to as the *Shekinah*, or the Glory of God.

"After you left with the woman," Peter said, "two of Jairus's servants arrived. They said Jairus's daughter had died. Jesus ignored them. Jairus collapsed and Jesus held him up and made him stand. He told him to stay calm and keep believing. When we got to the house, the mourners were already there, making a great din with their wailing, and playing their flutes.

"Jesus ordered them to leave. He said the girl was only sleeping. They jeered at him. He told some of us to send them away. Then he took James, John, and me into the house, with Jairus leading the way.

"As we went into her room, Jesus ordered all the relatives weeping around the girl's bed to leave except her mother." He paused remembering. "Ah, what a beautiful child she was, even in the stillness of death. Her hair was flaxen, her face like fine alabaster. Her hands lay crossed against her chest, her breasts childish promises of future womanhood. It saddened me so, that I nearly sank into despair.

"The Master took the unconscious girl by the arms and gently sat her up. '*Talitha cumi*,' he whispered. 'Wake up, little girl. I command you to rise from death.'

"She stood and opened her eyes, which were wide and blue and sleepy with confusion. Her mother embraced her with an exultant cry; her father fell upon Jesus in gratitude. The Master as well as James, John, and I shared in their joy. Then Jesus told them to give the child some food. Afterwards we assumed he said this to ground her more firmly to earth, for she seemed to be airy and fragile as if still between this world and the other. He also warned her parents not to tell anyone what had happened."

Peter shook his head slowly. "I walked out of the house on a cloud. But how long can a man remain airborne? Men of flesh were not made to dwell in high places. The atmosphere is too rare, too insubstantial." He laughed mirthlessly. "And we are nothing but dust—vessels of clay."

"Sleep, dearest," Deborah said soothing his forehead with her hand. "Think no more, just rest."

⚱

During the next few weeks Jesus and his disciples made an extensive tour of the cities and towns in Galilee. Large groups of people came out of the rural hamlets nestled in the folds of the hills to hear him.

Batasha and the other women followed along in their wagons with tents and supplies. Although initially against having the women along, Simon now admitted to himself, albeit grudgingly, that it had proven to be a good idea. The goatskin shelters protected against the occasional sharp-edged autumn wind that bit by night and nibbled by day. Considered altogether, however, the weather had held fair, and the coming winter promised to be a mild one as the last Sabbath in November dawned bright and crisp.

They were camped outside Nazareth, Jesus' hometown. Simon asked Peter why the Master didn't stay with his family inside the city. Simon remembered Batasha telling about the mother and brothers visiting Capernaum some weeks before and the Master's refusal to see them. Peter said it was no secret that there were serious divisions in the family. He hoped that during this visit healing and reconciliation could occur and had prayed for the favor of Jehovah on the matter.

On Sabbath morning they all set out for the synagogue ahead of Batasha, who would follow with Jonas and the other women. The synagogue was full to bursting when they arrived. As was often the case, the fame of Jesus had preceded his arrival. Apparently the townsfolk had conveniently forgotten his last visit home. Some of them had demanded miracles; he implied that their lack of faith prohibited God's blessings. Enraged, they had tried to attack him.

When officials asked him to conduct the service, however— an honor often conferred upon traveling rabbis who had gained respect—Simon relaxed. Perhaps a healing would take place between the Master and his hometown today as well as his family.

Simon assumed his usual state of Sabbath reverence to listen. As Jesus paused in his speaking, Simon heard a low hiss from someone in the congregation. There was a slight stir like the ruffling of feathers among the listeners after which Jesus continued.

When Simon heard the rude noise again, he turned and saw the smug young pup who had done it. He wasn't much older than Jonas. Jesus went on reading as if nothing had happened, but his authority had been undermined. People began to murmur and grow restless.

Jesus finished the teaching and opened up the floor to questions, as was the custom. In other towns this was when Jesus impressed many with his wisdom and knowledge. The Nazareth gathering posed no questions. A man asked in a loud whisper if this was the same Jesus who used to live among them whose father was the carpenter.

"Who does this man think he is?" another said.

"A carpenter's son. Ha! I'm a brickmaker. Does that make me a prophet?"

The women's gallery had begun to buzz. "Didn't his sister marry the tentmaker?"

Simon's jaw clenched as he tried to control his temper. Not only were these people demeaning his Master, they were ruining his Sabbath. After the service he spied the boy standing beside an older young man who appeared to be his brother. Simon made for them like a falcon diving in on prey.

"You disrespectful whelp!" he said addressing the one who had made the noises. "Someone should thrash you soundly."

The boy's eyes bugged with alarm as Simon grabbed a wad of his robe and began to rattle him. The older brother intervened. Simon grabbed him too, preparing to knock their heads together.

"Simon!" The Master's clear, vibrant voice cut through his anger like a steel blade. "Let them go. They're my brothers."

Simon released them instantly and stepped back. A crowd was gathering.

Quietly dignified, Jesus stood in the cool morning sunshine. "James. Joseph." He nodded first at the older, then the younger brother.

The oldest one burst out, "Why did you come back and involve us in your crazy pretense? Think of what you are doing to us with all this talk of being the Messiah?"

The Master's eyes filled with pain. "I didn't come here to tear families apart, to set brother against brother." In obvious distress, Jesus seemed to be pleading with his brothers to accept him and believe in his work. "But if that is the way it is, then so be it," he said in a voice of resignation. He moistened his lips as if thirsty. "It has always been so: a prophet is neither honored in his own country nor in his own house."

"Take your disciples and go," his brother James said harshly, "before there is trouble. You remember what happened the last time, don't you? They took you to the cliff and nearly threw you over. If it hadn't been for our sister Ruth's husband and me, they would have, and you'd be dead. Is that what you want?"

"It is not a cup I would like to drink," Jesus admitted wryly.

"Come along, Mother." The Master's brother motioned. The little woman beside Batasha obeyed, closing her eyes briefly against tears before following slowly. Two children broke away from her and ran toward Jesus. They were twins—a boy and a girl about six years old.

Laughing, Jesus knelt, catching and lifting them in his arms. They squealed as he put the boy on his shoulders and tucked the girl to his side like a mama bear with a cub.

"When are you coming home, Jesus? We miss you," the girl said hugging his side.

"Please come home again and ride us on your back and play the cloud game with us in the fields," begged the young boy with melting eyes.

Slowly Jesus set them on their feet, knelt, and kissed their faces. Sensing it was another goodbye, the children tried to climb upon him once again. Their mother called and Jesus ordered them to obey with a gentle push.

Simon was very moved as the children walked away knuckling their eyes. Strife within a family was often hardest on the children. "Let's get out of here," he growled, tossing his head angrily before setting off in a wrathful stride.

Chapter 12

He will be our guide even unto death.
Psalm 48:14 KJV

They had been back in Capernaum for a week. Jesus talked about making another tour of Galilee, but this time they would separate and go various ways. He told them there were many people that were hidden back in the hill country in little hamlets who had not yet received news of him. By separating, more could be reached. Some of the disciples were skeptical. What could they do without Jesus? They had no power to work miracles, and without miracles, would the people believe?

Jesus assured them by saying he would vest them with power. Simon reminded them that his father had been healed by the mere utterance of Jesus' name. If he had received his miracle without the physical presence of Jesus, so could many others. Faith took root in their hearts and burgeoned into enthusiasm.

Jesus counseled them daily on how they were to behave and what they might expect. "Don't take anything on your trip, not even a walking stick. No money, or anything with which to collect money. Don't take food or extra clothing either."

"But Lord," Judas protested, "with no food or money, how are we to survive?"

"The working man deserves support," Jesus replied. "Stay with a righteous family in the village and depend on their generosity. If a village won't receive you, shake the dust from your feet and be on your way."

"May James the Less and I go into Judea to see our families?" Simon asked.

"At this time I prefer that our ministry be mainly in Galilee. Judea's time has not yet come, but a brief visit to your families is fine. Under no circumstances are you to preach to the Gentiles or the Samaritans."

"But Lord," asked Philip, "shouldn't God's power to save be offered to everyone?"

Jesus answered with a smile. "Please understand that I shall do things in my own time. We preach first to the lost sheep of Israel."

Thomas's face had taken on a frown of perplexity. "This all sounds a little dangerous to me. You know how hostile people can be at times."

"Thomas!" Peter burst out. "What would we do without you always looking on the dark side?"

Everybody laughed. Jesus joined in before once again becoming serious. "I never promised any of you an easy time. I'm sending you out as sheep among wolves. Thomas is right to a certain extent. Be wary and wise as serpents. Be innocent, harmless, and guileless as doves. Know this—even a sparrow can't fall to the ground apart from the Father's will. So don't be afraid; you are worth more than many sparrows. If evil men deliver you up to be flogged, stand fast and be courageous; the Spirit of your Father will give you the words to say and the strength you need."

"Do we lay hands on the sick?" Matthew asked. He looked up from the notes he'd been taking on the Master's instructions.

"I send you to proclaim the Kingdom of God. I give you power to cure the sick, raise the dead, cleanse the lepers, and drive out demons. All this you can do in my name and by my power and authority."

He continued to instruct them, repeating many things over and over. On the day before their departure, he went out into the hills to pray as each disciple went his own way to say goodbye to family and friends.

Simon took Jonas to Magdala to stay with Batasha. Jonas argued that he was only a few years younger than Thad, and that Thad got to go. But Simon was adamant. Jonas relented, knowing that once Simon was set on a course of action, there was no changing it and that arguing would merely irritate him.

After the initial greeting and leaving Jonas in the spare bedroom to unpack his things, Batasha returned to find Simon standing in the front receiving room, his hands clasped behind his back looking out the window at the long shadows cast across the lawn in the winter afternoon sun. She understood how he must feel to leave the boy again.

"Sit down and relax, Simon. I'll have Suzanna bring us some sweet wine."

He made himself comfortable on some cushions. "I struggled with the temptation of taking him with us," he admitted with a sigh. "But reason won out. At his age it is imperative that he be about his studies every day. This trip may be dangerous. The Master has even admitted as much. Jonas is developing nicely, but he isn't quite a man yet."

"I'll see that he does his lessons every day," Batasha promised.

Susanna entered with a tray of wine and fresh-baked almond cakes. Jonas trailed behind her sniffing.

"You are not to spend your days eating and playing," Simon admonished him in a stern voice. "Batasha has agreed to help you with your letters. She has a library of books and I

shall expect a full accounting of how many you have mastered
when I return."

Jonas bit into a warm cake and grinned. "Yes sir."

"And make yourself useful around here. I shouldn't like to
return and find you've grown lazy and fat."

"Oh, I shall never look like Judas, sir."

Batasha stifled a smile. God must certainly forgive the
honesty of children. Indeed, Jonas would never look like Judas.
Of all the disciples, he most resembled John, straight and lean,
not muscular, but well formed. He also had the keen sensitivity
of John and that occasional brash audacity which came to the
fore at the most unexpected times.

"Be sure to say your prayers three times a day. Keep your
mind free of evil. Adhere to the laws of cleanliness, and, as
the Lord has charged us often, follow his teaching," Simon
instructed.

"Where will you go?" Batasha asked, diverting Simon from
his catechism.

"Judas and I are to go south. He and I have been paired
together, as James will be traveling with Thad." Simon's
clipped tones indicated he was not especially happy about this
arrangement. He reached under his belt and brought out a long
purse bulging with coins. "Here, I almost forgot. The others
told me to bring this to you. You are to be our treasurer while
we are away. It was difficult for Judas to part with the money,
but even he agrees that it would be foolhardy to take such a
large amount on the road where robbers and cutpurses may
attack. Since you and the other women donated much of it, we
thought it would best to leave it in your keeping."

Batasha spread the contents of the purse on the table. "I see
that Jesus authorized a large sum to be given to the poor," she
said lifting her brows quizzically.

"What makes you say that?" asked Simon leaning forward.
"He hasn't approved any extra expenditures lately."

She moved the coins around with her fingers in puzzlement.
"I gave Judas a silver talent last week. It is the newly minted

coin the Romans have recently issued to equal the value of seventy-five pounds of silver. It's not here."

"Are you sure?" Simon bent over the table.

She was certain. Alexes had written the transaction in her books. "Who has access to the treasury?" she asked grimly.

"Only Judas. None of the rest of us wants to be bothered by keeping accounts and carrying money around. Even Matthew, who would have been the most logical choice since he is a former tax collector, refused the job.

Simon straightened, suddenly offended. "Of course I might have taken the talent on the way here. Is that what you are thinking?"

"Don't be ridiculous!" she said heatedly. "You may be a lot of things. But I know you're not a thief!"

"What do you mean 'a lot of things'?" he said in an escalating voice.

A brow lifted, as she immediately shot back, "Stubborn, irritable, inconsiderate, and downright rude, to mention a few."

"Why are you two getting angry with each other," Jonas interrupted with the candor of a child. "It's obvious who stole the money—Judas. Blame it on him, if you have to get mad."

Batasha's eyes locked with Simon's then shied away as they both realized the truth—Judas was a thief. How could he do it as one of the Master's closest followers?

Simon abruptly ran his fingers through his hair. "I guess I'll have to tell Jesus," he said with an exasperated sigh, obviously reluctant to bring it to a confrontation.

"No! Please don't!" She leaned over the table grabbing his arm. "It would hurt him. And think of what it would do to everyone's enthusiasm." She let go of his arm and wrung her hands. "Maybe I was mistaken. Maybe my mind was playing tricks on me and I forgot to give it to Judas and merely assumed I did. Accusing someone of stealing is a serious matter."

Simon hit the table with his fist. Coins flew to the stone floor, tinkling and rolling and coming to rest in scattered disarray. "Don't make excuses. Judas has probably been doing this for some time. If the others knew they would tear him to pieces! Peter alone would beat him within an inch of his life. This sort of transgression cannot be excused. Sometimes I wonder if Judas hears anything the Master says, for he has told us time and again that the love of money is the root of all evil. And Judas is supposed to travel with me! How will I be able to bear it, knowing this about him?"

Batasha felt a great deal of antipathy toward Judas as well but ignored it as she tried to console Simon who was clearly heartsick. "Maybe he won't do it again. Maybe temptation got the best of him when he saw the talent and realized how much it was worth." She modulated her voice, again touching his arm. "And Simon, I could have been mistaken. It's possible as busy as we all are. Please, let's just forget it. You can't go about casting accusations and ruining everything on the eve of your departure. Think of what it would do to our Master."

"You're right," he said gathering his calm. "You're right, of course. It would be bad, very bad indeed, to bring this to light right now." He got up and headed for the door, still frustrated. "I have to go if I expect to make it back to Capernaum in time to get some sleep." He looked over his shoulder at Jonas, his love for the boy apparent in his expression.

"We'll walk you to the bend in the road," she suggested.

A few moments later she clutched the hood of her winter robe to keep the chill evening wind from mussing her hair. For some reason she loathed to part with Simon, although she realized it was unreasonable and unwise to allow herself to yearn for him.

"Is the tree house still there?" Jonas asked pointing to a far clump of laurel.

"Of course," Batasha answered. "Just as it was the last time you visited."

"I'm going to go see," Jonas said. "Goodbye, sir." He extended his hand to Simon. "I'll pray for you morning and night." Before he broke away and ran, Simon grabbed his shoulders and swept him into his arms.

"God bless you and keep you, my son," Simon said in gruff tones as he kissed Jonas on both cheeks. "I love you."

"And I love you, sir." Jonas touched his beard, then broke away crying.

"Will he find the tree house?" Simon asked smiling after him.

"Oh, yes," Batasha responded as they continued to walk.

When they reached the point where the road veered off and began to wind downhill, Batasha turned to face him. "I wish you well, Simon. I'll add my prayers to those of Jonas. Don't worry about him." Her hood blew off, releasing heavy golden flags to the wind. She reached back and tried to recapture them once again under the disarranged mantle.

"Leave it," he said in a whisper, his black eyes softening. He reached and cupped the back of her head, tenderly crushing the thick, perfumed hair in his hands. "I like your hair. I've always liked it." His words were barely audible. "It feels like silk." He pulled her forward. "I love the way you smell." Then he bent his head and kissed her, drawing apart to murmur, "I've wanted to do this." Again he gently ravished her mouth.

She closed her eyes. Tears gathered in her lashes like shimmering jasper. *Dear God, he cares for me*, she thought.

"I'll miss you," he said when he finally held her face away.

"I'll be here in the spring," she promised softly, "waiting."

Peter and Andrew traveled with Simon, Judas, James the Less, and Thad as far as Chorazin. These six disciples would be witnesses in the southern part of Galilee. Peter and Andrew planned to go as far west as Sepphoris and Cana, concentrating on the little pockets of farmers and shepherds tucked away in the hills. Simon and the other three were to dedicate their efforts to the plains east and south of Mount Tabor.

Evening descended finding them well cared for in the home of a believer in a little village near the town of Nain. They ate hearty Galilean victuals then enjoyed a time of singing and laughter with the family. Jemuel, the head of the house, had seven children, ranging in ages from six to seventeen. All of them were musically inclined and as eager to entertain as monkeys. His wife, Zina, was a particular housekeeper, and when the disciples retired to the spare room, small though it was, they found it swept clean, and free of lice and other insects which frequently inhabited the homes of some of the poorer folk.

Simon's rush bed was fresh and sweet and the rough blanket smelled of the soda the women used in laundering. Comfortable as he was, he could not sleep. Motionless, he watched through the high, open window as a cold, pale moon rose and looked down upon him.

Hello, you wizened old man, he thought. *What's the matter? Can't you sleep either? It must be because you have an ugly face and your head is very bald. They say you cause madness, but I'm not a superstitious man, so I can look you full in your puckered old face and not be afraid. What was the special mission the Great Jehovah gave you when He created you? Was it to wander all over the sky spying on people while they sleep, chortling down at them with your funny round mouth? Do you see my boy, Jonas, now? Have you noticed how he sleeps with his fingers over his nose? A vestige left over from infancy when he used to suck his thumb, I think. What do you think?*

Are you peering into Batasha's window as she sleeps? But she has winter shutters of thin mica to keep out your prying eyes. The image of Batasha asleep arrested his wandering internal monologue. Soft curves beneath warm silk. Silver hair on white shoulders. Dark lashes forming crescents against soft cheeks. Eyes closed, as they had been when he'd kissed her farewell.

He stifled a moan and got up abruptly. Quietly, he left the house through the back door. He walked through the dried and withered vegetation of what used to be a summer vegetable garden. Stopping at a stone wall, he leaned against it head first, feeling its hard iciness against his fevered brow.

"Simon, are you sick?"

He turned and straightened. Peter's face in the moonlight showed concern.

"No. I'm all right. I'm sorry I woke you."

"I'm a light sleeper. Deborah says the falling of the dew can wake me. What's wrong? You don't look as if you've been asleep at all yet." He touched Simon's shoulder in friendship, inviting confidence.

Simon lifted his hand and pinched between his eyes. Should he tell Peter? He wanted to tell someone. "The truth is, sometimes I have trouble sleeping. The truth is," he blurted out, "I sometimes want to be with a woman."

"Oh." Peter showed no surprise. "That is not unusual, Simon. You're a virile man. Many men your age are married. I am myself."

"But I don't want to get married," responded Simon. "My first priority is serving the Master. A wife would distract me from taking part in the kingdom he is going to establish in Jerusalem. I only want a woman in the way a man wants a woman to comfort his body."

"The Master has said that not everybody is cut out for celibacy," Peter said softly. "I myself would be a difficult man without my beloved Deborah, too pent up and restless to be of any use to anybody including the Master. Jehovah has created us with drives and needs. I know that marriage is sacred and right for me." His low whisper became cajoling. "You and I are a lot alike, my friend. Marriage will cool your passions and make you a better man. Get yourself a sweet little virgin. Is there not someone whom your parents in Emmaus have picked out as a prospective bride?"

Simon leaned his back against the stone wall and crossed his arms. "Perhaps you're right," he conceded. "My mother wants me to become betrothed to the daughter of close friends.

Perhaps I'll speak to my father about it as soon as I can go into Judea."

Peter smiled with the smug benevolence of one who thinks he has offered a friend the best advice. "What's the girl's name?"

"Lila."

"Is she comely?"

Simon dredged his memory but couldn't come up with a clear picture of her. "She's young and shy, quite attractive." Certainly if there were any blemishes or unsightly warts he'd remember. "She's from a strict family and her bloodlines are pure." Quite different from Batasha and imminently more suitable, he thought. And she was a virgin, of that he was sure. Old Jesse wouldn't allow one of his daughters to play loose, whereas, Batasha had been involved with the Roman centurion Marcellus and most likely had been intimate with him.

The two of them walked back into the house, their arms laid across each other's shoulders. Their silence was broken only by the swish of leaves underfoot.

Back in the bedroom, Peter gave a low chuckle. "Judas snores as if he's choking," he whispered. "I can always tell which one is he because he sort of bubbles."

Still unsettled, Simon said in a vehement hiss. "I wish I didn't have to be partnered with him!"

Peter yawned, at the same time stifling a laugh. "The Master is probably trying to build up your patience." He made more humorous sounds as he lay down and turned over. Soon both he and Simon were adding their music to the other men sleeping in the room.

It turned out to be a mild winter. The nights and mornings were brisk and clear, and the days warmed to an extent that one could dispense with the outer robe. Batasha and Jonas prayed daily for Jesus and the disciples, and Batasha often thought of

Simon. His farewell kiss had inspired a burgeoning hope that he cared more deeply for her than she had imagined, that he did not dislike her at all despite his gruff manner. That moment of touching had been sweet and sincere, and she looked forward to seeing him again and perhaps sorting out their differences. Perhaps love would bloom between them in the spring when dead things came to life and the earth put on her garments of joy.

She grew a winter garden of herbs and pumpkins and winter squash and kept her hands busy at the loom in the evenings making clothing. Jonas spent the mornings at his lessons, and then went into Magdala with Batasha to help in the shop, although business was usually scant during the winter months. Jonas had made friends with an elderly man named Ashima, one of her father's old friends, who spent many hours entertaining him with ancient gossip and old stories.

Jonas spent some time each day in the tree house. Batasha wondered what the fascination was, but remembered her own childhood and how she had liked to go there to daydream. Usually he was tardy for his evening meal and she had to call him more often than not. Alexes told her that Jonas fought Roman armies everyday, and that to date, he'd probably vanquished a dozen legions single-handedly. Using his imagination, he spotted them from his private lookout and came down to conquer them with short swords made of sticks.

She wondered if Simon had instilled such sentiments in the boy, but admitted that was probably not the case. Perhaps the tendency to find an enemy and engage in open warfare was innate in all males, especially Hebrew males, who were reputed to be born fighters. She often wished, however, that there were children Jonas's age close by. A boy needed friends, and other games to play besides war.

One evening when she called him, he pushed through the brittle winter shrubbery out of breath, ran toward her in urgency, and seized her hands.

"Jonas!" she chided. "You've been playing without your warm cloak. Shame on you! Your hands are like ice. Are you such a child that I have to dress and muffle you before I let you out to play?"

"There's an old man down by the laurels!" he informed her in a rush. "He's collapsed in great pain."

"An old man?" she asked closing her eyes for a moment. *No*, she thought shaking her head. *No, it couldn't be him.*

She allowed Jonas to pull her to the laurels. The man was curled on his side huddled in a torn, dirty robe. She pulled him over and their eyes met. She could only stare. She had recognized him in Sidon. She had known who he was when she had seen him looking down at her from the rocks on the beach. Now here he was again, and she could no longer deny that this was her father.

"Why did you come back?" she asked in a flat voice without welcome.

"I'm dying."

"What does that have to do with me?"

"You're my daughter."

"I'll send Alexes to fetch you. Come along Jonas."

The boy followed in silent puzzlement.

By the next day news had spread all over Magdala that Hillel, the father of Mary Batasha, the perfumer, had come home. Many of his old friends from the days when he had been a successful importer came by to see him and were shocked at how old and frail he'd grown. "But Hillel is still young, too young to die." They said this because they were his same age and frightened.

Grete fussed over him in loving sadness, Suzanna tempted him with her best cooking, and Alexes bent under his gnarled hand and wept openly, for Hillel had been the kindest of masters. Batasha stayed away from his bedside and wished fervently that he would go ahead and die without further ado. But he lingered. And day after day her resentment grew until it became something dreadful.

"Why don't you go in to see him?" her aunt asked one evening as Batasha sat in front of the loom working it with swift, noisy strokes. "He asks for you every hour. The physician says he won't make it through the night."

"Ashima is his best friend," Batasha replied in a leaden voice, keeping up the steady rhythm of her work. "He sits by his bed and provides comfort."

"It's not Ashima he wants to make peace with—it's you."

"I'll see him later."

"Later may be too late."

Sitting at her feet, Jonas looked up sharply. Accusation and confusion showed in his precocious black eyes. "He's your father! Don't you care?"

"You don't understand." She said in the patronizing voice one used with a child. "My father abandoned me when I was about your age. Just walked away without a word or a promise. One night he kissed me and sent me to bed; the next morning I had no papa. My father died then. That man lying in there bears no resemblance to him. I won't pretend to love him, for I've never been a hypocrite."

"It seems to me that you're just angry. Angry at him for not living up to your ideal. You're angry, so you won't bend or try to understand him the least little bit," protested Jonas in a stubborn voice.

"That will be enough!" Batasha said to him with uncustomary sharpness.

He scrambled to his feet, throwing down the leather belt he'd been weaving, standing against her as indignant as a slender flame. "So what if you only had him twelve years? That's more than some of us had. I don't even know my real father's name."

"Go to your room, Jonas," Batasha ordered coldly. "I won't tolerate this impudence from you. This is none of your business."

As Jonas ran out of the room, Grete made a distressed sound between her teeth. She had never heard her niece talk to the boy so harshly. Batasha went back to her weaving with mindless determination, the automatic *click, click* of the shuttle loud in the deafening silence. Eventually Grete also withdrew to her bed, leaving her niece alone, wrapped in her own tense blanket of bitterness.

Chapter 13

But you are a forgiving God,
gracious and compassionate.
Nehemiah 9:17 NIV

At midnight, Batasha slammed down the crosspiece of the loom nearly tearing the material asunder. She rose and walked to her father with slow, reluctant steps.

Suzanna was keeping watch. Her black, African eyes flew wide as Batasha approached. "Go on," Batasha said. "I'll stay with him for a while."

After her friend left, Batasha stood in a pool of cold yellow light cast by the bedside lamp. She stared at the man in the bed. This leathery, sun-baked creature with the sunken dark eye sockets was her father. His long grey beard was dingy and his hair, once thick and black, was now only a few straggling wisps hanging limply to a bony skull.

Heartsick, she turned her head toward the plastered wall, refusing to deal with reality. Better to focus on the fine oriental arras and the niche containing three costly Cretan vases. She willed her saddened mind to think on these details instead of the pitiful conglomeration of gristle and wasted flesh that was Hillel of Magdala.

Eventually she looked at him again, at the small rib-encased chest covered by grey skin and sparse, grey hair. Once that chest had been large and robust, full of laughter as he had held her close. Now it barely moved. She studied it, watching its lifting and sinking progress.

Suddenly his eyes opened. They were dull with pain and death. "Brighitta?" he called in a weak quaver.

She forced herself to remain composed. "No, it's Batasha."

"Of course, Mary." Incredibly, at this dire hour, humor lurked in his voice. He had deliberately called her by her first name, never having totally approved of the tribal name her mother had given her. "Standing in the light, you look just like your mother."

Impassively, she eased into the chair by his bed. "Are you in much pain?"

"No."

She knew he was lying. "I'll call the physician."

"No! He's a jackass like the rest of them. They don't know anything. Most of them are scoundrels and thieves. I don't need some heathen charlatan telling me what my problem is." He wrestled himself up, then fell back gasping.

His struggle for breath alarmed her. "Where do you hurt?"

"In my chest."

"Your heart?"

"Yes, my heart is disintegrating like an old leather wineskin, leaking blood into my chest and lungs and God knows where else."

Just like him to provide his own diagnosis. He always thought he knew everything. She found herself growing angry at this tragic and inappropriate time. "How do you know?"

"Because I just do," he said with some of his old, self-confident smugness.

She shook her head, casting him a sidelong glance. He hadn't changed at all in some things. Always willing to argue and insist on his own way. "So! I guess you know more than a person trained in these matters. And where did you get all this medical knowledge, Papa?"

"Will you argue me to my grave, Daughter?" He sighed and began to pick at the bedclothes with withered, claw-like hands. "I know because I've had two attacks before. The first one occurred while I was on board a ship coming back from Sicily. When we landed in Sidon, the pain was so great that I went to a Phoenician doctor. He gave me a potion of mandrake, charged me exorbitantly, and told me to rest. The woman I was staying with at the time told me I was having a heart attack. She had seen her husband have one and pronounced gloomily that I would die just as he did. I wasn't frightened, so I suppose I recovered out of sheer perversity." He gave a raspy chuckle. "Or perhaps Jehovah looked down and said: 'Ha! I'll be merciful and give you another chance, Hillel.' At any rate I recovered. Five years later, I had another attack, went and bought some mandrake, treated myself, and again improved." He seemed to sink into the bed helplessly. "But this time I won't."

Batasha's eyes felt dusty. Her mouth was so dry she could hardly swallow. "Why did you come back? Don't you have friends in Sidon to look after you? Didn't you ever remarry?"

"I have many friends in Sidon—the sort one acquires over a pitcher of beer. And no, I never remarried. Who could compare with your mother?"

"You mentioned a woman."

"She was just someone I was with for a while." He closed his eyes breathing erratically. She thought he'd dozed off until he asked, "Did you recognize me in Sidon?"

"Did you recognize me?"

"Why are you determined to vex me?" He made a birdlike sound in his chest that was supposed to be a chuckle. "Yes, I knew you right away. You're the image of your mother. Physically anyway. Otherwise, you are much like me, I fear."

I knew you by your eyes," she admitted. "I was in Sidon with Jesus and a number of his followers. We believe he is the promised Messiah."

"I saw him," said Hillel. "An ordinary fellow, although I'll allow that he has great drawing power. Messiah, bah! That's a lost hope, something the ancient prophets concocted to placate the people and something the politicians use today to keep an atrophying nation from shriveling into the dust."

"He really is the Messiah," she stated unequivocally. "I'll send Alexes to find him tomorrow. He's somewhere in northern Galilee now preaching and ministering to the poor. He'll come and lay hands on you and make you well. He healed me of the seizures."

"He did?" Hillel said in weak surprise.

"Yes. He has great power. I've seen many remarkable things."

"Well, my mind isn't closed. A very small part of my bleeding heart still hopes for a Messiah. But don't send Alexes. It's too late."

She withheld comment but silently decided to send for the Master first thing in the morning. "You've become cynical, Papa. Cynical and morbid."

He gave a twisted smile. "It comes with age, my daughter—and from having the most beautiful thing in one's life snatched away for no reason."

"So you hold a grudge against God because Mama died?"

"Perhaps," he said noncommittally. "It was senseless. You explain it," he challenged in a whisper. "She was young and beautiful and good, and she didn't deserve to die."

"I can't explain anything," she answered. "I don't know why Mama died and some filthy old thief or murderer lives on to walk the streets and hurt people. But I still believe in God. And I especially believe that Jesus has the power to stay the hand of evil that so often strikes people."

"Oh, I still believe there is a God, too," Hillel argued. "I just wonder about his intentions. He doesn't seem to be the kind and merciful Jehovah the Psalmist proclaimed. I've often believed him to be an unfeeling tyrant, playing a wicked game with us all. Testing, always testing. And only the most stoic—only those who can withstand all the torment and suffering here on earth—may go on to heaven. Yes, there is a God, all right. But I don't like him very much."

"Papa!" she said horrified.

He gave a dry cackle. "It's blasphemy, I know. But perhaps not. Perhaps it's the purest form of honesty."

"It is without faith. My Master, Jesus, wouldn't approve of your views. He tells us to hope, to believe always. He says that the Father has numbered the very hairs on our heads and loves us with a great unending love."

Hillel made a scornful sound through his lips. "This fellow sounds like a man who has never known pain. Let him lose something he loves with all his heart, and then we'll see how much faith he has. Let him have a heart attack and feel as if his chest is going to burst. Let life come at him like a wall of evil, and see how he holds up."

"He would not falter," she said with certainty, getting up to tidy the sheet around his emaciated body.

"Stop it!" Shifting restlessly, he waved her away. "Yes, I should very much like to meet your Jesus," he said combatively. "I'd like to see him face to face and have it out with him. Perhaps he'd say that Jehovah didn't destroy my faith at all. Perhaps he'd say that I destroyed it myself, with my weakness and unwillingness to believe in God's goodness. He'd say that I let resentment take the place of trust."

Tears began to gather in his weak old eyes. Batasha was grief stricken at seeing the father, who had been her idol in childhood, weeping and hopeless.

"I'm a pathetic man," he admitted. "I haven't the fortitude of Job. I ran away and turned my back on God. I raised my fist and called him names. I tried to believe that I knew more than he—that I was more just. And so I've come to this moment and now I know that he is God, and must be allowed to be sovereign in all." He laughed hollowly and tears broke from his eyes. "It's ironic. I will pray and say I'm sorry. Sorry that I, a mere man, set myself against the Almighty. And the Almighty, in his righteousness, will have to forgive me. After all, he is God; and God cannot hold grudges. I held one against him, but he can't hold one against me."

"It's all right, Papa." It stunned her to see him so broken. "Don't worry. I know God loves you."

"I've been wrong," he wept. "All this time so wrong, and down deep inside I knew it. But I was proud and angry."

She bent over him and smoothed his brow. He felt strange to her touch and cold with perspiration. At last he seemed to fall asleep, and she sat down and leaned her head against the chair. Why had he come back into her life like this to tear her apart? What did he want of her?

Time flowed into deepest night—interminably dark and lonely. Sand trickled grain by grain through the hourglass. The lamp burned low. Silent, dark shadows in the corners of the room crouched inexorably closer constricting the circle of light ever smaller.

When her father once again whispered, she leaned forward to listen. "What is it, Papa?"

The familiar, loving eyes opened, bleak and pleading. "Will you also forgive me?"

This was the question, the reckoning she'd tried to avoid. How could she lie and say yes, yet how could she say no?

"Will you forgive me, little Mary Batasha?" he asked again. The pall of death had momentarily lifted from his expression and he was lucid, aware. He searched her. He would know if she lied.

She searched deep for something to give. His hand lay on the sheet, all bone and brown leather. She slipped hers under it as a little child. "I'll try, Papa."

Suddenly he threw back his head and silently convulsed, as if his soul had risen up to escape his body. She ran and woke the house. In a few moments, Grete, Alexes, Suzanna, and several faithful servants were at his bedside. She stood back and watched with shocked dry eyes as his throat stopped working, his mouth closed, and the motionless sheet became a shroud.

What was the hour? she wondered. Someone must write it down. The hour her papa died. It should be written down and never forgotten. As the others began to mourn with sobs and loud lamenting, she turned and walked stiffly to her room. Going to the window, she pulled back the heavy winter curtain and unlatched the mica window. Dawn had arrived at last like a gaping, purple wound in the sky, cold and congealed. "Papa, I love you." She leaned out the window calling. "I forgive you!" Turning she saw Grete standing in the doorway with arms outstretched. As she ran sobbing, her aunt enfolded her. "He can't hear me now! I wish I had told him."

"He heard you," Grete said smoothing her hair. "He heard you on the way to Abraham's bosom."

Nine days after the burial of her father Batasha and Jonas went to Capernaum to visit Leah and Deborah. Grief had left Batasha's heart as bare as the winter earth. Her mother's death had been swift and decisive, like the mortal incision of a sword. She had never seen her mother's dead body, had never gone to the tomb until many weeks later; her father had spared her all that. She realized now the enormity of his consideration.

But with her father she had seen it all, had lived through every horrifying and numbing moment of it. Sickness, death, burial. They had left her with a deep sadness that gouged dark, mournful holes out of each new day.

Deborah and Leah welcomed her wearing masks of cheerfulness. As a way of offering comfort, they circumvented their pity and concern by avoiding any exchange that might bring Batasha remembrance and fresh sorrow. Jonas went out to play as the women sat and talked of mundane matters. Long, uncomfortable silences punctuated their conversation. Batasha found herself feeling sorry for them. She generously accepted that they didn't quite know how to respond or what to say. Courteously she avoided mentioning her father or recounting any of the dark convolutions of time she had staggered through in recent weeks.

Jonas entered the room during one of the painful lulls to announce that the Lord's mother was at the gate. Leah told him to admit her immediately as Deborah got up to fetch another cup of sweet wine. Batasha smiled remotely at their flurry. A part of her that wasn't buried beneath melancholy looked forward to seeing Jesus' mother again and understood Leah and Deborah's desire to show her the greatest hospitality.

With the woman's entrance, the room seemed to settle with a quality that Batasha could only identify as serenity. Leah took her cloak and offered her comfortable seating. Deborah hastened to fill two small cups with juice for the twin children that accompanied her. Jonas moved around the scene in the background eyeing the tableau guardedly.

"This is Jude and Judith, my youngest," said the Lord's mother introducing the twins with a smile.

Unable to contain his aspirations any longer, Jonas piped up, "May they play with me? I've made a palace of stones and I'd like to show it to them. I can see that they are smaller than I, so I'll watch them carefully."

The mother's warm grey eyes crinkled at the corners. She nodded as the children hurried to finish their drinks and make a polite, but hasty, exit.

"I'm looking for Jesus," she explained, turning to Leah and Deborah. "I understand that he stays here."

"He does. I…I mean sometimes he does," stammered Leah. "Right now he's away. They all are. Jesus could be anywhere in Galilee."

Her face fell. She took a drink hiding her consternation in the cup. "I see," she finally said in a composed voice. "When do you expect him back?"

"We don't know exactly," responded Leah. "Sometime in the spring."

"Is this an emergency?" asked Deborah. "Sometimes my husband Peter comes home for the night. I could ask him to locate Jesus and send him to Nazareth if it's urgent."

"There's no emergency. And I wouldn't want Jesus to go to Nazareth," his mother said with open honesty. The distant sound of children's laughter wafted into their presence from outside. "I have left that place and I won't be going back."

Feeling raw herself, Batasha sensed a gentle sadness in the woman, even though her heart-shaped face was strong and tranquil. She sensed that this woman had left Nazareth at great personal cost and that she had been through inner turmoil and hard decisions.

Batasha's eyes suddenly welled with tears that scurried down her cheeks before she had time to staunch them. "Please bring your children and come stay with me in Magdala," she urged in a broken voice.

The Lord's mother reached out and gently took Batasha's hand. "Why are you crying?" she asked softly.

"She just lost her father," Leah explained.

"Ah, yes." The pure, untainted sympathy of the Master's mother completely surrounded Batasha with comfort. "And tears flow at the most unexpected times," she went on. "At children's laughter, a kind look, an intuitive recognition of another in pain."

"Will you stay with me until Jesus returns in the spring?" Batasha asked.

"Certainly," said the Lord's mother with a smile. "And spring will come, my friend. You must cling to that and expect the sunshine and the joy."

The soul of the Lord's mother was like a gracious elm tree, gold-crowned by the sun, filled with the music of many birds, bending joyfully at life's breezes, and standing stalwartly against its many storms. Batasha took refuge beneath her spreading protection, rested in her quiet, sun-dappled shade, and absorbed her song like dry, thirsty ground.

She was practical and efficient, like her sister Salome, the mother of James and John, knowing how to stretch a measure of meal and the best way to arrange a freshly laundered robe on a rack to dry. Yet at times she seemed mysterious, as if pondering secrets kept deep within.

Batasha felt uncomfortable calling her Mary, which was her first name, and took to addressing her as Lady. The Lord's mother humbly accepted this title of respect without demurring.

Even though it was a mild winter, there were two light snows that melted off immediately. It rained a great deal, leaving earth and grass an indistinguishable, mottled pattern of gold and brown. But there were no driving sleet storms, which sometimes visited Palestine in its severest winters, and Batasha and the Lady gave prayers of thanksgiving for that.

One afternoon toward the month of March when the countryside lay fallow and quiet with expectancy, they heard a loud "Ho!" and the shrieking of excited children followed by deep masculine laughter.

"It's Jesus!" Batasha exclaimed. "He must have found out from Peter that you were staying here," she said to the Lady.

He entered the villa with Jude and Judith firmly clamped to his sides. His mother rose and turned, her eyes, so much like his, brimming with happiness. "What am I going to do with you, my son?" she pretended to scold. "You've turned into a vagabond."

His arms drew her tenderly to his chest; then he touched the dark, silver-winged hair as he held her away to kiss both cheeks. "Mother." The one word was both an endearment and a prayer of gratitude.

Her quiet eyes filled with tears. "I'm sorry I didn't come sooner. It wasn't that I didn't believe. You know that. It was that I didn't want any more quarreling. And I was afraid for you."

"I know." His voice was soft with understanding.

"I left the others well and safe. Simon is with Ruth. Joseph is still with James at the shop. They are angry with me, but I couldn't stay away any longer."

He eased her away and looked into her eyes seriously. "Can you bear all that will come to pass?"

"I must," she said smiling through her tears. "Now come along and let me get you some refreshment. You must be tired and thirsty."

Batasha stood in puzzlement as they left the atrium with the children. It had been a tender reunion, which was no surprise considering the capacity to love that both Jesus and his mother possessed, but what had Jesus meant when he referred to the future in such solemn tones?

Chapter 14

You open your hand
and satisfy the desires of every living thing.
Psalm 145: 16 NIV

Spring came early and the disciples returned to Capernaum two by two, weary yet robustly joyful with the success of their mission. They gathered at Peter's house enjoying what was turning out to be a grand celebration, with much kissing, boisterous greetings, and shoulder clapping. Batasha, Suzanna, and the Lady, upon hearing the news of their return, had come from Magdala with a banquet of covered dishes. Salome arrived with her husband Zebedee, who added his gusty voice to the teasing and general merriment.

Salome and the Lord's mother fell on each other's necks with cries of delight. It had been a long time since the two sisters had seen one another. Salome upbraided the Lady for not visiting Bethsaida since moving into the area. The Lady replied that she had been busy taking care of her two young children. Why hadn't Salome come to Magdala to visit her since having no little ones, she was free as a bird? Salome returned with feigned severity that she certainly would have if her sister had been considerate enough to send word that she was just across the lake and no longer in the hill country. They both burst out laughing and embraced again, the older sister whirling the Lord's mother around playfully, two siblings lost in the utter joy of blood being united again with blood.

They all ate and drank with appetite. Deborah brought out her flute and began to play a light, cheerful tune. The Lady accompanied on the zither, and Salome, not to be outdone, took up the timbrel, accentuating the beat with tinkling bells. Soon there was dancing, and Batasha joined the circle with excitement, her natural love of the dance urging her on. When Simon touched her hand briefly and impersonally, keeping his face averted. Batasha's happiness turned to anxiety. He had not looked at her all evening, or acknowledged her in any way. It was as if she didn't exist and their tender kiss of farewell in the autumn had never taken place.

She brightened, however, as Joanna and Chuza arrived. They had been at Herod's winter palace in Machaerus for the past several weeks, Chuza having been summoned there at Herod's special request. The circle broke and Batasha ran to embrace her friend. At this contact, Joanna burst into tears. The incongruous sound of loud sobbing among the laughter seemed to ring a death knell over the festivities. The music stopped and all sound and movement came to a breathless halt.

"The Baptist is dead!" announced Chuza, hanging his cloak upon a peg. Lines of fatigue and grief scored his face. "Herod had him executed."

"Dead? The Baptist is dead?" The news echoed around the room.

Saying nothing, Jesus groped for a chair, as if unable to see, and sat down hard, a painful moan rising from deep in his chest.

The Lady held her hand to her eyes as Salome came and put an arm around her. "Oh, how can it be?" the Lady mourned tearfully. "So young. Only six months older than my Jesus. It seems that only yesterday he was a boy going into the monastery at Quamran. Always so mindful of spiritual matters, always wanting to do the right thing. We all knew he would be a mighty man of God someday. A great prophet. I'm glad Aunt Elizabeth isn't alive to suffer this." Her voice gave way as she said to her youngest nephew, the disciple John. "You were named after him." John ben Zebedee went to his aunt and held her as she wept against his shoulder.

Salome raised an impotent fist. "Herod will pay for this! He has shed innocent blood, and, as a result, he will suffer the broadside of Jehovah's wrath."

They all looked at Jesus, who leaned forward in his seat bowing his head between his hands, apparently too deeply moved to speak.

"I can scarcely believe it," Peter said. Andrew and I followed him for a while before meeting Jesus. When did it happen?" he asked.

"Two weeks ago. I left as soon as I could to get back here. I told them my wife was ill. And she is. This whole sordid thing has given her nightmares and has destroyed her nerves."

"Oh, it was horrible!" Joanna cried feverishly. "Herodias' wicked child brought his head into the banquet hall. His eyes were still staring and there was so much blood!"

"They beheaded him," Chuza explained, his own voice gruff with horror as they all sought cushions and sat down in various postures of shock. "I never really thought Herod would kill him," he continued. "He liked John. His respect for the Baptist was well known."

"It was Herodias's doing," Joanna put in tearfully. "She and her wicked child conspired together to kill him."

"But I don't understand," said Philip, trying to milk a drop of reason from the situation. "If Herod liked John and respected him, what brought him to the point of doing such a terrible thing to him? It doesn't make sense."

"Does evil ever make sense?" Simon exploded. "I tell you, Philip, you'd debate Satan himself and try to pick him to pieces. Why don't you just accept that some men are truly depraved?"

"But everything isn't that clear cut," Philip protested.

Simon glared mutinously. "The evil of this deed is quite clear," he argued. "I hope Herod dies like his father did—with a belly full of maggots!"

"Tell us how it happened, Chuza," urged Peter, precluding further discord.

"It was the anniversary of Herod's ascension to the Tetrarchy," Chuza began. "We had prepared a great celebration. Herod's friends from Rome and every part of Palestine and Syria came. Every guest room in the palace was occupied and I had ordered a great deal of food and costly wines. The entertainments became quite lascivious and there was a great deal of drinking. I was about to remove Joanna from the scene when Herodias's daughter entered and began to dance, so I decided not to offend the queen by leaving at that time.

"The little girl performed in a most provocative manner. I won't go into a description, but it was seductive beyond your wildest imagination. She had the tongue of every filthy-minded male present lolling in drunken lust. I couldn't believe it—a mere child, the same age as Jonas over there."

"She knew exactly what she was doing!" Joanna cried. "How could she not, with her mother as her teacher?" Joanna turned back into Batasha's comforting arms.

"When she finished, she was quite naked," Chuza said. "Applause and stamping thundered in the hall. Herod called her over, took her on his lap, and began to pet her. It was"—he searched for a word—"disgusting. He told her she could have anything she wanted, even one half of his kingdom. She ran to seek counsel from her mother. When she came back, she hugged Herod and asked for the head of John the Baptist."

"Dear God!" Simon clenched his fists.

"I can't believe he agreed to it," Philip said. "To kill a man so brutally at the request of a mere child?"

"Oh, he was affected," Chuza remarked. "He sobered and became quite maudlin. But he couldn't go back on his word and lose face with his guests. He had sworn to give her anything and John's head was what she had asked for. And so he committed an atrocity in order to appear honorable among his friends," Chuza concluded on a note of irony.

"The executioner came to the entrance of the hall and handed Salome the platter with John's head on it," Joanna said. Her tears had dried, and now her voice was wooden instead of hysterical, as if she had relived these moments many times in her mind's eye. "Blood and gore splashed down her naked leg as her little-girl arms tried to keep the large oval dish steady. She was giggling when she set it before Herodias. I shall never forget the queen's look of triumph. She had finally gotten her revenge on the Baptist for accusing her of living in adultery. The great voice was silent. The cry in the wilderness lay dead in the gaping bloody mouth."

Batasha felt sick. She looked at Jesus who still sat with his head bowed, his eyes clenched, pinching the bridge of his nose. The women were crying and the men wore expressions varying from anguish to outrage. She looked past them to the debris of the once jubilant party. *Everybody had been so happy*, she thought mournfully.

Hearing voices outside, she left the room and walked to the gate. She hoped that word of Jesus' return to Capernaum hadn't gotten around this quickly and that the sick and afflicted weren't already coming to the door. But she was met by a group of about one hundred men, all of them standing quietly like hopeless shadows.

"Is this the home of Peter bar Jonah?" a man asked.

"Yes," she informed them in a soft voice.

"Is Jesus of Nazareth here?"

"He is, but this is not the time for healing and preaching. He has just found out that his cousin, the Baptist, was beheaded."

"We know," the spokesman said respectfully. "We're John's disciples. We've just come from burying his body. Now we want to follow Jesus, if he'll have us."

The Master received them kindly. Ravenous, they ate all the leftovers, being half-starved from grief and traveling. Peter told them to set up their tents in his courtyard since it was late and they were obviously weary. Leah grumbled a bit in her usual fashion, especially when she noted how one of her potted lemon trees had been cast aside haphazardly as the garden became a tent city of sorts.

They informed Jesus in hushed, fatigued voices that he might be in danger. News of some of his miracles had reached Herod's ears after John's death, and the conscience-stricken king had come to believe the John's spirit had somehow been resurrected in Jesus.

The disciples were aghast. They couldn't believe Herod's thinking had become so irrational. John's disciples replied that the Tetrarch was a superstitious man, even though not religious. He was suffering from guilt, and guilt worked strangely on a man's soul.

Furthermore, the Sadducees encouraged him in the illusion that John had come back to haunt him in the person of Jesus. This was ironic since Sadducees didn't believe in any form of resurrection after death at all. They held that when a man died, he simply ceased to exist altogether. The High Priest Caiphas had engineered the rumor, hoping to gain advantage over Herod by playing on his weakness and making him squirm. Caiphas loved power, and nothing would make him happier than to have a terror-stricken Herod blubbering at his feet.

At any rate, word was out that the king wanted to meet Jesus. His disciples, for once in unanimity, urged Jesus to withdraw for a time into Philip's Tetrarchy until Herod's sick madness over John abated. Jesus agreed to go with them across the lake the next morning to Bethsaida-Julius. There they all would get some rest and Jesus would have time to recover from the shock of his cousin's brutal murder.

☙

They camped in the grass of a wide plain just three or four miles north of the lake and east of the Jordan. To the south was Bethsaida-Julius, the city built by Philip the Tetrarch and named after Caesar's daughter. On down farther was the region of the Gadarenes, where Jesus had healed the demoniac Aulus the morning after he had calmed the storm.

The disciples watched an approaching multitude with some misgiving. There would be no rest today. The people had come from across the lake in ships and overland by way of Capernaum, fording the river about a mile from its mouth. Many were on their way to the Passover in Jerusalem and had decided to seek out the miracle-worker, Jesus of Nazareth, as a side excursion. Others came from the Decapolis where Aulus had spread his fame far and wide.

"Do you want us to send them away, Master?" James bar Zebedee asked.

Jesus answered with compassion, "No. Look at them, James. They're like lost sheep, crying, seeking a shepherd. I have to help them."

He walked to and fro over the wide plain, healing, comforting, talking to some in Aramaic, to others in eloquent Greek. To Galileans who had followed him across the lake, he spoke in the native guttural accents they were used to. An everyman's man.

Simon was amazed at his Master's capacity to give, to forget his own human requirements, his own need to grieve and weep. Jesus was willing to sacrifice everything he had to help humanity. Simon knew that Jesus would gladly spend his whole life walking the earth touching each person individually, if it weren't impossible for one man to do such a thing in one lifetime.

John's disciples came over and made a sad little group of forlorn-looking men. The chief Pharisee from Capernaum arrived with some of his friends from Jerusalem. Aulus, the Gadarene, restored to new life and purpose, darted busily among the people, considering himself a disciple too, as indeed he was in a sense. Simon was taken completely off guard when he saw his old Zealot friend Eleazer bar Samuel with some of his Judean revolutionaries moving about in the crowd.

Eleazer had a knack for stirring things up wherever he went, creating unhealthy excitement with his zeal. Simon watched him talking and gesticulating. He knew it was subversive talk—hatred toward Rome, war, and insurrection. Simon wondered if he himself came across so violently. He hoped not. There was something dark in Eleazer's passion.

It was early afternoon, what the Jews call the first evening. Jesus had been in the crowd all day and still had not seen them all. "Men, we have a problem," he said.

"What is it, Master?" asked Andrew.

"The people are hungry. They've been out here in this deserted place all day without anything to eat. How are we going to feed them, Philip?" He asked the one in the group who was considered to be the most educated. Then upon leaving the question in Philip's hands, he turned and walked purposefully once again into the crowd.

Philip's brow wrinkled in thought. "About how many people would you say we have here?" he asked Matthew.

"Close to five thousand men," Matthew answered, "and that many more women and children at least."

"Well, have you solved the problem?" Jesus said striding back a while later.

Philip seemed chagrined. "Lord, I figure it would take five hundred denarii to buy enough bread to feed this multitude, and even then, each would have only a morsel." He turned to Judas. "How much money do we have in the purse?"

"Not that much!" Judas exclaimed alarmed, laying his hand protectively on his belt as if to keep the hidden coins safe. "Let the people go into Bethsaida-Julius and buy their own food."

Simon watched without comment. He knew that Judas was a thief and wanted to confront him with it. When Batasha had returned the treasury purse, it had been full to nearly bursting because she had replenished it. Simon didn't know if there was enough money to feed a multitude, but he suspected that she had added several more pieces of silver to replace the one Judas had stolen.

Jesus paused, studying Judas thoughtfully.

"Lord," Philip protested in a voice of reason, "even if we went and bought bread, how would we get it all back? It would be too much for us to carry."

"We'd have to hire a wagon and donkeys," Andrew put in practically.

"Did any of you bring food?" Jesus asked suppressing a smile. He appeared to find their feeble attempts to solve the problem amusing.

"I did," Jonas piped up. "Suzanna stuffed a lunch in my shirt this morning before we left."

Simon laughed. "Suzanna has adopted Jonas's stomach, Master. She knows he's a growing boy and requires regular feedings throughout the day."

Jonas loosened the lunch from its hurried wrappings and held it out to Jesus. "It's not much, sir, but you're welcome to it."

"Master!" Andrew exclaimed in a despairing voice as Jesus walked over to accept the paper holding two fishes and five loaves from the boy. "What are five loaves and two small fish among all these people? It would be like pouring a bucket of water on the Sinai desert."

"Go and tell James, John, Peter and the others to make the people recline in companies of fifty and one hundred," Jesus said looking at Andrew pointedly.

Here was action, something Andrew could understand. He hurried off in unquestioning obedience, apparently refusing to think beyond the Master's immediate command.

"This is impossible!" Philip riveted his eyes upon Jesus in fascination.

After the multitude was arranged horizontally and vertically on the lush vivid grass, looking like so much cultivated farmland, Jesus raised his eyes to heaven and prayed: "Blessed art thou, Jehovah our God, King of the world, Who causes to come forth bread from the earth." It was the customary prayer of grace one said over a meal. Then he broke one of the loaves and his hands kept moving rapidly until the basket Simon had made with his robe was full to overflowing.

Philip was dumbfounded. The disciples filled their robes again and again, the bread mysteriously multiplying in Jesus' busy hands. Dizzy from watching, Philip had to accept what he was witnessing—Jesus could create substance out of thin air.

A woman came up with a baby clasped to her breast. It was the custom for women to travel carrying their infants in wicker baskets.

"Master, use my basket to help distribute the food while my baby feeds at my breast."

Soon other women offered their wicker cradles too. All of baskets became full to overflowing with broken bread and pieces of fish to the point of spilling over onto the grass. Sparrows came and fed at the Master's feet, then after taking their fill, rested on his shoulders unafraid.

Philip staggered down the hill, holding his head.

"Where are you going?" asked Simon. "Help us serve the people."

Philip—suave, urbane, educated Philip—turned, sobbing openly. "Do you know who He is? What He is?"

"He is Jesus, the Messiah," answered Simon.

"He is the Great Life Force, the Power that moves the universe and has since the beginning of time. He's the Creative, Life-giving Energy that breathes over the face of the deep and in the hearts of men."

Peter started to go after him, but Simon held him back, "Let him go. We have work to do."

After the people had eaten, the disciples gathered up twelve baskets of leftovers. They gave them to Aulus to distribute among the poor in the surrounding countryside.

Eleazer and his Zealots saw an opportunity to move among the people inciting them to action. Replete with food, they were more than willing to consider Jesus a political leader. They compared him to Moses who had called down manna from heaven to feed the people in the desert. Jesus could provide them with food and everything they wanted. What a king he would be! There would be bread on every table and safety and peace on the roads and highways. The Romans would no longer be able to burden them with heavy taxes; their soldiers would no longer beat and maim them, and rape their women.

Suddenly the crowd rose from the grass with a great exultant roar and began to converge on Jesus, Eleazer and his men leading.

"Master!" cried Simon caught up in the excitement. "They want to make you king! They'll carry you on their shoulders as they did Saul of old, and neither the Sanhedrin nor even the Emperor of Rome will be able to deny your authority to rule."

Jesus warded Eleazer off with a halting hand. "Stop! The time isn't right for me to ascend to my throne."

"But Jesus!" Eleazer cried. "Let us make you our ruler. Let us take you before us into Jerusalem so that everyone at Passover may know who you are!"

"Don't you understand," Jesus said lifting his head to address them all in a loud voice. "I don't receive glory from men. I crave no human honor or mortal fame. My Kingdom is not of this world."

With that, he left them and walked away toward the hills. Several hours later he returned after the crowd had dispersed. He told the disciples to take the boats and go back to Bethsaida in Galilee. He would come around by land and meet them there.

They boarded the largest ship of Zebedee's fleet, which easily accommodated them all. It was only six miles from one side of the lake to the other. Since the wind was contrary, James bar Zebedee pulled down the sail and they began to row. Simon put his strong back into it, thinking that rowing such a short distance would be a minor feat. With the others, he pulled and pulled until his shoulders throbbed and his arms felt limp as leather thongs.

"How far have we gone?" he called over his shoulder to Andrew.

"Not quite halfway! The wind is fighting against us."

"What time is it?" James the Less asked in a loud groan.

"The fourth watch," Peter answered from behind. "We've been at it most of the night."

"We'll never make it," Thomas pronounced gloomily. "Satan has sent a steady wind against us."

"Look, look!" Peter pointed a shaking finger off the starboard. They all ceased rowing as a white vision floated across the water some distance away.

"It's a ghost!" cried Judas cowering.

They all huddled in the bowels of the boat afraid. Even Simon, who considered himself a courageous man and one unscathed by superstition, caught their contagious dread.

"Take heart!" said a familiar voice. "It is I myself. Don't be afraid."

Peter scrambled to his knees peering over the side of the hull. "Master, is that really you?"

"Yes, I saw you from afar and came to help."

Peter began to laugh. "Lord, let me walk on the water too."

"Come ahead!" Jesus motioned with a sweep of his arm.

Without a backward glance and on sheer madcap faith, Peter immediately climbed over the side and began to walk upright. He used the toddling steps of a baby and was proceeding quite well until a particularly boisterous wave made a lunge at him. Suddenly he looked down at the undulating water and panicked.

"Oh, God! What am I doing?" Immediately he sank beneath the restless water and a wave obliterated his existence until he surfaced a moment later groping and choking. "Jesus! Where are you? Save me!"

Jesus grabbed his shoulders and hauled him up so that again only his feet touched the waves. Peter clung to him for dear life as the Master's chest rumbled with laughter. "What happened to your faith? Why didn't you come the whole way?" he asked.

The men in the boat had watched the event with avid interest. "Peter took his eyes off the Lord, and that is why he sank," Philip summed up. "Jesus is laughing, but I think he's a little disappointed. Peter failed him."

"Jesus understands," Nathaniel said generously.

"I didn't notice you going over the side to walk with the Master," Simon spoke up bluntly in defense of Peter.

"Nor I you," Philip pointed out in cultured tones heavy with sarcasm.

"Stop it!" John said exasperated. "You two are always at each other. It puts everybody on edge. Keep it up and I'll kick you both out of the boat. Being landlubbers, you would certainly sink. And good riddance, I'd say."

Simon and Philip had sufficient conscience at least to look a bit guilty. John didn't become angry often, but when he did, everyone took notice. They all remained silent as Peter boarded the ship ahead of Jesus, talking animatedly of his adventure and castigating himself for sinking needlessly.

Having been blown off course, they reached shore next to the plain of Gennesaret, one of the Lord's favorite spots. They slept soundly through the rest of the night, not minding that there were no comfortable beds and no roof over their heads—God's blessed, fragrant earth felt wonderfully solid.

During the next few days Jesus helped the people in the region. They brought their sick to the villages and marketplaces on pallets, and many were healed by merely touching his garment as he walked among them.

Eventually Jesus returned to Capernaum with his weary and footsore disciples. A mob of people awaited; many of them were the same ones he'd fed in Bethsaida-Julius. They were not in a good mood. They accosted him outside the synagogue. His evasions had irritated them, and they complained that they had spent several days looking for him.

Finally he spoke out in irritation. "Why have you been searching for me?" he demanded. "Is it because I showed you miracles and signs? Is it because I fed you bread and your flesh was satisfied? Honestly, you hurt and bother me. I know you're not interested in the real reason I help you—you have no interest in the things I can do for you spiritually."

Not listening, they shouted, "What are you going to do today? Show us something wonderful! Feed us again, and every day, as Jehovah fed our people manna in the desert."

Jesus shook his head in frustration. "But I am the Bread. Don't you understand? If you accept and trust in me, you'll never be hungry or thirsty again!"

The ones who had come merely to get a meal were disgruntled. Disappointed, they started moving away. They wanted something more substantial than a sermon in symbols. The ever-present Pharisees added to the unrest by further resentful comments: "How can this carpenter's son call himself the answer to the people's spiritual needs? We shouldn't allow him to make these outrageous claims. Something must be done." Eleazer bar Samuel and his band of malcontents, already angry with Jesus for not allowing them to set him up as a political leader, joined in the general grumbling.

"Why do you all complain against me?" Jesus challenged them drawing himself up to his full six-foot height. "Why do you close your hearts and try to find answers inside your flesh? Don't you know that only God can teach you? If you will listen to the Father and learn from Him, you will come to me. I am the Bread of Life that gives Life—the Living Bread. Yes, your fathers ate the manna in the wilderness. But they died. But if you eat of me, you will never die. Anyone who adheres to me and puts his faith in me will live eternally."

The crowd rumbled in discontent. The Scribes and Pharisees saw the falling away and took advantage of it. "Are you going to continue with him?" one of them shouted at the *am ha'arez*. "Can't you see he's insane? Only a crazy man would make such blasphemous claims. Go to Nazareth, his hometown. He's known as a madman. Even his own brothers have denounced him!"

In groups of twos and threes, the religious leaders pushed out of the crowd, gesturing with their arms as if to say "Bah!" Many of the common folk followed their lead. In quiet dignity, Jesus watched them go, his eyes clouded with disappointment. Then he turned and addressed those remaining, most of whom were his own close followers and John's ex-disciples, who stood together in the thinning audience shifting on their feet in indecision.

"I'm speaking honestly and seriously," he told them. "Please listen. You can't have any life in yourselves. You must eat of the flesh of the Son of Man and drink his blood. You must appropriate his life and its saving merit. If you feed on me and drink my life-giving blood, you will live forever, because anyone who does this dwells every moment in me, and I dwell every moment in him. I am your covenant with the living God." He pleaded with them to accept this simple, yet profound truth.

The leader of John's disciples, whose name was David, turned and walked away, his shoulders slumping. Over a hundred men accompanied him. Judas stepped out as if to join them, then seemed to think and change his mind.

"Does this offend you and cause you to stumble?" Jesus called after them on a pleading note, his arm outstretched in empty sadness. "Does this shock and scandalize you. Then how much more surprised you will be when you see me ascending to heaven. Will you believe then?"

Simon caught David's arm as he passed. "Don't go. Trust him. Stay with us."

David shook his head. "He's not like the Baptist. He's too strange. All this talk of blood. I don't want to hear it."

"He often speaks in parables and secret language," Simon tried to explain in persuasive tones. "We don't always understand him either. Please!"

"No!" David pulled away. "I'm going back to my old life."

Now the only ones that remained were the Twelve, scatterings of common people, and the faithful women, all of them standing in separate pools of silence. Jesus bowed his head and uttered a deep, barely audible groan of defeat.

"Will you also go away and leave me?" he said slowly lifting his head to address them.

Peter answered. "Master, we have no place to go, no one else to go to. You are our Messiah; you speak the words of Life. We can cling to no other."

"Yes, I hand-picked you all." His voice was rough with unshed tears. "And even at that, one of you is a devil." He covered his head with his mantle and walked out from among them.

Simon was stunned. The Master had called one of them a devil. He felt self-condemnation touch his heart like a cold finger. Had the Lord been speaking of him? Had he looked into Simon's heart and seen his unforgiving resentment of the Roman occupation? His tendency toward lust? His stupidity when it came to grasping important teachings? His wayward temper and refusal to remain quiet when offended? His complete and all-pervading inadequacy as a follower?

Simon felt upset and angry with himself. He was a failure. He must try to do better, to be worthy of his calling.

Chapter 15

... and a light for the Gentiles.
Isaiah 42: 6 NIV

Batasha knew that Alexes needed her in Magdala to help begin harvesting the flowers. She and Suzanna planned to leave Capernaum tomorrow although she didn't really want to leave Joanna's so soon due to the fact that Jesus was going through a difficult time since the collapse of his Galilean ministry. The desertion of so many of his followers had affected him immensely, causing deep hurt.

To make matters worse, the Pharisees had been hounding him on various minute points of the law. As a result, he had become quiet and spent more time than usual alone on the Plain of Gennesaret or wandering the shallow hillocks that lifted away from the lake. Often he stayed away from Peter's for two and three days at a time. The Twelve were also dejected and tried to talk the Master into leaving Galilee altogether for a while. Philip wanted them to go into the neighboring Gentile regions; he was sure that the heathens would accept Jesus much more eagerly than the Jews, who already considered themselves especially favored by God.

Jesus, however, apparently not ready to commit to a plan, kept a moody silence. Sometimes it seemed to Batasha that he was the loneliest man in the world. Even the disciples' feeble attempts at joking did not cheer him.

"What's he going to do now that so many of his own people have rejected him?" asked Joanna as she and Batasha moved among her newly awakened garden flowers. "Ugh!" she exclaimed bending over an opening rose bud. "Here's another one of those shiny blue bugs! Why do they sleep in my roses? Do you have them on your flowers in Magdala?" she asked Batasha.

"They are harmless," Batasha answered with a laugh. "It's the tiny green devils that get on the stems that you have to watch out for. They are aphids and must be washed off with soap and water." She sighed and plucked a rose to carry as they walked. "Do you think he'll quit now, Joanna?" she asked. "I know he's terribly hurt and disappointed. Sometimes I think his mother is afraid and would be relieved if he went back to his former life as a carpenter."

"Can you blame her for being afraid?" Joanna returned with uplifted brows. "You saw how the delegation from Caiphas went after him in the synagogue yesterday. They were after blood. You'd think that since most of his followers have deserted, the religious leaders would let up."

"They're nothing but a pack of jackals."

"But Jesus is a Jew. A brother Hebrew. How can they despise him so completely?"

"Jackals are known for turning viciously on one of their own. I was glad yesterday when Jesus gave them the tongue-lashing they deserved." She sat by the little blue pool her friend was so fond of and leaned back on her arms to bare her face to the warm April sun. "No, I don't think he'll give up. He has a destiny. A man with a destiny doesn't give up."

"Chuza thinks he will leave Galilee and begin to tour the Gentile cities now that many of his Hebrew followers have deserted." Joanna sat beside her and tested the water with her fingers. "Chuza says that sometimes it's easier to overcome ignorance than prejudice."

" I never believed Jesus would withhold his power from the Gentile regions anyway," remarked Batasha. "He is willing to help all people who call upon him in need. I do not agree with Simon that Jesus has come to be king of the Jews exclusively."

"Speaking of the Zealot, have you talked to him since he came back from Judea?" Joanna asked off-handedly.

"I didn't have a chance the night of the party with everything going on. Then the next morning they were gone to Bethsaida-Julius. I spoke to him briefly the day before yesterday, and he told me that he had legally adopted Jonas, giving him all the rights of a true son." She smiled. "That makes me quite happy."

"He didn't mention anything else?" Joanna asked surprised.

"No, what else is there?" asked Batasha asked puzzled.

"Well, according to Peter, the Zealot talked to his father while he was in Emmaus and asked him to initiate a betrothal arrangement with a young Jewish maiden whose family has been known to his for years. Peter says there has been an understanding between them for a long time."

Batasha went vacant. Every thought and emotion had fled, leaving behind an empty shell of silent disbelief. Yet although the news was a shock, it explained his air of detachment the night of the party.

"Isn't it wonderful!" exclaimed Joanna, unaware that her information had dealt Batasha a stunning blow. "So you see, everything isn't all doom and gloom among us."

Paulus had come out to sail his boat, and Joanna turned her attention to him, holding the back of his tunic so that he wouldn't slip headlong into the water. Batasha used this opportune time to make a hasty exit.

"Where are you going?"

"I...I think I'll go lie down for a while. I feel a slight headache coming on." Batasha held her hand to her forehead convincingly.

"Oh no! You haven't had one of those in months."

"It's nothing. Certainly not the seizures coming back. Just a normal headache, really," she explained in a rush. "Don't worry. Probably the bright sunlight caused it. I'm all right. Stay here and enjoy yourself."

"But you look dreadful!" Joanna protested much concerned. "May I get you something? Perhaps a cool drink?"

"N…No. I just need to lie down," she stammered escaping with her hand still pressed to her forehead.

Once alone she paced the floor, angry and wounded. *How could he! How could he kiss her lovingly in the winter, and then come back in the spring betrothed to someone else? Only an insensitive beast would behave like that!* She wanted to curl up like a garden grub and die.

She spent the rest of the afternoon in her room at Joanna's nursing her grief, feeling rejected and inadequate, and praying for the peace of acceptance. *What sort of woman had he chosen?* she wondered torturing herself. *What did she look like? She would be a Jewish maiden of pure blood with dark eyes and hair like Deborah, she thought. Shy and modest. Young.* She would be the total antithesis of Batasha with her foreign looks, her aggressive ways and mature years.

"Why do you sit gazing in the mirror?" Joanna asked delivering fresh linen to the room. "It is not like you to be so fixated on yourself."

"I'm getting old," Batasha said, touching imagined lines at the corners of her eyes.

"Oh dear. Is that what's bothering you?" her friend said with a wave of dismissal. "I'm three years older than you. I suppose you think I'm Methuselah's mother. Don't be a ninny." She placed the linens in a cupboard looking back over her shoulder. "But I know what you mean. Just thank Jehovah that you're not married. It's raising children that ages a woman. Paulus is driving me to an early grave. He just lunged into the pool after one of his boats and a servant had to fish him out."

She nudged Batasha aside and sat down beside her to peer into the mirror also. "I'm getting grey hair. Have you noticed?"

"Where?" Batasha bent Joanna's head to inspect. "Oh dear!" Her friend's crown was riddled with tiny silver threads. "You'll have to start using the dye of the pomegranate before long," she said in sympathy with an inward smile. The old adage was true: Misery loves company. "Just be thankful that we have cosmetics to help us stay the march of time."

Joanna laughed. "Really, Batasha, the years have been kind to you. Not that twenty-eight is old by anyone's standards."

"It is in our culture," Batasha reminded her. "I should have already been married and had children by now."

"So that is what this is about—wanting to get married," Joanna accused playfully.

"Sometimes I think about it," Batasha admitted.

Joanna gave her a knowing look in the mirror. "Philip likes you." She lifted her brows punctuating her next words. "He likes you very much."

"Please!" Batasha held up her hand amused. "Don't be ridiculous."

"Oh, aren't you the sly one?" Joanna teased. "Acting as if you don't know." They both laughed, and Batasha's constricted heart eased somewhat. It was good to have a friend.

Since it had been an uncommonly warm winter, the flowers were blooming profusely. Batasha had arrived at the villa and immediately gone to work. The lush fragrance emanating from the harvest scented her arms by day and wafted through her window by night like a familiar caress, lingering until dawn like a forgotten dream.

After being home four days, she settled into a routine, thinking of Simon only between tasks. She had been away from the business for so long that Alexes often had to remind her of certain details and measurements concerning the pressing and distilling process that she had forgotten. He even ordered her around a bit, a surprising development which she found rather amusing, especially when he realized what he was doing and nearly prostrated himself apologizing.

When her aunt interrupted her work late one morning with the news that Philip of Bethsaida had arrived unexpectedly, she hurried to the peristyle with a cordial greeting, extending her slender arms in welcome.

"Philip, how bad of you to come at this time when I look like a peasant woman," she teased.

"You are as beautiful as always," he said holding her away admiringly.

"And you are as flattering as always," she responded with a feigned look of accusation from beneath her brows.

"Not flattery at all," he said accepting the seat she offered. "I speak the truth. Your hair is windblown, your face is flushed, and you smell cool and sweet."

"And my toes are dirty, and thank you for not mentioning it," she said laughing. She did believe he thought well of her, though, and his regard was like a balm on a wound.

"We are leaving for Tyre and Sidon tomorrow. I wanted to come and see you before we left. Remember the halcyon days we spent there last autumn? I wish you could come."

"I do too," she said. "But the harvest has started quite early this year and I must stay home for a while to help manage."

"It won't be the same without you," he said in reproachful tones. "I'll miss you."

She gave him a bemused smile thinking what a nice man he was, how gentle, and considerate of her feelings. "The Master told me that he might come through here sometime during the middle of the summer for a short visit," she said brightly.

"Then I'll have that to look forward to when I'm walking the beach without you."

Suddenly bereft of banter and not knowing what to say, she remained silent for a few moments. Did he know what the religious leaders of Capernaum had said about her? Had he heard the gossip? If he hadn't, she thought he should be informed before their relationship proceeded any further.

"Philip," she began softly, "are you aware of my damaged reputation? I...I mean there has been some unfortunate gossip," she stammered.

He threw back his head and laughed. "This is extremely amusing. I think that you are actually trying to protect me from caring for you. What stories are you referring to? That you ran a bordello for Roman soldiers here in this sylvan paradise?" He waved his arm in derision. "Do you really think I would believe such rubbish about you? Apart from the fact that you serve an extremely virtuous Man of God now, I wouldn't consider you good whore material anyway. You're far too honest and straightforward, and far too self-possessed to give yourself away easily. And you also have a tendency to blush, which you have been doing very prettily for the past several minutes."

"But Philip, there are things that perhaps you should know."

"I already know all I need to." He cupped his hand to her cheek and covered her mouth with his thumb. "Please! I don't care about your past. Do you expect a recitation of every personal mistake I've made in my life? Believe me there have been plenty."

He rose and pulled her up to face him. "I have to be leaving if I'm going to make it to Bethsaida by nightfall. I still haven't yet said goodbye to my parents."

She walked him out onto the columned portico. He turned and, with polished sureness, bent and kissed her lips. "I'll see you in a few weeks. Think of me."

His chariot churned up dust and disappeared around the bend in the road. She looked after him smiling fondly. His kiss had been cool and gentle, and he had tasted of mint. Very pleasant.

⚱

In late August, Jesus and the disciples arrived in Magdala as promised. All work with the perfume ceased as Batasha ordered every hand to wash linen, prepare food, and polish the villa until it shone like a pink pearl. During the visit, she avoided Simon, addressing the air above his head when forced to ask him a question. Her feelings for him were still very raw.

In the evenings she walked with Philip to the bridge crossing the stream, and they talked. Their relationship was growing and she found him to be consistently good company. Most of the time they talked about the Master and his new ministry among the Gentile cities. Clearly pleased with the progress being made, Philip told her that all over the Decapolis, Greeks had come out in droves to be healed and to listen to his teachings.

Jesus had worked just as many miracles in Scythopolis, Capitolia, and Hippos as he had in Galilee. No narrow-minded religious bigots had heckled him there, for the Greeks were remarkably tolerant where religion was concerned. Outside of Hippos he had graciously fed a multitude of Gentiles in the same miraculous way he'd fed the Jews on the plain near Bethsaida. This proved to Philip that Jesus was unwilling to withhold any good thing because of race or tribe. That day he had fed four thousand men and several hundred woman and children with seven small loaves and a few fish. It was the same miracle performed with the same kind of poor food. Afterwards, the people behaved differently from those in Bethsaida. When Jesus urged them away to their homes, they went quietly with believing hearts.

At the end of the three-day visit in Magdala, Jesus made ready to travel north into the region of Mount Hermon, the site that gave birth to the headwaters of the Jordan River. Batasha followed him down to the lake and knelt at his feet as the others embarked and prepared to sail. "Lord, what wondrous things you have done both here and in the Gentile cities! My heart goes with you with great love." The early morning sun revealed his face in bright clarity—the sensitive features, dark well-groomed beard, his hair, also dark but sprinkled with copper filaments, his lean body toughened by traveling many miles with little rest and indifferent food. Hardship and disappointment had aged him, she realized with a pang. The wide-set, deeply mysterious eyes now displayed lines when they crinkled in a smile, and there was silver mingled with the gold in his crown as he bent to lay his hands on her head.

"Mary," he said. "I have great aspirations for you and all my disciples. Remain faithful. Always believe, for I am blessed by your love and obedience."

The voyage across the northern tip of the lake proceeded without incident. The disciples remained silent as they reached the shallow marshlands at the mouth of the Jordan, beached, and made camp. Upon leaving Magdala, Simon had begun to breathe more comfortably. Watching Batasha and Philip getting along so well had scattered his emotions in different directions. He'd had enough of watching Philip mooning over her. He knew Philip wanted Batasha, and accepted with a great deal of irritation, that she would in all likelihood accept a proposal of marriage should he offer one. The thought came as an unwelcome shock.

The next day, they traveled ten miles, and made camp near the Jordan Lake, or Merom, as it was sometimes called. It was a marshy terrain, little more than a swamp. In the morning, the Lord led them with sure steps through the seemingly impenetrable tropical growth. Once on the other side, they climbed a steep hill and viewed a fertile plain. Then they passed through olive groves and up a gentle slope and saw the gushing spring of ancient Kedesh.

A little over an hour later, they encountered an old road that the Romans had built. Huge mulberry trees and a tangle of clematis and honeysuckle walled it on both sides releasing sweet savors as they traveled. Soon the historic town of Abel Beth Maachah came into view, and then a verdant plain, which gave birth to numerous springs that flowed down and fed into the Jordan. Women bent over these streams washing clothes. Children, their brown bodies naked and shiny, played in them.

Great golden fields of wheat tossed in the breezes as they trudged on.

Climbing ever higher, they skirted huge boulders and trod over patches of wildflowers. They crossed a bridge and saw the city of Dan off to the right. Even higher, perched upon a hill of basalt was Caesarea-Philippi, Philip the Tetrarch's capital, gleaming like an amethyst in the setting sun. Around it rushed silver streams and waterfalls, and stone terraces glistened through a riot of oleander and bougainvilleas. The snowy head of Mount Hermon rose above it all, like a white-haired father.

Jesus led them to the left of the city a few miles upstream where the upper source of the Jordan River burst from a large cavern in a rock wall. Here is where they pitched camp and rested, the living music constantly in their ears. Here is where Jesus mothered them with his presence and nestled their spirits to his bosom as he prepared them for what was to come.

Although the capital city was predominantly Greek, it had a synagogue, and Jesus ministered there daily. He preached from its sunny colonnaded porches and healed the sick. The crowds were polite and didn't tear at him and dog his every step as those in Galilee had done. They treated him as a demigod that might have somehow arrived anew each morning on the back of a magical, winged Pegasus. As pagans they accepted him as much as they were able.

On the first day of the week following their arrival, he gathered his Twelve around him after arriving back in camp. "What do the people say about me?" he asked. "Who do they say I am?"

Simon had been mulling over this question for some time; he hadn't been able to formulize the profound identity of Jesus into conscience thought. On the day of the feeding of the five thousand, Philip had said that Jesus was a life force, a creative energy. But Simon had trouble grasping this abstract concept and didn't know exactly what it meant.

Thomas spoke up with an answer. "Why, Master, some in Galilee believe that you must be John the Baptist come back to life. Didn't his disciples tell us that?"

"Others say that you are the incarnation of the prophet Elijah because of your power to work miracles," put in James the Less.

"Then there are a few who think you are more like Jeremiah because you pronounced doom on the cities that wouldn't repent and turn from their wicked ways," Nathaniel spoke up rubbing the bridge of his nose.

"But who do you think I am?" Jesus asked them to be specific.

They fell silent. The living water gushed out of the heart of the mountain behind them, its currents swirling in the stream nearby, soaking tiny particles of dust, giving them life.

Peter stood up and took a deep breath before speaking. "You're the Son of God," he announced. "The Christ." He knelt before Jesus in homage.

Simon swallowed. Peter had said it. What they had all been thinking. Peter, in his impulsive obedience, had blurted it out. None of them could ever plead ignorance again or avoid naming the true identity of their Master. Peter's words had committed them to a higher plane of belief.

Jesus blessed Peter's fiery-maned head with his hand. "You didn't learn this from yourself or other people," he said softly. "My Father revealed it to you. They call you *Petros*, which means rock in Greek, but I tell you that on the *petra*, the rock of your confession, I will build my church. And nothing shall prevail against it. To you and your brethren I give the keys of the Kingdom. In spiritual knowledge, you'll let loose on earth what is already loosed in heaven. And you'll know what is bound in heaven and will likewise bind it on earth. And thus God will work his pleasure through you." Then he looked up and became stern. "Don't spread it around that I am the Christ. I need more time to prepare you."

He walked outside their circle to a nearby oak and leaned his arm against its ancient and gnarled bark. "I have to tell you something," he said. "Soon I have to go through an awful test. The Chief Priests and the Scribes will do unspeakable things to me, and I'll suffer." He raised his face toward heaven. "They're going to kill me."

"He's exaggerating" Simon whispered to James the Less. "If he is the Christ, how can they kill him? It would be impossible to kill a man imbued with the identity of God."

Jesus continued speaking, "But I'll come back in three days. As living proof that I AM." None of them listened. They had all begun whispering among themselves like inattentive school children.

Finally, Peter once again assumed the position as leader of the group. He took Jesus aside whispering vehemently. "Lord! Why are you saying these morbid things? God forbid that something should happen to you. Come on now," he said pulling him toward the circle of men, who looked on in alarm. "Sit with us and forget all this talk of death and killing."

Jesus pulled away wearing a look of astonishment. "How fickle is the human heart! It never ceases to amaze me. One minute you are moving in the Spirit, the next you speak out of worldly desire. Satan tempted me severely in the desert of Judea at the beginning of my ministry. He tried me sorely. The hardest temptation of all was his suggestion that I act in self-power and self-ambition, instead of on behalf of my Father. But I resisted and overcame him. You remind me of Satan right now, and I shall likewise overcome you. Get behind me!" He showed Peter his back and paced away. "Don't call me friend unless you are willing to abide by my words," he flung over his shoulder.

Then he turned to face them all, his voice strengthening and becoming emphatic. "I'm telling you the truth. Hear me well. If you honestly want to be my disciples you have to forget yourselves. You must accept your destiny and follow my example in living, and yes, also in dying if called to it. If you're set on having the comfort and security of the world at the expense of every other consideration, then you'll lose your heavenly inheritance. But if you let go of your earthly ambitions for my sake, you'll find fulfillment and peace here as well as in heaven. Decide for yourselves which is more valuable. What good is the whole world and the riches within, if by gaining them, you lose God?"

"Tell us when you will set up your kingdom here on earth, Lord," asked John.

Jesus' dark, all-seeing eyes seemed to look into the distant future, over centuries of time, over hordes of warring people clashing on battlefields, over great cities and civilizations, and then came back to the present. He gaze rested lovingly on them one by one, pausing when he came to Judas. "Most of you here will live to see me coming into my Kingdom. I have ordained you to help me set it up."

Simon felt relieved. Jesus hadn't meant it when he had predicted his death, for how could a dead man set up a kingdom?

Six days later as the Sabbath sun was setting, Jesus took Peter, James and John up the mountain to pray. They came back the next morning before dawn. Simon turned over in his sleeping bag and cracked his eyes as they entered camp. Jesus' face was glowing. Simon wondered how this could be when the sun had not yet risen.

"Don't tell anybody what you have seen," Jesus told his companions quietly, "until after I come back." He left them and walked up the mountain as if seeking a place to rest in some solitary place.

The three disciples were shaking. They huddled over the dead coals of the campfire as if to seek warmth. *Here is a mystery*, Simon thought to himself. John was shivering violently even though it wasn't cold, and James and Peter wore awe-struck expressions.

"Are you all right, John?" James put his arm around his younger brother's shoulders. John burst into silent, breathless weeping.

"He's overcome," Peter whispered. "He's been shaking like that ever since we saw the visions. Pull yourself together, John," he ordered briskly as one trying to coax another out of a state of hysteria.

"Leave him alone," said James. "Sit down, John. You'll be back to normal directly."

"He's too sensitive," Peter remarked with pity. "I was astounded too when I saw the Lord's raiment turn brilliant and his face become lucent with holy fire. The two personages with him were Moses and Elijah, you know. I nearly fainted when I realized that. Thank God I managed to keep my wits about me."

James snorted. "Keep your wits? You rushed up to them, our greatest prophet, our greatest national leader, babbling about building them some miserable tents to live in! Are those the actions of a man with his wits about him? If I hadn't been so dumbfounded myself, I would have been embarrassed for you."

"I just wanted them to know they were welcome," Peter defended. "I remembered how Jehovah lived in a tabernacle when He lead Israel through the wilderness and was hoping Moses and Elijah would stay on and help Jesus set up his kingdom on Mount Hermon."

James heaved a great sigh. "I'm sorry. I know you meant well. But sometimes I don't understand how you can be so impulsive."

"That's all right." Peter ventured a grin. "Sometimes I don't understand it either."

"Do you remember anything they said?" asked James. "It seemed that they were giving the Lord counsel."

"Yes, and encouragement too."

"That was before you so rashly interrupted with the pedestrian comment about the tents."

Peter lifted his hands apologetically.

"No wonder Jehovah himself overspread us with his Holy Presence and told us to listen to his Son and obey. He had to do something to shut you up."

Peter ran his fingers through his red mane in agitation. "Oh, I hope I didn't offend the Almighty too greatly."

James sighed in exasperation, taking pity on his remorseful friend. "If you had, you'd be dead. Don't worry about it. Perhaps Jehovah understands your habit of always sticking your foot in your mouth. Let us hope that He has a sense of humor."

Simon lay awake long after they had gone to sleep thinking about all he had heard. This was proof to his way of reasoning that Jesus was the Son of God and that he intended to set up a magnificent kingdom here on earth to rule in might and holiness with the sanction of Jehovah and all the ancestral fathers who had gone before. He would build a palace, perhaps, right here on Mount Hermon, as Peter had suggested, finer and grander than any ever yet seen by men, farther up the mountain than the Tetrarch's, perhaps on its very peak where it would be bathed in a constant fiery *shekinah* which would be visible the whole length and breadth of Palestine. Pilgrims would come from all over the world to bow down and pay homage.

Chapter 16

Starting a quarrel is like
breaching a dam.
Proverbs 17:14 NIV

A few days later they broke camp and headed home. On the way Jesus preached in the hamlets and villages of northern Galilee. Again he predicted his death, and again the disciples were grieved, distressed, and disbelieving. They assembled and agreed not to take his words literally. Simon expressed the notion that the Master would soon be setting up his kingdom from Mount Hermon. Why else would he have gone there if not to scout out the area as a possible headquarters?

The others liked this theory and began to embellish the idea with their own fantasies. Jesus would have a vast and glistening temple, each marble column so large in circumference that forty men holding hands couldn't circle it around. There would be hundreds of these columns holding up a roof glittering with jasper stars. The floor would be gold—a transparent gold that would shine like a mirror. Jesus would sit on a great dazzling throne in resplendent robes of purple and scarlet. His crown would be studded with pearls and precious jewels of every kind. From behind his head would stream blue rays of light. Six lesser thrones would be lined up on either side of him, where they, as his chosen Twelve, would sit as his generals, aiding him in decisions and in important matters of State.

"And I'll sit at his right hand," Peter announced with great enthusiasm.

"You!" James ben Zebedee cried. "Why you?"

"Because he favors me. You know he does. He was pleased when I confessed he was the Christ of God. He gave me the keys to the kingdom. You heard him."

"Then he will probably give you the job of minding the door," James snapped with acerbity.

"You can't deny that I'm his favorite," Peter went on rashly. "Why he even stays at my house all the time."

Old Nathaniel cleared his throat much perturbed. "If you ask me, he loves his cousin John the best. He's always looking out for him, and he asks John to look after his mother when he can't. I think John will certainly have a place of eminence in the coming kingdom."

"James too," John spoke up in defense of his brother. "James will sit on one side and I on the other. For we are his cousins."

"But my father is his cousin too," Thad pointed out. "And so am I, for that matter."

"But not his real cousins," John argued. "You're Joseph's nephews, and Joseph wasn't his real father. Don't we all believe," he said scanning the others for support, "that Jesus is the Son of God?"

"Of course we do," Philip explained, "but only in a spiritual sense. Jesus had to have had an earthly father. Any other notion is inconceivable." He smiled at his clever choice of words.

John's expression turned mulish. "But my mother told me that the Lord's mother was a virgin when she gave birth to Jesus."

James cut in hurriedly. "However, she forbade us to discuss it." He gave his brother a warning look.

"But it's true!"

"Oh, all this is getting us nowhere," Simon broke in. "It's enough that he will soon be establishing his kingdom. That's all I care about. I, for one, don't feel worthy to sit on his level and would be content just to be his cupbearer or a lowly palace guard. Let's keep our minds on his triumph and set personal considerations aside as he has requested. The Lord would be displeased if he knew we were fighting."

Philip folded his arms and cocked a brow. "Words of appeasement coming from the Zealot? That's a new one."

"I have always made my position clear," Simon replied in a voice without challenge but tinged with sarcasm. "Unlike a philosopher who analyzes every idea until it no longer has meaning, my view is simple: all I want, and have ever wanted, is for our Messiah to free the people so that we can live in peace and joy without oppression and hopelessness."

They squabbled the whole way back to Capernaum as Jesus walked ahead and said nothing. When they reached Peter's house, Jesus knelt, took his little sister Judith into his arms, and turned her around. "Do you see this child?" he said. "If you have to behave like children, then be soft and trusting and humble and teachable as she is. These are the qualities that will make you great in the Kingdom of God, not selfish ambition and pride. Arrogance has no place before the Father."

Much chagrined they went about their business in moody silence, still resentful of one another. The Feast of Tabernacles would be celebrated in Jerusalem the second week of October and Jesus told them to begin preparing for the trip to Jerusalem. Leah and Deborah announced that they would not be going as Deborah was in the early stages of pregnancy. Peter, both happy about the news and solicitous for his wife, who suffered from frequent bouts of sickness, proclaimed that he would also stay home. Deborah, however, would not hear of it and made him promise to go. She said that his place was with the Master, and that Leah would help look after her. Everyone knew that her urging was partly because Peter turned green every time he saw her get sick and that he would certainly become bedridden if he stayed home to function as a nursemaid.

They traveled from Galilee south into Judea by a direct route through Samaria, which was a bit unusual, for it had been deemed unclean territory to the strict Jew and its people an inferior race who had no part in Jehovah's blessings. Simon being a man of great prejudice, felt edgy during the journey, but didn't complain about soiling his pure Hebrew feet with Samaritan dust.

The sons of thunder, James and John, however, showed their tempers when the people of Yazith refused to let Jesus and his followers travel through their town. The two brothers told the Master to call down fire and incinerate the infidels for their disrespect and unorthodox departure from true Judaism. Jesus told them that they were the ones who were under the influence of a foreign spirit and rebuked them severely.

Many other Samaritan villages, however, received Jesus kindly, due both to his reputation as a prophet and their willingness to observe a centuries-old oriental custom that required extending hospitality to travelers. As a result, he made many friends among the Samaritans and many believed he was the Messiah.

They reached Jerusalem on the evening before the first day of the celebration which would last the next eight days. The Feast of Tabernacles, or *Booths*, as it was sometimes called, commemorated the Jews' wandering in the wilderness and expressed their thanksgiving for the ingathering of the harvest. To honor and venerate their forefathers' forty-year plight in the desert, Jewish families erected tents to live in during the festival; or they built booths of palm and juniper branches, festooned with brilliant flower garlands and sweet smelling vines.

Jesus and his followers walked down the busy, colorful streets of Jerusalem where rows of pumpkins and baskets of apples and nuts lined the makeshift dwellings. Children played unrestrained and took food from anywhere they pleased, since it was a time of great generosity and good will. The fragrance of fresh pine, cinnamon, fruit meat, baked bread, and roasted fowl, as well as happy Jewish music and the harsh sounds of strange tongues mingled in the cool air.

Jews from all over the world came to the Holy City for this holiday, many from as far away as Spain, Italy, and Lower Sarmatia, catching up on all their sacrificing in this one gala trip. They traveled during the summer months in order to arrive on time. Thus, the Feast of Tabernacles was a religious observance as much attended as the Passover, which occurred at the end of the often cold and rainy winter season when traveling conditions were rough.

The disciples erected their tents in the spacious courtyard of a recent convert named Daniel bar Ithamar, an elderly, well-respected man of Jerusalem who owned a grove of olive trees in nearby Gethsemane. His wife, Tabar, was a statuesque woman with a faith as stalwart and dignified as her figure. A widowed daughter lived with them with her young son, John Mark, who was the same age as Jonas. The two boys made friends immediately and became inseparable.

Daniel told Jesus that people in Jerusalem had been talking about him for weeks. Many Jews of the dispersion had not yet had a chance to see him and wanted to witness his works. He said that there were many of the am ha'arez who engaged in discussions and hot disputes about him. Some were saying that he was merely a good man; others believed his influence was bad and misled the people. The majority, however, hoped that he was the Promised Messiah. They dared not speak out too loudly in his behalf, however, because the Pharisees were openly hostile and had threatened to excommunicate anyone who professed to be a follower.

Batasha listened to the talk in Daniel's courtyard in silent, growing alarm. The Temple guards shadowed Jesus every day as he addressed the crowds, as if waiting for him to make a false step for which they could arrest him. She frequently turned to the Lady and Daniel's wife, Tabar, for strength and support, even though she sensed that they, too, were afraid that the

opposition of the powerful religious leaders of the City had
become dangerous.

At dawn of the seventh day of the Feast, Batasha, the Lady,
Tabar, and the children went to the Temple to take part in the
ceremonies. They carried palm, willow, and myrtle branches
in one hand and a piece of fruit in the other, waving them at
the proper time, as the litany progressed. At its conclusion the
priests poured wine and water together on the altar.

Jesus had been standing off to one side in silence during the
proceedings. After the sacrifice, he walked up the Temple steps
to the altar, turned around and addressed the people in a loud
voice: "If you're thirsty, come to me and drink! Then you'll
have a spring of living water in your innermost being that will
rise up in great peace and happiness." A woman standing behind
Batasha said, "Surely this is the Christ! Look at his face. Never
before have I seen such virtue in a man's countenance. This has
to be the Anointed One we've been waiting for.

"This man is from Galilee," scoffed the woman beside
her. "He can't be the Messiah. The prophet Micah foretold
that the Christ would come out of the City of David, which
is Bethlehem."

The Lady turned and stared, piercing this woman with her
calm grey eyes before departing with Batasha and the others
as the worshipers dispersed. "What's the matter?" Batasha
whispered as they walked away. "Did that woman offend
you?"

"No," the Lady replied quietly. "I merely wanted to look
into her face and see if there was any real desire to know the
truth. If there had been, I would have told her that Jesus was
born in Bethlehem, not Galilee."

Later that day Batasha cast aside her reluctance to have
any social contact with Simon and approached him seeking
information. He sat apart from the others who were talking with
an elderly man named Nicodemus, a member of the Sanhedrin.
He had come to report that the authorities had met together

and accused Jesus of blasphemy. Such a declaration was against Jewish Law without a proper hearing.

"Simon?" she asked hesitantly. He raised his dark head to look at her guardedly as she sat on the bench beside him. "Do you think Jesus is in danger?"

"Yes," he answered shortly before continuing to carve on a piece of wood with a carpenter's knife. "But Peter and I have made a commitment to protect him at all costs. If the Pharisees want to do him harm, they will have to go through us first."

She breathed a sigh of relief. Simon and Peter were the strongest of the disciples physically. And neither one of them was afraid to fight. She remembered how Simon provided himself as a bulwark for Jesus in the crowds in Galilee. He didn't shrink then, and he wouldn't now if a confrontation arose.

"Do your Zealot friends in Judea join you in your devotion to Jesus?" she asked curiously, changing the subject.

He concentrated on his carving without looking up. "I've broken with them. They're following a man named Jesus bar Abbas. He's nothing like our Jesus."

"Isn't he the one rumored to have murdered three Romans on the road to Jericho?" she asked attempting to engage him in further conversation. If a personal relationship with Simon was impossible, she wanted to go back to the time when they had at least been friendly. The hurt she had suffered at his rejection could be kept private and hidden.

"According to Eleazer, the leader of the Jerusalem Zealots, the rumor is true. Eleazer doesn't like our Jesus because he teaches peace and love. He prefers to support bar Abbas who finds joy in murder and violence."

"And you don't condone overthrowing the Roman government by force anymore?" she asked tentatively.

"I've changed." He bent over the wood molding it delicately with the tip of his knife. "Of all the disciples, I'm probably the most transformed. And the more I change, the more I become aware of my inadequacies and my unworthiness to be a follower. I look forward to the time when the Master sets up his kingdom, but I do not expect a position of importance as many of the others do. He has chosen me and I don't know why, for I am unclean."

She had never seen Simon like this. His quiet vulnerability moved her. She reached and opened his hands. "What are you making?"

"It's nothing. Just something to keep my hands busy."

"Why it's a carving of a fish," she said softly. About palm-size, it was rough and unpolished, yet perfect in every detail, each tiny scale stylistically joined to the next. Engraved deeply from the head to the tail were the Greek words: JESUS CHRIST, SON OF GOD, SAVIOR. The first initial of each word stood out as an anagram: ΙΧΘΥΣ "Why it's beautiful!"

"It's worthless," he said moving restlessly. "I'm used to carving in stone. Wood is too soft."

Sensing an imminent departure and knowing the abruptness with which he usually moved, she spoke quickly without thinking. "May I have it?"

He placed it in her hand with a self-deprecating shrug, as if puzzled at her request, and got up and walked away, eating up the flagstones of Daniel's courtyard with his usual brusque energy.

Batasha showed the carving to Daniel's wife, who liked it so well that she took it to an artisan friend and had a copy made. She, in turn, showed it to her friends, who also had copies made. Unbeknownst to Simon, soon several hundred people all over Jerusalem had copies of his little wooden fish, the number growing every day. Somehow in the process of replication, the words had been dropped off, leaving only the mysterious anagram ΙΧΘΥΣ. *This was probably a good thing,* thought Batasha, *because the enemies of that message were desperate and powerful. This way only the friends who held a fish knew what it meant.*

After the Feast of Tabernacles, Jesus and his party dismantled their tents and went to Bethany, a lovely little suburb two miles south of Jerusalem. They stayed at the most spacious and beautiful Palestinian inn Batasha had ever seen, a two-story affair with a balcony running entirely around the second story. Potted palms and trailing philodendron sat between each of the several archways giving entrance to the stable on the ground level.

As they entered the shaded area and tethered their horses and donkeys, Batasha noticed its cleanliness. There were no offensive odors of dung and hide. The water troughs and stacks of fodder were neat and tidy and the stalls were clean with fresh-smelling hay in the mangers.

A man about the age of Jesus came out to greet them. Upon seeing Jesus, he swallowed him in a bear hug, nearly knocking him to the ground. His exuberant joy was infectious, and everybody smiled as the Master returned his affectionate greeting with much laughter.

"So you finally came to see us!" the friend said in good-natured accusation. "I was beginning to think your fame had gone to your head and you'd forgotten us."

Jesus gave him a rough masculine kiss on each cheek. "Forget you, Lazarus? How could David forget Jonathan?"

This mystifying reference seemed to throw Lazarus into deeper paroxysms of joy. "Ah, so you still remember what our mothers used to call us when we were boys." He circled his arm around Jesus' shoulders hugging him to his side. With his other arm he gestured to the members of the party. "As friends of my best loved friend, you are welcome." With that he bowed in courtly subservience and everybody laughed.

Batasha took to him at once. He was genial and happy with that intense vitality one finds in a person who loves people. Further elevating him in her regard was his playful, and almost puppyish, hero-worship of the Master.

"We'll have a feast, eh?" He held Jesus away, nodding for his approval. Jesus laughed and shook his head as if arguing with his friend would be futile. "Eh? A young lamb, cooked to perfection by my sister Martha, fresh vegetables from the garden, the best wine!"

He had turned and was leading Jesus up the stairs motioning for the others to follow, and talking the whole time. They went up another flight of steps and out onto a beautiful rooftop terrace decorated with stone tables and benches with colorful cushions. Dotted everywhere were large urns of flowering shrubs and tropical fruit trees. Vines bloomed on arched trellises and climbed the waist-high walls.

Lazarus had spotted the Lady and was now giving her kisses punctuated by questions concerning her health and well-being. He excused himself from the group of men and led her down some stairs exclaiming how glad his sisters would be to see her. Batasha stood aside in confusion. She and the Lady were the only women who had come on the trip. Suzanna had gone to meet her husband and sons in Damascus for a time of reunion, and Joanna was at Machaerus with Chuza. She didn't want to stay and try to fit in with the men, so she tramped off after Lazarus and the Lady uninvited.

Once in the kitchen, she saw the Lady being embraced and fussed over again by the two sisters, each as different from the other as night from day. The older one was large-boned and ruddy with a friendly grin from which her teeth protruded slightly. The other was smaller and younger with dark flowing hair. She had the fragile, mystical air of an oriental princess.

Lazarus turned around and seemed to notice Batasha for the first time. "Forgive me!" he exclaimed slapping his forehead, signifying he'd been a rude idiot.

He pulled her into their circle and the Lady made proper introductions, after which, with another apology to Batasha for his oversight, Lazarus bounded back up the stairs two at a time.

The women began to talk about cooking pots and the best sauce to serve with lamb. Maria, the enchanted one, didn't enter into their animated conversation, but sidled away unnoticed and ascended the stairway to find Jesus.

Martha had dismissed the servants from the kitchen calling them *dunderheads* and undertook the preparation of the meal personally. The Lady and Batasha dived in to help, and soon they were perspiring profusely—Martha most of all. Her large capable hands were everywhere at once, demanding perfection. After a considerable amount of time, dishes of cheeses and olives were ready to be served. Martha insisted on doing it herself. Batasha was surprised, for the lamb was ready for saucing, and Martha had been as careful of that lamb as a queen with her jewels.

She returned from the roof with astonishing swiftness, however, just in time to take the ladle out of the Lady's hand and commence with the basting. "Just like Maria to shirk her duty," she complained. "Lazy child! I always have to do everything around here. She's up there listening to Jesus, as if there isn't a thing to do. I think this is done." She sliced perfect, uniform pieces from the lamb's hindquarters and began arranging them prettily on a huge oval platter, burning her fingers in the process, Batasha was sure.

Wisely, the Lady went to another part of the kitchen and began placing loaves of bread in a napkin-lined basket. Batasha followed her example and dished up the vegetables.

"My own sister!" Martha fumed hovering over the platter. "Just sitting there on her pretty little backside." Batasha and the Lady exchanged telling looks. "If Mama were here she'd give her a smack! And then my sister would have to stand to be lazy because she wouldn't be able to sit down for a week! Leaving me to do all this work …" Her voice trailed off into inarticulate grumbles.

"I'll handle this." She lifted the huge dish with its pyramid of meat. Her arms bulged and her shoulders shook. "You two get the rest."

The Lady and Batasha gathered what they could manage and all three of them staggered up the steps, Martha panting heavily.

"She's an ox!" Batasha whispered in a hiss, at which the Lady shushed her.

The picture on the roof was serene. Lazarus, the disciples, and other guests of the inn had gathered around to listen to Jesus talk. Close to his feet wearing a rapt expression was Maria, cool and beautiful, the breeze fanning her hair.

An explosion seemed to take place inside Martha. She bustled through the group of men and kicked Maria roughly with the side of her foot before placing her burden on the table. Her naturally ruddy complexion had suffused to deep red, making her freckles almost invisible.

Batasha and the Lady also arranged their food on the table. Then sighing in relief they reclined with the others who were in the process of adjusting themselves more comfortably as they talked and anticipated the feast ahead.

Only Martha was still on her feet. There were a few empty plates from the appetizers that went before, and she began gathering and stacking them, making a great clatter.

As her arm reached in front of Jesus, he captured her wrist and held it. "What's wrong?"

Her chin trembled. "I'm tired. I've done all this work."

"Don't get upset over nothing. It's just food. We're simple men. You don't have to impress us with all these fancy dishes."

"Well, it wouldn't have been so bad if Maria had helped!" She shot her sister a fulminating look. "I do all the work around here and she has all the fun," she said unable to keep the tears from her voice.

Complete silence descended on the group. Embarrassed, Martha tried to pull away. "I...I'm sorry."

Jesus refused to yield his hold. "Where are you going?"

"Back to get more. Tell *her* to help me." She tossed her head toward Maria.

"Maria has chosen to spend time with me. I'm not going to send her away." His voice was kind but firm. "What's more important, spending time with me or worrying about the sauce?" he asked with a gentle smile.

Martha hung her head. "I just wanted everything to be right," she said in a quaver. "I wanted you to have your favorite things."

"Martha, Martha." He reached and brushed a damp tendril from her forehead. "You haven't even given me a welcoming kiss. You haven't even said you love me." His rebuke was tender.

"But I do," she whispered earnestly. "You know I do." She knelt and hugged him in wild abandonment. "I'm so glad you're here." She kissed one cheek, then the other. "It's been over a year since we last saw you, and I've missed you so much."

"Then sit down and eat with me," he ordered with rough affection. "Maria, give your sister a little room."

In the ensuing days the Bethany inn became Jesus' headquarters in Judea, in much the same way as Peter's house had been in Galilee. His fame had spread all over Palestine and had seeped beyond into Mesopotamia, Syria, Thrace, and Italy in the West. Frequently men from these faraway places came to the inn to hear Jesus teach. He always received them kindly, even though many were astrologers or students of other religions or philosophies. They would go back to their own cities and cultures saying that he was the Messiah promised in Jewish Scripture who would bring peace on earth. Then others would come to see for themselves. The word spread until the mere utterance of his name made hearts stop and listen, hope and believe.

Rich and important men from nearby Jerusalem also visited him, most of them surreptitiously, wanting to keep their established positions in the City and have him too. Nicodemus ben Gorion and Joseph of Arimathea were such men. During one of their visits, Joseph of Arimathea spoke at length concerning the High Priest Caiphas.

"His main purpose in life is to preserve the priesthood," Joseph said to the disciples one evening. "From that obsession, fear has sprung. He frequently bemoans the fact that the whole world is chasing after Jesus. Although he despises the common folk, he knows he needs them, for without their support of the Temple and the priestly traditions, his power and wealth would crumble in the dust. The people are listening to the Master's condemnation of our sect for its meaningless rules and its lack of true religion. They're tired of the many burdens and impossible obligations religious officials put upon their hardworking shoulders. Caiphas knows he's losing power and influence, and that realization has turned him cruel and evil."

Nicodemus turned to Jesus confidently. "But don't worry, Rabbi. Caiphas may complain all he wants, but he can't condemn you without a trial. Joseph and I are your friends, and some of the others also are beginning to believe you are the Messiah. Caiphas can't do anything without unanimity, for it takes all of our votes to get any measure cleared in the High Court. That's the Law, and even the High Priest must abide by it. He and his cronies may challenge you to debates in the Temple every time you go into the City to teach, but he can't harm you. Nor can he sentence you to death, for that authority belongs only to the Roman government. Caiphas's hands are tied and he knows it."

Chapter 17

Your eyes will see the king in his beauty.
Isaiah 33:17 NIV

Simon often walked the seven miles from Bethany to Emmaus to spend the Sabbath with his parents. Sometimes his father would come back with him to sit at the Master's feet and enjoy the company of the other disciples. Simon's betrothal with Lila bas Jesse had not become official, and this was just one of the many unresolved issues that had been weighing upon Simon of late as he traveled with his father one Sunday morning.

"What is causing the delay?" he probed. "I asked you to begin negotiations weeks ago," he reminded his father.

"My son, the child is still young. Jesse says that she's too shy to think of marriage at this time. Perhaps if you visited her more and showed her some tenderness. Perhaps if you gave her gifts."

"Yes," Simon muttered. "I should have given her gifts by now," he admitted. "I didn't think of it. But, Father, I am not a tender man. I have never studied the art of courtship. I don't know how to flatter a woman and make myself appealing."

Cleopas shook his head in sorrowful agreement. "Jesse says that Lila is afraid of you. Being a father more indulgent than most, he is loathe to insist upon an official engagement until she is more amenable to the idea."

Simon snorted with impatience. "Afraid of me!" he exclaimed. "I've never given her reason to fear me."

"I know, my son," Cleopas replied. "Perhaps it is your size and ferocious demeanor that intimidates her." He hid a smile. "I have decided not to speak to Jesse about the matter for a while. You must trust me, my son, to do what is right on your behalf. A good Jewish father always wants the best for his son in an important matter like marriage.

"Very well, Father," Simon agreed dismissing the topic from his mind as they approached Lazarus's inn. Simon went up on the roof to find Jesus, who usually met around a stone fire pit with his disciples this time of day even when the weather was cool. Cleopas headed for an upper room where the women habitually congregated in front of a glowing brazier.

Batasha welcomed Simon's father with a smile and motioned for him to sit on a cushion nearby. She had come to look forward to his visits because of his ready wit and his tendency to launch into entertaining and often exaggerated stories about all manner of subjects including his only son. She found it interesting that an easy-going, congenial man like Cleopas had sired a son like Simon, whose dark intensity tended to put people off. Also, it surprised her that, even though their faces bore some resemblance, there was a noticeable difference in their size. Simon towered over his father by a good six inches.

After Cleopas had settled down with a cup of mulled wine, she broached the subject, not bothering to disguise her curiosity. "How did your son come to inherit his imposing dimensions?" she asked. "Does his mother come from a family of tall men?"

"Quite the contrary," Cleopas replied leaning back and crossing his legs. "Hannah's people are quite short." His black eyes took on a mischievous gleam and his voice became droll. She recognized these mannerisms as signs that he was about to start one of his amusing stories.

"Actually, it's interesting that you should ask," he said. "Of course, what I'm about to tell you must remain in the strictest confidence. You mustn't ever discuss it with my son, for I've kept it a secret even from him."

"I see," she replied, stifling a smile. "I assure you I can be trusted. I'm not the sort of woman who goes about gossiping behind her hand." She leaned back also crossing her legs, arranging her face into a mask of seriousness. Her steady blue eyes met his, which were dark and lurking with humor.

"Many years ago," he began, "centuries ago, actually, one of my forefathers met and fell madly in love with a Philistine woman. Understand that my son doesn't know anything about this heathen affair and I shouldn't want him to find out," he added in warning tones. "I've been very careful to expunge it from our genealogies."

"My lips are sealed," she assured him.

Cleopas sighed gustily and made a gesture with his hand signifying that he trusted her. "The men in my family have always been known for their passion," he confided in a low voice. "My ancestor, Marchishua, loved this heathen woman so much that he married her, defying the ancient law that requires us to keep the bloodlines pure. The ceremony was beautiful and quite pagan. As the story goes, Gormla—that was the woman's name—wore a garment of flowers arranged in such a way as to leave her greatly exposed. On her head, she wore a crown of woven clematis, and from her shoulders down her back flowed a train of hundreds of roses in full bloom. About her hips she wore a girdle of scarlet anemones."

He paused adding, "Being a perfumer, you can appreciate the fragrance she emanated as she walked." At Batasha's sardonic nod, he continued, "They said their vows under an ancient rain tree bursting with yellow sunshine."

"Very romantic," Batasha remarked.

"Yes, Marchishua was an incurable romantic, I'm afraid. He forsook his own people to live among hers. They dwelt in a cave, and for three years they were very happy. Gormla gave birth to a son, whom they both loved dearly. During a tribal war Gormla was killed and Marchishua left for dead with a grievous wound. The male child lay safely under a heap of flax where his father had hidden him at the beginning of the onslaught. Marchishua recovered and brought his son back to his own people to be raised as a Hebrew." He paused for effect. "But he never remarried, for he had given his heart to Gormla."

"Deeply touching." She reached for her wine to hide a soundless laugh in the cup. "But what does this have to do with Simon's height?" she asked setting it down again.

"Oh, didn't I mention it?" Cleopas slapped his forehead. "Gormla was a giantess, and Marchishua was only as tall as her waist. Their son grew up to be a semi-giant, and every tenth generation since, our bloodline has produced a semi-giant."

"Really?" She produced a look of wide-eyed credulity. "Well, I must certainly thank you for this fascinating revelation. I always thought Simon to be something of a throwback."

He stood to his feet, indulging himself in a low chuckle. "Well, I must begin the walk back to Emmaus, or my dear Hannah will worry."

"When you have more time," she suggested sweetly, "you must tell me how your son came by his ungodly belligerence."

Cleopas grinned, taking her hand. "Ah, yes, there's also a little Hittite blood in us, I'm afraid. Hamar the Hittite fell madly in love with a Jewish princess. He was a strong warrior, who was fearless on the battlefield. But he had the heart of a lamb, gentle and tender within and capable of great love." He lifted his brows significantly.

"Humph." She didn't try to disguise her skepticism concerning the possibility of Simon inheriting such qualities. He squeezed her hand and walked away laughing.

☩

Every morning Jesus turned his face solemnly toward the Temple. Simon had come to dread going into the Holy City because he knew the Master's enemies would be lying in wait to heckle him and jeer at his teaching. Early on a Sabbath afternoon, as they were going into the City by way of the Fountain Gate, they came upon a blind man chanting pitifully for alms.

"O people, have mercy! I came out of the darkness of my mother's womb into the darkness of this world. Merciful Jehovah, take pity on a poor man who has never seen the light of day!"

He was quite young, about John's age. Simon felt sorry for him, for fate had robbed him of a normal life and the joy of his youth. "Lord," he asked, "who sinned, this man or his parents? Why was he born without sight?"

"It isn't that somebody sinned," Jesus answered. "This man was born blind so that God's power could be manifested in him today." He stooped and took up some dust. "I'm going to create eyes for him. Then people will believe I am the Light of the World."

He spat in the dust and made mud. He spread this as an ointment on the man's eyes and said, "Go wash in the Pool of Siloam."

The man turned in instant obedience, searching along the city wall with his hands and passing through the gate. Simon started go help lead him the short distance to the pool. Jesus held him back indicating that it was important for the man to find his own way, even if he had to stumble and grope before receiving his healing.

The next afternoon Nicodemus visited the inn. He spoke with excitement. Everyone in the City was talking about the miracle of Enos, the blind man. It had caused such a stir that the Temple officials had brought the man before the court to investigate the incident. Enos had explained that a prophet had put mud on his eyes and told him to go wash in the Pool of Siloam. The unbelieving priests called in his parents for interrogation. Being afraid of excommunication, they would only say that their son had been blind from birth and that they couldn't account for his sudden ability to see. Then the officials called for Enos again. They tried to get him to deny that a man had created eyes for him out of mud.

Jesus, who had been listening attentively to Nicodemus, broke in with a question. "And did Enos deny me?"

"Indeed, Lord, he did not!" answered Nicodemus. "Never before have I seen one of the am ha'arez stand so boldly before the court. Enos told Caiphus that if he was as smart as he claimed to be, he wouldn't be asking such stupid questions. He said that since the beginning of time no one had worked such a miracle as this, except perhaps Jehovah who made Adam from the dust of the earth. He told them that if they didn't know who you were, then they were the ones who were blind. Caiphas ordered the Temple guards to throw Enos out. They did so with great fanfare and the poor man landed ingloriously on his backside in front of a large crowd of witnesses."

Jesus gave a soundless laugh. "Let's go back into the City," he said to the disciples. "I want Enos to see me so that we can become friends."

As excited talk of Jesus and his miracles spread like wildfire into every stratum of Jerusalem society, Pontius Pilate became concerned about Jesus' political ambitions and sent a delegate to the inn of Lazarus. This envoy was none other than Joses, the brother of James the Less.

Upon finding out that he was the brother of one of the disciples, Martha welcomed him warmly. James the Less was somewhat cooler, and Simon kept an icy silence as Joses entered the room where they were staying.

"How is our mother?" James the Less offered Joses a chair by the brazier. "I haven't seen her since you sublet our business and moved her to the City."

"Mother is well. Her only complaint is that you have never come to visit us in our new apartment. She thinks you're jealous of our newfound wealth."

"Please assure her I'm not jealous," James the Less said acidly.

"Assure her yourself." After taking a seat, Joses meticulously arranged his ornate winter robe. He oozed with nard, and his close-cropped hair dripped with a sickening spicy oil. "I've come to speak with Jesus of Nazareth. Where is he?"

"He's gone to his favorite garden spot to meditate. What do you want with him?"

Joses gave his brother a patronizing smile. "As you know, some my closest friends are Pilate's advisors. They've been keeping the governor informed of Jesus' movements and the unrest he is creating among the Sanhedrin."

"Jesus doesn't create unrest," James the Less countered sharply. "If there's any unrest, it has been created by the Pharisees and Sadducees who oppose him."

"A moot point," Joses said dryly. "The situation is getting out of control and Pilate is concerned. He has sent me to—shall we say—talk reason with the rabbi. But since he isn't here, I suppose I'll have to appeal to the leader of your group. What's his name? Peter bar Jonah?"

"Peter has made a quick trip to Galilee," James the Less explained. "His wife is with child, and he wanted to check up on her. He won't be back until next week."

"So why don't you just leave?" Simon put in acidly. "We don't want to hear anything you have to say, and your pretty-boy stench is ruining my digestion."

Joses's polite façade crumbled away like a clay mask. "Take care how you speak to me, Simon. Or you'll find yourself cut down like the Galilean Zealots who came into the Temple a few weeks ago to start trouble. Pilate made short work of them and he could make short work of you, too, if I should tell him you belong to the Zealot movement. It's only because you're my brother's partner that I've held my silence thus far."

"And the fact that you're my partner's brother is the only thing that's kept me from pulverizing your stinking little face!" The fragile threads holding Simon's temper snapped. He had always distrusted Joses. And since Joses had recently sublet the business they had left in his care, Simon had been nursing a desire to have it out with him. "Do you think your puny threats scare me?" he said with a menacing laugh. "Do you think I'm afraid of that heathen Spaniard you serve? I'd like to throw him and every Roman in Palestine into the red chasm surrounding Masada and add every adulterous Jew who supports them to the heap. Then I'd take a torch and light them like so much dry stubble."

Joses sprang to his feet, his lips curling. "You're a swine! Low and common and liking the dirt too well to try to rise above it. You and my brother think you've found a Messiah in the self-deluded rabbi. You're both too stupid to realize we've already got a Messiah—the Roman Government! Pilate and Herod would rule us with justice and peace if radical Jews like you and the rabbi would let them. Prosperity and fair government lie within the grasp of all Israel if the Jews would only reach out and embrace a new way of life."

Simon was shouting now. "Do you call cutting down innocent men in front of the altar an act of justice? Do you call using Temple taxes to divert an aqueduct into the palace good fiscal policy? Pilate's wife Claudia gets to bathe her lily white body while Jewish women have to walk a furlong just to get drinking water for their families." He stepped away from Joses and waved his arm. "Bah! It's a pity you and all your friends weren't standing under the aqueduct recently when part of it collapsed. That would have been justice."

Joses's face glistened with oil and perspiration. "I don't have to stand here and put up with these insults. Be assured, though, that I will tell Pilate about this, and I will also inform him that you are a dangerous Zealot. Then I will watch with great pleasure, Simon, when they crucify you as an enemy of the State."

As the threat was issued with true venom, and knowing his brother's capacity for spite, James the Less spoke up hastily. "They'll have a hard time proving anything against Simon. It's been over two years since he's had any dealings with the Zealots. They're supporting a false messiah."

"We know all about bar Abbas," Joses said. "Soon we'll arrest and execute him. The same fate awaits your rabbi, and even if he is my kinsman, I shall appreciate the beautiful spectacle he'll make hanging on a Roman cross."

Rage engulfed Simon, completely obliterating all rational thought. He went for Joses with outstretched arms. Philip and Nathaniel rushed from another room and helped James the Less pry Simon's fingers from Joses's throat.

"Martha told me that one of my kinsmen had come to visit." The Lady's serene voice cut through the melee. Simon pulled back, shaking his head, trying to restore his self-control. The Lady came and took one of Joses's cold, trembling hands in hers as if nothing unusual had been going on. "You must be Joses," she said, "the son my sister-in-law Miriam had late in life. We've never met. I am Mary, the mother of Jesus. I married your father's brother Joseph."

Her gentle mien demanded respect. Joses bowed. "You must come and visit her," Joses said in a shaken voice. "My mother has an apartment now in the Holy City; it's in a brand new complex on East Street, the third building. My name is on the lintel. Just the other day my mother expressed a desire to see you again after so many years."

The Lady smiled. "I'll certainly visit Miriam before I go back to Galilee if she wants me to."

"I think it would please her greatly." Joses again nodded respectfully, shot Simon a blistering look, and took his leave.

☥

Batasha and the Lady found the building without any problem, and Miriam, garishly overdressed, invited them into her apartment. Batasha's eyes rolled in wonder as she saw that the room was even more tastelessly adorned than the woman. It was filled with the latest fads and bric-a-brac from the stalls in the marketplace. There were gaudy figurines of naked goddesses clustered incongruously around marble busts of Roman statesmen. Hideous birds made of colorful feathers perched on tables and sat in corners. A huge stuffed eagle, symbol of the Roman government, cast a beady stare from a place of prominence, its horny talons embedded in a blue-veined pedestal.

"The years have treated you kindly, my sister," Miriam remarked to the Lady as she offered them cushions around a low table. A tall, smirking slave served them wine with great flair. Ignoring him, Batasha focused her disbelieving gaze on the centerpiece, a wildly glued-together conglomeration of shells and faux pearls, fuzzy with dust.

"Beautiful, isn't it?" Miriam remarked, noticing what she assumed was Batasha's admiration. Joses bought it in a shop that deals exclusively in Mediterranean imports."

Batasha nodded and smiled. "It's breathtaking."

"It's wonderful to see you doing so well," the Lady said after introducing Batasha to her sister-in-law. "I'm glad you told Joses that you wanted to see me. It has been a long time."

"Yes, far too long to harbor misunderstandings and hard feelings," Miriam returned politely. "With both Alphaeus and Joseph gone, I saw no reason for us to remain strangers. I always liked you."

Ever generous, the Lady reached over the mountain of shells to clasp her sister-in-law's hand briefly before letting it go.

"How many children did you have after Jesus?" Miriam asked. "I heard about the second, James, whom you named after our husbands' father. But after that, I lost touch with you completely."

The Lady's voice assumed its customary soft gentleness as she set out to reacquaint herself with her kinswoman. "After James, I gave birth to a daughter, Ruth. She married a prosperous tentmaker in Nazareth and now has children of her own. Then came Simon, who decided he'd rather make tents than be a carpenter. He works with Ruth's husband in his shop. Next came my Joses, who, by the way, reminds me a little of your youngest son. James is teaching him the art of carpentry in Nazareth. My twins, Jude and Judith, are my youngest. They are ten years old. They've been a great blessing to me, for I discovered I was with child just after Joseph's sudden death, which was a terrible shock. The months of my pregnancy were a mingling of grief and happy expectancy. I continually comforted myself by thinking of the baby soon to be born into the world as a final gift from Joseph. Imagine my joy when I delivered two lovely infants in rapid succession with very little pain. God in his mercy had blessed me with a double miracle. He'd given me two loved ones to help replace the loss of one."

"You were more fortunate than I," said Miriam sadly. "I lost four babies between James and Joses. Two through miscarriage; two were stillborn."

"I'm so sorry," said the Lady with sincerity.

Never having had children of her own, Batasha was unable to contribute to the conversation. Not that she minded listening to women talk about childbearing. Sometimes she longed to nurture a child in the womb, and hold it to her breast. Now that she was free of her affliction, she knew she could have a baby without fear of passing along the condition to the child. But having a baby required having a husband, and every time she thought of being with a man in that way, she thought of Simon. Thus, her thought processes always brought her to an impasse, for he was going to marry the girl in Emmaus. Shaking herself out of her reverie, she asked Miriam if she'd met Jesus.

The elderly woman briefly fondled her heavy necklace. "Oh, I've seen him, of course. Everybody in the City has." She leaned forward, took an almond from a bowl that matched the centerpiece, and worried it with her few unfortunate teeth. "I must compliment you, Sister, on what a fine-looking man you have for a son," she said to the Lady. "He's quite majestic in his robes although they're not at all stylish. Yet he moves with great authority and his dark hair and beard are always immaculately groomed. I know very well where he got his coloring because you have the same eyes, and your hair is also that rich, ripe date color. But all of the men in Alphaeus's family were uncommonly short. I wonder where your eldest got his height. But then it was never decided if Joseph was actually the fa … er … um." Embarrassed, she quickly changed the subject. "Of course, Jesus never recognized me; I was just one of many in the crowd. And how could he, never having met me even in his youth? But I must tell you how proud I am of having a nephew who is called the Messiah by so many."

Yes, Batasha thought, *worldly acclaim would impress Miriam beyond anything else.*

Miriam went on after pausing to sip from her cup. "Having one son who adheres to him as the Messiah and one who does not has created some problems in our family," she confessed. "I'm afraid that James is offended in Joses and vise-versa. But even Joses can't fault your son for his kindness. One merely has to look to see that he is a good man."

She took another nut into her sunken mouth, once again making a job of chewing. "And he has the gift of healing!" she exclaimed. "I've seen that for myself. Joses still doesn't believe it, but I do, for I saw him heal a woman of crippling arthritis. Joses says it was a trick, but I know it wasn't, because I had seen that woman many times in the marketplace. Every time I did, I thanked Blessed Jehovah that old age had not visited me with an infirmity like hers. Wrinkles and a few missing teeth one can tolerate, but never being able to look up and see God's blue sky … ah, well … that's a real affliction. How would you like to go around day after day looking at people's dusty feet?" She turned a sudden gaze on Batasha.

"Oh, not at all," Batasha assured her quickly.

"Well, neither would I, nor would anybody. I heard from people in the crowd the day she was healed that she had been that way for eighteen years. Just imagine! Eighteen years of never being able to sleep on your back! And what a trial it must have been for her to shop for food? Never being able to look a merchant in the eye. Think of all the times she must have been cheated. But your Jesus fixed her quickly enough." Miriam grinned at the Lady, revealing four teeth, crooked and grey as stone monuments. "Straight as an arrow she became. And threw away her walking stick which was as poor and gnarled as she was, and the handle just as bent as her back."

Batasha smothered a smile, thinking that there was something quite likable about the garrulous old woman. One just had to keep a sense of humor and a safe distance.

"When did you first notice your son's remarkable powers?" Miriam asked the Lady.

"Why, I always knew Jesus was very special, even before he was born. So did Joseph," the Lady said without going into specifics.

Miriam gave a "humph" and avoided looking the Lady in the eye. Batasha became aware that there was some mystery here concerning Jesus—some secret that had caused dissension in the family—something that had pitted brother against brother. Whatever it was, neither Miriam nor the Lady was ready to address it openly.

"Jesus was a good child in every way," the Lady said, not without a trace of maternal pride. "He was born with a pleasant disposition and showed a great eagerness to learn as he grew up. Joseph loved him with a great tenderness and spent many hours in the shop teaching him the skills of carpentry. Our other sons sometimes felt that Joseph favored Jesus over them. I didn't realize how much they resented him until recently," she said with sadness.

"Yes, there's always a bit of jealously among children in the same house. That's been the way of it since Cain and Abel," remarked Miriam sympathetically.

The Lady nodded and went on to reminisce about Jesus' early years as a child. "Although he always loved to be around people," she said, "he spent a great deal of time walking out in the countryside alone. I believe that he gained much of his knowledge directly from God through meditation and prayer. He was also a voracious reader."

Batasha listened with interest. "I wasn't aware that the synagogue in Nazareth had a large scriptorium," she said.

"It doesn't really," the Lady answered. "Just the usual scrolls of Jewish Law and histories of the patriarchs, which Jesus had mastered by the age of twelve. We were fortunate, however, that nearby Sepphoris, where Joseph had his shop, was located on a busy trade route between the East and the West. Many times Joseph borrowed scrolls from business acquaintances, travelers, and traders who had been to far away places with different cultures and religions. Joseph used to say that Jesus had a mind like a sponge and never forgot anything he read." She stopped and smiled as if afraid of monopolizing the conversation.

While their elderly hostess had returned her attention to the bowl of nuts and appeared to be half listening, Batasha was riveted by everything the Master's mother had said about Jesus, trying to imagine what he must have been like as a boy. Far different from Jonas, she suspected, who fell out of trees on a regular basis and jumped into water at every opportunity, unless it was bath water, of course, which he shunned like the plague.

"Jesus must have been a wonderful child," she said, "never causing you a moment of grief or worry."

"He was wonderful," the Lady agreed, "but there was a time when I became quite vexed with him. And as for being worried, I thought I would die of it. It happened here in Jerusalem during Passover when he was twelve years old."

Miriam's ears perked up. "I always wondered if you and Joseph ever came to Jerusalem to observe the festivals."

"We did, of course," responded the Lady. "We always traveled with my sister and her family, making a celebration of it and having a good time. But this particular Passover ended in three days of horror."

"Did something happen to Jesus?" asked Batasha. "Did he get hurt?"

"We imagined all sorts of things," the Lady answered. "We had already been traveling a day on the road back to Galilee when we discovered Jesus wasn't in the caravan. I thought he was with my sister Salome and her boys, and she thought he was with me. When we realized he was missing, I went into an absolute panic. Joseph and I began backtracking, searching frantically along the way. We'd had James and Ruth by then and Simon was just a nursing infant. We finally got back to Jerusalem and began checking everywhere. I was convinced that slave traders had stolen him. Fears of how evilly they would abuse my gentle son made me sick, and my breasts went dry. That made Simon cry constantly, which upset Ruth who was only three. James, always a jealous child, said that we should forget Jesus and go home, that he didn't like him anyway. That was the only time I ever saw Joseph raise a rod to one of the children. On the fourth day, we went into the Temple to make prayers of supplication, and there was Jesus, well and whole, amid a group of learned teachers debating the Law."

"What did you do?" Batasha asked.

"I rebuked him severely. He put his arms around me and said that he must always mind his Father. I knew he was referring to Jehovah, and it was then that I remembered something I had not consciously thought about often due to my many responsibilities as a wife and mother—birthing babies, raising a family, and keeping the household orderly and clean."

"What did you remember?" asked Miriam

"I remembered the visitation I'd had from an angel before I became pregnant with Jesus, telling me that Jehovah had chosen me to be the mother of the Messiah." Miriam sat back and drew a deep breath. "And so you really believe it?" she asked. "You who nursed him at your breasts, rubbed his teething gums with camphor, and washed his soiled napkins—you really believe he's the Messiah promised to us by the prophets?"

"Yes," the Lady answered. "Definitely. I tried to avoid thinking about it for several years. For a long time I wanted to protect him by encouraging him to live the life of an average man. But there came a reckoning, a time when I had to make a decision and stand by it. My decision was to adhere wholeheartedly to what I knew was true. Perhaps I will suffer. Long ago an old prophet said that Satan would drive a dagger in my heart." She gave her sister-in-law a long, penetrating look and added, "Even so, I will always be faithful to Jesus and his identity."

Miriam seemed to shrink back into the cushions. "I want to have your faith. Faith is beautiful, ageless. But I don't. I don't believe."

The Lady smiled and reached over to pat her withered hand. "There is still time, my sister. And if you want to believe, sometime soon that desire will birth a small faith, which will grow and mature, and then your soul will rise up with great peace and joy."

Chapter 18

The Lord turns my darkness into light.
II Samuel 22:29 NIV

In the depths of December, when the days were shortest, the Jews celebrated another holiday—the Feast of Dedication. During these eight days, hundreds of blazing candelabra lit the cold darkness of the Temple. Sometimes called the Feast of Lights, this festival commemorated the 25th Chisleu, B.C. 164, when the patriot, Judas Maccabeus, with a band of Jewish warriors recaptured Jerusalem from the Hellenistic domination of the Syrian, Antiochus Epiphanes. The Maccabee, or "the hammer," as he was called, cleansed the altar of the defiling blood of heathen sacrifices and rededicated the Temple to Jehovah. This was a great victory for the war-torn Hebrew homeland and was forever after celebrated joyfully as proof of the fighting spirit of the Hebrew people and the will of Jehovah to preserve the Nation.

On the last day of the Feast, when the lights blazed more numerously and brightly than at any other time, Jesus went to the Temple and walked on Solomon's porch to teach the people.

The Jews, lead by Caiphas, kept harassing him and asking him the same questions over and over. "Come on," they sneered.

"Tell us who you really are. Don't keep us in suspense. If you are really the Christ, just say it plainly."

Simon's mouth went dry with anger. Jesus had already told them many times and in many ways who he was. Yet they kept stinging and pestering him like a swarm of noxious insects, hovering and waiting for an opportunity to charge him publicly with blasphemy and bring him before the courts for sentencing. Looking around, Simon noticed that the audience today was sparse; it was cold, and many chose to stay home by a warm brazier instead of congregating on the Temple porches in the cold wind.

"I have told you who I am," Jesus finally answered them with calm dignity. "But you won't believe. I have worked many miracles in the City, but still you won't believe I operate in the power of God." He filled his chest then exhaled slowly. "But you aren't my sheep. My sheep know my voice and come running eagerly when I call. They know I'll gather them to my bosom and care for them, for they belong to me. I have promised to give them eternal life. And they shall never lose it, and they shall never perish. And no one," he said accusingly, "can take them away from me."

The small group of common people standing by nodded in agreement. Many of them were people he'd healed and comforted, such as Enos the blind man, the lady who'd been bent over with arthritis, and a prostitute he'd saved from stoning several weeks ago. These and many others adored him openly.

He lifted his arms to heaven and the ivory robe fell away, revealing capable, manly forearms, sinew and muscle tense and strong. "My Father is greater and mightier than all else. No one can take my followers away from me, and no one can take them away from my Father." Then raising his voice, he shouted. "I and the Father are One!" His proclamation echoed through the corridors of the Temple and even into the very Holy of Holies.

Caiphas shrieked and smote his breast. He whirled around renting the beribboned ephod on his chest. "Blasphemy!" he screamed. "Kill him!"

To Simon's utter amazement, the Priests and Pharisees accompanying Caiphas brought out chunks of granite from the folds of their robes where they had been hiding them. Simon couldn't believe that their hatred of Jesus had driven them to plot murder within the very confines of the Temple.

His heart gave a great thud of fear. He rushed at the nearest Pharisee, who held up a jagged rock poised at Jesus' face. But before he reached him, Jesus' voice rang out again.

"Stop!" All movement was caught in tableau. Even his enemies had responded instinctively to his tone of authority.

The ensuing silence was thick and tense. As he stared at them, a whole range of emotions fleeted across his face—hurt, anger, disappointment, frustration, grief. Finally he spoke, "I have shown many acts of mercy in your presence," he said in lower tones. "For which of these do you mean to kill me?"

"None of them!" Caiphas spat through the foam of bloodlust on his lips. "We want to stone you for blasphemy! It isn't right for you, a mere man, to make yourself out to be God."

Jesus looked down from his place on the steps. His imposing height and dignified bearing rendered Caiphas mute. Jesus' next words were directed specifically to him. He spoke kindly and with no hatred or ill will. The contrast between the two religious leaders was stunning.

"I'm the One whom the Father dedicated to this world and sent into this world. I do His work so that you can know I am one with Him. But you won't believe this. I am telling you the truth, if anyone is a blasphemer, it is you because you want to kill me for saying that I am the Son of God."

"Stone him!" The High Priest spat out.

But the moment for action was over. The Pharisees' arms already hung limp at their sides. One by one the stones thudded to the pavement. Satan's courage drained out of their hearts, leaving them weak and helpless. Jesus walked away, and the crowd began to disperse.

Caiphas grabbed Simon's arm angrily as he passed by. "I'll see him crucified! It's better for one man to die than for God's chosen race to perish in anarchy. We are the religious leaders of the nation, and I"—he pointed to his chest—"am the chief one. Form and ritual must be preserved. I won't let a man like Jesus completely destroy us."

Simon looked down at the High Priest's white hand. "Don't touch me," he menaced softly. Caiphas let his arm go. "You're not a man of God," he accused. "You only care about worldly power and the offerings the people throw into your coffers."

"What's your name?" Caiphas demanded.

"Simon bar Cleopas."

"Well, then, Simon bar Cleopas, you shall die also, for supporting an insurrectionist and a blasphemer."

"And someday, Caiphas" Simon grit his teeth and replied, "you will split Hell wide open with your priestly descent. There you will strut about in your finery in a dazzling flame. You will want to cry out to the Master for mercy, but your mouth will be like a furnace. Only hot air will come out as it does even now."

"You will die, Son of Cleopas!" Caiphas called out as Simon left. "All of you! In torture and shame. Twelve traitors on crosses with your leader in the middle. That will be the final fulfillment of your false hopes."

They walked back to Bethany in silence. It had begun to rain, a cold, sorrowful drizzle, mixed with sleet. Simon clutched his rough robe to his shivering body, and drew the hood over his face as he drove into the wind. In the dark northern sky winter thunder rumbled ominously.

When they reached the inn, Jesus called a meeting. Without mentioning the violent incident in the Temple, he announced that he and the disciples were going east to sojourn a while in the region of Perea. He told Simon to go into Emmaus immediately if he wanted to say goodbye to his parents before their departure. He instructed Batasha to accompany his mother back to Galilee, taking Jonas along with them. Philip, who had recently gotten a message that his father was ill, would travel along with the women to Magdala and then go on to Bethsaida from there. After visiting his father, Philip could return to Judea by way of the east side of the Jordan and rendezvous with the rest of them in Perea. He suggested that they all reunite in the spring to celebrate Passover together in Jerusalem. According to the Lord's wishes, Batasha and her party left the next day after many embraces and fond farewells to Lazarus, Martha, and Maria.

After three days, they approached Magdala in foul weather. Batasha's warm pink villa with it many braziers and piles of freshly laundered woolen rugs and blankets was a welcome relief. Suzanna, who had recently returned from Damascus, made them soup, and Grete clucked over them like a mother hen over half-drowned chicks.

Dressed in a dry robe, Philip was the last one to arrive at the table. Taking advantage of the marble bath facility attached to Batasha's bedchamber, he'd washed up and shaved.

"Now you look more like the Philip I know," Batasha teased, "instead of a highway robber."

Philip smiled, rubbing his smooth chin. "I had decided to let it grow. Jesus and the others have very fine beards in the traditional Hebrew style. But alas! It had begun to itch and bother me. I don't think I have the patience to get beyond the scratchy stage. I've shaved ever since my university days at Alexandria, and I suppose I'll always resemble a Greek or Roman in appearance more than a Jew." His tone was apologetic.

"You must dress and groom yourself in the manner most befitting and becoming to you." The Lady sipped from a cup of hot tea spiced with cardamom before continuing. "God looks at the heart; whether or not the outward appearance is conventional, stylish, or acceptable to society is of little importance. Frankly, I can't picture you any other way than as you are."

"Lady, you are the soul of kindness." He turned to Batasha. "Do you also think I look fine the way I am?"

"I'll withhold my opinion," Batasha answered, smiling mischievously. "The Lady's compliment has already made you conceited."

He sighed, feigning deep injury. They continued to eat in congenial silence for a few moments before Philip spoke. "When did you plan to fetch Jude and Judith from Bethsaida?" he asked the Lady.

"I'll set out for Salome's the first sunny day. I'm very anxious to see them, but I wouldn't want to expose them to this bad weather for any reason. I know they're well and happy with my sister. The only thing that worries me is that Zebedee tends to spoil them terribly," she added with a laugh.

"Why don't I fetch them for you?" he suggested. "After I visit my father, I'll bring them back in my chariot before setting out for Perea."

A week later the rain stopped, and the sun came out from behind the clouds bathing the brown muddy landscape with a thin yellow light. The occasional gust of wind, however, still had an edge of bitterness that smote the cheeks with surprise making the eyes water. Philip arrived in his ornate chariot drawn by two mettlesome horses. Jude and Judith were with him, one on each side, cocooned in heavy woolen wrappers. Only their pink noses and excited eyes were visible.

Batasha and the Lady grabbed their cloaks, running to meet them. The children flew into their mother's arms uttering wild cries of delight. "Where's Jonas?" Jude cried exuberantly.

"I think he's in the tree house," said Batasha.

Jude let out a war whoop and set out for the copse hiding the tree house. There was an answering shout from Jonas and distant laughter. Judith stood immobile, her eyes filling with forlorn tears.

"Come on, dear." The Lady took her by the hand. "We'd better follow along and make sure they don't get into any trouble." Judith clung to her mother's hand, more confident now and smiling.

"Stay out of the wind," Batasha warned.

"We shall," the Lady assured with a backward glance. "They won't want to play for too long, I imagine."

Philip and Batasha made themselves comfortable in the front room as Suzanna brought them a hot chamomile tea and wafer thin pastries smoothed with honey butter.

"How is your father?" she asked.

"It was as I expected—an attack of gout. I dismissed mother's Greek physician and threw out his ridiculous remedies. Then I kept strict surveillance on what my father ate and how it was prepared. Within three days the swelling had gone down and he was walking around."

"I'm glad it wasn't serious." She sensed an underlying tension in Philip that was uncharacteristic of his usually unruffled demeanor. Unable to imagine what must account for it, she became apprehensive and uncertain in her responses.

He removed a cushion that was lodged between them, slid closer, and encircled her shoulder with his arm. When she bent her head, he lifted her chin and kissed her. She remained still, waiting for something deeper than the mere intellectual acknowledgement that she was being kissed rather nicely. Nothing stirred within her. Her thoughts drifted to Simon—his fiery, unexpected passion on the sands of the Great Sea, his intense farewell before becoming engaged to the Emmaeun girl.

"Marry me," Philip said moving away to hold her gaze.

"No," she whispered without stopping to think. "I can't."

"Why not?" he asked drawing back. "We're compatible. We get along well. I thought you cared for me."

"Oh, Philip, I'm so sorry. Of course I care for you. But ..."
She paused searching for words. "But I have decided not to get
married at all. It is not as if I am a young maiden whose father
must arrange a betrothal according to our customs. I don't have
a family. I have been on my own for years. I have the freedom
to choose for myself what I believe is right."

"And you don't think it's right for us to be married?" he
asked, clearly hurt and becoming agitated. He got up abruptly
and began to pace.

"Oh, I didn't mean it that way," she said, leaning forward,
her eyes begging for understanding. "I just meant that I don't
feel about you the way a woman should about a man she intends
to marry."

He groaned. "Too honest. Always too honest."

"Oh, I've been so stupid," she said in distress. "I know I led
you on, but I do like you, Philip," she assured him. "I thought
I might love you and marry you if you asked me. But I can't.
Please forgive me and let us go back to being friends."

"No!" he said emphatically grabbing for his cloak. "Don't
ask me to be just friends. My feelings are too raw right now to
swallow that pap."

"Oh, I've lost you completely," she mourned following him
to the door. "How you must hate me."

"I don't hate you. You must understand how disappointed
and upset I am at this point in time. But I don't hate you." His
voice gained some of his old self-assurance as he began to analyze
his feelings. "I'm just wounded. This is an unfortunate day for
me. But I am a philosopher, after all," he asserted. "This doesn't
mean that all the days to come will be equally disastrous." He
pulled his cloak tightly about him and sashed it. "All things
are relative. One must keep a perspective. Perhaps we can be
friends in the spring after a period of time has passed. No," he
said holding up his hand, "don't embrace me!" He quickly quit
her presence and called for Alexes to bring his chariot.

Batasha prayed faithfully for Jesus and the disciples. She petitioned fervently that Philip would forgive her and meet her in the spring without grudge or malice. At the very end of her prayers she always mentioned Simon, and then she would become mute. Her prayers for him were wordless, without structure, without beginning or end.

Children's laughter filled the house and echoed through the marble halls, the Lady's quiet serenity giving order and discipline to all. Jonas helped Jude and Judith with their lessons, and Judith proved to a more apt scholar than her restless brother who only cared about carving chariots and soldiers out of olive wood.

Batasha purchased several large spools of thread imported from the East. She and the Lady, in a joint effort, were making Jesus a fine lightweight robe for spring. The Lady worked on it during the daylight hours, since her eyesight wasn't what it used to be, and Batasha took over in the evenings. The garment, which they wove on a hooked needle in the Galilean fashion, would be all of one piece, without seams. She asked the Lady if she had chosen the color wisely. After all, his winter cloak was white. The Lady assured her that it wasn't as white as this; when they held up the newborn fabric, to the winter sunlight, it glowed with a pearlescent sheen. Batasha had developed a rapid rhythm, pulling and looping the fine thread with the single needle, working by the light of an oil lamp often well into the night. She wanted to get it done by Passover.

The weather warmed intermittently, and she and the Lady took these opportunities to visit Deborah and Leah in Capernaum. The once petite Deborah showed her condition quite obviously now as she began her last trimester of pregnancy. Every time they visited, Leah would tell the same horror story of how her sister had died in childbirth.

"Oh, I shall never forget her cries of agony!" Leah said launching into the familiar, but unwelcome narrative, her eyes rolling tragically. "I was only fourteen when it happened. What a horrible way to die! The baby was stillborn and my sister had hemorrhaged delivering it. As I slipped into the room where she lay, I thought I would faint. There was blood everywhere. The infant was lying to one side, a mere scrap of discolored humanity, hardly looking anything like a baby. My mother was sobbing in my father's arms. My poor sister lay bleeding on the sheets, her husband weeping at her side. The midwife had lifted her bloody arms toward heaven in helpless defeat.

"But you'll be all right." She leaned over and gave Deborah's hand a worried pat. "The midwife has been able to acquire some of the essence of the poppy. I've instructed her to give you plenty when your time comes. If I hadn't taken it when I gave birth to you, I don't know what would have happened, for I was two days in hard labor. Thank God, the medicine allowed me to sleep most of the time."

In a flurry of nervous anxiety, she got up to get some refreshments. Batasha felt somewhat queasy and wasn't sure she could stomach drinking wine. Deborah sat woodenly as if in a trance, patches of white on either side of her mouth. Only the Lady remained untouched by Leah's gruesome tale.

The Lady reached out and took Deborah's listless hand, surrounding it with warmth and assurance. "I had seven children," she said in a soothing voice. Deborah tried to focus on her as if from a great distance. "Listen to me!" The Lady shook her hand gently, but insistently, trying to get her to pay attention. "I'm alive and so are all my children. I had Jesus, my first, with only the help of my husband and God Almighty. He was born in a stable. There was no attending midwife, and certainly no poppy medicine. You must have faith. Your child will be born healthy and alive. You will experience some pain. Pain is natural when the body is opening up to bring forth new life. You must work with it when the time comes. By fighting and being afraid, you'll only harm yourself and that fine child you're carrying." She gave Deborah a loving smile, adding in a soft voice. "I believe it's going to be a boy, a very healthy, lusty boy, and quite large by the looks of your progress so far."

"I think so too." Deborah's eyes lit up. "I told Peter on his last visit home that it would be a boy."

"A mama usually knows." The Lady chuckled and squeezed her hand.

"But sometimes I ... I'm scared," Deborah confessed in a stammer. "A ... And the midwife my mother has hired to help with the birthing ... I don't like her. She has dirty fingernails. Oh," she moaned looking down at her swollen stomach, "I wish Peter were here. He'd know what to do."

"You're wrong about that!" Leah breezed into the room placing a tray on the table. "Men are totally worthless when it comes to birthing babies. But I have told you over and over not to worry," she said anxiously, her entire demeanor emanating a near state of panic. "The woman I have contracted is very good. And as long as you drink vinegar and eat the prescribed eggshells, I'm sure you and the baby will be safe."

"Egg shells? Vinegar?" the Lady's voice escalated as she rose indignantly from her seat.

"Why yes," Leah answered. "Eggshells make the baby's bones strong and vinegar will keep evil spirits from entering Deborah's womb to do the baby mischief."

During the entire year Batasha had known her, she had never heard the Lady raise her voice, or seen her lose her temper. Her present display of anger was awe-inspiring.

"The only evil spirits doing your daughter and her unborn child harm are you and that ignorant woman you call a midwife!" the Lady exclaimed in a towering rage. "Stop making her eat things that will make her sick!" She grabbed her cloak and stalked to the door. "Egg shells and vinegar indeed! Don't listen to them," she ordered Deborah over her shoulder. "Eat and drink whatever you please. Mind your body and listen to what it tells you. Pray to Jehovah in faith and believe in his unfailing love. Be still and confident. And above all, don't take the juice of the poppy or powdered mandrake either. Drugs only retard the natural process of the body." She gave a snort of disdain, wrapping in her cloak with quick sharp movements. "No wonder Leah was two days having you," she muttered.

Still stunned by the Lady's uncharacteristic behavior, Batasha also retrieved her cloak and prepared to leave.

"Well!" Leah stood glaring with her hands on her hips.

Deborah ran after them, maneuvering clumsily around the furniture. "Wait! Don't be angry. Peter would never forgive me if the Master's mother was offended in our home."

The Lady turned. All her wrath seemed to evaporate as she heaved a deep sigh. The only emotion left was love and concern for Deborah. "I'm sorry, child." She reached out and cupped Deborah's stricken face. "I wasn't angry with you, truly, or your mother either really. I was angry at fear and what it does to people. Batasha and I shall pray for you daily. And when your time comes, you will deliver a beautiful son in the strength and the favor of God." She smiled and promised gently, "If you ever have need of me at any time, day or night, you have only to send word."

Chapter 19

Behold the virgin shall conceive,
and bear a son.
Isaiah 7:14 KJV

February winds blew in more cold weather, and it seemed to Batasha that this unusually severe winter would never end. Every day she asked the children if they'd noticed any flowers during their play, referring to them as brave heralds of spring. At last they reported that they had spied one. Wrapping in a warm cloak, she rushed across the thawing ground to see for herself. It was a crocus, a stalwart little soldier wearing a sturdy yellow helmet. She laughed and declared she'd never seen such a beautiful sight.

Zebedee and Salome stopped by on their way to Passover. They were going early this year and planned to lease a house for the duration. Joanna, Paulus, and Chuza also visited traveling to Tiberias, for it was time to open Herod's summer estate. Since the Tetrarch always spent Passover week at his ancestral Hasmodean home in Jerusalem, however—either to observe religious festivities or to spite the Judean governor Pilate—they promised to meet her the first of April at Lazarus's inn.

Batasha and the Lady waited patiently for the passing days to unite them once again with Jesus. The robe was done and lay in the bottom of Batasha's cedar chest awaiting the journey. They expected Peter to come with a summons from Jesus the week before Passover, since Deborah's time was drawing close, and he had planned to be with her during the birthing.

One afternoon in mid-March, Alexes came back from town unexpectedly. A letter addressed to the Lady had been delivered to the shop by courier. The Lady unrolled it with trembling fingers. Disbelief and heartbreak gathered in her expressive grey eyes as she quickly read through the message.

"Merciful Jehovah!" she cried sinking into a low chair. "He's dead! I can't believe it!"

Batasha's heart leaped against her ribs like a frightened animal. She took the letter from the Lady with trembling hands.

> To Mary, the mother of Jeshua H'Mashiach, Jesus the Messiah, greetings from Martha bas Saul of Bethany:
>
> Our beloved brother passed away early this morning. By the time you receive this missive he will have been in the tomb of our fathers two days. He fell ill of a dreadful fever ten days ago. We sent for Jesus, who is in Perea, to come and heal him. But he never came and Lazarus died. Maria and I are beside ourselves with grief. We still await Jesus, for we need him now more than ever. Many of the high officials from Jerusalem have come to mourn with us since our inn has served their many friends and family from afar in past years. Nicodemus and Joseph of Arimethea are in constant attendance, but only Jesus can help us now. Our love for him has not wavered even though we can't understand why he didn't come.
>
> I knew you would want to know what has transpired, my friend, my second mother. Maria and I know we will see Lazarus again in the Resurrection. It is this, and this only, which keeps us from utter despair.

Our beloved Lazarus, kind, gracious, and cheerful to all, poor and rich alike—how we will miss him! We weep without ceasing from sore hearts. We know you grieve with us for the babe my mother was carrying in her womb when your Jesus was born, the dearest friend your son ever had. May the grace of God be with you, as well as with us, in this sorrow.

Batasha couldn't believe it. Lazarus was dead. He had been so vital and alive the last time she'd seen him.

"I must go to them." The Lady rose to her feet wiping her tears.

"We'll leave immediately," agreed Batasha. She called for Alexes, telling him to prepare the wagon and see to the donkeys right away. Suzanna fetched the children from their play. Batasha decided that they would take the direct route through Samaria. With steady progress, they would be in Endor by nightfall. Alexes must leave the shop to Suzanna and go with them, for it wasn't safe for women and children to travel long distances alone.

Grete interrupted Batasha's personal packing to announce that Leah had arrived from Capernaum. Batasha felt irritated. A morbid visit from Leah was all she needed at this time. She went into the hall wearing a mask of welcome, determined to get rid of Leah as quickly as possible.

Noting Leah's distraught appearance, however, she quickly changed her mind. She led her into the front receiving room and made her sit down. Leah's hands were shaking as if with the palsy. She asked her aunt to bring a cup of uncut wine, for it was obvious Leah was badly in need of a restorative.

"Where is the Lady?" Refusing to stay seated Leah jumped up and began to move about frantically. "I must see her. Deborah's time has come, and she insists that no one can deliver the child safely but the Master's mother."

"But we're getting ready to go to Bethany! One of the Lady's friends has died and we have to console the family."

"No! No!" Leah's voice shrilled as she paced in a small circle. "I have to bring the Lady back to Capernaum. Deborah needs her."

"What is going on?" The Lady entered the room dressed in warm robes and carrying a rucksack. "Leah!" she exclaimed surprised. Then she paused and smiled. "Ah, yes, it's Deborah, isn't it? Her pains have begun." She took Leah's hand, offering the panic-stricken woman reassurance. "I thought the baby might arrive early," she said unruffled. "I believe there must have been a miscalculation concerning the predicted date. It happens quite often. Don't worry."

"Oh please!" begged Leah. "She doesn't want anybody but you to help with the birthing. Please forget your anger and come help my daughter."

"I forgot my anger long ago. I've stayed away because I didn't want to cause further trouble." The Lady took the cup of wine from Grete and held it to Leah's trembling lips. "Now here, take a drink, and sit down."

Leah obeyed seeming to collapse. "But there isn't time. Deborah might be having the baby right this moment as we sit here dithering. And I left her with servants! Oh, God! What if she dies?"

"She won't die." The Lady patted her shoulder. "How bad were her pains."

"They were bad! Very bad!" Leah sobbed. "I don't see how she stayed on her feet."

"Then she was walking around?" the Lady asked.

"She's been doing nothing else. Yesterday she cleaned her bedchamber from top to bottom, and made sure the baby's crib and swaddling clothes were in order. The floors are so clean you could serve dinner on them. It was very late last night before she went to bed. I was dreadfully worried." Leah's words came out in a disjointed tumble. "I checked on her frequently as she slept. Then this morning she said her pains had started and she wanted you. She told me that the baby would be born tonight. Please, we have to hurry!"

The Lady, picking through Leah's ravings for meaning, asked quietly. "Is that what she said—that the baby would come tonight?"

"Yes, but she's just a child herself. How could she know?"

"Sometimes God gives an expectant mother special wisdom. We should be able to get there in plenty of time."

"Then we're going to Capernaum instead of Bethany?" Batasha's mind was whirling from this sudden turn of events.

"We must." The Lady went over to the writing desk and took out pen and parchment. "How can I go and mourn the passing of a friend when a young mother needs my help in bringing new life into the world? There will be time to weep for the dead afterwards." She scribbled a hasty note, then rolled up the letter and sealed it. "Will you have this sent by messenger to Martha? It expresses my condolences and the regret that I shall be delayed in getting there."

"I'll have Alexes deliver it personally. He can explain the circumstances to Martha and Maria more fully."

"I want you to come to Capernaum with me," the Lady said to Batasha. "I'll need help and Leah is in no condition to give it."

Batasha nodded and went to give Alexes his new orders and tell Aunt Grete and Suzanna that there had been a change of plans and to look after the children while she and the Lady went to Capernaum. Leah stepped into the hired chariot that had brought her and ordered the driver to make haste. Batasha, accompanied by the Lady, followed behind. A competent driver, Batasha assumed the reins of her own vehicle after waving to Alexes, who headed south on Mercury with the letter.

They arrived at Peter's house in record time. As they approached Deborah's chamber, Leah hung back and huddled in a darkened corner in the hall. She refused to enter the room for fear of what she might find.

Deborah was lying on her side in the fetal position, her eyes closed, her face beaded with perspiration. When she opened her eyes to see the Lady's loving expression, she gave a helpless little smile. "I knew you'd come. I haven't been frightened. As long as I pray, I'm able to bear it."

A wave of pain hit her and she scrunched up more tightly, neglecting to breathe. The Lady bent over the bed. "Don't run away from it," she said gently. "The pain is natural and to be expected. All the great matriarchs of the race have experienced it, so you are in good company. You must relax and breathe deeply." She made Deborah sit up and lean forward. Then she massaged her back and shoulders before propping her against the pillows, explaining that most women found a half-sitting position to be more comfortable than lying down.

The Lady spoke calmly and without excitement. Batasha realized that she was deliberately infusing the room with her own special serenity. "Go inform Leah that everything is all right," she said to Batasha. "Tell her she will have a grandchild in about eight hours, I think. Tell her we need water, clean cloths, and a flask of oil. And bring us a bowl of lightly honeyed water with a sponge." She turned back caressing Deborah's forehead. "She'll get very dry and thirsty before this is over."

Batasha did as she was told and came back to the room. Time crawled as Deborah's pains increased in intensity and frequency. There was some blood. The Lady changed the pad under her often, and Batasha helped her take off Deborah's soiled gown.

"Was it this bad with you?" Deborah asked the Lady coming out of a particularly gripping contraction.

With a cool cloth, the Lady pressed the sweat from Deborah's brow. "The firstborn usually hurts the worst. With Jesus I thought I was dying, for I was a virgin and had never even known a man." She continued to bathe Deborah as she was seized with another pain. "Women were never meant to suffer like this," the Lady said sympathetically. "God never intended it. Look at the animals. How they have their young without crying out or groaning. That is the way it should have been with humans. But Eve sinned, thus bringing us all to this."

She waved indicating Deborah's plight and gave a sardonic little laugh. "I have been quite vexed with our first mother at times for her disobedience."

Batasha's mind had halted at one of the Lady's statements. "Did you say you were a virgin when you gave birth to Jesus? I don't understand."

"Neither did anyone else. Joseph and I were engaged, which is as legally and morally binding in our law as marriage. I began to increase with child. My family was embarrassed. Because they thought I had been sinful, they sent me away to my mother's Aunt Elizabeth in the hill country of southern Judea. She had conceived in her old age and was also pregnant. When she saw me, her own unborn baby, six months further along than mine, turned over in her womb preparing itself for birth, and the Holy Spirit revealed to her that I was carrying the Messiah. I stayed with her several weeks and she gave me much comfort, for I was very young, only fifteen at the time. Her baby was John the Baptist," the Lady said sadly, "whom they killed over a year ago in Machaerus."

She continued to bathe Deborah, the sound of her voice, a crooning comfort. "While I was gone, Joseph's brother Alphaeus argued with him and took his wife and moved away. He was sure that I had been unfaithful to Joseph. That is why Alphaeus, his wife Miriam, and their son James the Less, who was ten years old then, went to live in Emmaus. Alphaeus took up stonecutting and never spoke to Joseph again, hating him for the scandal and shame he thought I'd brought down on the family. I kept in contact with Miriam for a while, hoping that somehow I could mend the breach between the two brothers, but eventually we lost contact altogether until my recent trip to Jerusalem."

"But how could you have been with child while yet a virgin?"

Deborah moaned and asked for water. The Lady moistened her lips with the sponge, but wouldn't let her drink, explaining that anything on her stomach right now might make her sick.

She instructed Deborah again to breathe evenly and told her to relax. Deborah's eyes were dazed with pain, but she nodded in obedience.

The Lady sat back in her chair as Deborah continued to labor in silent bravery. Batasha waited for an answer to her question but wouldn't press by asking again.

"I can't explain it," the Lady finally replied. "It was a mystery. An angel came to me one night and told me that I had found favor in God's sight and had been chosen to bear his son. I was afraid and wondered how this could be. But the angel told me not to be frightened or troubled. He said that a son would come from my virgin womb and that I should name him Jesus, which means Savior, and that he would rule the house of Israel forever and that there would be no end to his Kingdom."

"What did you do then?" Batasha asked.

"I believed," she answered simply. "I was overwhelmed with gratitude that God had chosen to bless me, a poor village girl, with such an important vocation. I went about for days with a song of praise in my heart. I don't know when God sparked the seed within my womb with Holy Life, but soon I began to increase.

"Then I had to tell my parents what had happened. At first they didn't believe. Then I think they did, but not completely. Their fear of scandal interfered with their faith. Salome argued with them on my behalf. She had just married Zebedee and sensed intuitively that I was still a virgin. I shall always love her for standing by me at that particular time in my life. In her uniquely practical, steadfast way she never wavered, never doubted."

"But you were engaged. How did your betrothed feel about all this?"

"At first he thought as his brother did—that I had been with a man. Knowing that he was not responsible for the pregnancy, he decided to repudiate me quietly by sending me away and never going through with the wedding ceremony. Then an angel spoke to him in the middle of the night, and he believed. When

I came back from Aunt Elizabeth's, he made preparations to travel with me to Bethlehem. It was the year of the census, and although my pregnancy was quite advanced by that time, he wanted to protect me and would not let me out of his sight."

Batasha got up to light the lamps. It was a fantastic narrative, but as the glow of lamplight chased the evening shadows from the room, her doubts went with them. It all made sense really.

The Lady continued when Batasha sat back down. "Joseph was a godly man. He remembered that the prophet Isaiah had foretold that a virgin would bring forth a child. We didn't come together as husband and wife until some time after Jesus was born in Bethlehem."

"Oh, yes," Batasha said remembering. "The woman in the Temple the last day of the Feast of Tabernacles mentioned that Bethlehem was to be the birthplace of the Messiah."

"I gave birth to him in the stable of Saul and Lydia's inn—the parents of Martha, Lazarus, and Maria. The inn was full with all the people coming from different places to register for the census. Every Hebrew male had to go to the city of his forefathers, you see, and Joseph was a direct descendant of King David. Recognizing that I was in labor, Lydia, who was in the first months of pregnancy herself, hastened to make me a place in the stable beneath the inn. It was there on a bed of clean straw that I suffered as poor Deborah does now and delivered into Joseph's astonished hands the infant Jesus." She laughed and gave Batasha an amused look. "We didn't realize until later that we had fulfilled the Scripture of the prophet Micah by having Jesus in Bethlehem. True prophecy is not accomplished by human design.

"Even so, news of Jesus' birth became widespread. Many believed, even then, that he was the Messiah. They came to the inn to worship. Some shepherds from surrounding fields saw a vision and followed a star to find us. Three Zoroastrian astrologers had also seen the strange sign in the heavens and were amazed because there was no rational explanation for it on their charts. They came with gifts, believing that something wonderful had happened. They were learned men and, upon seeing my child, even in his poor makeshift cradle, remembered the ancient writings that a King would be born to bring peace on earth. Their rich robes whispered in the hay as they knelt and paid homage.

"Herod the Great, the father of the present Herod, heard of it and asked the Priests and Scribes where the Christ would be born. When they told him, he went mad, and ordered every male child in Bethlehem killed. So even then, forces of evil were working against my son. And him just a babe."

Batasha murmured. "When I was a child, my father often spoke of that massacre with horror."

"Babies were slaughtered in their cribs and ripped from their mothers' breasts. Jesus would have been one of them if an angel hadn't warned Joseph in a dream. We immediately fled to Egypt, using the gold the astrologers had given us to pay our way. Before we left, we told Saul and Lydia what was going to happen. Lazarus had just been born. They fled with Lazarus and Martha, who was eleven years old at the time, to Lydia's parents in Bethany where they later built a new inn. A few years afterward, I chanced to meet Lydia again in Jerusalem at Passover. As we renewed our friendship, she told me that they had tried to warn other parents in Bethlehem, but had been scoffed at. Lazarus grew up to be my son's best friend through the years when we visited the Holy City." She sighed in sadness. "And now he lies dead in his father's tomb."

Deborah made a strange sound in the back of her throat, different from the whimpering that had gone before. The Lady bent over her immediately and began another litany of comforting words.

"I'm going to die. I can't go on." Deborah moaned.

"Breathe deeply. The pains will be constant now, but not for long. This is the stage before pushing begins."

Deborah didn't seem to hear. She lifted her hands in front of her face as if to reassure herself that she was still alive, perhaps thinking that the pain had completely consumed her existence. Suddenly she reared up and gave a loud piercing shriek, every tendon in her neck straining in agony. Then she went limp and fell back.

"Good!" the Lady said happily. "Now you must do that on every pain. But try to be quieter. It's not the noise we want, but the effort." She lifted the sheet, and the pad underneath Deborah was soaked with blood and water."

"I didn't know it would be like this," Batasha said in a weak voice.

"The baby will be here very shortly." The Lady was all business now. She shoved the sheet above Deborah's thighs and rushed around to support her back as Deborah rose up again to push. "Go tell Leah to get ready to tend to her grandchild. He will have to be swabbed and oiled and I'll be too busy to do it."

Batasha left the room in a flurry, coming back immediately with Leah whom she'd found in shambles outside the door. Deborah worked hard now with every contraction, too busy to complain or focus on anything other than the present task of ushering her baby into the world.

"There! There's his head!" the Lady cried. "He's going to make short work of this last stage. Good for you, Deborah," she said excitedly. "Look at his hair!" She laughed looking up at Deborah briefly. "It's red!"

Batasha was both shocked and awed by what she was witnessing. One more push and his head was out. When the Lady asked for a swab, Batasha quickly provided it, but the baby was already crying and choking, clearing his own air passages. *Not all the way out of his mother's womb,* Batasha thought amazed, *and already fighting.*

The Lady asked Deborah to push again more gently, and the baby was born. Batasha and the Lady sobbed happily. Deborah was laughing. Leah fainted dead away.

"Let me see! Let me see!" Deborah held out her arms working her fingers.

"Wait until the Lady finishes with the cord," said Batasha.

In a few moments the Lady placed the naked newborn on Deborah's breast. "Oh, he looks just like Peter," she said cuddling him close. "Mama, look! I have a son! Oh ... poor Mama."

"You'll have to clean him, Batasha. Leah can't," the Lady ordered in a brisk voice.

"Me?"

"Yes. I don't have the time. There's still work to be done. The afterbirth is coming. Take him and put him in his little bed. Swab him good and then oil him. I'll do the swaddling if you don't know how." She handed the infant to Batasha and dismissed her with a wave.

Batasha stood staring down at the squirming newborn, feeling helpless. She had never taken care of an infant in her life. Then she laughed, and a sort of tenderness took over, a sort of universal motherly instinct. She laid him down and began to clean his tiny body with all its nooks and crannies. "Oh, what do you mean by that sweet little scowl?" she crooned lovingly. "I must oil your toes whether you like it or not."

At Deborah and Leah's request, they stayed in Capernaum four more days. Little Jonah was a handful and kept them all busy. Leah recovered and turned proud, showing signs of becoming an indulgent grandmother. The Lady helped Deborah feed the infant and laughed as their first efforts failed. The fiery little mite would have none of it. He doubled up his fists indignantly and pulled his head away.

"See how strong he is!" the Lady exclaimed.

"He doesn't like me," Deborah wailed in unison with her offspring.

"He'll like you well enough when your milk comes in. He's a fine boy. And smart. He knows you don't have much yet. But he's getting a little, and that's all he needs right now."

On the third day the Lady and Batasha left for Magdala as Deborah bent her head maternally over her son who had finally discovered where to get his nourishment. They promised to relay the particulars of Jonah's birth to Peter as soon as they saw him, for it was agreed that they would set out for Judea as soon as possible. There was still the need to comfort Martha and Maria, and Passover was only two weeks away.

"Leah is a lucky woman to have such a grandchild," the Lady said wistfully as they rumbled along in the chariot. My daughter Ruth has two children. I love them dearly. But none of my sons have had children. There is something special about the son of one's son, I think. At one time I had hoped that Jesus …" She stopped, cutting herself off. "But there's no use in thinking of that now."

"What were you going to say?" Batasha asked.

"Oh, I suppose at one time, several years back, I hoped that Jesus would get married and live the existence of an average man. I had even picked out a wife for him—Maria bas Saul. You see, for a long time I kept his true identity so well hidden that I almost forgot it myself. I wanted him to be safe—anonymous. A mother trying to protect her young. That instinct never goes away, you know, no matter how old they get or how famous and important they become."

"Did you tell Jesus you wanted him to marry Maria?"

"I hinted. He merely gave me that mysterious smile of his as if he understood my desire for his human side to take precedence. I don't know if it was a temptation for him or not. Soon afterward, he struck off for the Jordan and was baptized by John. Then he went into the wilderness and didn't come back for forty days. When I next saw him he was lean and gaunt, and imbued with an inner power I didn't understand. It seemed that all fleshly desires had been burnt out of him in the desert. He told me that he had undergone many temptations and that he had confronted Satan face to face. He wouldn't go into much detail about it though. He merely said that he had learned to put away human desires in order to do the will of his Father implicitly.

"After that, I never spoke to him of Maria again. I believe he loves her. But it is with the same overpowering, all-encompassing love he has for all individuals. He'll never alter the course of his life now; his actions will always be in accordance with the Father's will. Sometimes my heart is struck numb with fear—fear of what the world will do to him."

"But they can't hurt him," Batasha argued. "Jehovah God is more powerful than Satan and must want to protect Jesus as any earthly father would."

"I know," the Lady said sighing. "But I can't forget an old prophet Joseph and I met as we dedicated Jesus in the Temple when he was a baby. He said that Jesus was destined to separate those who believe from those who will not. Then he gave Jesus back to me and said that a sword would pierce my soul.

"I hugged Jesus to my breast. I was frightened. I didn't know exactly what the prophet meant, but I sensed that tragedy would befall us some day. Evil beyond my control—that it would break my heart into a thousand pieces."

"He was an old man," Batasha reasoned in an attempt to make her feel better. "Don't let anything he said worry you. It was a long time ago."

"But he was a prophet," said the Lady. "Prophets know the future. And down deep inside I've always known his words were the beginning of my preparation. I'm still trying to prepare for what I know, but would rather not accept, is the inevitable."

Batasha didn't get a chance to reassure her. They had arrived home. Jude, Judith, and Jonas came running to meet them. She frowned. They didn't have on their woolen cloaks. Then suddenly she realized that it was no longer cold, that the sun was warm and brilliant. The trees were studded with tiny green buds, and some of her flowers had begun to bloom. It happened this way every year, and she could never pinpoint the exact moment. Spring had arrived unseen, like a mischievous child with a paint box of new colors.

Alexes rode in later that evening, dust-caked and weary from traveling. He was bursting with excitement. Showering the clean marble floor of the kitchen with grime and sand, he collapsed in a chair. "Lazarus is alive!" he announced to members of the household who gathered around. "Jesus called him from the tomb. I saw it myself."

The Lady offered him a cup of wine to moisten his mouth as Batasha asked him for further explanation. "I found the inn with little trouble, and the servants told me the direction of the tomb where the mourners had gone, led by the two sisters," he explained. "When I arrived, Jesus was there. The stone had been removed from the mouth of the tomb. The crowd had ceased weeping, and a hush had fallen over them. Suddenly Jesus called out loudly, 'Lazarus, come out!' The dead man walked out of the darkness into the sunlight, staggering from the weight of the layered grave-clothes and spices. He held his hands out groping, for the linen swathe still covered his head.

"The crowd was struck motionless as stone statues. Jesus ordered me to take the napkin from Lazarus's face. My hands shook, and I fumbled badly. There was no stench of death about the man, only the perfumed scent of a freshly opened alabastron. His face was full-fleshed, and he was smiling as if just awakening from a restful sleep. Upon seeing Jesus, he laughed in immediate recognition and stumbled forward, dragging strips of linen behind. Jesus caught him in a hug, and kissed both his cheeks. The astonished witness broke apart and started to move around, most of them close friends of the family. Hushed sounds of joy filled the air and began to swell.

"Everyone went back to the inn, led by Jesus with Lazarus and his deliriously happy sisters, and a celebration took place. Later two members of the Sanhedrin came to the inn to report that news of the resurrection was all over Jerusalem. Caiphas had called a special meeting of the High Court. Caiphas informed the officials that Jesus must die for the sake of the nation, as well as Lazarus, because he was a walking testimony of the extraordinary power of Jesus. Jesus decided that he and the disciples, including Lazarus, should go to the village of Ephraim to stay at the home of the disciple Thomas for a while."

Chapter 20

See, your king comes to you,
righteous and having salvation,
gentle and riding on a donkey.
Zechariah 9:9 NIV

According to plan, everyone gathered in Judea the week before Passover. The women and children had made the sixty-mile trip from Galilee without incident. Batasha and the Lady stayed at the inn in Bethany while Suzanna went into Jerusalem to be with her husband and two sons, who had taken time from their journeys to observe the Holy Week. Jesus and the disciples arrived the next day from Ephraim, gaunt and tense. Their mood had lightened, however, upon hearing of little Jonah's unexpectedly early arrival into the world. Peter became the recipient of much friendly teasing and congratulatory comments.

On the Sabbath before Passover a prominent man of Bethany whom Jesus had healed of leprosy invited Jesus and his party to dinner. During the meal, Jesus remarked that his time was short. As the disciples responded with their usual disbelieving comments, Maria, the sister of Lazarus, entered

271

with an alabaster box of spikenard, broke it, and anointed Jesus as he reclined at the table.

Judas spoke out against her extravagance, and Jesus rebuked him. A dark look of defiance fleeted across the disciple's face, noted by Simon who observed silently. James the Less had recently told Simon that Judas was saving money to buy an estate in Kerioth, his hometown, and spoke of little else but his desire to have a house and lands. Simon wondered if Judas was still pilfering money from the treasury and was hoarding it to finance his personal ambition. He kept his suspicions to himself, however, as jealousy and strife broke out often enough among the disciples without bringing forth accusations of thievery.

Now there was a rift between Peter and James bar Zebedee. Peter had gotten upset when Salome had begged for Jesus to set her two sons on either side of him when he came into his Kingdom. The whole argument was foolish to Simon's way of thinking. He felt that he was the least of the disciples, but at the same time, he didn't think that any of them were good enough to demand special favors.

Simon knew that Jesus was under a great deal of pressure. His powers had not diminished, but his human strength had. He was thinner than he'd been two years ago when Simon had first met him. Now the dark hair was sprinkled with silver, and care had hollowed his cheeks. Though he still walked with the same determination and energy he'd always had, his pace was somewhat slower, and his smiles were now fewer.

Was it the danger in Jerusalem that bothered Jesus so deeply? Simon wondered. He had always thought that he could protect the Master, but he wasn't so sure of late. The chaotic state of Simon's soul had robbed him of self-confidence. For the first time in his life, he had begun to acknowledge his limitations as a human being. He often prayed that Jehovah God would send angels to protect the Master should there be an attack, for he wasn't at all sure that his human effort would be sufficient.

Or, perhaps it was the spirit of strife among the disciples that weighed heavily upon Jesus? It seemed that they weren't able to come under one roof together without quarreling. Even now they stayed in separate houses. James and John were in a rented house with their parents in Bethphage. Andrew, Peter, and Matthew were staying at Daniel bar Ithamar's home in Jerusalem. Simon, Jesus, and the rest of the disciples lodged at the inn in Bethany along with Batasha, the Lady, and the children.

On Sunday, the first day of Passover week, Jesus met with his disciples on the road outside of Bethany near the Mount of Olives. A large crowd of Passover pilgrims began to gather around them curiously, many having heard about Jesus raising a man from the dead. As Simon watched the milling crowd, he felt a great sense of expectancy. The morning was bursting with spring sunshine and his spirits temporarily lifted. Jesus looked resplendent in the new robe Batasha had given him. Simon hurried forward when the Master motioned to him.

"You and Peter go into the village," he said pointing to Bethphage in the distance. "On the outskirts you will find a colt tied up. Bring him here. If anyone asks what you're doing say that the Lord has need of a colt."

The two disciples did indeed find a white colt tied to a fence. But when they began to lead it away, they ran into some difficulty. The animal dug his hooves into the ground and wouldn't budge.

As Peter pulled him by the neck, Simon pushed from behind, all to no avail. "Come on, you stubborn mule," Peter said with a grunt. Simon slapped the donkey's hindquarters, which elicited an indignant bray, but still no movement. "Don't hurt him," Peter warned. "We don't want to incur the owner's wrath."

"But the Lord is waiting for us! What are we going to do?"

"I don't know." Peter stopped his futile wrestling and stood back to give the donkey a scowl. Unconcerned, the animal lowered his head to crop the grass.

"We might be able to carry him," Simon suggested desperately.

Peter looked alarmed. "He looks rather heavy. And the hill is steep in places. Oh well, it's worth a try," he said with a shrug. "I'll take his front quarters and you take the back."

"Why do I get to be the lucky one?"

"Don't complain. At least you get to walk forward. If I should stumble and fall I'll be buried under two hundred pounds of braying donkey."

"What in the name of Merciful Jehovah is going on here?"

Grunting, they set the beast down and turned to see a man who was obviously the donkey's owner. "The Lord has need of this colt," they said in unison.

"Oh, yes, the Rabbi told me he might want to borrow it today. His aunt and uncle are renting one of my houses. He visited them yesterday, and they invited me over to meet him personally. It was a great honor."

"Then you don't mind if we take the colt?" Simon bent down to pick him up again.

"Not at all. But you won't get anywhere with him unless you take the mama too. He has never been ridden and he's wary of people."

"Uh oh," said Peter *tsk*-ing and shaking his head. "I'm afraid the Master might have a time trying to ride him then. When the man gave Peter the reins of the female, he led her toward the garden where Jesus was waiting. Simon came along behind with the colt, which followed his mama happily.

The Lord amazed them both when he mounted the colt without a problem and began to descend the Mount of Olives toward the Holy City. The crowd followed gathering more pilgrims like a widening river. Excitement leapt from heart to heart as news spread among those who didn't know, that this was the miracle-working prophet from Nazareth.

As the procession mounted the last craggy hill before descending into the Valley of Kedron, the people began to chant Hosannas, and exultant praises calling him the Son of David and naming him as King. They spread a carpet with their cloaks, and women and children broke off branches to wave in the air, shouting that he was the Messiah.

This was not quite the glorious entry into the City that Simon had always imagined. There were no fiery chariots, clashing swords, or battle cries. There was only Jesus surrounded by a joyous throng acclaiming him with praise. Simon remembered the prophecy of Zechariah which foretold that the Savior of the nations would ride on a colt in humility. Gentleness, peace, and righteousness would be his path to power. Once again Simon was confused and couldn't fully comprehend how the Master's ascension to the throne would be accomplished.

At the top of the hill, Jesus paused. All Jerusalem lay glistening in clear view. The golden dome of the Great Temple flashed in the morning sun. He reached out as if wanting to grasp the shimmering city in his hand. "I wish you had accepted me," he whispered, "for this was your time of reckoning." His eyes gathered with tears as he surveyed the streets, teeming with humanity dressed in colorful holiday raiment, the occasional glint of a Roman helmet moving among them as soldiers kept order. "But you did not recognize God's visitation. Now the day will come when you will be surrounded. Your enemy will besiege you. Then they will attack and dash you to the ground and all the children within you." Weeping, the Master urged the colt forward, a temperate breeze drying his tears.

Only his close followers had witnessed this anguished pause in the procession. Undaunted, the crowd continued to shout and sing along the way as they dipped through the Kedron Valley and approached the northeast gate of the City which led directly to the Temple steps. Some of the priests, hearing the din and perhaps viewing the approaching celebratory throng from the high platforms of the Temple, came out to meet him.

"Reprove the people," they demanded in loud voices. "They shouldn't be calling you King and Messiah. Can't you hear what they are saying? They're calling you the Christ!"

"I hear them," Jesus answered. "And I tell you that if they kept silent, the very stones along the way would cry out." He dismounted and told Jonas and John Mark to take the colt back to its owner. Then he walked through the arched gate and up the steps into the Court of the Gentiles, his white robe glistening in the sunlight as he lifted his arms to signal he was about to teach.

Caiphas looked on, grinding his teeth in frustration. If he set the Temple guards on Jesus today, the people would rise up in revolt. Roman soldiers, summoned from outlying towns, patrolled the streets and the immediate vicinity, ready to spring to action if a riot broke out. The Chief Priest did not want trouble with the Roman authorities. Jesus had won this battle. The whole world seemed to be following him, and his enemies could only stand by helplessly and watch as he took over the Temple.

That evening at the inn Batasha helped serve supper. Having no appetite herself, she went through the kitchen and left the house through the back door. A shady bench sat under a gnarled old sycamine tree, and she went there to hide in the cool gloom.

"Mary?"

It was the Lord's voice—the familiar way he said her name. The robe she had given him rustled as he sat beside her and remained quiet. His loving presence reached out and enveloped her with understanding and concern.

"Oh, Master!" she cried softly, turning toward him tearfully. "When you love someone so much, why do they reject you?" She was speaking of Simon. Seeing him again had stirred her heart with longing. "Everyone I've ever loved has abandoned me. My mother died when I was a child. My father left soon afterwards. And now someone I care very deeply about has cast me off. I feel so lonely, as if I will never be complete or experience true joy."

Jesus drew her head to his shoulder, holding her gently. "I understand. Your griefs are common to me also. I have been rejected and cast off too. Never think that I am above the pain and anguish a human being suffers on this earth."

He continued to hold her without further comment. She felt his pulse beneath her cheek, the warmth of his lifeblood. The fragrance of Maria's anointing still lingered on his skin and clung to the robe she'd made for him. She sighed and opened up to his peace. Her soul settled down, and she put her arms around him as she would a father or a big brother who had come to soothe her hurts. "Don't ever leave me, Rabboni."

"Don't worry." He chided softly, then promised. "I'll never leave or forsake you."

The next day was Monday. Jesus again convened with his disciples near the Mount of Olives preparing to go into Jerusalem. Jesus looked pale and drawn in the morning light. He'd refused breakfast this morning at the inn, and Simon couldn't remember the last time he'd seen the Master eat a really hearty meal. He wondered if Jesus was weak from hunger. Whatever the case, it was apparent that he was in not in a good mood. Sensing this, the disciples kept a wary silence as they walked with him down the road to the gate in the wall of the City which led directly onto the Temple porches.

When Jesus spied a fig tree in the distance, lush with foliage, he quickened his steps. A fig tree was supposed to produce fruit along with green leaves, but this one was a hypocrite, for it was barren when they arrived. Perhaps the Master's stomach chose this moment to contract with hunger, because he became irate and cursed the tree for being a pretender.

Startled at his vehemence, the disciples walked on a little distance, daring to cast surprised glances at one another as Jesus shook his fist at the tree before walking to catch up with them. Simon realized that something more than just a barren fig tree was distressing the Master. But instead of focusing on what might be the Lord's concern, he became lost once again in his own sense of inadequacy and barrenness.

Even as they arrived at the Temple, Jesus was still fuming. When Caiphas tried to block his way into the Temple enclosure, Jesus brushed him aside without acknowledgement and went directly to the Porch of the Gentiles where the officials were selling animals to be sacrificed and changing foreign money into Jewish currency. He grabbed a whip from the man assigned to watch over the sacred lambs and whirled it in the air around his head. Then he popped it near the head of one of the moneychangers. The man staggered back astonished. Jesus continued to snap the whip as, one by one, he drove them away from their tables. If they tried to grab stacks of money before retreating, he cracked the whip in front of their greedy fingers. Then he reached, and with one arm, turned over one of the heavy four-footed tables continuing down the line, crashing them over one after the other. The men beat a hasty retreat, slipping on rolling coins as they ran.

Jesus shouted after them shaking the whip. "God's house is a place of prayer! You've made it a den of robbers!" Then he tossed the whip aside and stalked from the premises, his dark eyes sparking with anger, his face set with holy indignation.

Once again the religious leaders could do nothing but look on helplessly. The scene Jesus had made was bad enough, but if they added to the melee by trying to arrest him, the Roman magistrates would be displeased. They appeared to be biding their time, looking for a way to apprehend him, perhaps in a secluded spot at night when the throng who loved him were nowhere around.

As he walked in the colonnade, Jesus seemed to settle down, touching the people individually and answering their personal questions. When Philip and Andrew approached him in the company of three young strangers, he welcomed them without protest. Simon could tell by looking at them that they were not Jewish.

"Lord," Philip began humbly, "some of my friends from the university at Antioch heard about you and have come all this way to meet you."

Jesus motioned them forward, and Philip made the introductions: "These two men are Sylvanus and Petronius. Both are students of philosophy." He indicated a clean-cut blond young man about the age of John. "And this is Luke. His father was my favorite professor. Luke is studying to be a physician."

Jesus gave Luke a smile before addressing all three of them. "You've come to meet me at a time of crisis. I'll tell you the same thing I've said all along. If you want to serve me, you have to stay with me. A servant will stay with his master and his master will stay with him. If you adhere to me, God will honor you."

He looked up as if to scan the clear blue sky. "So, you are philosophers," he said in a low voice, tinged with melancholy. The men strained forward. "I'll tell you a little philosophy then," he said looking at them. "A grain of wheat falls to earth and dies, and then it produces many more grains of wheat. But first it must die." He took a deep breath then leaned against one of the columns with an extended arm, bowing his head. "What can I say? You've come all this way to see a man suffer agony." He looked up to search the heavens again. "Oh, what pain I have in my soul!" he whispered. "Sometimes I want to ask my Father to rescue me! To say I can't go through with it. But I know I must because it is why I was sent." His distressed, lucent eyes filled with tears. "Oh, Father, may I honor you."

The cloudless sky gave a deep rumble as if it were fragmenting into pieces. The Temple floor shuddered. Simon's legs turned to water, and he nearly fell to his knees. Luke covered his face with his sleeve, and the others assumed various postures of awe.

Some said they heard thunder; others proclaimed it to be the Voice of God saying "I have already honored, and glorified, and brought praise to you. And I will do it again."

Jesus turned and addressed them: "That wasn't said for my sake; My Father said it for yours. Many Jews heard this Voice when I was baptized; some of my disciples heard it one night in Bethsaida-Julius; and so now have you Gentiles heard it." He gestured to encompass Luke and his companions and other Gentiles who'd gathered around. "It is my Witness. When I am lifted up on the cross, I will draw and attract all men—Gentile as well as Jew. You will remember what you have seen and heard today and it will help you bring people to the cross where I can cast the evil genius of this world out of their hearts."

"But Rabbi," said Luke, "we have learned from Scripture that the Christ is to remain forever. How then can you say you will be lifted on a cross? A dead man cannot live and rule forever."

"Our Lord frequently talks in symbols," Philip explained, speaking up for Jesus.

Jesus sighed and began to walk away. "You'll have the Light just a little while longer." He looked back over his shoulder. "Cling to me while you can; learn while there's still a little time. Then afterward you too can become sons of Light and Truth."

He left the Temple confines and did not return to Bethany for supper. Simon ate in silence, with Peter, Andrew, Philip, and Nathaniel. A sense of imminent doom had darkened their spirits, and no one wanted to probe it. Nathaniel finally spoke up saying that Judas was back from Kerioth.

Simon looked up sharply at hearing the news. "It's about time," he said with brusque disapproval. "Judas has been spending more time in his hometown than he has with the Master. How can he be considered a true disciple?"

"He has some important business dealings afoot." Never one to pass judgment, Nathaniel spoke up in defense of Judas.

Simon made a rude sound between his lips, went back to his food without comment, and further conversation died.

The next day Jesus and the disciples went into Jerusalem again, taking the same path they had traveled the previous morning. It was Peter who first noticed the fig tree. He walked over to examine it more closely, breaking off a dry leaf that crumbled between his fingers.

"Look, Master! This is the tree you cursed yesterday," he said in tones of awe. "It has completely withered away. Even its roots." He kicked one of the protruding roots, and it scattered into dust. "It's as if a great fire has consumed it."

"Prayer can do mighty things," Jesus said. "It can evoke tremendous power. Through confident and trusting prayer, even that mount"—he pointed to Gethsemane—"could be lifted up and thrown into the sea. Remember this lesson. But when you pray," he added, "be sure you have forgiven your enemies. You mustn't hate. If you forgive them, your heavenly Father will forgive you also of your own failings and wondrous things will result from your prayers."

When they arrived at the Temple, Jesus went into the Court of Women, which was also the Treasury. It was still early in the day, but the great room was filled with pilgrims coming to give tithes and offerings. Jesus stood and silently watched people casting their coins into the trumpet-shaped coffers. The disciples, encouraged by his relaxed attitude and the absence of the Scribes and Pharisees, began to wander about.

Simon noticed Judas standing by a column talking to someone. Peering closer, he recognized Caiphas, the High Priest, minus his entourage of sycophant Pharisees. He elbowed Peter and nodded. "I wonder what Judas is up to."

"Maybe he's asking Caiphas to donate to the Lord's treasury," Peter answered wryly.

Simon toyed with the notion of telling Peter what he knew about Judas, but refrained. It looked as if Judas might be in process of eliminating himself from their ranks anyway if his frequent desertions to Kerioth were any indication. "I wonder what percentage of all these Passover proceeds Caiphas siphons off into his personal accounts," Simon speculated.

"More than you and I will see in a lifetime, my brother," Peter answered slapping Simon's back. Simon's eyes narrowed once more on Judas before he followed his friend out onto Solomon's Porch where Jesus had already begun to teach. More people had assembled each day as the tide of pilgrims coming into Jerusalem increased. Time was short. It was already Tuesday and the Paschal would be eaten on Friday night. If visitors wanted to find a place to stay and purchase their sacrificial lambs and the other items for a traditional Passover supper, they had to arrive in the City today.

Groups of Pharisees spotted strategically in the crowd continually interrupted Jesus in his discourses in an attempt to discredit him, or merely to harass. "Who gave you the authority to teach here? By what power do you do these things?" one of them shouted.

"You answer me a question first; then I'll answer yours," Jesus said. "Where did John the Baptist get his authority? From Heaven or from men?"

Simon smiled. If they said from Heaven, they would be sanctioning the Baptist and all he had said about Jesus being the Christ of God. If they said from men, the people would rise up against them, for many knew John had been a true prophet.

"We don't know," the Pharisee begged off.

Jesus motioned with his arm as if brushing away flies. "That's no answer. And so I won't tell you by what power of authority I do my miracles." Turning back to his audience, he said in a voice tinged with disdain. "The Scribes and Pharisees sit in seats of authority. It's all right to respect their authority. But don't be like them," he instructed, gesturing in their direction, "for they do everything for show. They carry Scriptures around in little boxes tied to their foreheads and arms, and wear dazzling robes, lengthening the fringe every year to attract admiration. They take positions of honor at feasts and the best seats in the synagogues. Oh, yes, they eat up the respect you give them and feel proud when you call them 'Rabbi.' But just remember: you are all brothers and sisters put here on earth to serve God and one another, and your only true leader and Rabbi is the Christ"

Slowly his outstretched hand closed into a powerful fist, which he then shook at his enemies. "How terrible it will be for you, Scribes and Pharisees. Pretenders! Hypocrites! You steal from widows, then go make long prayers in the Temple. You miserable blind men! You travel over sea and land to make one convert. Then when you get him, you turn him into a son of Hell like you! You give a tenth of every little herb in your garden to the Temple, yet you have no faith, justice, or mercy in your hearts. Does God care about how well you follow rules? Or is it more important to show kindness and generosity to the poor and afflicted? You are doomed! You are careful to strain a harmless gnat from your drinking water; then you turn around and swallow a camel."

Simon and Peter looked at one another with uplifted brows. "If they had seen that fig tree this morning, they would all be running for their lives," whispered Simon.

"Spiritual wretches! You take such care to perform the ceremonial washings!" Jesus continued relentlessly. "Don't you know that is futile when you are so dirty inside? First make sure your hearts are clean, then worry about the outer man. You're nothing but whitewashed tombs! You appear to be pure, but within you're full of the stench of death.

"You say you would not have killed the prophets of long ago if you'd been alive then. But remember, you are the sons of murders! The spawn of vipers! How can you escape Hell? Listen to me!" His voice reverberated from the marble halls in waves. "Don't ever forget what I'm telling you today. In times to come I'll send prophets and wise men to contend with you again. You'll flog them in your synagogues and pursue and persecute them from town to town. Their blood will be on your heads just as the blood of the righteous prophets of long ago is on the heads of your fathers."

Tears fell from his eyes even as he was shouting. "Oh, Jerusalem, Jerusalem! Stoner of the prophets and murderer of those God sends. How I wanted to gather your children under my wing as a mother hen gathers her chicks! But you wouldn't have me." He descended the Temple stairs cowling his head with the hood of his robe. "I leave you alone to your empty house," he said turning momentarily to gesture toward the Temple. "You won't see me again until you mourn the one you have pierced."

Wordlessly, Simon and the others followed him to his favorite garden where he dropped to the grass and leaned against the twisted trunk of an olive tree throwing his head back in weariness. The disciples gathered around and also reclined.

Realizing that Jesus was terribly upset and apparently wanting to ease his inner turmoil, Peter gestured toward the Temple in the distance. Its golden dome blazed, and sunset had struck its white marble porches and columns with dying fire. "Look, Master! Isn't it beautiful?"

Jesus replied in a weary voice. "A time is coming when that building will be cast completely down, and not one stone will sit upon another." Then he closed his eyes and began speaking of what would happen at the end of the age. Matthew took out his notes and began to record the Master's words.

Chapter 21

God will provide himself a lamb.
Genesis 22:8 KJV

"Joanna! It is good to see you! Did you have any trouble finding us?" Batasha embraced her friend and knelt to hug Paulus and ruffle his hair.

"I saw James the Less outside the Temple Monday and he gave me directions. My but this is a nice inn! Quite the nicest I've ever seen." She removed her mantle and made herself comfortable at one of the tables. "They've made this whole rooftop into a lovely garden. And such nice people! Tell me, is this where Lazarus lives? The man whom Jesus raised from the dead? News of it has spread even as far as Tiberias."

"Yes. He and Jesus have been best friends since childhood. But how did you get here?" Batasha asked. "Where is Chuza?"

"We came in the chariot. Chuza couldn't take time to drive us because he's busy getting the palace in order for Herod's Passover celebration. I can tell you for sure that the Tetrarch isn't planning to observe this holiday in the manner of a good Jew. I just hope he'll have the decency not to turn his party into an orgy. A slave named Troilus drove us. Herod thinks very highly of him and trusts him to come and go pretty much as he pleases."

"Troilus!" Batasha instantly remembered the noble Greek who had come to her rescue in Tiberias two years ago. "Is he dark-haired and good-looking? An artist?"

"Why, yes," answered Joanna. "Quite the most talented and intelligent slave I've ever encountered. Do you remember him from the banquet?"

"I certainly do! Where is he now?"

"In the stable below tending the horses."

Batasha told her she'd be right back with refreshments and quickly went down the two flights of stairs to the stables. She found Troilus brushing a chestnut mare with slow gentle strokes.

"Has the most notable belly-painter in the world become a groomsman?"

He turned surprised, his dark eyes flashing with recognition. "Lady!" He bowed.

"I've brought you some wine." As she held out the cup he made no move to take it. "It's not permitted for a slave to be served by a lady."

"Then I'll set it on the bench and you can have it when you like."

The corner of his mouth lifted as he apparently remembered that Batasha did not mind breaking rules when it involved showing courtesy to a fellow human being. Thirsty, he took the cup from the bench and drained it.

"How have you been?" she asked. When his eyes flitted around the stable to various disinterested servants giving attention to their masters' horses, she added. "Don't worry. You can talk freely to me. No evil will befall you here."

He visibly relaxed. "I've been well."

"Do you still paint?"

"Not stomachs," he answered with a wry grin, continuing his chore of brushing dust from the horse's coat. "Herod has ordered me to do a fresco on one of the Hasmodean palace walls while we're here. Body painting went out of style."

"Thank blessed Jehovah for small mercies." At his look of obvious relief, she chuckled. "Or perhaps I should say, thank Zeus. Isn't Zeus the name of your Greek god?"

"Not mine," he countered bringing a bucket of water under the horse's nose so that he could drink. He glanced around again briefly making sure that nobody was listening. "I believe in the invisible God, the one of goodness and mercy. The one who Fathered the man Jesus. That's why I volunteered to drive the wife of Chuza today. I've heard that the Divine Man stays here sometimes." He set the bucket aside. "Is he here now?"

"Jesus is spending the day in prayer. It has been stressful for him in the City of late," she explained. "Oh, Troilus, I'm so glad that you have become a follower of our Master!" When he grimaced and held up his hands as if to ward off her loud tone, she laughed. "Don't worry. The people here are believers too. The people who own this inn are close friends of Jesus."

"Forgive me. It's very different in Herod's palace. Some of the slaves are believers, and we talk among ourselves. But we never speak in front of anyone else for fear it will get back to Herod. He would kill a disloyal slave as easily as stepping on an insect."

"You can talk to Joanna and Chuza," she informed him with a smile. "They've been followers of the Master for almost three years."

"It is not permitted for me to converse with them. I am a slave."

"You are a believer," she corrected him gently. "The Master commands us to love one another without prejudice. By loving each other, we express our love for him. Remember that. Joanna and Chuza would not betray you." She turned to go, then paused looking back. "God be with you."

"And also with you." He lifted his hand and nodded, signifying they were in accord.

When Batasha got back to the roof with a tray of food and drink, Joanna was in a pout. "Here I've come all this way and you run off and leave me."

Batasha laughed. "I'm sorry. I just found out something very interesting. The slave Troilus is a follower of Jesus."

Joanna sat up amazed. "But I had no idea!"

Batasha gave her friend a cup and they drank in silence for a moment watching Paulus explore among the pots of flowering shrubs. "I wonder how many there are like Troilus?" Batasha mused. "Secret, silent followers who go about their daily business without ever mentioning the name of Jesus, yet who wholeheartedly love him and adhere to his teachings?"

"Several legions, I should think," responded Joanna, "enough to make an army perhaps."

Their conversation turned to personal matters as they caught up on one another's news. Batasha told her that Philip had proposed and that she had refused, but that he seemed to bear her no grudge and still regarded her with friendliness. Joanna called her a fool in the fond way someone berates a close friend. Joanna said that Chuza was retiring from public life and had bought a farm near Capernaum. Batasha expressed surprise and delight, yet mentioned that she couldn't picture her friend milking goats for a living.

Paulus ran over to them, his hands cupped together, his eyes alight. "Guess what I've got, Mama."

"Oh, I do hope it's not a frog."

"We don't get many frogs up here," Batasha said wryly.

"It's a butterfly," Paulus announced delighted.

"Well, let it go! You'll smother it."

Paulus seemed to agonize for a moment before opening his chubby hands. A gorgeous scarlet and purple butterfly lifted lazily heavenward, dipping a path in the sunshine then disappearing over the wall of the roof. "Oh, I wanted to keep it!" Paulus exclaimed beginning to cry.

After Joanna left, Batasha walked across the terrace in back of the inn carrying a basket of laundry to the tubs beside the well used for washing clothes. She passed Jonas, Judith, and Jude playing with a little white lamb.

"Where did that come from?" she asked with a smile as it frolicked from one child to the next.

"Lazarus just brought him home." Jonas hugged the lamb's neck. "Isn't he beautiful? Pure white. There's not a mark on him."

Judith kissed his muzzle. "Oh, he's adorable! I love him!"

Batasha went to the well and began to draw water for the washtubs. She heard Simon's baritone voice and went on with her work as she listened.

"Don't you children allow yourselves to fall in love with that lamb," he warned. "It'll just break your hearts."

"Why?" asked Jonas.

"Because it must be slaughtered tomorrow. Hundreds of lambs will be killed on the altar in the Temple, this one included."

"Oh no!" Judith wailed. "This little lamb is too precious. How could anyone kill it?"

"It's the Law," Simon answered, regarding the Master's little sister with tender eyes.

"But why?" Jonas asked again, standing up. "Why does the Law require the killing of innocent animals, beautiful animals like this one? What did they ever do to deserve such cruelty?"

"God commanded it," Simon replied. "Now take my advice and stay away from the little fellow, or you'll be sad when Lazarus has to take him away."

Judith knelt, hugging the lamb. Jude hung back in silent observation, while Jonas took a stance of defiance. "I still don't understand," said Jonas.

"You've read the Scriptures, son," Simon reminded him. "You know the importance of blood sacrifice in our religion."

"I've read the Scriptures," Jonas conceded. "But I never understood the senseless killing of innocent animals." His eyes took on a stubborn cast. "It seems we serve a very mean God!"

Batasha waited for a show of temper from Simon, and was surprised when he merely sighed and sat down on a stone bench, motioning for the children to come forward. "It's all right to question, my son," he said to Jonas. "But take care how you do it. God has ears."

He made Jonas sit down beside him and took the two younger children into the circle of his arms. "Many hundreds of years ago," he began, "God created man from the dust and breathed life into him and gave him a soul. He told the man he could have the whole earth and everything in it. He only asked that the man love and obey Him in return. If the man didn't, he would die. The man rebelled and went his own way, immediately becoming miserable and unhappy at being separated from his Creator. He longed for the former close relationship he'd had with God, but since his heart had been blackened with the sin of disobedience, God could not communicate with him as a Father because God is good and cannot be friendly with sin."

He pulled Judith on his knee and Jude sat down at his feet listening. "And so God grieved. He saw that his creation would perish; yet he couldn't go back on his judgment of death as the penalty for sin, for God cannot make himself a liar. In his mercy, he devised a way to make a substitution for the death that man deserved. That substitution has always been expressed down through the ages with the killing of innocent animals. When God sees their blood, he counts it as the death of the man and the payment for his sin." The lamb had come up tamely, and Simon reached to fondle its ears. "This little one, innocent though he be, must pay the price."

Jonas was somber. "Look at him. I think he knows and doesn't want to die." Tears choked his voice. "It's very sad."

"Yes, but never blame God. This is man's own fault. If he had never wandered his own way, there would be no death."

"But why must I worry about what Adam and Eve did?" Jonas argued. "I'm not bad. I'm not a vile person."

"You're a sinner," Simon answered. "You were born with sin in your veins. It is our inheritance as human beings. With man's first disobedience, it became a part of all of us, to be passed down from generation to generation. Corruption, suffering, death. And don't feel resentful toward our first parents for the way they behaved. If given the same choice, can you be sure you would have done differently? I'm not. Man is a creature capable of making wrong decisions, of acting in base selfishness, without considering God at all."

He let Judith down and she followed the boys down the hill. In the pasture beyond, they began petting the lamb again, unable to resist their affection for him. Batasha shook her head then concentrated on the task before her. Unexpectedly, Simon's large hand descended in front of her eyes and took the bucket of water she'd lifted to fill the washtub.

"This is servants' work."

"I don't mind. The inn is full because of Passover and all the servants are very busy."

He drew more water to finish filling the tubs, handling the heavy bucket as if it were a toy. She scented him and moved back, disturbed by his nearness. "You did a good job teaching the children just now," she said. "I always thought you were gifted that way. Everything Jonas knows, he has learned from you."

"Thank you," he said with a self-deprecating smile.

"Why didn't you and the others go to the Temple today?" she asked sprinkling soda into the tub.

"Jesus said he wasn't going back." Simon sat down on the grass beside her as she worked. "He mentioned that he would come back at a much later date though," he added. "Some of us are hoping that he will set up a kingdom on Mount Hermon and quit contending with the religious leaders in Jerusalem. Is that my robe you're washing?"

"Yes, it was with Jonas's things," she answered applying it to the scrub board. "What did you do, take a mud bath in it?"

He laughed. "We were wrestling."

She slid him an amused glance, and then changed the subject. "Are the disciples still arguing among themselves about who will be greatest among the Master's closest followers?"

"There is always an undercurrent," Simon admitted. "I cannot understand it. I feel extremely honored to be considered a lesser companion. I used to think he called me to be a disciple because of my physical strength and fighting prowess, but a man with the Master's supernatural power has little need for the protection of a mere mortal. In a moment he could apply to God for legions of angels to fight on his behalf. I feel at times like a sham and have considered going back to the stone."

She was shocked. "Oh, Simon, how could you leave him?"

"That's just it," he admitted. "No matter how useless and unworthy I feel, I know I can't turn my back on him. I love him like the brother I never had. I've decided to remain and be content serving in any small way he needs me."

"Have you told him about your confusion and self-doubts?"

"No," he answered shaking his head. "I didn't think it important enough to bother him."

"But Simon," she scolded him gently, "Jesus is interested in all our personal concerns." She sought his eyes with her own. "You must go to him privately and tell him how you feel. He will clarify your purpose in life and give you comfort." Her gaze sidled away. "I recently had a conversation myself concerning a matter that was ruining my peace."

"Was it about Philip?" His voice took on an edge of challenge. "About marrying him?"

She wrung out more laundry, placed it in the basket, and reached for the Lord's white robe. "No, it wasn't about Philip," she replied testily, "and certainly not about marrying him."

"Is that the robe you made for the Master?" he asked in a suddenly cheerful voice.

"His mother and I made it during the winter months." She looked up briefly. He was grinning, obviously pleased about something. She put the Lord's robe into a fresh tub and began to squeeze the wash water through the finely woven fabric.

"It's very beautiful."

When she glanced up again, it was to find him wearing a particular look. She had seen it before. She made quick work of rinsing the Lord's robe and rising to her feet, using the heavy basket as a barrier. When he reached toward her face, she pulled back. "Don't touch me, Simon," she ordered in sharp tones. "It's unseemly for a betrothed man to touch a woman the way you want to touch me." She hoisted the basket to the side of her hip. When he moved to help her, she turned quickly saying, "I'll do it!" and walked away.

As he watched her retreat, the side of his mouth lifted in crooked smile. Perhaps he was not doomed to total failure in his relationships after all. He had not lost her to Philip. He would find a way to let her know that his betrothal to Lila had never materialized. Then he would set about wooing her to the best of his ability, with gifts and gentleness as his father had suggested. But where was she going with the clothes? His smile became an amused grin. The drying racks were out here.

The next evening Jesus led the disciples into Jerusalem. He had arranged for them to take the Paschal Feast together in a little-used upper room of Daniel bar Ithamar's house. Simon wondered why the Master had not freely discussed ahead of time about where the meeting place would be. Judas had asked him repeatedly. The Master had not answered, but had apparently informed Peter and John, for he had called them aside, and soon after, they left to help with the preparations.

They entered the well-furnished room hidden at the back of the second level of the wealthy merchant's home and found a U-shaped table covered with a white cloth and reclining couches arranged in the customary fashion. Apparently some of Daniel's servants had helped and also his grandson, John Mark, who was always eager to do any service for the Master. Daniel welcomed them with the courtesy of a good host and many declarations of how honored he was that his house had been chosen for the celebration of their feast. Then he withdrew to preside over the Paschal meal he would share with his own family. He pulled John Mark behind him, the youngster giving every indication that he would prefer to remain with Jesus and the disciples.

Immediately after they left, a quarrel broke out between Peter and Judas, both of them wrestling for a position beside the Master. "You are not to fight for places of honor as if you were in the court of a Gentile king," Jesus ordered without anger. "My Kingdom isn't like that. Let the greatest among you become the least; let the chief and leader become lowly. You must know by now that even I, your Master, have come to serve."

Peter was abashed. Immediately he let Judas have the couch and hurried around the table to take the lowest seat. In the u-shaped arrangement, it was directly across from John, who was at the Master's near right. Simon silently chose the couch beside Peter.

Soon everyone settled down and Jesus rose and spoke: "I have earnestly and intensely desired to eat this Paschal with you before I suffer." He bowed his head and blessed the food. A melancholy seemed to settle over him. The lamps on the table cast the company in an ethereal light, and the scene took on a sad, dreamlike quality.

The first cup was passed according to tradition as the disciples murmured intermittently among themselves. They had resented Judas taking such an important place, forcing poor Peter away from the Master's side. They admired Peter and felt the need to defend him in this injustice. The discussion developed into a round of general criticizing and accusations that flew around the table.

Jesus rose abruptly. They had already washed before sitting down and Simon didn't understand why the Master went to the water pots standing beside the door. As the others debated among themselves, Simon silently watched Jesus remove his garments down to his loincloth and wrap a towel around his waist. He noted the Master's gaunt frame. How had he become so thin? While there were no signs of weakness or illness in Jesus, he was no longer the robust and hearty man who'd gone swimming with them in the Great Sea two years ago. Now he was rangy and angular, his chest less deeply muscled. His arms were tough and knotty, and his shoulders, although still wide and masculine, were raw-boned.

Not in a very high mood anyway due to the sense of failure he continually felt, Simon sank into a deeper gloom. His eyes followed as Jesus carried a basin of water and knelt at Peter's feet.

Busily talking, Peter halted in mid-sentence and looked down in startled amazement. "Lord, what are you doing?" Jesus reached for his ankle and Peter jerked it away. "Master, no! I can't let you wash my feet. You're my Lord!"

Jesus clasped Peter's ankle more firmly and unlatched his sandal. "You don't understand this now, but you will eventually."

Peter protested again mortified. "I can't let you do this!"

Jesus sat back on his haunches and looked up. "We can't be friends unless I wash your feet."

Then Peter thrust out his feet as impulsively as he'd withheld them. "All right! But wash my head and hands as well. If there is some hidden meaning in this, I'll need a thorough job."

Jesus smiled. He wiped Peter's feet with the towel tied to his waist. "Your heart and hands are already cleansed; it's only your feet that must be made ready for service."

Simon cringed inwardly as the Lord came to him next. He didn't pull away as Peter had done but silently and motionlessly broke into a thousand pieces as he felt the Master's gentle touch. *Oh, God,* he thought, *my heart is black with unconfessed sin. Oh, Master, how can I be worthy of you. I had hoped my secret thoughts and failures would go away in time like a vapor.* He gazed down at Jesus' bent head. In the lamplight, he wore a golden halo. *How could I ever live up to the standard of excellence that you have set before me?*

"There, Simon." Jesus gave his foot a final, gentle caress with the towel and looked up, his patient eyes penetrating the deepest recesses of Simon's soul. Simon swallowed and bowed his head humbly. As the Master moved on to the others, Simon remembered Batasha's advice. Perhaps he should find a way to talk privately with Jesus to explain his feelings and ask forgiveness for a heart that could never be good enough.

After Jesus had gone around the table washing each disciple's feet, he put on his robe and sat down again. By now they had quit arguing among themselves and had fallen silent.

"Do you understand what I just did? I did it as an example. You call me Teacher and Lord. If I can wash your feet, the least you can do is minister to one another. Serve each other as I have served you. As I have become humble and stooped to your needs, so you become humble and stoop to the needs of one another.

"But you also have rights," Jesus went on. "You've stayed by me in my ministry. As my Father has given me honor, so do I also confer honor upon you. You may eat and drink at my table in my Kingdom, and sit on thrones, and be as judges."

Peter laughed impulsively in triumph. Jesus regarded him with a sad look. "Peter, listen! Satan wants to sift you. He wants to test all of you." His gaze swept around the table. "But I have prayed—especially for you, Peter, that your faith will not fail. You'll stumble, but then you'll come back and be stronger. Use that strength to establish your brothers."

"Not me! I'll never turn from you, Lord. I don't care if they put me in prison or even kill me! No, Lord, I'll be steadfast!"

Jesus closed his eyes briefly and shook his head. "I'm telling you the truth plainly. You're going to pretend you never knew me. Before the rooster crows tomorrow morning you will have already denied me three times."

"No." Peter was visibly upset. "How can you say such a thing? I would never do that!"

Without arguing further, Jesus reclined and they began to eat the traditional Passover meal of bitter herbs in vinegar, roasted lamb wrapped in bread, and crisply curled unleavened cakes. A sort of strained gaiety ensued in which Simon refused to participate. He sensed a deep inner disturbance in the Master, a sad distress. It seemed to him that darkness was closing in on their little assembly as the lamps burned low and the warm circle of light grew smaller. Even now Judas was completely in shadow.

"One of you is a betrayer," announced Jesus. As the others expressed surprise at this statement and began to ask questions, Simon simply bowed his head and remained silent. He dimly took note when Judas bolted from the table suddenly and left in a hurry, Jesus looking after him as if watching someone who had fallen into a deep chasm.

After the departure of Judas, Jesus addressed the rest of them: "My dearest friends, our remaining time together is short before I must leave you."

"Where are you going? May I go too?" Peter asked.

"Not this time. You can follow me later."

"But let me come with you now," Peter argued.

"There's no need to worry," he said to them all. "Just continue to believe and trust in me, no matter what. Where I am going there are many dwelling places. I wouldn't have led you all this way for nothing. I'm going to prepare a place, so that we can all be together again. Then I'll come and get you." He smiled at their puzzled expressions. Simon didn't understand a thing he was saying. Apparently some of the others were confused too.

"Just relax," Jesus said reassuringly. "You know where I'm going and you'll know how to get there."

"But Lord!" Thomas was clearly at a loss. "How can we know if you don't tell us ahead of time? And how can we get there if we don't know the way?"

"Because I am the Way," Jesus answered. "I'm the only Way to my Father."

"Lord," put in Philip, "I'm beginning to understand that you are not talking about going to some solitary place on earth to pray like you did yesterday. You're speaking of another realm that can't be seen with the human eye where God dwells. But, Lord, if you could only show us a glimpse of God, maybe we would be able to visualize these things you are saying."

The Master's eyes clouded with sadness. "Oh, Philip, have I been with you all this time and you don't know me even yet? Anyone who has seen me has seen my Father. How can you ask this question? Believe me—believe that I am in the Father and the Father is in me. If you can't adhere to that, then remember the works you have seen me do. I assure you most solemnly that anyone who believes in me shall do great and wondrous exploits he never dreamed of doing. I'll grant whatever you ask if it is asked for the sake of my identity as the Christ."

His mood dropped profoundly. "It grieves me that you all are still so immature. I've asked the Father to give you a Comforter to warm your spirits and teach you from inside your hearts. He will recall many of these things I've said to you after I'm gone and help you understand what has come to pass and what you are supposed to do."

He rose and took an unleavened cake between his hands. After giving thanks he broke it and handed it to John indicating that it should be passed from hand to hand. "This is my body which I'm laying down freely for your salvation. Eat it. And perform this ceremony as a remembrance from now on in my honor."

Then he lifted a cup of wine. "This is my blood, the new promise of hope, healing, deliverance, and prosperity from God. Drink it, and do so from now on to commemorate how I generously shed my life's blood for you."

Simon tried to comprehend. Why did the Master keep bringing up the subject of death? Certainly they knew he was in some danger, but they also knew he had great power and could deflect any attack by merely calling upon God for deliverance. And why this symbolism concerning the bread and the wine? Simon wondered if he would ever understand the Master's cryptic language that was so often cloaked in figures of speech.

Jesus lifted his arms offering a long and passionately tender prayer for their safety. Then he led them in the hymn that customarily closed the Paschal Feast, his voice harmonizing pleasantly with theirs.

Chapter 22

Dogs have surrounded me;
a band of evil men has encircled me.
Psalm 22:16 NIV

Somberly, they walked together to Gethsemane. Jesus ascended the hill toward his favorite garden spot accompanied by Peter, James, and John. The others trudged a little distance behind. Simon hung back, glimpsing the Master's white robe catching the moonlight as he moved through the trees to his favorite place of safe solitude. Without thought or plan, Simon turned and walked back into the City, seeking the mindless activity of the holiday crowds, the torchlight and gaiety

A Roman detachment assigned to the gate watched pilgrims leaving the city going into the suburbs to their rented lodgings for the night. They stopped anyone who entered, however, for questioning. A soldier, not much older than Jonas, stepped forward to inquire of Simon why he was going into the City at such a late hour. Simon waited for the familiar hatred to bloom in his heart and engulf his thinking, but it didn't. He seemed to be devoid of emotion.

"I grew up here and thought I might like to revisit some familiar places," Simon explained. The unseasoned youth was barely man enough to grow a beard. Simon gave him a smile, wondering where his parents were and why he was so far from home.

"Stay in the marketplace, fellow," the soldier advised in a friendly, but self-important manner. "There have been several incidents this week. Small gangs of robbers walk the streets at night looking for victims among the revelers."

"I'll be careful, son." He gave the boy a nod and said, "Shalom."

He passed through the narrow streets, standing aside for pockets of Passover revelers coming and going from private parties, and made his way to the street market. Many of the booths and shops were still open for business, and the whole area blazed with torches as people milled about looking for souvenirs and good things to eat.

Not everybody celebrated the holiday by religious observance. The taverns were doing a thriving business, and there was a great deal of drunken merriment. Raucous laughter poured from a lighted café decorated with holiday garlands of glass and tinkling metal trinkets. Simon ducked under the awning and ordered a cup of *shekar*—clear liquor made from the palm. Then he sat down to watch the teeming streets while sipping the fiery beverage.

His father had thrashed him soundly once when he'd come home after drinking too much shekar, he remembered fondly. It was during his teen years, and although he was taller than his father by six inches, he had submitted to the punishment without complaint as Cleopas quoted a Proverb with every stroke of the rod. He had been a rebellious boy and had deserved it.

He tossed off the rest of his drink and headed out of the marketplace toward the narrow winding streets where he had once run with a group of hooligans. That was how he had learned to fight. Led by Eleazer, his gang had brought opposing factions under subjection and had ruled the back alleys with the patronizing arrogance characteristic of the conqueror. Later they had become Zealots, and after that, Simon had forsaken them to follow the Master.

Lost in reverie, he sensed rather than heard a rush from behind. His reflexes had been rendered a fraction slower from the effects of the liquor, and he turned too late. Something struck his head hard. He closed his eyes to blackness. Before completely losing consciousness, he saw a brief vision of Jesus looking toward heaven, his agonized face bathed in a bloody sweat.

It was past midnight and Batasha couldn't sleep. Jonas had mentioned after the Passover meal that Simon wasn't betrothed, that the negotiations had never become final and had recently been abandoned altogether. The news, delivered off-handedly by the boy, had surprised her beyond coherent thought. She didn't know what to make of it, and lay awake in the dark daring to hope.

Suddenly she heard a strange scrabbling on the outside wall of the inn. She rose up, fetched some fire from a low-burning sconce in the hall, and lit a lamp by her bed. Then she heard it again. She thrust her head out the window looking for the source of the sound. She saw a boy rising out of the ground fog, crawling spider-like up the vine-covered wall. It was John Mark, distinct in the moonlight. Too distinct. His adolescent body shone completely bare.

Grabbing the lamp she rushed to Jonas's room just as John Mark tumbled through the window in paroxysms of fear and trembling. "What on earth are you doing?" she demanded in a whisper.

Jonas sat up in his bed rubbing sleep from his eyes. "John Mark!" he exclaimed groggily. His friend tried to talk, but merely issued forth with tearful stuttering.

Batasha silenced them both with a gesture of her hand. "Both of you lower your voices or you'll wake the whole house. John Mark, compose yourself. Jonas, give him a robe before he shakes to pieces from the cold. He's as naked as the day he was born."

Jonas reached for a garment and flung it to John Mark, who caught it with a spastic movement and hastened to wrap it around his body. Once fully covered, he rose completely from his crouching position. "I ... I'm sorry, ma'am. I didn't mean to wake you. The Roman soldiers tried to hold me, and I ran away in panic. I came here because I wanted to talk to Jonas."

"What in heaven's name happened to your clothing? And what do you mean you were running from Roman soldiers?" Batasha asked the flustered boy. "Your grandfather will be vexed if he finds out you've gotten into trouble with the authorities."

"The soldiers grabbed me, when they arrested Jesus. But I twisted and got away, leaving them holding only my robe."

"Arrested? Jesus!" She collapsed on Jonas's bed. "Sit down, John Mark, and tell me exactly what happened."

"We had all gone to bed after the Passover meal," he began. "Jesus and his disciples had already left. Then Judas came to our door, and my grandfather roused out of bed to receive him. I had also awakened. Instead of fully dressing, I covered up in a loose robe without even a belt. I heard Judas ask where Jesus was. My grandfather answered that he didn't know. I crept down the stairs, and told Judas that I thought I had heard them mention something about going to Gethsemane. Judas seemed satisfied and left. When I got back to my room, I looked out the window and saw Judas going to join a large group of men farther down the street, many of whom were soldiers and Temple guards bearing torches and weapons. Fearing that Jesus was in danger, I followed them without my grandfather knowing.

"I took a shortcut to Gethsemane hoping to warn Jesus before they got there. I found some of the disciples asleep, but couldn't locate the Master. Before I knew it, the soldiers had arrived, and I hid behind some bushes.

"The disciples roused up, and there was a great deal of noise and confusion. Jesus came out of the darkness with Peter, James, and John. Judas stepped forward and kissed him and addressed him as Lord. This is the manner in which he pointed out which one was the Master."

"Oh, how could he do it?" Batasha said in disbelief. "To betray the Master with a kiss of friendship?"

"The soldiers seized Jesus roughly. Peter lunged forward, brandishing a sword and struck one of the men in the crowd. The Master rebuked Peter and the other disciples who were advancing to fight."

"Where was my father?" Jonas asked.

"I don't know," answered John Mark. "I didn't see him."

"What happened then?" asked Batasha.

"Jesus told the soldiers he would go with them quietly and to leave the disciples alone. He asked the priests, captains of the Temple and elders of the Sanhedrin, who had come with the soldiers, why they had come after him in the middle of the night with swords and clubs as if he were a common criminal. He said that he had always done his works openly and the fact that they had come out to arrest him in the darkness proved that the Powers of Darkness were controlling them.

"The soldiers fell on him angrily and bound his hands. When they started for some of the disciples, panic set in. The disciples fled, Peter in the lead. Don't ask me why he was willing to fight one minute and running the next. Perhaps the Master's calm surrender made him feel helpless, I don't know. All I know was that I was silly with fear myself.

"In the confusion, one of the soldiers stepped back and tripped over me. He pulled me up by the scruff of my robe, and I could see the malicious glee in his eyes at finding so handy a victim. That's when I slipped out of my robe and ran away naked. The soldier cursed, and then burst into laughter. My cowardice had amused him."

"What will they do to Jesus?" Jonas asked fearfully.

"Nothing!" Batasha answered. "They wouldn't dare put him on trial in the middle of the night. Caiphas will probably only question him and let him go. You two get some sleep. John Mark, you're going to have to explain all this to Daniel early in the morning. Jonas will go with you for moral support."

"I'm worried about Jesus." John Mark said brokenly as he climbed into bed. "I feel guilty, for it was I who told Judas where he was."

"You mustn't condemn yourself. Judas would have gone to Gethsemane looking for him anyway. Everyone knows it is his favorite spot for prayer. Rest now. Jesus will be released in the morning, and all will be well."

Three hours later Batasha was still awake. She hadn't been able to close her eyes at all. She thought of rousing Lazarus, but with the way the religious officials felt about him, she hesitated. He would be in danger too if he went into the City to try to help Jesus.

Hearing a soft, but distinct ringing of the bell on the outside gate, she rushed to see who was there. It was the disciple John, obviously in a state of distress. "What in God's name is happening?" she demanded. "John Mark came here a while ago with the most bizarre tale about Jesus being arrested. Tell me it's not so!"

John came into the stable complex and crumpled on a low stone bench. "It's true. They took him to Caiphas' palace.. Peter and I followed at a distance. I talked our way into the High Priest's courtyard identifying myself as a Levite interested in the what was happening," he said. "There was a lot of confusion. I've come to tell my aunt about it and to comfort her. Will you call her for me?"

"But the Lady ate the Passover with your mother and father. Didn't you know?" She sat down beside him numb with shock.

"No. How could I? I haven't seen my parents since"—he brushed his hand across his eyes—"since Wednesday night." He rose to his feet. "I'd better be going. The Master would want me to be the one to break the news to her."

"How is he?" she asked. "Surely they don't mean to harm him."

"They have already struck him in the face. One of his eyes is swollen shut and his lip is bleeding." John ran his fingers through his hair. "I can't believe this is happening. I have to keep my wits about me. I have to think of my aunt and what I can do for her."

"Where are the others?" she asked. "Where is Simon?"

"We all scattered when they arrested him and led him away." John's brow furrowed. "I don't remember seeing the Zealot in the garden at all after we ate the Paschal supper."

"But Simon and Peter made an agreement to defend Jesus at all costs," Batasha argued.

"Peter denied even knowing him," John said. "He was with me in the courtyard and a servant girl asked if he was a follower. He said 'no' and cursed. After that, he left. I waited around to watch Caiphas and a delegation from the Sanhedrin take Jesus to Pilate. An unruly, drunken mob of Passover revelers followed, desiring to be entertained. The Jews wouldn't go into the fortress because it was the home of a Gentile, so Pilate came out to them. He wasn't in a good mood. Caiphas told him Jesus was a criminal. Pilate retorted that he should try Jesus by Jewish Law. Caiphas answered that it wasn't lawful for the Jewish court to sentence a man to death."

"Death?" Batasha's voice pitched to the level of panic. "Death!"

John's relatively calm demeanor cracked. "That's what they want. They want to get rid of him once and for all. Permanently."

"But they can't! He hasn't done anything wrong. This is totally against the laws of God and human decency." She rose to pace the straw-strewn floor of the stable, disturbing the animals and making them restless. "Did Pilate say anything else?" she asked whirling around on her heels.

"I don't know. I left. Jesus had given me a look, and I knew he was silently telling me to go to his mother." John got up and stumbled to the gate in weariness and grief.

Batasha flew up the stairs. Lazarus must be told without further delay. Perhaps he could find Nicodemus and Joseph of Arimethea. They were members of the Sanhedrin. They could use their influence to save Jesus.

Upon being informed of the news, Lazarus quickly left for Jerusalem. Both weeping, Martha and Maria joined Batasha in the receiving room of the inn. Dry-eyed, Batasha tried to console them as they waited. Upon hearing the bell on the gate once again signaling a visitor, she rushed to see who it was. The slave Troilus greeted her while trying to catch his breath. She opened the gate allowing him into the stable.

"I ran all the way," he said groping to sit down. "I was afraid to draw attention to myself by harnessing a horse or preparing the chariot." He wiped the sweat from his brow. "I have come from Herod's palace. The noble Chuza sent me to inform you that they have brought the God-man to Herod for sentencing."

"What happened?" Batasha asked trying to make sense of the situation.

"Herod was finishing a night of festivities as the Chief Priests and Scribes asked for an audience. The king was bored and drunk. He apparently hoped that Jesus would entertain him with some trick of magic. The Chief Priests and Scribes began to accuse the Divine Man. But when he remained silent throughout their denunciation, Herod became impatient and began to scoff and ridicule and call him a fraud.

"Chuza sent me to tell you these things and to give you hope," Troilus rushed on. "Herod has refused to condemn Jesus, although as a Galilean, Jesus comes under his jurisdiction. The king still has nightmares about the Baptist and doesn't wish to compound his guilt by shedding more innocent blood."

"But what about Pilate?" Batasha asked. "What will he do when Jesus is brought before him again?"

"I don't know, mistress. But the Romans take pride in their legal system and boast that they have brought order to the world. We can hope that Pilate will decide justly according to his Roman training and refuse to condemn Jesus as well."

"How was Jesus? Did Herod's men treat him cruelly?"

"He had been abused before he reached Herod. Then Herod's soldiers dressed him up in a bright red centurion's cape and made a crown from the branches of a thorn bush and forced it on his head. It made several gashes in his forehead, which bled freely. Then they struck him about the face and mocked him."

"Has all the world gone mad?" Batasha exclaimed horrified. "I don't understand why they would do such a thing!"

"Because the Chief Priests accused him of claiming to be King of the Jews," Troilus answered. "The soldiers made sport of that by dressing him up like a king. Herod was amused, but soon afterward, dismissed Jesus to be taken back to Pilate. He sent his favorite centurion and a troop of soldiers to provide escort, saying that he was lending Pilate his best men to carry out whatever sentence Pilate decided upon. At that point, he merely wanted to be rid of the problem, being desirous only of his bed."

Simon roused briefly to hear voices, faint and distorted through the pulsating pain in his head: "What are we going to do with him? We can't just leave him outside the door, perhaps to die."

"Don't get involved. Leave him alone. He's probably just drunk. Let him sleep it off."

"Remember the story of the good Samaritan that the Master told us? How can you say 'don't get involved'? Look, he's a Jew, a fellow brother. And one of pure birth by the looks of the profile and the dark, glossy beard."

"Veronica! We can't take this stranger into our house. I'm sorry I stumbled over him coming home just now and told you about him. Come back through the door."

"Oh, look! His head is bleeding. Someone attacked and robbed him. Please, my husband, we must bring him inside. I must clean his wound with oil and give him some nourishment when he wakes up. God will surely be displeased if we don't at least try to help."

"Oh, all right! But you'll have to take care of him. I must go back and find out what is going to happen. Help me get him up. Merciful Jehovah, he must weigh a ton!"

A murky dawn had replaced the darkness of night. Servants admitted Joses to the room where Batasha, Martha, and Maria were awaiting news. "I'm looking for my brother," he said grimly. "Is he here?"

"No," answered Batasha. "Neither James the Less nor young Thad is here. They didn't come back last night after Jesus was arrested," she added.

"I was concerned for their safety. I've just come from the Praetorium where Pilate is holding court."

"Then you've seen Jesus!" She led him further into the room. "You must tell us what's going on. We're frantic with worry. Lazarus is out now trying to rouse Nicodemus and Joseph of Arimethea to action."

Martha and Maria latched onto Joses as persons drowning. "Is Jesus all right? Please tell us!"

"Pilate is trying to save him," Joses answered. He keeps repeating that he can find no fault in him. My friends woke me early this morning with the news that he'd been arrested. Of course my mother became alarmed for James and Thad and sent me to find them."

"Do you think Pilate will let Jesus go?" Batasha asked leading Joses to a chair.

"He's sick of all Jewry," Joses said sitting down, "and the false piety of the High Priest and his supporters. Pilate is not at all pleased with this turn of events. Say what you want, but Romans operate on justice and are not nearly as religiously inflexible as our own people. I really don't believe Pilate will execute Jesus. I fervently hope not," he added shaking his head in regret, "for I have been very wrong. And I am deeply sorry for having taken sides against him."

"What did Pilate say?" Batasha probed insistently.

"He wanted to give Jesus back to the people. You know about the custom of releasing one prisoner during the Passover Season? Pilate had the soldiers bring out Jesus with the criminal bar Abbas whom they've had in prison for several days. He thought that the mob would choose Jesus over the infamous criminal, bar Abbas. But the common people who follow Jesus were still abed and the mob that had gathered was full of drunken miscreants and prostitutes who had followed the action all night and weren't about to let Jesus go before seeing his blood. The priests had been mingling among them the whole time inciting them to riot, telling them that Jesus had blasphemed Holy Jehovah by claiming he was equal with God. Eleazer ben Samuel was also there with his band of Zealots shouting, "Give us bar Abbas! Crucify Jesus!" It became a chant. So Pilate released the criminal and kept the innocent man in custody."

Batasha's throat constricted with fear. "But you don't think he will order Jesus executed," she said, reminding him of his previous words.

"No." Joses heaved a deep sigh and seemed to deflate. "After he let bar Abbas go, he tried to appease the crowd by ordering that Jesus be scourged."

"Scourged!" cried Maria hysterically, dissolving into uncontrollable crying.

"Well, it's better than the cross," Joses reasoned. "I can see Pilate's logic. He was faced with a crowd demanding blood, and religious leaders determined to kill him. Pilate knows that Jesus is an innocent man. I think he ordered the scourging to avoid the more extreme alternative—death by crucifixion."

"Thirty-nine lashes," Batasha whispered horrified.

"Try not to worry. Both Herod and Pilate seem to agree that Jesus should not die. They've even become tentative friends. Herod lent Pilate his favorite centurion and band of soldiers to follow this thing through. Just be patient. When the crowd sees Jesus after the whipping, they'll be satisfied and leave him alone. He'll come back to you beaten, but at least he'll be alive."

"But many men have perished under the whip!" Martha exclaimed, holding her weeping sister. "They strip them naked and make them get on their knees. And the whip has bits of metal and glass in the thongs. It cuts a man until the whites of his ribs show. Oh, dear God, help your Son, your Anointed One!"

Chapter 23

*His appearance was so disfigured
beyond that of any man.*
Isaiah 52:14 NIV

Simon opened his eyes, grimacing against the pain in his head. Nausea threatened to rise in his throat. A woman stood looking down at him wearing a worried expression. A mantle of cerulean blue covered her head, its vibrant color muted by the thin, watery light coming through a window. His vision blurred and he closed his eyes against dizziness.

"Where am I?"

"You're safe. Go back to sleep."

"What's all that noise I hear coming from the street?"

"A man is being taken to Golgotha to be executed." Her voice broke on a sob. "Everybody is running to see it. But you rest. You'll feel better later."

Simon frowned and then drifted off.

Batasha stood in front of the inn waiting for Lazarus. Surely he would be returning soon bearing Jesus, wounded from his scourging, but still alive. Suddenly Jonas crested the hill running at full tilt. "They're crucifying him!" he announced crying. "He's carrying a cross to Golgotha right now! I ran all the way from John Mark's to tell you."

She began running toward Jerusalem immediately, her uncovered hair flying. "Tell Martha and Maria!" she screamed. And you stay here!" She waved hysterically. "This isn't something a child should see!"

When she reached the Holy City, she plunged through the crowded narrow streets until she spied the procession heading toward the west gate. Her arms had the strength of iron as she pushed people aside and dug into their shoulders with talons of steel. "Get out of my way! Let me by!" she ordered, relentlessly determined.

When she finally saw him, he was staggering under the weight of the cross; blood from his lacerated back soaked through the white robe in bright slashes and dripped from the hem onto the stones. She struck her way through the soldiers surrounding him and went directly for the centurion in charge, her fists flying. "Stop this! Murderer! Swine!"

The soldiers laughed. "The women never could resist you, Captain. It must be your pretty face."

She kicked him and tried to hook his eyes with her fingernails. "Let him go this instant!" she yelled.

"Are you crazy? Stop it!" He shook her shoulders until her teeth rattled. Then he held her still and stared in disbelief. "Batasha!"

"Marcellus? Is it really you?"

"Have you gone mad? I could have you thrown in prison for attacking me like this."

She grabbed his arms begging. "Oh, Marcellus, don't crucify this man. He's innocent! Please, for God's sake, let him go!"

"I can't do that; I have my orders. What is he to you anyway?"

"He is my Lord and my God."

The soldiers jeered loudly. "Then take a good look at your God. See? He bleeds like a man."

"Go away, Batasha." Marcellus set her aside firmly.

She folded her hands before her face pleading. "Oh, Marcellus, please stop this!"

"But I didn't condemn him. Go beg your precious High Priest."

One of the soldiers poked Jesus in the side with his short sword, and the procession began to crawl again. She saw his profile, his beautiful, noble head now beaten and disfigured. The warm odor of fresh blood filled her nostrils. "Oh God," she whispered. "What have they done to you?"

A hand grabbed her shoulder and urged her back into the anonymity of the crowd. It was a woman dressed in cerulean blue. Upon looking closer, Batasha remembered her as the woman she had helped touch the hem of the Master's garment. Her name was Veronica; Batasha remembered the incident well.

She handed Batasha her mantle, which she had moistened in water. "You know the centurion. See if he will let you get through again to wipe the Master's face."

Batasha took the mantle and fought her way again through he wall of men. Seeing her intention, Marcellus halted the soldiers and allowed her to kneel before Jesus. Tenderly she sponged the gashes and abrasions on his face and the blood out of his swollen eyes. The front of his robe was scarlet where his chest oozed from the claw marks of the whip. He seemed to be fractured, like a shattered alabastron, still whole, but seeping from within. There was no way to staunch the blood.

"Don't let them do this," she whispered. "Don't let them do this horrible thing."

"No man takes my life. I give it freely." He lifted his battered face to the women lamenting in pity. "Don't weep for me. Weep for your children, for one day this wicked city will be destroyed. If it didn't repent while I was here, how much worse will it be when I'm gone?"

Marcellus pulled her away and ordered Jesus to get up. He rose under the weight, and then fell again, crashing his knees against the pavement, bowing his head and remaining in a pool of blood on all fours. "I said get up!" He grabbed Jesus roughly by the arm.

"No!" Batasha put herself between Marcellus and Jesus. "Can't you see he's bleeding to death?"

"The other two men are carrying their crosses," Marcellus said, pointing ahead to two criminals also sentenced to be crucified.

"They haven't been cut to shreds with a whip!" she cried in his face. "Marcellus, don't make him carry the cross any farther." She scanned the crowd for help. Her eyes fell immediately upon Suzanna, her husband, Simeon, and their two sons, Alexander and Rufus, who had been watching from the sidelines. Simeon was a broad-shouldered man of dignified mien. "Help him," Batasha begged softly with pleading eyes.

Simeon stepped out, and Marcellus shoved him roughly toward Jesus. Ignoring the aggressive treatment, the African man knelt beside Jesus and gently nudged his shoulder under the one-hundred-fifty-pound cross, lifting it steadily from the Master and beginning to walk.

"Very good," Marcellus mocked. "You have performed a kindness today. Perhaps your God will reward you for it."

Batasha groaned. Her eyes closed as they drove the spikes. She heard a faint crunch as his wrists gave way, and then the fragile, tender bones of his feet.

Someone screamed behind her. She looked over her shoulder as the Lady approached holding both fists between her breasts. Stark terror had whitened the hair at her temples and cut lines of shock in her face. "Satan has driven a sword in my heart. I knew this would happen. Oh, my boy, my beautiful, gentle boy!"

The soldier's sweated as they lifted the cross. Jesus' body swayed out, his hands and feet remaining pinned to the wood. Then the cross sank into a deep hole with a resounding thud.

Jesus let out an ethereal moan as the joints in his body tore apart.

"He always had such lovely hair." The Lady's voice was struck toneless with horror. "Remember when he was a baby?" she said to her sister Salome. "His hair used to curl about my fingers when I combed it? Soft, dark little ringlets with a bronze sheen. Remember?"

"Yes." Salome put her arm around the Lady's shoulders.

"Look at it now. The blood, the spittle. That's my baby, my sweet little boy. So good—always so good."

Martha came up beside Batasha, her eyes red, her face swollen from weeping. "Is God watching this? Why doesn't he do something? This is his Son."

Marcellus heard her. "You foolish women. This is an ordinary man, although I must admit that he dies more bravely than most. He wouldn't even accept the sedative we offered him."

"You're wrong, Marcellus," Batasha said.

He cursed and swaggered away, picking up a wineskin and slinging it over his shoulder to drink. When he was through, he held it up. "Would you like a drink, O great king?"

Jesus blinked the blood from his eyes and focused on him with sorrow.

"No?" asked Marcellus in sarcastic tones. "Well, of course not. It's the poor quality we soldiers get. Not fit for royalty. Do you know Pilate had us nail a placard above your head? It says in three different languages that you are King of the Jews." He bowed deeply, nearly pitching forward. The soldiers laughed boisterously.

"Father, forgive them. They don't know what they're doing."

One of the criminals hanging with him called out. "Aren't you the one who claimed to be the Messiah? If you really are the Christ, get down from there and set us free." He gave a pained laugh that became a groan. "Then we'll believe in you."

"Be silent!" ordered the thief on the other side of Jesus. "Don't you have any reverence even in your dying hour?" He looked over at Jesus begging. "Lord, I deserve what I'm getting. But you don't. I know you're innocent. Lord, remember me when you come into your Kingdom."

"Be assured," Jesus said, "you will be with me in Paradise."

Stoically, Batasha witnessed all that was going on. Unshed tears dammed up behind her eyes, swelling her face and forehead. She had decided she wouldn't cry. Tears would not help him. She knew he was going to die and was determined to accompany him to the last moment without thinking of herself.

The Pharisees came to mock him with smug comments. "Ha! You said you could destroy the Temple and rebuild it in three days. What are you going to do now? You can't even save yourself."

The Lady came closer to the cross, held by John who kept her from collapsing. "My mind is dizzy with memories," she said. "All the good times, the laughter. He always loved to laugh and have a good time. So loving to the children after Joseph died and he became head of the house. Never complaining. Working hard in the shop to provide for us. So good, so patient and strong." Her eyes widened and stared at the mangled figure on the cross. "A son to make a mother proud."

Batasha's heart broke for her. A mother shouldn't have to see this kind of horror.

"Look at him now. Thin, mutilated, tortured. He was always a sturdy, healthy child." She shook her head, her brows pulling together. "I can't remember ever seeing his blood before. He never cut or scraped himself as I recall. But I can see it now. Look. See how it drips down the tree, soaking the earth. That's his life draining away."

Batasha embraced her. She looked over the Lady's head beseeching John with a look. "Oh, take her away. This is killing her."

"Dear Lady," Jesus called down to his mother, his swollen tongue making his words indistinct. "John is your son now." He focused his pain-glazed eyes on his cousin. "Take care of her."

The Lady lifted her empty arms toward the cross—a mother wanting to hold her child one more time. "My son, my son!" she cried out in anguish. John made her turn and leave with him.

☩

The room was dark. Silent. Simon wondered what time it was. He had a vague remembrance of two kind people dragging him from the alley through their back door and laying him on a pallet. But it should be morning by now. It seemed he had awakened once and it had been light. He remembered the woman dressed in blue. Had he slept through the day and into the next night? Or was it still night and the woman had been something he had dreamed? His head felt better, but he was confused. Sighing deeply, he dozed off again.

☩

"I don't understand this darkness," said the blond, youthful Greek who had come to the foot of the cross with Philip. "It's not time for an eclipse."

"Philip, where have you been?" Batasha asked without accusation. "Where are the others?"

"I don't know." Philip's face was haggard and he kept his haunted eyes averted from the cross. "Last night Peter and John told us to wait for them in the garden, but they never returned. I went to be with my friends. The next thing I knew this was happening. So Luke and I came."

"Why?" she asked mournfully. "Why does he have to die?"

"Why?" He looked up at Jesus and shuddered with horror. "I don't know why. Can this bloody mass of humanity be our Master? " He covered his face with his mantle and turned away.

Time passed like a black sludge. Jesus suffered. He struggled for each indrawn breath, having to press against the nails as the weight of his own body was suffocating him. The thieves screamed and cursed in their pain, but Jesus gave only soft moans. Batasha watched the hollow beneath his ribs as it moved in and out. She knew the movement would eventually stop. She knew that moment would come shortly, for he was weak and beginning to swoon.

Miriam, the Lady's sister-in-law, came to the cross. "I believe now, but it's too late," she told Batasha softly. "I always knew down deep that he was the Messiah. I knew his mother was a virgin when she had him. But I wouldn't speak up. I wouldn't try to persuade my husband Alphaeus to believe also. The world could have had him, but we wouldn't believe or commit. Now it's too late for me, too late for everybody." She went a little distance down the hill, sat down, and wept bitterly.

Marcellus was frightfully drunk. So were his men. True Romans, they loved to gamble and did so now for Jesus' robe. They cursed the strange darkness that had blotted out the light of an already gloomy afternoon, making it difficult to see how the dice were cast. With benumbed disinterest, Batasha watched them play for the robe she had so painstakingly made.

When she focused on the cross again, she caught a momentary vision. A thick murky cloud had descended around Jesus. It pulsated with a green glow and rolled internally like a slow macabre dance. She saw her old enemies, their reptilian, serpentine bodies entwining and writhing in a malignant, mocking ring of ridicule. They were happy with spite as they made sport of him, laughing, tormenting. Chemosh, Dagon, Anammelech, Nergal, Siccuth, Meni, Malcham—they were all there—spewing their hateful venom upon the Lord's bleeding head.

"No!" she screamed, closing her eyes. When she looked up again, she saw only a mutilated, dying man lifted on a cross, surrounded by darkness. But she knew they were still there in that other realm, celebrating the agonizing death of God's Anointed One.

"*Eloi, Eloi, lama sabachthani?*" Jesus suddenly shouted.

"That's ancient Hebrew," Philip said. "The beginning of the Twenty-second Psalm: *My God, my God, why have You forsaken me?* Our father, David, predicted all this—the mockery, the suffering, the piercing of his hands and feet, even men gambling for his raiment—all of it was foretold two thousand years ago."

"I'm thirsty," Jesus moaned.

"Marcellus, give him something to drink!" Batasha's voice snapped.

The centurion had lost his swagger. The liquor had not drowned the image of the man on the cross. He kept looking up at the bleeding stranger, his tawny eyes anxious and fearful. The eerie darkness had descended even deeper on the scene unnerving him further. Wordlessly, Marcellus fastened a soaked sponge on the end of a reed and lifted it up.

Jesus drank from the sponge with parched lips; then his head fell back against the cross and he shouted. "*Tetelestai*! The debt has been paid! Father, I release my spirit into your hands!"

His agonized breath trembled; then he sighed. His head fell forward. Batasha was stunned. She stared at his chest waiting for it to lift, but it remained still. Moments passed. Her heart hammered. *Why does mine still beat and his doesn't? He's gone. It's over. I'll never have him again.* Her shock and desolation were indescribable.

A profound silence enjoined the darkness. No one spoke. Batasha thought she heard him still breathing. She peered closely at him once again. He was grey and dead. Her eyes mourned over his corpse. No movement. Nothing! It bore no resemblance to the young, vital man she'd known. Yet still, she continued to hear the sound—a soft inhaling and exhaling. It filled her ears like a soft wind. Was it the giant breathing of the universe?"

"Why do they have those clubs?" Luke whispered to Philip.

Philip answered wiping his eyes, "Sunset begins our Sabbath. It is forbidden for a man to hang on the cross on the Sabbath. The club is to pulverize their legs so they can't push up to catch their breath. They will suffocate within moments."

The soldiers went to one thief and then the other bludgeoning their legs with the heavy club. Their cries were pitiful. When they came to Jesus, Luke called out, "Stop! That man is already dead. I know. I'm a physician. Don't desecrate his body by crushing his legs needlessly."

"We have to make sure." One of the soldiers swung back the club.

"No!" Marcellus shouted. "Don't hit him. That's an order!" His voice broke on a sob.

Before anyone could react, another soldier drew his sword and thrust it full force into Jesus' side. Blood and fluid gushed out.

"I forbade it!" Marcellus staggered back and turned, covering his face with his forearm. "What have I done? This man was the Son of God."

Simon sat at the table eating hungrily. "We seem to be in an eclipse," he said to the lady in blue.

"God is grieving," she commented listlessly. Her face was marked by weeping.

"What is your name?" Simon asked.

"Veronica."

"You're a good cook, Veronica." He smiled. "Thank you for taking care of me after I was attacked last night. Where is your husband?"

"Still west of the city at Golgotha."

"Oh, yes, you mentioned something about a crucifixion. You must have known him. I can see you've been crying."

"He was a good man. Once I touched his garment and his power flowed out and healed me." She began to cry. "He was the Messiah. What hope is there for us when the evil forces in this world can kill even the Messiah?"

Simon's stopped chewing. The bread in his mouth turned to dust. He stared at the woman in disbelief, slowly shaking his head like a dumb beast. "What was his name?" he asked in a trembling voice.

"Jesus."

"No!" he cried staggering to his feet like a wounded animal. He backed away in stricken horror. "This can't be!" He turned and ran, tearing through the streets toward Golgotha. The earth began to shake. The pavement rumbled beneath his feet. People streamed out of the shops and houses screaming. "It's the end of the world! The hour of doom! Earthquake! Run for your lives!"

Simon charged against the tide of panic with the single-minded purpose of getting to Jesus. Foundations of buildings shifted and blocks toppled from roofs. A young priest flew from the Temple beating his chest. "The veil in the Holy of Holies is rent from top to bottom! Surely God has sent judgment on us this day!"

When Simon arrived at The Place of the Skull, it was forsaken. Three empty crosses stood in the distance against an angry sky, the one in the middle most prominent. He turned and saw Peter watching him sadly.

"Where is he?" Simon asked.

"Joseph of Arimethea begged Pilate to let him bury the body before the Sabbath set in," answered Peter.

Simon looked up and heaved a defeated sigh. "Then he's really dead? I can't take it in. We ate supper with him last night. How could it have happened so quickly?"

"Judas brought them to Gethsemane. They paid him thirty pieces of silver."

"My God! That's not even four months wages. He sold Jesus cheaply."

"Afterwards he felt remorse and went and hanged himself."

Simon fell to the grass and leaned forward with his head in his hands. "I feel sick."

"He had no one to defend him in his dying," said Peter. "We all ran. I denied I even knew him, and he heard me do it, for he looked up at me." Peter closed his eyes and tried to pinch away the tears. "My little son is not even three weeks old. I wanted to hold him before I died. I wanted to kiss Deborah again. So I became a coward."

Simon gave a soundless laugh. "I behaved no better. Feeling sorry for myself, I went into the City looking for diversion instead of staying at my post beside our Master. I drank shekar and was too befuddled to fend off a gang of criminals who attacked and robbed me. I slept all day while Jesus was dying."

"What are we going to do now?" Peter asked.

"Mourn," answered Simon in a broken voice. "It's all over."

As Peter turned and silently walked away, Simon pulled himself to his feet and walked up the craggy, desolate hill toward the rough-hewn cross. He stared appalled. The blood of Jesus was still wet upon it. Then he threw himself down prostrate. "Oh, Jesus, forgive me. I'm sorry." He lay at the foot of the cross, the loneliest man in the universe, alone in his repentance, alone in his surrender, unable to do anything but weep.

"They're embalming him too hastily," said Salome.

Batasha rubbed her grainy eyes. "Be thankful that Joseph of Arimethea asked Pilate for his body and offered his own tomb for burial."

"They're not even using perfume," Miriam remarked indignantly. "The cloves and aloes will not be enough."

"Perhaps that is all they could find at this late hour. They're doing the best they can," said Batasha.

"Did you bring some perfume with you from Magdala?" asked Salome.

"Yes, of course."

"I have some myrrh," said Salome. "Do you have anything to offer?" she asked Miriam.

"An alabaster box of nard," she answered. "I would be honored to give it to him. His body should get a proper embalming. It's only right after the way he died."

"Then let's meet here tomorrow with our gifts," said Salome.

"Tomorrow is the Sabbath," pointed out Batasha. "It will have to be Sunday."

"Very well, then," persisted Salome. "Sunday before dawn. The three of us."

Eventually Simon became aware that he was no longer alone in his grief. Another man was lying at the foot of the cross on the other side. His hands were beside Simon's clutching the blood-soaked earth. The stranger's sorrow was as deep and uncontrollable as Simon's. When he lifted his head and sobbed brokenly, Simon recognized him.

"What's wrong, man?" Simon asked.

"I'm miserable," Marcellus answered moaning.

"This is a day of miseries," Simon agreed.

"Who are you?"

Simon realized that Marcellus didn't remember him from the incident in the wine shop two years ago. "I was one of his disciples," he answered.

"Where were you when he was suffering? I saw mostly women followers at the crucifixion."

"I was asleep. I've asked God to forgive me. He is merciful, and I believe he will do so."

"Will he forgive me too?" asked Marcellus. "I killed his Son."

"We all did." Simon reached out in compassion and helped Marcellus to his feet. "We all failed him."

"Did you know the God-Man well?" asked Marcellus allowing Simon to lead him down the hill.

"He was like a brother to me." Simon wept softly. "He taught me many things."

"Will you stay with me for a while and tell me about him?"

Simon nodded as they walked away from Golgotha together, their arms supporting one another.

Chapter 24

He will swallow up death forever.
Isaiah 25:8 NIV

"Where's the Magdalene?"

"In her room."

"How is she?"

Simon watched Martha's tear-swollen eyes fill. "She won't eat, and she hasn't slept for two nights. She won't join us in our grief. She doesn't cry."

"I'm going to talk to her."

Martha shrugged. "Go ahead. But it won't do you any good. She hasn't spoken a word to anybody since coming back from the burial last night."

He found her sitting in a darkened corner, shrunken, forlorn, and unkempt. It was the first time he'd ever seen her without her hair brushed and cosmetics on her face. She was pale and her eyes stared ahead, dull, dry, and unblinking.

He sat beside her on the couch and gently took her hand. "I've just come from Daniel's upper room. Everybody is praising you for remaining faithful to Jesus yesterday." He paused when she tilted her chin and found another spot on the wall to stare at. At a loss for words, Simon pleaded, "Batasha, why won't you weep?"

"Because if I started, I wouldn't be able to stop," she said stiffly. "My whole universe would be consumed with it."

"Batasha, I can't bear to see you like this," he said painfully. His own eyes filled with tears. "Is there anything I can do for you? Can I bring you anything?"

"I need Jesus," she said stonily. "Bring me back Jesus."

He sighed. Tears fell unchecked from his eyes. He reached next to his chest to bring out the garment Marcellus had given him. "I brought back the robe—the one you made."

Slowly she reached for the crumpled, bloodstained robe, once so white and pure, once beautiful like the man who wore it. Her hard expression began to disintegrate, starting with a few scalding tears that quickly became a raging, uncontrolled torrent.

"Oh, Tasha." He gathered her in his arms and gently rocked her shuddering body as if she were a child, petting and soothing her with his large, rough hands, whispering words of comfort and love. He kissed her face and her eyes, and buried his face in her hair and wept with her.

"He left me," she sobbed. "He promised he would never leave or forsake me. Why would he tell me that and then die?"

Simon wanted to give her an answer but he had none. His arms tightened protectively. His lips whispered, "I love you." He went on to repeat it over and over with kisses until she gradually gentled and rested against him.

"Is this all there is?" she asked brokenly. "Just two people holding to one another?"

"For the moment," he answered softly into her hair, "it is enough."

"Oh, I'm tired." She held him close burying her face against his chest, sighing and snuffling like a child. Within moments her arms relaxed and she fell into a light sleep, breathing through her mouth quietly.

Gently he extricated himself from her arms and turned to make her comfortable among the pillows. This was how it felt to love a woman—this sensitivity that broke a man with its tenderness, this willingness to give oneself completely. "My beloved," he whispered, bending to touch her lips briefly before leaving.

Ϙ

Miriam and Salome met in the garden of the tomb a shortly before dawn. Batasha was late.

"Where have you been? The sun is nearly up."

"I'm sorry. I overslept." Weeping had ravaged Batasha's face, and her hair was loose and unbraided beneath her mantle.

"Did you bring the perfume?" asked Miriam.

"Yes."

"Good. Salome was able to obtain spices."

They began walking in silence toward the tomb. "How are we going to move the stone?" Batasha asked.

"I didn't think of that," said Salome, seemingly vexed at herself for overlooking this most important consideration. "Perhaps if we all three pushed together ..."

"Ha! It took four men to seal the tomb Thursday evening," Miriam said shaking her head.

Batasha spoke up, "Martha said that soldiers had been assigned to keep watch. The officials were concerned that the disciples would come and try to claim his body. Perhaps Marcellus is in charge, and I can persuade him to have his men move the stone so that we can go in to anoint the body."

"If they won't, Peter and John might be able to help us. They're supposed to be here in a little while," said Salome.

"Look!" Miriam pointed. "Someone has already opened it." The huge sealing stone lay some distance away from the marble entrance as if tossed aside impatiently.

Salome began to run forward. Getting to the tomb first, she bent and looked in. "He's gone!"

This news hit Batasha hard. The murderers hadn't been content to just kill him; they'd had to desecrate him further by taking him out of the tomb. She stumbled away blindly, sobbing.

"Batasha, what's wrong?" Peter and John approached her in a pre-dawn haze.

"Oh, Peter, they've stolen our Master's body. Go see for yourself."

Batasha collapsed on a bench, dissolving into a fresh fit of weeping. After a while she was able to get up and again approach the rich marble burying place that Joseph of Arimethea had donated for Jesus' burial. The first rays of sun touched the delicate white alabaster carvings decorating the entrance. Apparently Salome and Miriam had already left, for they were nowhere in sight. As she bent to look inside, another wave of grief washed over her fevered eyes. Two men stood within the dim confines of the tomb. They weren't Peter and John.

"What are you so upset about?" one of them asked.

"They've taken him. They've taken him," was all she could manage between sobs. She turned and walked several paces away, then cried out childishly. "Oh Jesus! Where are you?"

Utterly desolate, she tried to gather sufficient strength for the long walk she knew she must make back to Bethany. Dawn had christened the eastern sky with a rose-mauve crown. The garden had burst into birdsong, and the early morning flowers had begun to unfold their perfume.

Suddenly a man walked out of the sunrise to meet her. She assumed he was the gardener come to do a day's work. His brightness blinded her sensitive eyes causing her to squint.

"Woman, why are you so distraught? Surely so much crying will make you ill."

She made an awning with her hand. "Sir!" She inhaled deeply trying to compose her watery voice. "If you've been a part of this robbery or know anything about where they've laid my Master, tell me right now, for I must get him back!"

He gave a soft laugh. "Mary."

Astonished, she blinked, then stumbled forward holding out her arms. It was Jesus, saying her name in the old familiar way. He was alive. "Rabboni!" She clung to him with all her might to make sure she wasn't dreaming, to make sure he didn't leave again.

"No, don't hold me. I can't stay. I have to go to my Father. Go tell my brothers that I am alive."

She released him and knelt at his feet to pray in thanksgiving. When she opened her eyes, he was gone.

⚱

That afternoon Simon walked with his father on the way to Emmaus. After seeing his father safely home and visiting a short while with his mother, he planned to go back to Bethany to see Batasha. She had reported to several of the disciples this morning that she had seen Jesus alive. He wanted to be on hand to comfort her grief until she began to think more rationally.

"But John believes it, and so does Peter," Cleopas said continuing the argument they were having along the way.

"Father," Simon admonished him softly, "why hope when there is no hope? We must all accept what has happened to Jesus. We can continue to follow him by living by his example. That's the heritage he left us and the way we must honor him now that he is dead. All this talk of resurrection is foolishness."

"But he predicted that he would come out of the grave in three days. Matthew has it in writing. John remembers it now too. Jesus mentioned it just after the trip to Caesarea-Philippi. Nathaniel says he remembers other times. Even Philip is entertaining the possibility that Jesus has been victorious over death."

Simon asked wearily, "What's Philip logic this time?"

He says that Truth and Goodness cannot be killed. God is greater than Satan by Universal Law."

Simon remained silent. A small bud of hope began to unfurl in his breast. What if it were true? What if the Master had conquered the grave? What if he had beaten Satan in the last great arena all humans must face? As he walked, he pondered, half-believing. A gentle spring rain began to fall—liquid jewels mixed with sunshine. They put up their hoods and lowered their heads.

"Ho!" They turned around and beheld a figure approaching, his hooded head bent as he walked. "Where are you two fellows going?"

"To Emmaus," said Cleopas.

"Wait! I'll walk with you."

"Glad to have you," welcomed Simon. Something in the set of the stranger's shoulders was disturbingly familiar. "This is my father, Cleopas, and I am Simon. Have you just come from Jerusalem?"

"Yes," the man replied. "What were you and your father arguing about? I could hear your discussion as I approached."

A certain timbre of the man's voice resonated with Simon; it was a strange, profound echo of another voice he had known. He tried to see beneath the man's hood as they all three began walking together. He caught a glimpse of the stranger's hair; it was the color of lamb's wool. Yet the man didn't seem to be elderly, for his steps were sure and energetic.

"You mean you've just come from Jerusalem and haven't heard about Jesus?" Simon asked astonished. "The entire population is talking about what happened to him."

"Suppose you tell me," the stranger suggested as they trudged together amid the jasper raindrops.

"I thought everybody in the Holy City was aware of the events that have taken place these past few days!" Cleopas exclaimed. "Enlighten him, my son," he said to Simon.

"Yes, Simon. Enlighten me," said the stranger. "Then perhaps I'll enlighten you."

A familiar humor. Simon knew this man from somewhere. He wished it would stop raining and the man would remove his mantle and reveal himself.

☙

"Of course it's true," said Lazarus. "If he could bring me out of the grave, he can certainly do it for himself. Everyone is surprised and skeptical because they didn't realize the extent of his power and the vastness of the Father's love."

"The disciples are still gathered in Daniel's upper room mulling it over," Martha remarked. Simon bar Cleopas has also seen the risen Lord and is trying to convince them. I suppose Jesus will have to appear to them all together before they will truly believe."

"Simon has seen the Lord?" Batasha asked.

"Yes, on the way to Emmaus early this afternoon," answered Martha. "It is reported that he and Cleopas invited the risen Lord into their house to eat with them without realizing who he was. When he broke the bread with his hands they saw the fresh wounds, and then the Lord's mantle fell back from his face and they beheld him. Simon reports that the Master's countenance has changed somewhat due to the glorification of his resurrected state, yet he is still clearly recognizable as the Jesus we all knew and followed."

"This is only the beginning," predicted Lazarus. "Future generations will look back to this day with faith and joy, and many millions will believe."

They spoke further of the miraculous events that had taken place, then retired. Batasha stayed up. She knew Simon would come. After a while, she heard the gate bell. But instead of Simon, it was Jonas, running into the room disheveled, his robe flying out like wings. *No wonder his clothes always look like the wrath of God,* thought Batasha.

"Jonas! What on earth has gotten into you?" she whispered vehemently. "People are asleep!"

"I had to talk to you." He panted catching his breath. "I ran all the way from Daniel's."

"You smell like a copper penny. When was the last time you had a good bath?"

"Please don't start in on me again about bathing."

"Someone must. What you need is a mother."

"I know. That's what I came to talk to you about. Please don't nag, and just listen a minute."

He had grown into that sassy stage of adolescence, and she didn't like it. "Nag! You concern me, Jonas. I'm afraid you're going wild. Racing the streets at all hours unchaperoned, tearing your clothes to pieces in the process?"

He squirmed. "I'm sorry."

"That's better. Now sit down and tell me what's gotten you so excited."

He sat beside her, grabbing her hands. "My father is going to ask you to marry him."

"How do you know?" she asked curiously, but without surprise.

"I heard him mention it to my grandfather. Grandfather was much pleased. He said you are a woman with grit and will make my father a fine wife. My father is coming here tonight to discuss it with you. Please say you will," he pleaded squeezing her hands. "I could never think of Lila as my mother. Why, she was only a few years older than I. When their betrothal ended, I was glad."

She ruffled his hair. "If Simon asks me, we'll have a long talk about it. Don't worry. Now run along to bed. And please wash down before you get under the covers."

"But you know how gruff and impatient my father is at times. I think I should stay and help."

"You will certainly do no such thing. Go to bed," she ordered in a tone that brooked no further debate.

She shook her head *tsk*-ing as Jonas raced up the stairs in his customary clambering manner. Then she groomed her hair, freshened her face, rubbed her arms with lotion, and began to pace the floor. The bell, when it finally rang, startled her.

Simon came through the door of the sitting room without waiting to be admitted. He swept her into his arms. There was no mincing around for permission or further courtly preamble. He gave her a wild, all-consuming kiss that lasted several moments. Then he set her away by her shoulders. "Marry me."

She arched an eyebrow. Obviously there would be no long talks and lingering, lover-like sighs. "Very well," she agreed.

He kissed her again, greatly pleased. Then he made her sit down beside him on the couch. "We are meant to be together."

"Did the Master tell you that?"

"Not precisely, but I know. You are to be my partner since Judas is gone. There is much work to be done. I believe Jesus will stay a while longer to further instruct us before ascending to his Father. But he will not live among us as he did before. He has promised to send us a helper to reside within, a spirit to guide and empower us. I don't fully understand that part, but I suppose I will in time. And then we must go and tell everyone what has happened."

"I heard that you and Cleopas saw him on the way to Emmaus today," she said.

"Yes, he explained many things. He was very patient with me and quoted numerous Scriptures from Moses and the prophets concerning himself. He was sent to be the suffering Messiah, to provide a blood sacrifice for all the people for the remission of sins. He never meant to become a temporal king as we all assumed. Whenever he spoke of his Kingdom, it was in reference to his virtuous power living within people individually who by praying and working together might change the world."

"I was the first woman who saw him in his risen form, and you were the first man. This is a great honor for us," she pointed out.

"He means for us to be parents—first parents in a sense—to help birth children from the water of repentance and the blood of atonement into new life with him." He gave her a dazzling smile and got up. "I have to go back to Daniel's to spend the night with my brothers."

She followed him to the door as he continued to talk, "My father will have the marriage contract drawn up tomorrow. I know it is customary to allow time between the legal agreement and the claiming of one's bride," he said turning to her abruptly, "but I will take you to myself immediately, without lengthy courtship." He tested her with a look from beneath his brows.

"As you wish, my love." Her submissive expression held a note of wry humor.

"Then we are in agreement?" He pulled her close and she melted.

"Total agreement."

What he saw in her eyes made him tremble. He cupped her face in his rough, stonecutter's hand. "Dear God, I shall love you with my life." A brief, ardent kiss to her lips and he was away, full of hope, purpose, and a sense of destiny.

EPILOGUE

A.D. 68

I, Jonas bar Simon, servant of God to the churches in Brigantia and Atrebatia, send greetings to our children, Benjamin, Bethany, and Jerusala and their families. Health, peace, and prosperity from God, our Father and his Son, Jesus Christ.

The days of summer have passed quickly and not as uneventfully as I had anticipated. It has been only twelve weeks since my last letter. So much has happened that your mother and I can scarcely take it in. Vast legions of Roman soldiers, under Proconsul Titus, son of Vespasian, have encamped about Jerusalem in heavy siege. My good friend Gaius Valerius, whom I mentioned in my previous letter, hears from old acquaintances that Titus plans to completely destroy the Holy City and kill the Jews within, scattering what few survive to the four winds of the earth. I am painfully reminded of our Lord's words concerning the Temple—"not one stone will be left upon another." Could this be the beginning? It is difficult to imagine that enemy hordes would take the time to cast down the huge Temple blocks which, in some cases, are sixteen feet thick and twenty-four by twelve feet in length and width. But perhaps they will do so in order to get to the gold covering the dome.

The war has crept upon us by inches. One hears of a battle in Capernaum where several hundred died, or a massacre over in the Decapolis. On a sunny day in the marketplace, one sees the regiments marching through town going south toward Judea, their boots drumming cadence against the paving stones. People stop and pause. They shake their heads. Then they resume the business of buying nuts and melons, trinkets and wine. But a moment comes when alarm rushes in like a sudden wave, nearly drowning one with the realization that there is going to be a bloodbath. The Romans are tired of dealing with the intractable Jews. They are determined to crush instead of correct, not only in Judea, but here in Galilee as well.

Your mother and I will depart tomorrow for home. I must leave behind the parchments I worked on all summer, for we will be traveling light. Gaius has secreted the seven scrolls in amphorae within a cave on his property and will look for a way to transport them by caravan to Britannia at a later date. I did not weep to think of sealing them into safe obscurity for a time. All my tears were spent in the telling.

During my work I learned that a distant memory sometimes arcs to another in one's mind, jumping over years to more recent events. I kept thinking of how my father died four years ago in the Roman Circus while on a visit to the Apostle Peter. Nero condemned him with a hasty trial and set the lions on him. Then John Mark buried his body and came all the way from Rome to tell us how bravely he had fought, for even at the age of sixty-five, Simon bar Cleopas was still a mighty warrior. Only two months after hearing it, my mother, known far and wide as Mary, the Magdalene, went to be with him in her sleep.

But I laughed too as I scribbled their story, remembering that after their marriage, my mother and father had many discussions—one might say arguments—about the wisdom of having children. My father was against it since theirs would be a life of constant travel and hardship. He said repeatedly that my mother should not undertake the bearing of children at her age. My mother would reply testily that he, not she, was the one who had grown ancient and cranky. Nevertheless, she kept a careful calendar and produced no babies. But natives all over Brigantia called her Mother because she helped with many birthings, and an opportunity to hold an infant or assist a mother with her young never passed her by. But these are things you already know.

My lovely Judith, childhood playmate and half-sister of the Lord, reproaches me with her sweet grey eyes. I am lingering by the lamplight when I should be helping her pack our rucksacks and prepare the villa for desertion. We will be traveling by chariot overland to Egypt. John Mark has established a church in Alexandria; I desire very much to visit my old friend and share news with him. Then we will go west along the coast to Cyrene where Suzanna and Simeon live, whose sons, Rufus and Alexander, have become well known in the church at Rome. I hope I can persuade Suzanna to make me some of her famous honey cakes. From there, we will board ship and sail through the Great White Gates up the coast of Spain and further on until we reach Atrebatia.

You will receive this letter before we arrive, for I am entrusting it to Joseph of Arimethea who leaves for Tyre tomorrow to sail straight for Britannia. He desires to establish missions in the tribal territory of the Dobunni. He will bring with him the Holy Cup. Please greet him with kisses of Christian love and encourage his endeavor. Perhaps some of our men would be interested in helping his work.

The Good News is covering the earth; churches exist from Parthia in the East to Hibernia in the West. Despite cruel persecutions, we are many thousands strong. But your mother is growing impatient with me. All her thoughts and actions converge on one goal—embracing her beloved children once again and taking your little ones, who call her Nonnie, upon her lap for kisses and hugs.

May the peace of God that passes all understanding keep your hearts and minds in Christ Jesus. And may Jehovah *Rapha*, our Father who heals, have mercy on this war-torn land. Pray

for the peace of Jerusalem. May our Lord Jesus Christ soon
come again according to his promise.